Chant of the Hawk

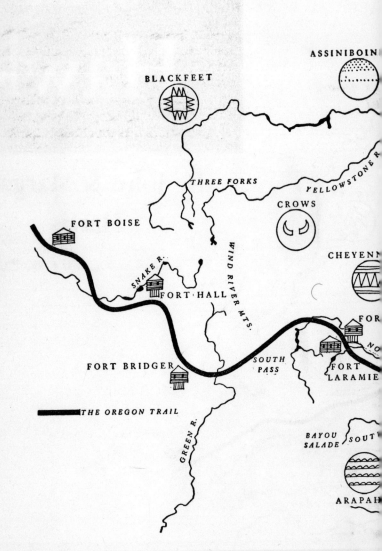

ASSINIBOIN

BLACKFEET

THREE FORKS

YELLOWSTONE R.

CROWS

FORT BOISE

CHEYENN

SNAKE R.

WIND RIVER MTS.

FORT HALL

FOR

FORT BRIDGER

SOUTH
PASS

NO

FORT
LARAMIE

THE OREGON TRAIL

BAYOU
SALADE

SOUT

GREEN R.

ARAPAH

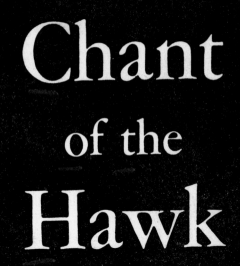

Chant
of the
Hawk

by John & Margaret
Harris

RANDOM HOUSE, NEW YORK

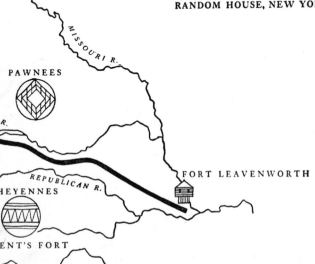

RT UNION

SIOUX

MISSOURI R.

TE

PAWNEES

TTE R.

R.

REPUBLICAN R.

CHEYENNES

FORT LEAVENWORTH

BENT'S FORT

ARKANSAS R.

Books by John and Margaret Harris

Arrow in the Moon
The Medicine Whip

To John and Duff

The hawks turn their heads nimbly round;
They turn to look back on their flight.
The spirits of sun-place have whispered them words,
They fly with their messages swift,
They look as they fearfully go,
They look to the farthermost end of the world,
Their eyes glancing bright, and their beaks boding harm.

An Indian Chant

Chant of the Hawk

Set in the Rocky Mountain West of the 1840's, this is an account of the enmity of two trappers.

George Stroud ceased his blaspheming and glared at Maud. The day was starting out just like yesterday and the day before and all the other days since they broke winter camp. Ey God, he was tired of it. Maud had fought him all the while they worked their way down the Laramie, and unless they had it out she'd keep it up till they hit the forts on the Platte. Stroud looped the tie rope around his body. His close-cropped, bearded jaw was set and his gray eyes were glinting below heavy, joined brows. Even his braids, stiff and shoulder-length beneath his flexible low-crowned hat, had an obstinate look.

Glaring back at him from the other end of the rope was Maud, wicked and beautiful and mouse-gray as a good Mexican mule should be. Ears backed, neck elongated, and tail between her legs, she whined again from the irritation of the newly cinched packsaddle; then she lifted her hind quarters in a tentative jump. Stroud turned his back on her, braced his buckskin-clad legs, gritted his teeth, and threw himself forward, feeling the rope cut into his ribs. He knew he could bring the mule to taw by fastening the rope with a half hitch around her nose. And he knew that the others knew he knew. Let them think what they liked. A half-dozen times Stroud lunged forward, but he failed to move the mule any nearer the cache. He paused and glared at the others from beneath his brows. Seeing that the men had all quit their work to watch, he felt a sudden irritation with them, too. They were supposed to be opening up the cache of trade goods they had buried last fall. But look at them. Ey God, after two years with them day in and day out, he could tell what they were thinking.

3

That young gentleman-adventurer Wyatt, conspicuous in his well-tailored St. Louis hunting clothes, should be packing the mules, but he stood beside several of the large, roped bundles of trade goods wrapped in skins, watching with unconcealed curiosity. He'd be betting on Maud and wondering if it was a fairly common way of bringing a mule around that he had missed up till now. Standing with him was Mozay, slouched as if he were half asleep, though his snapping black eyes between beard and beaver cap were intent upon the tug of war. Mozay would rather tell lies on credit than the truth for cash, so he'd be making up a whopper about how he'd outstubborned a mule. At the edge of the bank overlooking the stream, the swarthy, foxlike face of Partout was visible above the edge of the excavation. Half-French, half-Indian, and all durn fool, Partout would be thinking it was funny but be afraid to laugh. Hobart, who had been receiving the bulky, skin-wrapped bundles from Partout, appeared to have taken root. His shaggy red beard was the only thing about him that looked alive. He had once been a circus rider and thought he still was one when he got good and snapt. Hobart would have ideas that Maud hadn't been trained right in the first place.

Stroud's glance swept the rest of the camp. A few yards back from the stream the Indian women, Mozay's Madame Jack and Hobart's Emma, were busy taking down the two tipis. At a little distance Hobart's boy on a bareback mule worried a loose tooth with a thumb and forefinger as he played more than he worked at herding the pack animals. Several dogs nosed about. The women, the boy and the dogs, at least, were doing what was expected of them. Stroud's glance moved to the highest point of the bank, where even lank, grizzle-bearded old Greenberry had relaxed his vigilance to watch. Greenberry, who'd been in the mountains so long he wasn't fit to live among whites,

4

would be thinking a tug of war a waste of time; he might as well shoot the varmint. Mostly Greenberry was the sensiblest of the lot.

Stroud threw down the tie rope and pulled a revolving pistol from his belt. It was a newfangled Colt's six-shot repeater, and at one hundred and thirty dollars apiece they weren't plentiful among trappers. "You ungrateful, hell-fired, iron-jacketed . . ."

He placed his thumb on the hammer to draw it back when there came an exclamation from Greenberry. "*Wagh!* Visitors! Do 'ee hyar?"

Stroud was more exasperated than alarmed by the interruption. "What's the count?"

"Three whites."

Stroud lowered the pistol to his side. "Packs?"

Greenberry studied the approaching riders a moment. "Trade goods." As if for confirmation, he added in his thin, high voice, "No pelts, do 'ee hyar?"

"Looking for Shonka's band, I'll wager," muttered Stroud. News of a band of Indians who hadn't gone into the forts to trade for two years was bound to travel fast, but Stroud hadn't expected it to travel this fast. He had discovered Shonka's band himself only two days ago, saw them moving north up the basin. Likely they'd been in the mountains for spruce to replenish lodgepoles and for ash to renew bows and lances. Now they were probably heading to the north end of the basin for their spring buffalo hunt. The surround would keep them busy for days, Stroud knew. Riding among the herd and picking out the choicest cows, the hunters would make a great slaughter with bows and lances. Then, when the plain was littered with the huge black carcasses, the women and children would do the bloody work of skinning and butchering the meat into long strips and loading it on horses. In the camp, the racks would be heavy with meat and back fat drying, and around lodges, skins would be pegged down for fleshing and thinning. It was a good time to trade. The Indians would have to stay put and they'd be celebrating the surround. But by the looks of it somebody else had seen Shonka earlier and had carried news to the forts. Both Fort Laramie and Fort Platte would have parties out trying to get Shonka's trade. In the face of a new worry, Maud was forgotten. She took a few steps forward and stuck her nose into the thick grass.

"Hell's full of lookin'," scoffed Greenberry. Sending a small avalanche of rocks before him, he came slithering down from his vantage point.

Stroud was intent upon the approaching party—three mounted men and fifteen or twenty pack mules, an outfit of about the same size as his—which had come into sight a half-mile down the stream that wound along the base of the hills. It was likely a party from either Fort Laramie or Fort Platte—there was no free trader in these parts, other than himself, with that big an outfit. "It's Cebull," Stroud observed presently. Cebull had as mean and money-loving a pair of eyes as ever stared at the eagle on a dime. "And Old Man Rem," Stroud added without enthusiasm. Old Man Rem had outlived a half-dozen sons and almost that many squaws and was too ornery to die. They'd both been trading for Fort Platte since Wyatt, Croteau and Company built it four years ago only a mile and a half from Fort Laramie, the American Fur Company's Mountain Division post. It was an old trick of smaller firms to build a post near one operated by the Company, hoping to be bothersome enough to get bought out. But you can't be bothersome if there's no trade, and the trade in pelts had fallen off about that time. It looked as if young Wyatt's uncle, old Charles Wyatt, the head of the firm, had put as little as possible into the investment since then, operating by sending rascals like Cebull and Rem into the field, who'd trade the robes off an Indian's couch in the dead of winter.

Stroud kept his attention on the approaching riders, watching the third man, who was in the lead. There was something familiar in the way he sat his horse. He wore a sky-blue capote with the hood back, revealing a mass of yellow hair. Then, as the riders came nearer, Stroud had a moment of incredulity. By all rights, the man riding toward him shouldn't be alive. For seven years he had thought Jesse Reeshar dead. But it was Jesse Reeshar, right enough. Now, seeing Reeshar, the old torment rose up again: What had happened that time seven years ago after he left Reeshar with their squaws? What had happened to his own squaw, Batchika?

Looking back on it, it seemed plain enough they had been heading for disaster of some kind—he and Reeshar and their squaws, Batchika and Wicarpi—each new misfortune compounding the next. Until the first piece of bad luck they had spent a good summer and fall. They had been making their way toward winter rendezvous on the Powder River after having trapped the Belle Fourche, when an unseasonal storm caught them crossing open country to the north of the Bear Lodge Mountains. Stroud remembered how they had had to feel around with their feet for wood beneath the snow, where they were camped beside the frozen stream until the weather cleared enough to start on. There had been no question of staying camped to wait out the freeze. Not on the open plains where game was scarce and the freeze might last the winter. Afterward there had been days of floundering through the deep drifts, days of either cheerless gloom or blinding sun, of calm, icy air or of knifelike winds blowing snow that formed ice on their lips and eyebrows. There was a time when even the horses had been too exhausted to break a path in the snow, and Reeshar had thrown himself down in despair. He refused to move on until Stroud had taken the lead alone to break a path. It had been a hell of white monotony.

A few days after the blizzard they had come upon a plateau where the snow was swept shallow. About thirty Arapahoes had come into view, a war party swathed in robes and furs, on a raid into Crow country. The Arapahoes had barred their way and could easily have lifted their hair and stolen the women. But for some reason—probably because of their Hawken's rifles, which the Arapahoes knew would claim two of them if they tried—the Indians had gone on with looks of contempt. But not without driving the trappers' horses in with their own, first stripping them of packs and saddles and pole drag. They had been on foot then, forced to leave all their belongings behind, proceeding with nothing but the clothes on their backs, their rifles, and the small store of pemmican and dried meat they had had in their packs. When the second blizzard struck, they had been fortunate to find shelter under a large ledge of rock. But they had finished the pemmican and dried meat, and for three days while the blizzard raged they had been without food. Even their beaver plews, which would have eased their hunger pangs, had been left behind. It was on the fourth day, Stroud knew, that he had gone off alone to hunt for meat, agreeing somewhat doubtfully with Reeshar that one of them should stay with Batchika and Wicarpi.

Stroud remembered clearly the camp as he had left it, with Reeshar hunched over the fire with the women. And the camp as it was when he returned the next afternoon. An empty camp. A dead fire. Scattered human bones— the small bones of a woman. Wolf sign everywhere in the

8

dark-spotted snow. And two sets of human tracks leading off into the frozen nowhere: one large—Reeshar's; one small—a woman's. But which woman?

A new storm had already gathered and snow was starting to fall, a rising wind driving it into his face with the sting of buckshot. Stroud remembered dropping the frozen hindquarters of antelope he had brought back, to crawl on his all fours searching for sign, the question *Which one? Which one?* stabbing him as if he were a bull pecked by lances, but the howling wind was shifting the snow too fast for him to tell whether the smaller tracks were Batchika's or Wicarpi's. He remembered yelling then, calling Batchika's name over and over again, with the wind snatching the words from his mouth and losing them in the turbulent world around him. And afterward the questions stabbing at him again in the long wait for the storm to blow itself out. Which one? How had she died? Had Reeshar taken Wicarpi, his own woman, and left Stroud's companion, Batchika, to die by herself? Had Batchika been deserted because she was too sick or too weak to leave? Or had Wicarpi died and Batchika gone off with Reeshar? It had been hard to believe of Batchika, though the threat of starving and freezing could make a body do fool things—and it had been a fool thing Reeshar had done to leave camp. But why had they left at all? And how could either of them have survived the blizzard that followed? They had all been lucky before to find shelter under the ledge of rock. But nobody could hope for that kind of luck twice on the open plains.

Stroud continued to watch Reeshar, the revolving pistol hanging forgotten in his hand. Reeshar must have recognized him, too, for Stroud saw his head come up, showing the familiar, square-chiseled line of his jaw and the leonine quality of his head with its manelike yellow hair. Reeshar reined in a few yards away.

"God damn you!" said Stroud.

Reeshar looked down at him with a flat, unblinking stare. "What for?"

"What do you think what for? Why didn't you let me know you were alive?"

Reeshar's expression was bland. "Why should I?"

"That's a fool question." Stroud had an uneasy feeling. There was something different in the man. Something apart from the suggestion of fleshiness which had slightly dulled the sharp edges of his face. "Unless you never intended to tell me," he added.

Reeshar shrugged. "You went off to look after yourself. So did I."

Remembering how he had staggered and fought his way through the drifts to bring back the meat, Stroud felt a fresh surge of anger. "You knew me better than that."

"Who knows any man well enough to trust his life to him?"

The queer notion came to Stroud that this man before him wasn't Reeshar at all, but someone who might be his twin. It seemed beyond belief that they had spent a year together. "You knew I'd come back for Batchika."

"For Batchika?" Reeshar seemed slightly amused. "She was only a squaw."

Going back in his mind, Stroud could see Batchika and Wicarpi racing their ponies out to meet them as they returned from a hunt; could hear their laughter and see their wet, coppery bodies glisten in the sun as they swam in some still pool. He had never thought of Batchika as "only a squaw." He wondered if she had gone off with Reeshar and survived to be "only a squaw" as long as it pleased him. "That's how you thought of Wicarpi, too?"

"Squaws," Reeshar said. "To be had for a few trinkets."

Stroud could only regard Reeshar in amazement. "What in the name of common sense has happened to you?"

Reeshar smiled. "Nothing has happened to me. But I was sick of your common sense. Of your sturdy virtues. That blizzard didn't come any too soon."

"My common sense saved you more than once," Stroud said evenly, though it was a wolf-mean thing Reeshar had said. "I want to know what happened to Batchika, Jesse."

"You're foolish to want to dig up the past," Reeshar said. "A man has too many other lives to lead to cling to dead ones."

Stroud finally realized that Reeshar had no intention of telling him anything. "You're hiding something."

Reeshar shook his head. "It was a bad time and best forgot."

"It's like you to taunt a man," Stroud said. "I should have remembered that about you. But I wouldn't have thought you'd go this far. I don't know why you're doing it. I don't know what's come over you. But you alive, and not wanting to tell what happened . . ." He paused and looked steadily at Reeshar. "It doesn't shine, Jesse. I'm not going to forget it. I'll ferret it out."

Stroud stuck his revolver into the belt of his knee-length hunting shirt and turned away. It was easy enough for Reeshar to say it was "a bad time and best forgot," Stroud reflected bitterly. But Reeshar knew what had happened. He hadn't come back to the mystery of a cold camp with nothing but cleaned bones, wolf sign and two sets of tracks. Thinking the two who had left camp had died in the new storm that came up, Stroud had managed after a while to forget it pretty well. But with Reeshar turning up alive now, everything was changed. His refusal to tell what happened was enough to drive a man crazy.

Maybe that's what Reeshar wanted, and if it was he'd succeeded. But there must be some way to find out what Reeshar was hiding. And Stroud vowed he'd find it, though it would have to wait on this trade with Shonka. Stroud looked up and saw that the others—his own men as well as Cebull and Old Man Rem—were intent, respectful of whatever it was that stood between him and Reeshar.

"Let's have news of the forts," Stroud said to Cebull.

Cebull's mean little eyes looked from Stroud to Reeshar and back to Stroud. "Chardon shot himself in the arm and had to have it cut off. Went under anyhow. His squaw's gone with Perkins." He paused to dart an appraising glance over Stroud's camp, noting its opened cache with the bulky, irregularly shaped bundles of trade goods and farther back from the stream the pile of smaller uniform packs of beaver pelts ready to be sold. "Texas is one of the States now, and the greasers are hoppin' mad and fixin' to fight. Drips is the new Indian agent. Some dragoons are comin' this way."

"U. S. Dragoons?" asked Hobart.

"The First Regiment," Reeshar said.

"Why are them pork eaters comin' here?" Hobart wanted to know.

"To scare the Injuns away from the movers." Cebull gave a short laugh. "Next thing you know they'll be carryin' 'em to Oregon piggyback."

" 'Scare' be damned," mumbled Hobart. "Only scare them dragoons breeds is among durned fools."

Greenberry also had his doubts. "*Ti-ya*. I've seen 'em on the Arkansas."

"When'll they be here?" Hobart asked.

"A month maybe." Cebull wasn't much interested. His attention had settled on the ten packs of beaver skins, bound tightly with buckskin rope. With eighty pelts to a pack and each pack averaging around a hundred pounds, they were worth noticing. "You didn't trap all them, that's certain."

"Trapped and traded," replied Stroud. His tone didn't invite conversation.

"A trader from Taos said beaver's bringin' eight dollars a plew," remarked Greenberry.

Cebull motioned toward Reeshar. "He didn't hear it in Taos."

Stroud wasn't entirely convinced. The trade in pelts was coming back, and even at six dollars a plew his beaver would bring nearly five thousand dollars. And it was just as well that they didn't know he wore that much more around his middle. Four times during the past months he had swapped furs for trade goods and cash to other traders without going near a fort.

Cebull had given a possible answer to one question, at least. Stroud looked at Reeshar. "So that's where you've been. Taos."

"There and the States," said Reeshar. He had also been observing the packs of furs. He indicated them with a jerk of his head. "I'll take them off your hands. Five-fifty a pound."

"You trading for Fort Platte?"

"Not just trading for it. I'm running it. I'm the boss—the *bourgeois*."

"I'll do my business with Pryce." Stroud turned his back on Reeshar. He traded with Pryce at Fort Laramie whenever he could, and he'd eat his furs before he'd sell them to Reeshar. Stroud remembered the way Reeshar used to belittle trapping as a means of getting ahead in the world. Stroud felt he'd taken his first step up that winter when they struck out for themselves as free trappers, and he considered himself successful in having gone on to become an independent trader. Now, he thought, Reeshar shows up, having somehow managed to talk old Charles Wyatt into putting him in charge of a trading post—even though it was a skinflint one like Fort Platte. But maybe he shouldn't be surprised. He always had felt that Reeshar expected to start at the top in anything he did. Take Emlyn Pryce though, the *bourgeois* at Fort Laramie. As good a man as ever gnawed poor bull in spring. He'd been in and around Fort Laramie from the first, working up from clerk to trapping brigade leader to trade caravan captain to *bourgeois*. He'd be finding Reeshar pretty hard to stomach.

Stroud walked over to Maud, who was still cropping contentedly. He wished Reeshar would shut up and be gone, giving him needed time to get used to the idea that Reeshar was alive. He led Maud, unprotesting now, to where Wyatt and Mozay still stood beside the bundles.

He had met Reeshar eight years ago at Bent's Fort, when they had joined up with a fur brigade headed for the valley of Taos and the Bayou Salade. That had been Stroud's second winter in the mountains and Reeshar's first. That early winter as they had moved up the Purgatory—not really so long ago—Stroud had felt that they could hunt and live in wild freedom forever. Reeshar had seemed well pleased with the arrangement, too. Common sense and sturdy virtues—whatever they were—hadn't come between them then. What a fool he'd been. In his memory Stroud could see the valley of the Purgatory, with its loamy soil so deep the horses sank to their fetlocks, the snakelike coilings of the stream traceable by the groves of dead cottonwoods along the margin, cliffs and prairie alternating, far up to the mountain gap from where it emerged. He took up a rope, made a large single loop, and tossed the loop over Maud's *aparejo* so that it hung down on the off side below the mule's belly. "Let's get these packs on," he said to Wyatt. He lifted up one of the roped bundles and waited for Wyatt to carry his bundle to the other side of Maud. Mozay went to get another mule.

Reeshar, who had been watching Stroud's broad back, looked now at Greenberry. "What about your share?" he asked, contemptuously ignoring whatever agreement might be holding Stroud and his men together.

"This coon'll pack it on down, do 'ee hyar?" said Greenberry.

Reeshar shrugged and glanced questioningly at Partout.

"*Non, m'sieu'*," Partout explained. "I am also free trapper. I am go *le* Platte down. I am trade *avec le bourgeois* Pryce." Partout paused and then added, as if to convince himself, "Free trapper make very much dollar. Very much if it is not *pour le* dam' *rascalite* 'Rickaree *et le* dam' Blackfoot."

Hobart was not as quick as the others to turn down Reeshar's offer. He scratched his chin through his bushy red beard and eyed Reeshar speculatively. "Aye," he said finally. "Pryce'll raise the ante, I'm thinkin'."

Reeshar looked then at Mozay. "Want to sell your share?"

Mozay gave a negative shake of his head. "If I didn't think Pryce'd pay more, I *would*."

Reeshar turned his attention to Wyatt, whose downy beard was flecked by the early June sunlight, taking in the details of the young man's worn but well-cut clothes— dark corduroy breeches tucked into expensive boots, belted half-coat open, revealing a soft red wool shirt. A small clay pipe was stuck into the band of his felt hat. "You must be Alfred Wyatt," stated Reeshar. "Your uncle's worried about you."

"It'll do him good," said Wyatt cheerfully. He threw the loop over the top of the packs to Stroud, who passed the end of his rope through the loop and drew it tight.

It seemed to Stroud that everybody worried about Wyatt except Wyatt himself. Wyatt refused to worry about anything. That was part of his trouble. He had come out for the summer two years ago with a hunting expedition of sportsmen and healthseekers from St. Louis and had surprised his uncle and guardian, old Charles Wyatt, by staying on. Stroud had always doubted that it was a love of the wilderness that kept Wyatt away from St. Louis—maybe something connected with gambling or a girl, since he just wouldn't stand up to things and seemed susceptible to both.

Reeshar had been regarding Stroud's pile of trade goods, which included two ten-gallon kegs of whiskey. He looked over at Stroud. "Shonka has enough for both of us."

Stroud finished knotting the sling rope that now held the two side packs together. He stepped behind Maud to see if the packs were balanced. Then he picked up a lash rope, passed one end over Maud's croup and handed the *cincha* beneath her belly to Wyatt. "Maybe. But you'll have to find him to get any of it," he said.

"You're going to find him for me."

Stroud clenched his fists and turned on Reeshar. "You managed to lose two women, but you've hung on to your old arrogance, haven't you? You never did see any wrong in using people. And you'll keep it up till the devil sends a subpoena for you. But by God you've used me for the last time!"

He turned his back again and drew the rope between the packs, made a loop, and passed it over the packs. He wouldn't have thought Reeshar would try a trick like that. He guessed he didn't know what Reeshar was capable of— that he never had really known him.

Wyatt, as well as the others, had interrupted his work at the exchange between the two men. The boy looked from Stroud to Reeshar. "You better come with us," Reeshar said to him. "It might be a lot safer."

After a moment Wyatt said, "Thank you. I'll stay with George."

Stroud's attention was drawn by the sound of a dog yelping in pain. One of the camp dogs came tearing through the tall grass, making straight for camp. When the dog got close enough, Stroud could see the animal's nose stuck full of porcupine quills. With sharp yelps, the dog ran right on through the camp and straight between Maud's fore and hind legs. The sudden clamor of the dog seemed to recall to Maud her recent ill temper. She bowed her neck, jackknifed her hind legs, and pulled free. Before anyone could head her, Maud bounded off, kicking loose the unsecured packs and trailing streamers of scarlet squaw cloth between Stroud and Reeshar like wide streaks of blood.

Two

It was Wyatt who finally went after Maud and caught up with her where she was snared in a thicket. Having asserted her independence, she meekly allowed Wyatt to lead her back to camp. Reeshar and his men had withdrawn a couple of hundred yards upstream, where they were making coffee and lounging insolently while they waited for Stroud's party to break camp.

Stroud's men had all had their say about Reeshar and had simmered down into a tight-lipped silence as they worked to get packed, with the exception of Greenberry, who still muttered and swore as he tightened the lash ropes on one of the mules. Stroud and Hobart were packing the next animal. ". . . infernal, low-down, rot-mouthed, scaley-heeled, whiskey-wastin' potheads!" Greenberry was saying. "I'd split their skulls clean down to the swaller. I'd jump down their throats and gallop ever' chitterlin' out of 'em afore they could say quit!"

Stroud, who was working with his teeth clamped tight on his pipestem, didn't say anything. He knew the old man was just working off steam. There wasn't anything that could be done about Reeshar now, short of a pitched battle, and that would only get somebody killed. Greenberry gave a final yank on the rope. "All I know is, them cussed, no-count, good-for-nothin', dad-drotted sonsabitches beat anything in the mountains or out!" Greenberry went off toward Wyatt and Maud with renewed mutterings.

When the pack train was ready, Stroud gathered up his belongings and took time to check the contents of his or-namented deerskin possible sack—flint and steel, whetstone, and awl and sinew, plus a few nonessentials. Then he slung

18

it from his shoulders, along with a powder horn, bullet mold and shot pouch. There were certain things a man had to have and he by God better make sure he had them. Way things had gone around camp this morning was enough to make a man forget his head. Stroud knocked the ashes from his pipe and jammed it into the wide belt of his hunting shirt, which also held his sheathed Green River knife, hatchet and Colt. Taking up his rifle, Stroud swung into the saddle.

"Now listen here," he said to his men as they waited for him to move out. "I'll settle my trouble with Reeshar myself. Until then he's an opposition trader and nothing else." After a moment Stroud added, "And if anybody knows anything about him I don't, tell me now."

Stroud waited, but when no one had anything to say, he started off downstream, and the pack train, like a centipede in disjointed sections, began to stretch out along the stream until at full length it extended for a quarter of a mile. Stroud rode for nearly an hour before he permitted himself to look back. Reeshar was barely within sight.

This was the pattern of the next week, a period in which Stroud tried every device he knew to lose Reeshar. They moved in the dark of night leaving dummy camps behind; they muffled the hoofs of their animals with buffalo hide and tried doubling back past Reeshar; they traveled day and night without rest, taking tortuous trails; they concealed themselves, leaving Reeshar to follow false trails; they tried to run off Reeshar's animals. But at the end of the week Reeshar and his men were still sticking like hungry wolves. Never close, never very far.

Stroud reined in and glanced back at the hills through which they had ridden. Forbidding they seemed now, their shadows lengthening and their partial cover of pine and cedar assuming darker hues in the late afternoon. As he thought of the game of follow-the-leader Reeshar had been playing with him among the cut-rock walls and timbered bottoms and unwooded valleys, he muttered an oath. After all his big talk Reeshar was using him again and there didn't seem to be anything he could do about it.

A week lost trying to shake Reeshar loose! But a man could remember a lot in a week. And worry a lot, too. It was one thing to vow to get the truth and something else to know how to go about it. Could be that Batchika or Wicarpi—whichever one had left the camp with Reeshar seven years ago—was alive, too, Stroud reasoned. And if he could find her it would save a deal of trouble. But where? It was a lick-skillet business all the way around. With Reeshar acting the way he was, a man hardly knew what to suspect him of.

Stroud turned his attention to the old man in his worn buckskins whom they had come upon seated on the rocky edge of a soda spring. "It's Merk," he said.

The old man had barely taken notice of their approach, so absorbed was he in staring at the phenomenon of the effervescent water. "Thar's devils in them dancin' waters," the old man muttered.

It was always a surprise to run across old Merk. Each time seemed as if it would probably be the last. Nobody knew when he came to the mountains, where he came from, or a time when he hadn't been here. Stroud observed the old trapper's camp. In a jumbled pile were saddles, packs and trap sack. An Indian pony and two mules grazed hobbled among the cottonwoods which formed a grove around the spring. He studied Merk's horse, with its ewe-neck and tucked-up flanks and frayed tail. "Hard doings when it comes to that." Stroud raised his voice slightly. "*Hoú-kola!*" he said, using the Lakota greeting. But the old man's attention was still on the bubbling spring.

Wyatt was staring at the old man. "I should think an Indian would've had his scalp."

"It's winter-kill that'll put Merk under, not Indians," said Stroud. "They think he's a holy man. He's been this way long as I've been in the mountains, though he gets worse all the time."

"Crazy or not, he's done all right," observed Wyatt. He was eyeing a sizeable pack of beaver pelts and another generous bundle of dressed skins.

Greenberry shifted his cud of tobacco. "*Wagh!* Time was that'd be a poor catch for one hunt. He's been out for three snows."

"*Sacrebleu!*" said Partout. "He go under t'ree, four, ten time, he come up twenty time!"

Stroud tried again. "Where from, Merk?"

The old man finally turned his head, his hair yellow-gray and stringy, his pale-blue eyes cloudy, his face and hands barely distinguishable in texture from his buckskins. "Ye ain't fools enough to camp here," he said. "No good comes of sleepin' here." After a moment he remembered Stroud's question. "Wind River—bound to Laramie fork to trade."

"What's the sign?"

Merk scratched his head thoughtfully. "War party of Shoshones crossed the Divide maybe a week ago."

"Any Sioux?"

Merk shook his head.

"Buffalo?" Stroud prompted.

Merk nodded. "Heap buffler. Seal-fat." His eyes, which had seemed clearer for a moment, clouded again.

Wyatt had walked his horse over to Merk's packs and saddles and was examining the bundle of dressed deerskins. They were of particularly good quality. He called to Merk. "Will you sell me enough of these buckskins to make a suit?"

Merk looked around and his watery eyes reflected a shrewdness. "Them's Crow-dressed. Ain't none finer."

Wyatt smiled. "Name your price."

"Coffee? 'Bacca?" Wyatt nodded. Merk looked at the pack mules and saw the two kegs. "Whiskey?" Again Wyatt nodded. "Have your pick," said Merk, getting painfully to his feet and going to his packs.

"Can't blame you for wanting to get rid of those fool clothes," Stroud said to Wyatt. "But every time you start planning to get respectable buckskins made, you bring on disaster."

Wyatt grinned. "This is only my third start." He dismounted and went to join Merk.

"And the 'Rapahoes got the first set of skins and the Snake River the second," Stroud reminded him. "What kind of Injun sign you going to conjure up for this one?" He turned to Merk. "Like to sell your whole catch?"

"Aim to trade at the forts," mumbled Merk, giving his attention to the bundle of skins he was untying.

Stroud lifted his eyes and looked off to the northeast. Beyond the benchland he could see the high, rolling plain stretching out past the long reaches of hogback and coulee, and shimmering like a sea of light in the afternoon sun. This was the northern end of the Laramie Basin, the region he had been heading toward since breaking winter camp. They had moved down the Laramie beyond the mouth of the Little Laramie and had crossed the divide to the Medicine Bow. It was there that Reeshar had interfered as they were digging out the cache. For a week now they had traveled through the Medicine Bow range. Another two days would bring them well across the basin, where, if any of the buffalo Merk saw had ranged down from the Sweetwater, Shonka's band should be making its spring buffalo surround. And

Shonka hadn't gone north out of the basin or Merk would have seen him.

"Why am I camped here then, ye ask?" Merk was responding to Wyatt's attempt to humor him. He had returned to sit cross-legged by the spring, holding a pint cup full of whiskey, and by his side a bandanna knotted up at the corners bulged with coffee beans. He stared into the bubbling water. "Been downed a sight too often to be skeered by what can come out of them waters."

Stroud fixed his attention on a far point of crimson sandstone around which they had passed an hour earlier. He glanced next at the setting sun. "We'll camp farther down. Merk's all right."

Hobart spat in disgust. "Ain't we all half froze for sleep and grease? I'm sick of campin' cold and eatin' pemmican."

"Your squaw and the boy should've gone into the forts when Partout's woman did," Stroud said. He nudged his horse into a walk, his rebuke leaving Hobart glaring after him.

"I ain't no show animal to be worked hungry," Hobart growled.

Stroud paused by Wyatt, who was preparing to roll up the skins he had bought from Merk. Stroud's attention had been caught by a mark burned in with hot metal on the flesh side of one. He reached for the other two and upon examination saw that they were branded the same way, each skin at the middle, with a mark resembling a three-tined pitchfork. It was a curious way for Merk to mark his furs. Stroud returned the skins to Wyatt. "What's the mark?" he asked.

Merk spat into the bubbling water and wiped his mouth with the back of his hand. "The devil's mark. Ain't a devil as hisses can shine with this child." He laughed. "Tried 'em onc't. Fought 'em clawin' from here to hell and back again."

Stroud nudged his horse into motion. Behind him, Hobart sullenly sat his horse while the pack train passed. Hobart's Emma did not even glance in his direction. "*Cheyáya.* He is always crying," she said to Mozay's Madame Jack. They laughed. Hobart kicked his horse angrily and rode on to join the men, but as he passed Emma he gave her a backhanded blow that snapped her head back.

Looking back, Stroud saw what Hobart did. He was surprised. It wasn't like Hobart. He was a rough man, for a fact, but a reasonably good-natured one until lately. Stroud raised his eyes to the point of crimson cutrock by the trail. He had already taken too much time trying to lose Reeshar. Time in which another trader might find Shonka first, or in which the old chief might decide to go into the forts to trade. Maybe he was putting a strain on the others, who weren't getting as much out of it as he was. Stroud was considering the only stratagem possible when Wyatt came up beside him.

The younger man cast a backward glance, too. "What if Reeshar spoils your trade with Shonka?" He had mounted without tying the skins to his saddle, so he attended to it now.

"I've waited two years for Shonka." For two years the old chief had kept his people away from the forts. Even before that they had traded only for necessaries. Shonka's dislike of going to the forts to trade had gained him the reputation of being an "unfriendly" Indian, but Stroud respected the old chief. He wanted to keep to the old-time ways and this could be done only by staying away from the forts with their unlimited whiskey and, when there was nothing left to trade, the temptation to idle and beg— or to steal.

The stubbornness reflected in Stroud's voice amused

Wyatt. "You're in for it," Wyatt said. "Uncle Charles would skin an ant for its tallow."

Stroud remembered the account he had heard of the rich cache that suddenly passed into the hands of old Charles Wyatt—traded for, or stolen, or murdered for—it was long before Stroud had come to the mountains—maybe more legend than fact now. Old Wyatt was ruthless all right. Maybe he'd found something kindred in Reeshar. Stroud thought again of Reeshar's offer of five-and-a-half dollars a pound for his beaver. That came to about seven dollars a plew. Not a bad figure. With the trade in pelts coming back, and with Reeshar showing up as *bourgeois*, Stroud wondered if old Charles Wyatt hadn't decided to try and make Fort Platte pay off.

Stroud's party pushed on down into the basin where, just before dark, they saw a few buffalo grazing out on the plain. His decision made, Stroud indicated the buffalo and motioned the others on. He spurred his horse, and the men followed, whooping and hollering. In a matter of minutes a cow was slaughtered, the carcass was braced on its belly, and Stroud was skinning off the hide from neck to rump. As if summoned by the sound of the shot, a half-dozen large gray wolves came close and waited while Stroud severed the hump ribs from the vertebrae, parted the two-inch-thick fleece-fat, or *depuyer,* from the tough flesh of the back, and cut out the tongue. Everyone, including the boy, fed upon slices of raw liver sprinkled with gall bitters.

Stroud glanced distastefully at the wolves. Predatory cowards they were, cunning and evil. A pack no bigger than this could devour a deer carcass in ten minutes or less, leaving nothing but cleaned bones and a few scraps of hair. He guessed it wouldn't take that long on a smallish woman. Suddenly Stroud hated having to leave the rest of the buffalo for them. He turned away abruptly and mounted, the others following. It seemed to Stroud that his back was scarcely turned before the wolves were growling and snapping at the carcass.

They made camp. Soon the fire was ringed by hump ribs planted aslant on sharpened sticks, and *boudins* were roasting in the coals, the long, sausagelike pieces of small intestine knotted at the ends to keep the chyme from running out. The lengths of *boudins* cooked in a few seconds. Stroud fished a puffy coil from the fire, the steam escaping from little punctures, and ate it silently. Then, securing a frying pan from one of the squaws, he cooked some of the fleece. The others also ate quietly, each tending his own needs, until only the roasts were left. Stroud stood for a while watching the sizzling roasts, and occasionally he would scan the dark outlines of the benchland. Presently a pinpoint of light appeared in the distance—Reeshar announcing himself. Stroud moved into the dark and found his horse. Removing the hobbles, he led him back to the packs and saddles. The others watched him saddle up. When he was finished he said, "Greenberry, you know the sink of Deer Creek?"

"Do 'ee hyar now!"

Stroud realized he had ruffled the old man. Greenberry fooled you to look at him. Could be forty or seventy. He'd been at the Three Forks with Andrew Henry, and was the first with Robert Stuart to cross the Divide at South Pass and follow down the Sweetwater. "Wait for me there," Stroud said. He fastened on bridle and bit and then let the reins hang while he walked over to the packs. "Where's that fofarraw we fixed up for Shonka?" he inquired generally.

Hobart's Emma arose and soon found the parflêche that Stroud wanted. It contained articles of personal finery, plus an ivory hand mirror Stroud had got especially for

Shonka. Emma was a handsome woman, with a perfect oval face and glossy black hair parted severely and stretched tight to her scalp. There was a black bruise on her cheekbone from Hobart's blow. Stroud took the bulky oblong container and began to tie it to his saddle. The horse shied. Emma stepped up quickly. "*Mayúza*. I hold," she offered, grasping the reins.

Stroud secured the parflêche, took the reins from Emma, and mounted. "Much obliged."

"Aren't you taking someone along for company?" asked Wyatt.

"Hell's full of company. See you at Deer Creek." Stroud rode off, disappearing quickly into the night.

Wyatt listened to the receding hoofbeats. It took courage or self-confidence—maybe they were the same—to ride alone in the wilderness. Wyatt was thoughtful as he pulled the pipe from his hatband and filled it from a pouch which hung around his neck. He wondered what kind of predicament he was in. He supposed if real trouble developed between Reeshar and Stroud, his uncle would expect him to side with Reeshar. But Wyatt had never seen the man until a week ago and he'd been with Stroud for two years now. There hadn't been any reason to anticipate trouble when he stayed on after that first summer by choosing to go out with Stroud. Certainly there'd have been no fun in hanging around Fort Platte with Old Man Rem and Cebull or in going out with any of the *engagés*. Company trappers were rarely choice companions. And Stroud was his pick of the free traders even though he did do his business at Fort Laramie. Stroud was a good trader, mostly good company, and it had been a good two years. Better even than Wyatt had hoped. With the help of a little sign language an Indian camp could be mighty entertaining.

Wyatt lighted his pipe from the fire. All he could do was

wait. But if anything did happen, he'd keep out of it—just refuse to take sides. It wasn't his fight. Wyatt turned to Greenberry. "This old quarrel between Stroud and Reeshar," he said. "What's the whole of it?"

Greenberry looked up from the moccasin he was mending, a task calculated to take his attention from the roasts. "Do 'ee think we know, boy?"

Hobart said sullenly, "A man's past is his own." He impatiently pared a thin slice from the edge of a hissing roast.

Mozay, who to all appearances was asleep with his head on his possible sack, opened his eyes. "Not with it flashin' afore us like the behind of a antelope, it ain't," he disagreed. Mozay, by his own admission, had been at one time or another a gunsmith, an itinerant peddler, a flatboatman, a hog drover, a blacksmith and a stagecoach driver. But he had come to the mountains before he was twenty, so it was an obvious conclusion that the truth was too small for his imagination.

Hobart glared at the wiry Mozay. "Antelope be damned! Bears on a chain we are. Bein' drug around so's Stroud can blow his take in St. Louis, I'm bound, on soft beds and fancy gals." Hobart licked his fingers and sat down, much like a shaggy animal settling itself on its haunches. The fire glinted in his curly red beard and thick, tangled hair, which hung loose over his shoulders.

"*Wagh!*" said Greenberry. "Anybody can go to St. Louis if that's the way his stick floats." He paused and then added, "Besides, ye're on shares."

"Cabin fevers he have and no cabin," Partout said of Hobart. He laughed merrily at his own witticism.

"They sounded like they might have been friends at one time—George and Reeshar," said Wyatt. "Though Reeshar doesn't seem especially likeable."

"He *was*." Mozay stretched and rolled over on his side,

propping his head on one arm in a half-elevated position. He seemed oblivious of the curiosity that his statement had created.

"*Enfant de garce!* He sleep on his wedding night, this one," said Partout.

Greenberry looked at Mozay accusingly. "*Wagh!* Ye are plain trap-mouthed."

"Jest saw him once, old hoss," Mozay explained. "Rendezvous of '37. He was sashaying around nice as you please. A little green. But the likablest sort of fellow you'd ever want to see."

Greenberry eyed him suspiciously. Though truth was in Mozay, a body had to feel around to make certain when and if it was coming out. "Do 'ee hyar now!" Greenberry said. "And where was I?"

"Livin' with the Crows, I heered," Mozay replied. Though his body remained relaxed, Mozay's face with its crescent of beard had the bright, quick look of a chipmunk.

Greenberry cut the sinew with which he was sewing and put on his moccasin. "*Ti-ya,*" he agreed finally, convinced that Mozay knew what he was talking about. "And a bigger fool never cut red meat 'cross the grain."

Hobart, interested in spite of himself, remained unconvinced. "I was there."

Mozay nodded. "You were *that*. And 'tarnal drunk for a week." He turned to Wyatt. "He's *one*, Hobart is, and sometimes two or three. Rides standin' on the saddle and drinkin' whiskey, he does. Then tosses up a *pomme blanche* and catches it on his old Green River. All at full speed, mind ye. Then durned if he don't ride standin' on his head. 'Tain't often he chambers that much raise-devil."

"Aye," admitted Hobart. After a moment his doubt returned. "And you were drunk, too, I'm thinkin'."

"If you can get drunk with no beaver and no credit, I

29

was," contradicted Mozay. He shook his head. "So horrid sober I sold Reeshar two traps jest afore they went off."

For the first time in the conversation Wyatt found something to seize upon. "Reeshar and Stroud? Trapping together?"

Mozay gave an affirmative grunt.

"That would be the time they were talking about, I expect," Wyatt thought aloud.

"*Ti-ya*." Greenberry looked at Mozay. "And I suppose ye know what women they were quarrelin' over?"

"If they're the ones that left rendezvous with 'em that year, I *do*," said Mozay. He was silent a moment. "Though you couldn't really call 'em women. Not more'n fourteen, fifteen at most. Jest the age Injun gals are ripe for pickin'. Crows they was. And if anything'll snap a man's head around, them little Crow squaws will."

Mozay sat up and hugged his knees, looking into the fire. "Jest to see Stroud with that Batchika made a man feel young all over again. Don't suppose he'd ever been in love before—he couldn't've been twenty yet hisself. Him and spring was bustin' out together thar on the Green River."

Mozay paused and smiled into the fire. "It was a good rendezvous. Injuns all done up in their feathers and fofarraw—Crows, 'Rapahoes, Bannocks, Shoshones, Utes. Even a few Blackfeet come down, and some Hudson's Bay men from Fort Hall. And them Injun ponies—musta been four, five thousand—spreadin' out spottylike on the plain, and off to the east them Wind River Mountains holdin' up their snowy tops jest to show how much space there was. That Scotchman hunter come with the trade caravan that year. Brought a artist fella along to draw everything he seed. Even brought a suit of armor special for Jim Bridger. Long towards the last the Bannocks took to thievin' and we had

30

a three-day runnin' fight with 'em." Mozay gave a long sigh. "It was *some*."

"What about George and Reeshar?" asked Wyatt.

"Never seed Reeshar or them Crow gals again."

"And George?"

"Next rendezvous he's alone. And there warn't none to amount to much after that," Mozay explained to Wyatt. "Funny thing about that last big one. It was swarmin' with missionaries. Two on their way back to the States to get more, and four others with their wives on the way to Oregon to join up with Whitman's mission. If it warn't for the drinkin' and the cussin' and the fightin' and the gamblin', you'd've thought it was a revival meetin'."

"*Wagh!* Missed that one, too," muttered Greenberry.

Mention of the old-time big rendezvous had a silencing effect. It was not the same, taking furs into a fort, as meeting to trade with the Company representatives once a year on some green mountain meadow a thousand miles from nowhere. Greenberry returned sinew and awl to his possible sack and grasped a stick of hump rib. "Hyar's the doin's, and the child as does," he said. He began cutting off rib bones. "Freeze into it, boys."

"A hell of a way to live," grumbled Hobart as he took one of the long meaty bones. "Starve all day like a coyote, then stuff yourself like a snake that's swallowed a frog."

The interrogation of Mozay was forgotten while everyone ate ravenously. Food disappeared quickly, as if the marrow, raw liver, *boudins* and fleece had never been. Juices seeped into the beards of the men, and the piles of cleaned bones mounted. There was suddenly an exclamation of distress from the boy, young Hobart. The others paused and watched as he began exploring his mouth with a thumb and forefinger. After a moment he grinned and showed them a small tooth which he held in his hand. He was a sturdy child with a mop of unruly red hair and olive skin. He rolled the tooth in the palm of his hand. "Why do they come out?"

His mother, Emma, smiled. "There's a story why. An Old-Man story."

Young Hobart looked at her expectantly. He knew many Old-Man stories. Old-Man-Coyote made the world and everything in it and was always making mistakes and forgetting. Young Hobart had even overheard the story of why Old-Man-Coyote came to sleep with his mother-in-law. He sometimes wondered if there was a story why the Great Spirit, Wakon Secha, gave so much work to funny Old-Man.

"It begins by Old-Man walking beside a big river, carrying his songs in a bag," Emma said.

"Don't fill the boy with your heathen nonsense," growled Hobart.

Across the circle Greenberry wiped his mouth on his sleeve. "*Wagh!*" he said. "Happened on a day when Old-Man was half froze for meat. He come to this marshy place by the river, where some ducks was swimmin' around amongst the reeds. They asked what was in his pack, and when Old-Man told 'em it was songs, they wanted him to stop and sing so's they could dance. Old-Man figgered them ducks'd be tasty a heap—most as good as panther or beaver tail. '*Ti-ya*,' he said. 'I'll sing ye a medicine song if ye keep your eyes shut, do 'ee hyar?' Old-Man commenced singin', and when the ducks commenced dancin', Old-Man took a stick and knocked 'em on the head one by one. The last duck, though, suspicioned somethin' wrong and opened his eyes in time to fly away and save hisself.

"Then Old-Man built a fire and buried the other ducks in the coals. The one that got away, though, was tarnal tantalizin', so Old-Man went off to look for him. Whilst he was

32

gone a wolf come along and feathered into them roastin'
ducks. Ate 'em all, do 'ee hyar? Then, to be ornery, he
filled their empty carcasses with stones and put 'em back
into the coals afore he slunk off. D'reckly Old-Man come
back empty-handed, hungrier than ever. He raked the birds
out of the fire, bit into the first one, and busted off all his
front teeth. There he was, hoppin' around, spittin' blood
and teeth and madder'n a she bear with two cubs and a
sore tail."

Young Hobart laughed.

"And that's how it was," concluded Greenberry. "Warn't
no one else around to get even with, so Old-Man picked
on all young 'uns like you. He 'lowed that from then on all
young 'uns would lose their teeth." Greenberry resumed
his eating.

Hobart threw a bone into the fire. "Times you sound
more Injun than white."

Young Hobart, who was staring into the fire, said to
Greenberry, "Old-Man-Coyote really busted his teeth for
bein' a greedy-gut, didn't he?"

"*Ti-ya.* Unhonest, too, boy." Greenberry finished a
hump rib and tossed it aside. "Anyhow, buffler still shines."
He wiped his Green River knife clean on the leg of
his buckskins.

"Might've been any fool thing started trouble with
Stroud and Reeshar." He was talking more to himself now
than to the others. "Holed up for a winter, folks get touchy,
do 'ee hyar?"

"Where there's women or liquor mixed in," said Hobart,
"you're sure to be throwed some way."

"Not liquor," said Greenberry. "But the women now,
bein' Crows . . . Ain't hardly a night clear enough, even
in this rarefied air, a one of 'em can tell their own husbands
from Belteshazzar's off ox."

"You really mean that?" asked Wyatt.

"*Wagh!* Mozay's right. The Crow women are powerful pretty, but no more choosy than she-wolves in heat. Most of 'em anyhow." Greenberry picked up a stick and started whittling it aimlessly with his Green River.

"Beauty and virtue don't always go together even in St. Louis," said Wyatt.

"*Ti-ya.*" After a moment Greenberry continued, "Some things Injuns do makes more sense than the whites. But most of the tribes have a trick or two that give a body a turn, do 'ee hyar? The Crows, now. They're hell on societies. The Foxes and the Big Dogs are two of 'em, and every year jest after the thaws they make a sport of wife stealin'. Not jest any wives, do 'ee hyar? They only steal ones they've bedded with and only from the men of the other society." Greenberry gave a vicious slash with his knife at the stick in his hand. "And then, by Jesus, with a wife snatched from under him, a man's supposed to act like he don't give a damn or he loses face. Ye're expected to act like bein' cuckolded ain't nothin' to fret about, do 'ee hyar? And with the Crows I reckon it ain't."

Mozay eyed Greenberry for a moment. "Don't sound like anything worth missin' a rendezvous for," he said.

"Missed two, by beaver," muttered Greenberry.

Partout stood up and stretched. As he looked out into the night he saw the glow of Reeshar's fire. "*Vides poches!*"

"Wisht they'd start a fight," said Hobart.

"They won't," said Mozay. "That'd be like callin' off the hounds jest afore they treed the 'coon."

Young Hobart was reluctant to give in to the sleepiness coming upon him. "Tell about when you were in the circus, Pa."

"The tents was full of patches and the ropes full of

knots," muttered Hobart. "Go to sleep." In a moment Emma got up and led the boy off to his robes.

Wyatt tried to assess what he had learned as he finished eating, but it didn't amount to much. He decided it was useless to speculate as to what the trouble was between Stroud and Reeshar. Yet it seemed impossible to dismiss it from his mind, and off and on for the next two days he found himself wondering about it after all as they traveled across the north end of the semi-arid basin with its plats of bluish salt grass and sage and dotted with the white blossoms of the *pomme blanche,* the turnip of the prairies. At noon the next day they made camp among the cottonwoods and marsh grasses of the sink of Deer Creek. While they waited for Stroud, the men mended gear and the squaws scraped down the green hide of the buffalo. The women had hung up some meat for safekeeping, the scent of which attracted several wolves. One, larger and bolder than the others, twice provoked Mozay into throwing rocks at him to remind him to keep his distance.

Stroud arrived just before sundown. "Where'd you find Shonka?" Mozay asked.

"North Fork of the Laramie."

"Will he trade?" asked Wyatt.

Stroud lifted his leg over the saddle horn and slid to the ground. "Shonka's willing enough." He began uncinching the double-rigged saddle. "But some of his soldier-chiefs are damned and determined to go to the forts." He loosened the other cinch and dragged the saddle and blanket off, depositing them with the row of packs and saddles.

"Where there's a heap more whiskey, and movers to Oregon to steal from," said Mozay.

Stroud kneeled down to fasten a hobble to his horse's forelegs. "But not until they get a feast from us and Reeshar. They know he's out, too."

35

"*Wagh!*" Greenberry was disgusted. "They'll ask ye both for powder and ball and a palette of vermilion and a lookin' glass, and fofarraw for their squaws. Then they'll say their medicine ain't right for tradin'."

Stroud grunted as he buckled on the leather hobble. This world was all wrong anyhow. A week spent trying to lose Reeshar, and now Shonka wouldn't talk business unless they were both there. Stroud straightened up and removed the bridle and bit. Then with a slap on the horse's rump he sent the animal to join the others grazing in the marshy meadow. Stroud looked out across the basin. Snow still topped the ranges both to west and east, though not as much as last year. The Platte would be low this spring. He draped his bridle over the saddle horn, spread his saddle blanket, and stretched out on the ground.

Reeshar must have seen Stroud ride in and would guess where he had been. The idea of having Reeshar in Shonka's camp made Stroud restless. Trading was a ticklish business at best. Custom and the nature of the Indians had set a pattern for it. First upon entering camp would be the distributing of trinkets, like a drummer handing out samples. Then the feasting, a toll the Indians collected because they knew they could get it. Afterward, the council with the chiefs, angling for their approval to trade with the band, when a wrong word or a breach in etiquette could lose you the trade quicker than greased lightning. Even if permission to trade was given, there were still plenty of pitfalls. The knives and whatever guns were in camp had to be collected and kept under guard. Even the Indians knew that weapons and whiskey didn't mix, so at least Shonka would take a hand in this. Then the trade itself—judging the quality of the pelts and skins, deciding how much they were worth in trade and sticking to it. To pay too much to one Indian would have the rest of the band quarrelsome enough to fatten wildcats. Last was determining the exact time to stop the trade and get out: too soon and the Indians would be after your scalp for taking their furs without satisfying their thirst; dally too long and they'd have it. All the hazards of trading were complicated by whiskey, and a rival trader in camp at the same time multiplied the danger all along the line. The next few days were going to be a caution to slow dogs.

Mostly Stroud liked trading with the Indians. Getting the trade and seeing it through was a challenge, made more exciting by the dangers. But the whiskey was an abomination. What whiskey did to an Indian rested heavy on a man's conscience, if he had a conscience. Besides, it gave nothing of value for the rich pelts which meant days, weeks and months of work. Trinkets, yes. The Indians valued trinkets. But without whiskey Stroud wouldn't be in business. And maybe he shouldn't be. Sometimes it made him wonder what he was doing out here.

He couldn't remember exactly how or when it was that he decided to come. Born on the Cumberland plateau in the shadow of the mountains, it had been natural to turn west. The mountains were higher and the open stretches wider. The laurel and azaleas and rhododendrons of the mid-South turned into cottonwood and sagebrush and pine. But to a Tennessee boy raised with a gun in his hands, hunting the rugged hills and deep ravines of Fentress County, it was a logical choice.

Stroud glanced toward the west at a low ridge about a hundred yards away. Then abruptly he grasped his rifle and sat up. Sharply silhouetted against the sunset sky were the half-dozen wolves that had retreated on Stroud's arrival in camp. Taking a quick aim, more as if he were throwing a shot at the wolves to drive them off, he fired. The large wolf leaped up and fell back, the others disappearing as if suddenly swallowed by the ground. Stroud reloaded his rifle with a certain deliberateness, then lay down again. He knew what the others were thinking. In a country where wolves were almost constantly in sight, a man didn't waste powder on them. It was a fool thing to do.

Three

The sun was high when Stroud sighted Shonka's village. The camp crier had announced the approach of traders, and by the time they arrived the whole band was assembled in the center of the camp circle. Stroud inhaled the familiar smell—a blend of green hides drying, old leather, smoke, cooking meat, dogs and grease. Not unpleasant. Just Indian.

He decided at least to try to gain favor by distributing gifts before Reeshar caught up with him. He was just finishing when Reeshar rode into camp. Between them they contributed *paezhúta sapa*, the black medicine, sweetened with the white juice of the box elder, and liberal quantities of flour to make *aguiápi*, the brown-all-over bread that came hot from the iron pots buried under the coals. Then they met with the chiefs in solemn council in Shonka's big lodge. While the pipe was making its passage around the circle, Stroud kept his eyes upon Shonka, knowing that it was with this flat-headed old savage that his chances of trading rested. The Oglalas, Stroud knew, were split since the drunken murder of Bull Bear by Old Smoke himself in Smoke's village four years earlier. Many of the Bear People, such as Shonka's band, stayed away from the forts, holding the Smoke People in contempt as beggars who turned their backs on the old-time ways. But in Shonka's band the young chiefs of the *akicíta*, the warrior societies, were discontent. Strongest in his opposition to Shonka during the council was Shonka's son-in-law Eahsapa, the Black Bear, chief of the society known as the Bowstring Soldiers.

Eahsapa was short for a Lakota, as the Sioux called themselves, being several inches under six feet; but this was com-

39

pensated for by his luxuriant hair, which hung loose and thick to his hips, except for the scalp lock at the crown of his head, which was braided and secured in a loop with a metal disk. He was well-muscled and broad of shoulder and his chest and upper arms were tattooed, unusual for an Oglala Sioux, with vermilion and gunpowder worked into the skin. At a little distance it gave the appearance of embroidery. In profile his head had a half-moon shape, jutting chin, beaked nose and low forehead curving in an almost unbroken line, which somewhat spoiled his fine appearance. His mouth looked as if it was mortised into his face like a mule's shoe, heels down. From the minute he first opened it, he meant trouble. Eahsapa said it was good to count *coup* on their enemies and steal their best horses. But it was also true that the trading houses of the whites had many good things the people needed, things better than the people could make by following the old-time ways. They had robes and furs with which to buy more than the trinkets of the mule-pack traders.

Then Shonka brought into the open the thoughts he knew lurked in the young men's minds; of the white-topped wagons raising the dust along the Shell, which the white men call the Platte; of the timorous whites so easily frightened by the naked young warriors in their glistening paint; of the herds of horses easily driven off into the hills; of the stragglers yielding easy scalps; and of the whiskey afterward at the trader houses. They thought the firewater would make them feel good toward one another but instead it always made them as mad dogs in their own lodges.

The young chiefs grew sullen as Shonka went on to speak of how Wakon Secha, the Great Spirit, had been kind to his people. There was food in the parflèches, skins and robes piled in the lodges, and when Wakon Secha spread his white robe over the hills, Shonka's people were warm and well fed around their lodge fires. If there was trading to do, let it be done away from the mud forts on the Shell, in their own village, where the traders would not be foolish enough to cheat them. Surely with two traders in the village, there would be enough of the bright cloth and the blue blankets, enough of the finery to make their women proud to be wives of Lakota men. His warriors had taken many scalps and many fine horses from their enemies, the Snakes and the Crows and the Pawnees. The strong hearts of his warriors did not need the whiskey of the white traders to make them stronger.

Big murmurs of dissent passed around the circle that ringed the lodge fire, and when the young men, led by Eahsapa, arose and left Shonka's lodge without another word, Stroud understood the Indian temperament well enough to know that nothing was likely to change their minds. It amounted to a clear-cut victory for Reeshar. Not that Reeshar would get all the trade. With Fort Platte and Fort Laramie so close together, Reeshar couldn't hog it all. Pryce was bound to get a share. But it didn't leave anything for a free trader.

As he went over all this in his mind, Stroud clenched his fists. He had come close to combining two winters' good catch with a big trade. By September he could have been in St. Louis. Now he'd have to stay another winter. It was "another winter" that had kept him in the mountains for nine years. And each year beaver was scarcer. It was either cut foot or drown.

Stroud filled his pipe and struck a light with his tinderbox. The village was still celebrating the buffalo surround, and he was watching the bobbing, weaving dancers. Two tipis had been pitched together, the poles crossed and the lodge skins rolled up to form a large pavilion. A half-dozen men beat time on a hollow-log drum, while another half-dozen squatted in a row and played on hand drums. The dancers and watchers sang in a high-pitched chant. It was the eating dance they were doing. A person of one sex was supposed to invite someone of the opposite sex to dance by offering food, and Mozay's Madame Jack provoked a laugh when she invited a toothless old man to dance by offering him a huge bone. Stroud noted by the light of the many small flares that Wyatt, usually to be found dancing with the young women, was nowhere in sight. The others were all watching though—Reeshar and his men, as well as Stroud's.

After a while it occurred to Stroud that there was more than one way to skin an Indian—and a company trader. Not what he'd hoped for maybe, but a way to split the tribe's trade. As a plan grew in his mind, Stroud left the dancing and began walking through the camp, which ranged for more than a mile along the creek bottom. The skin lodges glowed like yellow lanterns, and the camp noises mingled to form a subdued clamor. Stroud listened particularly to the many songs characteristic of an Indian camp, especially a prosperous village which had completed a successful buffalo surround, with the scaffolds sagging from the weight of meat and back fat drying, and the area around each lodge covered with skins pegged down for thinning. As the song of the dancers lost its dominance, Stroud heard the minor chant of a medicine man singing to the favorable spirits. From another direction came the sweet and weird notes of a love song played upon a flute. Then Stroud distinguished the music he had been listening for—the lively rhythm of a gambling song. He followed the song to a large tipi at the south edge of the camp. Without hesitating Stroud pulled back the flap and entered.

A noisy game of "hands" was in progress. It was a game Stroud had played many times—the Indians' variation of the old shell game. Or more likely the shell game was a variation of "hands." Two people who sat facing each other did the actual playing, and they took turns being the one-who-hides-something and the one-who-guesses. Those who wanted in the game sided with one or the other of the two contestants and placed bets much like gamblers around a dice table. Drummers beat time on hand drums and everybody sang a noisy accompaniment to the rhythmic movements of the one-who-hides-something, who manipulated a small, polished bone.

At the moment Wyatt was the one-who-guesses. Playing against him was a young girl. Stroud realized with some surprise that it was Shonka's younger daughter, Tasina, suddenly grown up—or thinking she was. Instead of the usual deerskin clothing, she wore a flaming red dress of cotton squaw cloth, wrapped toga-fashion and belted with a wide belt dyed black and studded with flat brass buttons. And she had fancied up her hair by knotting her braids at each ear and fixing them with quill-embroidered deerskin and sprigs of sage. She was some, and ready for a man, Stroud guessed. Just like any girl when she started prettying herself up and hoping.

Stroud looked around the group. Enough maybe to get something under way. "*Iyuts*. I play," he said. He motioned Wyatt back, sat down in his place, and laid his tobacco pouch on the blanket. The other players put their bets down. Shonka's daughter tossed in two silver dollars. Stroud agreed, the singing commenced, and Tasina moved her hands in time to the singing, allowing occasional glimpses of the bone as she passed it from one hand to the other. Stroud concentrated on the girl's hands, and when she stopped, he pointed to her right hand, but it was empty.

"*E-ya!*" exclaimed those who had bet on Tasina. But the round was not over, the girl having merely gained the advantage. She smiled as she handed the bone to Stroud, who took his turn. If she guessed right, she would win. If she didn't, the round would be a stalemate, more bets could be placed, and they'd start another round. Tasina guessed right and won. Both the girl and Stroud guessed right on the next round, so no bets were exchanged—although some additional wagers were made by the onlookers—and the game was repeated. The third round Stroud won. It was fairly even for a while, then Stroud began winning more consistently. After a long losing streak, Tasina looked at Stroud admiringly. *"Wayan tatánka maníye.* He is a buffalo bull walking," she said.

Stroud's glance rested briefly on the girl. Batchika had said the same thing about him once, except it had been said in the Crow language, and it hadn't had anything to do with gambling. As quickly as he had been diverted, his attention returned to the game. As the stakes increased, Stroud spoke aside to Wyatt. "Fetch Greenberry. Tell him to bring the makings for higher stakes."

When Wyatt returned with Greenberry, followed by Partout and Mozay, all burdened with trinkets, squaw cloth and blankets, the game had moved outside, where fires had been set for both light and warmth. When the Indians sighted the trade goods, clamor disrupted the game and continued as the packs were put down behind Stroud. He opened a parflêche container and scattered the contents— beads, vermilion, looking glasses, shells, awls, iron buckles, steel rings and bracelets, copper wire, buttons, ribbons and other trinkets—the length of the blanket. It worked. An Indian couldn't resist the white man's fofarraw much better than his whiskey. The Indians began leaving the circle of light to reappear soon carrying furs, and the game resumed. New betters continued to arrive and others entered or withdrew as their luck prompted them. Besides quantities of trinkets, Stroud was soon betting bolts of cloth and his best three-point blankets to entice them to risk their whole winter catches of beaver and mink.

Shonka's daughter played it cautiously, sometimes sitting out a game or two. At the first sight of her beautifully tanned antelope skins, Stroud gave an appreciative grunt. "Even finer than Merk's." The games had been fairly even and the Indians were well satisfied until Stroud had a run of luck and took three games in a row. Because of the number of Indians betting against him and also the size of the stakes, Stroud's winnings were beginning to make an impressive pile. "A couple of hours more of this and Eahsapa can go to the forts alone."

Greenberry lifted the pile of furs and skins off the blanket, and as he did so he looked up. "*Ti-ya!*"

Stroud raised his eyes. Pushing through the opposite group of betters were Reeshar and Eahsapa, the young warrior-chief who had opposed Stroud at the council. They glanced across at Stroud and the pile of furs behind him. "Any objections if I play?" Reeshar inquired.

Stroud looked at him without expression. "You've nothing I want."

Reeshar turned to the Indians. "*Anagoptánpi yeto*. Listen to what I have to say." He turned back to Stroud, speaking still in Lakota. "Horses and mules. My animals against yours."

"*He wastéko lo!*" exclaimed the Indians. "That is good!"

Stroud glanced around. It was no wonder the Indians were for it. They could sell horses at their own price to the loser. As he studied the dark faces, he knew it wouldn't take much to start trouble. Trading parties had had their hair lifted for less. He shrugged and tossed the short length of polished bone to Reeshar, who had already sat down opposite him. "One mule, name of Maud," Stroud said. He

45

broke a stick in two and set half of it, to represent the mule, at the edge of the blanket.

Reeshar matched the half-stick and nodded to the Indians to begin the song. Reeshar's dexterity drew comments of approval. Stroud chose Reeshar's left hand and missed, but when he too succeeded in concealing the bone, Reeshar lost his advantage. Stroud passed the bone back to Reeshar and the game began again. Reeshar placed a whole marker at the edge of the blanket. "A horse." Stroud matched the bet. But again the round was deadlocked, and so it went for several rounds, the whole sticks and half-sticks representing horses and mules increasing until both Stroud and Reeshar had bet a good fourth of their animals. Finally Stroud guessed wrong and Reeshar guessed right and won the game. A shout went up from the Indians.

Stroud placed another marker on the blanket and tossed the bone to Reeshar. "Start it off," he said.

Again neither man was able to capitalize on his advantages for several turns. When again Stroud at last lost a round and was minus a good half of his horses and mules, Mozay shook his head. "This child's done everything 'cept wear a packsaddle."

Stroud resumed the game. He won the round, and another, but then the stalemate began to build up again. Stroud felt a light touch on his shoulder. He turned and found himself looking up at Shonka's daughter. Tasina had withdrawn from the game when Reeshar began to play, but she indicated now that she wished to enter—and on the side of Stroud and his trappers.

"*La belle sauvage*," murmured Partout, who was sitting at Stroud's right.

Stroud studied the girl, wondering what prompted her. "That's a good name for her—Belle," said Stroud. There seemed no reason for her wanting to enter the game, but it

46

certainly couldn't do him any harm to have Shonka's daughter on his side, Stroud decided. He shrugged, and the girl wedged in between him and Partout and put her bundle of fine skins on the blanket. Eahsapa gave a grunt of displeasure. Ignoring him, the girl looked along the line of betters opposite her, letting her blanket drop from her shoulders onto her lap. "Against the two superior horses of the Yellow-Haired-One," she said, indicating Reeshar, who nodded his agreement. "I will be the one-who-is-hiding-something," she added, picking up the bone.

Stroud looked at the girl and then at her hoard of skins. Maybe she'd change his luck. "Go it, Belle," he agreed, signaling for the song to begin.

But the stalemate continued, the bone changing back and forth between the girl and Reeshar, until Stroud had bet the remainder of his horses and mules, Belle leaving her wager unchanged. Greenberry, who irrationally blamed the stalemate on Belle, muttered, "Damn a fool squaw."

Stroud was getting more and more impatient to get Reeshar out of the game and go back to gambling with the Indians for furs. He was losing more than the value of the horses by wasting time with Reeshar. "This is the last round, win or lose," said Stroud.

"Why should I agree to that?" asked Reeshar, who was only interested in prolonging the game.

"To hell with what you agree to," said Stroud. "I'm not gambling my horses and mules to please you. We'll put it up to the Indians." He'd already lost half his animals and had bet the rest. All he wanted was a chance to break even —or go broke. He asked the Indians and they grunted their agreement.

Reeshar shrugged and began manipulating the bone. The air was full of tension as Belle successfully guessed the hand in which he held it. He tossed the bone to the girl. Reeshar followed her movements with intense concentration, then pointed to her left hand.

It was empty. A rumble of disappointment arose from the Indians. There would be no sale of horses. Stroud had won back all of his animals.

Reeshar looked across at Belle and began making arrangements for delivery of the two horses she had won from him. Stroud listened to the flow of words, remembering that this was the third time in Shonka's camp that Reeshar had spoken Lakota in his hearing. Yet Reeshar spoke none of the Indian languages when he first knew him. And though Reeshar had learned quickly from Wicarpi, a man didn't learn Lakota from a Crow wife. Nor in Mexico or the States. Somewhere between, Reeshar must have spent time with the Sioux. If he had been captured by—or found refuge with—some Sioux band before that last blizzard hit after he left their camp, it would certainly explain how he had survived. Stroud gradually became aware that the Indians were leaving. He ceased his speculations and stood up. "You warriors! Will you play against me again at 'hands,' or must I make a game with the women?" At the taunt some of the men seemed on the point of returning.

"Play again," Eahsapa jeered. "Be tricked like foolish beavers to lose your furs. I have many furs left. I will go to the big mud houses alone to trade."

In the quiet moment of indecision, gunfire and voices shouting alarm were heard from beyond camp in the direction of the horse herds. As the shouting became nearer and the alarm was relayed through the camp, Stroud distinguished cries of "Horse thieves!" "Many horses stolen!" Instantly there was pandemonium. Stroud was forgotten as Eahsapa and the group of young men broke apart and scattered for their lodges. Stroud and Reeshar stood looking after the departing warriors. Belle, noticing this, dipped her hand into the fold of her blanket, recovered the bone she had dropped there during one of the lightning-quick passes of her hands, and in the continuation of the same movement tossed it onto the gambling blanket. Only Greenberry, who had been bundling up some of the peltries Stroud had won, saw what she did. She had cheated Reeshar that last guess, the old man realized. The bone hadn't been in either hand. Greenberry's eyes narrowed. A man didn't hanker to be beholden, especially to a fool squaw, but sure as the hinges of hell opened easy, Stroud owed a string of mules and horses to this tricky one. Greenberry watched while Belle followed leisurely in the direction the warriors had taken; then he hoisted a bundle of furs to his shoulder and went toward the traders' camp.

Stroud turned away from Reeshar. With horses driven off by enemy raiders there would be a chase and likely a fight. Stroud felt in luck. If he could help the Sioux to recover their horses, without doubt they could be stampeded into trading with him instead of going into the forts. In the joy of victory, Indians would do anything for a brave warrior—Indian or white. It wouldn't be the first time Stroud had curried favor with a band of Indians by going out with a war party, and some of the trappers, like Hobart and Greenberry, would do it just for sport. Hobart and Greenberry would go along, Stroud knew. He'd ask Partout and Mozay to stay behind to watch camp. Wyatt could do as he pleased. Stroud went off to saddle up.

When he returned leading a saddled horse and an extra one to change to, the war party was not yet ready to leave. The warriors had taken time to paint themselves and were just beginning to come from their lodges to paint their fleet war ponies. The squaws, old men, boys, and others not going on the chase milled about the camp circle.

A few of the warriors soon completed their preparations,

49

among them Eahsapa who mounted and, leading his painted war pony, rode among the lodges exhorting the others to hurry. When he came near Stroud he paused, glanced from Stroud to the saddled horse with displeasure, then pushed his right hand toward Stroud, thumb between index and second finger, in the gesture of scorn. At Stroud's side a voice said, "While that war party goes one way, you'd better go the other."

Stroud glanced around to see Reeshar. "Not this child," said Stroud. He had no desire to talk to Reeshar. He looked back at the activity in the camp. Many of the braves were mounting and beginning their war songs.

"Still determined to be the typical mountain man," said Reeshar after a moment. There was a derisive tone to the words that made Stroud turn again. Reeshar was smiling. "Remember Miller's sketch of you?"

Stroud remembered. The year that he and Reeshar had gone into rendezvous together—after the winter in the valley of the Purgatory and the Bayou Salade—there had been an Easterner named Alfred Jacob Miller, an artist with the hunting party of the Scot sportsman William Drummond Stewart. Everybody had to look out for Miller, who'd get so all-fired busy with his paints he could have had his hair lifted and not missed it. Having to keep an eye on him made Stewart almost sorry he'd brought him; it distracted him so from his hunting. That rendezvous of '37—the time he brought Miller—was already Stewart's fifth. He'd been all over, from Fort Laramie to Fort Vancouver, from Taos to the Yellowstone, and had killed more meat in four years than most trappers did in a lifetime. There was hardly a man in the mountains who hadn't met up with the hawk-nosed, mustached Captain Stewart, the half-pay officer who spent his time adventuring around in the West while he waited to come into his inheritance. Stroud saw him at rendezvous again the next year, which everybody thought would be his last, for he finally did come into his title. But he showed up again, only two years ago, with the biggest outfit of sporting gentlemen, health seekers and St. Louis dandies the mountains had ever witnessed. That was when Wyatt had come out.

A lot of the mountain man had rubbed off on Stewart though, and behind his temper and his arrogance was as true-girt a man as any who gathered that summer of '37 on the Green River. Stewart had hired Miller in New Orleans to come along and sketch what he saw. Stroud remembered Miller as a quiet fellow with a thick nose and a soft, rounded chin and a thin wispy mustache. He had been so busy sketching scenes at rendezvous he hardly took time to eat. He had sketched Stroud sitting with his back to a tree, not knowing he was one of the greenest of the lot.

"He made you a typical mountain man," Reeshar went on. "Remember what a joke we thought it was? But I guess it caught your fancy. You've tried to grow to fit it." He paused while he seemed to assess Stroud. "I've heard about you. Killing a grizzly with an axe to save lead; bringing the Shoshones to trade by promising your scalp if they came to harm. Nobody but the man in Miller's sketch would be that big a fool."

"You asked a lot of questions before you came crawling out of your hole," said Stroud.

"Curiosity. And I know why it was you haven't talked about that winter. It was the man in the picture. You felt you failed him then. You still do."

Stroud flushed angrily. "You have something on your conscience, Jesse. You must be taking a risk showing up here. I hope the stakes you're playing for are worth it."

"One-third the value of all the furs I send to St. Louis. Then when I've run Fort Laramie out of business, a partnership."

"A trade war?" asked Stroud.

"With forty barrels of whiskey to fight it."

"Forty barrels!" With that much whiskey to squander, Stroud guessed the spring fur shipment from Fort Platte would be some. Here he'd risked his hair for nine years and Reeshar would outstrip him in a few months. That's what Reeshar was rubbing in—why he was being so free in talking about his arrangements with old Wyatt. "You always were one to gloat."

"It's hard to swallow," Reeshar said, "but you'll have to choke it down."

Stroud turned his back on Reeshar and mounted. Reeshar was right about one thing. Stroud did feel he had failed in that winter of the blizzards, though he wasn't sure even yet just where. There wasn't much any man could do about the weather. If he could only find out exactly what had happened to Batchika, he'd know whether he was at fault or not. The way things stood it made him look as if he was hardly fit to take a wife. Maybe he hadn't been then. That was a part of the torment. But pride or no pride, there hadn't been any use in bringing it up now, as long as he thought the others were dead. It couldn't do them any good. He had the fleeting notion that maybe Reeshar's refusal to tell what happened to Batchika was for much the same reason—because it wasn't to his credit. But that didn't seem likely somehow. Surely he could have lied enough to smooth over his own shortcomings. And that was strange, now he thought of it—why hadn't Reeshar tried some sort of whopper?

Stroud sat his horse for a moment, turning his attention to the activity of the camp. The warriors were parading around the circle, with Eahsapa and the other three soldier-chiefs in the lead. From the war songs of the braves and the cries of the women, Stroud gathered that the raiders had been identified as Snakes. There were some thirty mounted warriors in the party, mostly Eahsapa's Bowstring Soldiers. With their paint and flowing hair they looked as wild and shaggy as the paint-streaked war ponies. As they approached, Stroud had to admit to himself that Eahsapa didn't look companionable, for a fact. But Reeshar ought to know better than to try to scare him off. This was something he had to do.

Stroud glanced down at Reeshar. "Gloat all you want," he said, "but I'll get Shonka's trade." He kicked his horse into motion and fell in beside Eahsapa.

Four

The wide trail of the ponies stolen by the Snakes was as plain to follow as a turnpike, even at night. It was the head start the Snakes had that would cause trouble, and with fresh mounts to change to, even though slowed down by driving a herd, they could be hard to catch. The pursuers pushed steadily on through the night, the trail leading west across the basin.

Ahead of him, Stroud heard a horse break wind. In the moonlight he could see the arched tail and then there was a series of plop, plop, plops. It reminded Stroud that he was riding at the rear of the war party—he and Greenberry and Hobart. With one commanding gesture Eahsapa had motioned them back when they first started out. Stroud didn't like it. It had been quite a while since he had had the rear position in anything. Once a man got used to riding ahead, it was a satisfying habit galling to break. Damn Eahsapa. But there was nothing Stroud could do about it —or getting the trade, either—until he could prove himself in the eyes of the war party. And this might be hard to do. Nothing was more uncertain than when or if an Indian would choose to fight. Wasn't anybody could do more talking beforehand and afterward, and less fighting, than an Indian. Though that couldn't be depended upon, either.

They stopped at dawn to rest, then moved on again, and by noon came to the Platte, where the Sweetwater flows into it from the west. Here they stopped again and watered their ponies and ate from the bags of pemmican slung from their shoulders. The trail led west across the Platte and along the south bank of the Sweetwater. Not long after the war party crossed the Platte, the three scouts who were riding in advance reported back to Eashsapa that they had sighted the Snakes about four miles ahead. They had got close enough to tell that there were eleven of them and nearly a hundred ponies.

The Sioux stripped to leggings and breechcloths and changed to their war ponies. Leaving the tired ponies in charge of two young boys who had been brought along for that purpose, they all started off again at a canter, Stroud, Hobart and Greenberry having also changed to fresh mounts. Presently they saw a cloud of dust ahead and to the right across the river, although at this point the trail of the ponies was still on the left side of the stream. With excited yells, many of the war party started to cross the Sweetwater, supposing that the enemy had crossed farther ahead and were driving toward the hills to the north.

A sharp command from Eashsapa stayed them. He had followed the trail farther upstream. After crossing a little tributary stream that flowed in from the south, he stopped to stare down intently. Stroud rode up to see what Eahsapa had discovered. Stroud saw pony tracks in single file leading off south up the bank of the creek. He leaned down from his horse and looked more closely at the tracks. At the edges, grains of sandy earth were still sliding down into the deep imprints, indicating the tracks were made only a few minutes before. The Snakes had tried a trick that had almost worked. It appeared that the main party of Snakes had turned off up the creek, leaving a few warriors to drive the horse herd on up the Sweetwater and across, where they would probably abandon it as a decoy and then rejoin the main party.

Sending a half-dozen warriors after the stolen horses, Eahsapa led the rest of his war party up the small tributary stream. Going at a rapid rate for nearly a mile, they came to a rise. There were the Snakes, nine of them, about a half-mile in advance, riding toward a grove of aspens where the creek apparently had its source. If the Snakes forted up in the aspens, there'd be hell to pay getting at them.

Stroud saw that the Snakes had made a mistake keeping to the rougher ground near the stream, even though their course was in a direct line to the grove. He signaled to Hobart and Greenberry and veered his horse to the right, where there was a level bench between the stream and a coulee which angled into it farther up near the aspen grove. He broke his horse into a run. Several of Eahsapa's men saw Stroud's plan and followed along. Just then two mounted Snakes burst into view from over a ridge to the west, reined up in surprise, and started back. The Sioux who had followed Stroud took off after the two Snakes, crying, "*Hokahê!*" and blowing their war whistles. Stroud, Hobart and Greenberry, riding as if they were running a quarter race, continued toward the grove while the main group of Sioux led by Eahsapa, in pursuit of the nine Snakes, were bunched up like a pack of hounds. The nine Snakes were now dropping blankets and robes and war sacks, bright splashes of color, either hoping the Sioux would stop to pick them up or that the load of their horses would be lightened enough to enable them to reach the aspen grove.

When the Snakes saw that they would be cut off from the grove, they settled for a patch of willows and stunted box elders on the near side. Stroud reined in and watched as Eahsapa and his warriors halted about a hundred yards above the thicket on the brow of a small hill. One of Eahsapa's men fired into the thicket, and the Snakes returned the fire, wounding this man in the thigh.

When Stroud, Hobart and Greenberry came up, Eahsapa and his men had dismounted and were shouting insults and taunts at the Snakes, occasionally firing a shot or sending an arrow into the willow patch. At that distance, though not great, the old fusils that some of Eahsapa's warriors had were not as effective as bow and arrow.

Stroud dismounted. "*Wan le wan!* Look at this!" he said in sarcasm to Eahsapa. "It takes more than barking dogs to drive the fox from cover."

Eahsapa regarded Stroud with an expression of contempt. "You talk fire, but your deeds are ashes."

Stroud knew that an Indian admired a braggart who made good his brag. Noticing a quantity of boulders close by, he asked Hobart and Greenberry to help him roll them down the hill closer to the Snakes. Then he told them to stay behind the boulders and keep shooting into the thicket. Taking his rifle, Stroud used the coulee to work his way to the aspen grove, careful to conceal his movements from the Snakes, and cached himself there.

Seeing the wisdom of Stroud's plan, some of Eahsapa's men joined Hobart and Greenberry behind the boulders. The Sioux who had gone off over the hill after the two Snakes, rode back with two fresh scalps dripping from a lance tip.

Under the fire of Hobart and Greenberry, it didn't take the Snakes long to yearn for the better concealment of the aspen grove. All nine of them suddenly burst out on horseback and made a dash for it. Stroud waited at the edge of the grove behind a deadfall. When the Snakes were within fifty yards he opened fire with his revolving pistol. He hit two before they could stop, two more as they wheeled their ponies, and another as the remaining Snakes fled in panic. He missed with his last shot. Sticking the empty revolver into his belt, he took up his rifle and ran to the edge of the grove. He paused long enough to take the five scalps.

Three of the remaining four Snakes were being cut down by the Sioux as they tried to get across the stream. The fourth, charging back upon Stroud, was a magnificent rider. He hung from the far side of his horse, offering no target save his left foot, and discharged an arrow from under his pony's neck. Stroud had his rifle to his shoulder, ready to fire. The arrow struck the stock of his rifle a glancing blow, knocking the rifle from his hands and ploughing a furrow in his cheek as it flashed past. Stroud knew he didn't have time to retrieve his rifle. As the rider bore down upon him, Stroud leaped forward, waving his arms and shouting. The Indian's pony reared and the Snake fell hard to the ground. In an instant he was up, reaching over his shoulder for an arrow, but before he could fit it to bow Stroud had his gun. The rifle roared and the Indian fell backward. The savage sport was over.

Later, his face mirrored in a still pool of the creek by which he and Greenberry knelt, Stroud examined the red furrow beginning under his right cheekbone and ending just below the lobe of his ear. The fight had also cost him most of the few cartridges he had left for his Colt. Cold water from the creek stopped his face from bleeding and Stroud smiled as he got to his feet. "You hear what they call me?" Zapétah Wechashápa. Five Scalps. That'll be worth a galore of fur."

"Do 'ee hyar now?" said Greenberry. "One day ye'll trade your scalp for a beaver plew."

Hobart, who stood near by watching the Sioux where they were gathered downstream, said, "From here it don't look like Eahsapa's doing any cheering."

Stroud looked downstream. Eahsapa was squatted down fashioning a hoop from a willow twig. He didn't look happy, for a fact. More like his mother had just died owing him a dollar and a half.

Stroud noticed that the warriors had turned their ponies out to graze and had started small fires of *bois de vache*.

Others besides Eahsapa were fashioning willow twigs into hoops, and Stroud knew that the fresh scalps were laid out upon buffalo chips and would later be stretched over the hoops. As he watched, three Sioux rode out of camp. "They're heading for fixings to paint robes," he said. He went to his horse and began uncinching the saddle. The crazy Indians had spent less than an hour fighting, and now they'd spend the rest of the day and night getting ready to return to their village. In order to make their black paint of rejoicing, the Indians would have to kill a buffalo for a gut-length of blood to mix with cottonwood buds. "We'll be here the night."

"You plannin' to ride into Shonka's village at the head of this war party?" Hobart asked.

"I've earned the right," said Stroud.

"Eahsapa'll have something to say about that, I'm thinkin'," Hobart said.

"He can say it," Stroud said. "But he'll have to watch my horseshit going back."

The three warriors returned before nightfall, bringing a wolfskin, a circular piece of buffalo hide, and fresh blood of the buffalo contained in a length of gut. Because members of a successful war party were always stealthy as wolves, the robes of the warriors were bordered with narrow strips of the wolfskin. Then, using the hide as a vessel, they mixed the buffalo blood with cottonwood buds to make the black paint of victory, which was applied in parallel lines on the flesh surface of the robes. Between the lines, wolf tracks were painted. Preparing the scalps and painting the robes, with dancing interspersed, occupied the night.

As Stroud lay unsleeping in the robes he shared with Greenberry, the howl came again—the deep, painfully penetrating cry of a male wolf calling his kind to the hunt, scenting quarry too strong to tackle alone. The dismal sound stabbed through Stroud and screamed along his nerves. Other wolves took up the call, the piercing howls changing to higher pitched cries as the pack pursued the hot scent. The pack was getting farther away, and Stroud was glad. He had lived with the sound of wolves for nine years in this country, and before that, in Tennessee, wolves were not uncommon.

Now he was acting like a mover scared at the sound of his own dog. A man didn't soon get over the sight of human bones abandoned by wolves. Not when he had been living with the flesh that should cover them. Nor did he soon get over being followed and howled at by the wolves that did the eating. The refrain of a song that Partout sometimes sang started running through his mind: *"Jamais je m'en irai chez nous; j'ai trop grand' peur des loups*—Never shall I bid home adieu; they have me scared, those wolves."

After a while Stroud was aware that the Indians were dancing again. Beside him Greenberry muttered curses and tossed impatiently. It had occurred to Stroud that Batchika or Wicarpi—whichever one had left camp with Reeshar the winter of the blizzards—might somehow have got back to her own band. Without preamble he said, "You've spent considerable time with the Crows."

"More'n enough," admitted Greenberry. "A year and a half."

"Were you with the Crows the winter of '37?"

"*Ti-ya*. Missed rendezvous two years running—'37 and '38."

"What band was it?"

"War Eagle's," said Greenberry.

"Ever have anything much to do with Plenty Coup's band?"

"More'n enough," said Greenberry. "The two of 'em

—War Eagle's and Plenty Coup's—camped together the winter after the plague let up." Stroud sat up and a cold stream of air chilled Greenberry's spine. "Dammit to hell," he fumed. "If ye expect to set up the night, go paint yourself a robe, do 'ee hyar?"

Stroud lay back. "Did a young woman return to Plenty Coup's band that winter or spring? Batchika or Wicarpi, her name would be," said Stroud.

"Which winter do ye mean, boy?"

"The one after the plague."

Greenberry turned on his back and was silent for a while. "Can't recall hearin' the names," he said finally. Tactfully he added, "Acourse I left for the forts in midsummer. Thirty-eight, that'd be. Summer-hunted that year on the Wind River."

"It might've taken a long time," said Stroud. Then he decided this wasn't true. They had been close enough to Crow country. It wouldn't have taken any year and a half for Batchika or Wicarpi to find her way back to her band, if free to do so. And there would have been enough commotion about it that Greenberry would remember if either of them had returned.

"*Ti-ya.* Ye've taken a long time gettin' curious," remarked Greenberry.

Stroud said nothing. He knew Greenberry was aware that his questions had something to do with the reappearance of Reeshar, and the old man would like to know more. But one explanation would call for another.

Greenberry seemed to realize that as far as Stroud was concerned the conversation was finished. "*Wagh!* It's a big country for locatin' one wanderin' squaw, now."

"One possible wandering squaw," amended Stroud.

"Ain't a one of 'em worth it, do 'ee hyar?"

"I'll try." Just supposing he was right that Reeshar had

61

lived a while with the Sioux. Since the woman hadn't gone back to her tribe within a reasonable time, maybe she was still a prisoner. "Didn't you ever feel that something you planned to do was right, Greenberry? That it would turn out like you wanted, even if it was a little daft?"

"*Wagh!* Mostly mine turned out dafter than right."

"I've felt all along I was going to get Shonka's trade," Stroud reassured himself.

The first faint light of dawn was diluting the darkness, and there was the tantalizing smell of roasting meat. "Ye can have Shonka's trade," said Greenberry, crawling out of the robes. "This nigger's half froze for meat." He went off toward the Indians, muttering, "First sensible thing they've done all night."

Unable to sleep now, Stroud waited while it grew light. The Indians finished eating. They dressed themselves as they had been dressed during the fight. Then they began to paint their faces with charred willow branches. Stroud watched from his position upstream, knowing it was their way of announcing, as far as they could be seen, that the war party had been successful, had taken horses, had killed an enemy and had lost no warriors. An argument developed among the braves around the campfire. Some of them turned to look and gesticulate in Stroud's direction. A harangue by Eahsapa terminated the disagreement and the warriors resumed painting their faces. It was as clear to Stroud as if he had been able to hear their words; that Eahsapa was reluctant to invite him to blacken his face and ride with the war party. Ey God! Nothing came easy.

When the warriors were catching their ponies and were mounting, Stroud rode the length of the forming column until he came to Eahsapa, who was still near the campfire. As the young chief prepared to mount, Stroud looked down at him. Though some of the warriors only drew black lines on their faces, Eahsapa had painted his entire face black. Bare from the waist up except for the newly painted robe which hung from his shoulders, with his broad expanse of tattooed chest exposed and his long hair glistening in the early morning sunlight, he presented a wild and formidable appearance. "*Aksáka*. It is too bad," Stroud said. "The soldier-chief forgets why his warriors blacken their faces in victory." There were grunts of agreement from Eahsapa's war party.

Eahsapa hesitated, dangerous and menacing and full of resentment. Then with one quick motion he stooped and picked up a short piece of burning willow branch from the edge of the fire and tossed it up to Stroud, saying, "Blacken your face with this!" Only one tip of the branch was charred and Stroud was forced to grab the burning end with his bare hand. As it seared into his flesh, Stroud's expression didn't alter, but he silently goddamned Eahsapa, the whole goddamn Sioux nation, and every other goddamned Indian that ever tried himself thinking up devilish tricks. He knocked off the live coal on his rifle butt and crushed the charred end in his hand. With his index and middle fingers, he drew parallel lines horizontally on his forehead and vertically on each cheek, then wiped his hand on his legging. In surly silence Eahsapa mounted and immediately a half-dozen braves left the main party to ride ahead.

The afternoon sun was at their backs as Stroud and the others came in sight of the village. Through the long grass the people of the camp came running, crying, "*Ahi-ye! Now they are here!*" The main party of returning warriors rode in two lines. Alone at the front, in the place of greatest honor, was Stroud. The name Five Scalps had preceded him, and now the women sang songs about his bravery. Stroud didn't feel this attention particularly due him, yet he had anticipated it and didn't find it unpleasant. The press of people about him became so great that his horse could scarcely take a step. Seeing Belle and Wyatt together, he motioned to the girl, and when she had come up beside him he asked her to take him to her father's lodge. Belle grasped Stroud's horse by the bridle and began pushing her way through the crowd.

On the fringes of the crowd Stroud saw Reeshar. The eyes of the two men held as the distance between them narrowed. Reeshar shifted his position in order to intercept the rider. "You'll get the trade," Reeshar said bluntly, "but I'll sow a wind you'll have trouble reaping." Stroud did not reply, and Belle continued leading horse and rider toward Shonka's lodge.

Soon afterward the crowd dispersed. For the remainder of the day the camp took on an air of preparation. The people painted themselves black and dressed in their finery and brought wood for the great fire that would light the dances. Just after sundown, two halfmen-halfwomen, hermaphrodites who were thought to possess spiritual powers and who were often taken on war parties for their value as oracles, lighted the fire and the singers and drummers began the songs. Stroud did not appear until the first of the scalp dances—the sweethearts' dance—was nearly at an end. The unmarried men and women were in two long lines, the men dancing behind the women. Wyatt was dancing with Belle.

To begin the next dance, the women chose their partners, giving the name of their choice to the halfmen-halfwomen. One of them led Stroud to Belle. Though he usually preserved the dignity expected of a trader by not dancing with the Indians, he took his place beside her without comment and the dance commenced. He did think the girl might have done better to ask Wyatt, who looked disappointed.

Belle was very pretty, Stroud reflected as he glanced down at her. Knowing the lively, independent way of the Indian women toward their men, he decided that this one would make a good wife for somebody. Too bad that she would be wasted on Eahsapa. At least, as her brother-in-law, he would have first choice.

His thoughts were interrupted by Belle. "*Shi!* You are long-faced for one whose praises are sung," she said.

Stroud realized that he was neglecting her. "Not as long-faced as my friend Wyatt, because you choose another."

"Your friend is not the giver of gifts," Belle said promptly.

Stroud grinned. "You dance with me only in gratitude?" He supected that she had something in mind other than the fofarraw he had distributed upon his arrival in camp.

Belle glanced the length of Stroud's lean figure as they danced slowly backward now on the balls of their feet and with their legs bent at the knees. "I have two fine horses without hawk's bells for their bridles."

Whether she meant to remind him or not, Stroud thought of the "hands" game and the luck Belle had brought him. Her request was easy enough to grant. Every trader packed a generous supply of the tiny silver bells used in the now almost defunct sport of falconry. "So it's hawk's bells. Do you always get what you want?"

"If the time is right."

Stroud smiled. "Before the women's trading begins to-morrow. Come to me then."

"But the trading is to be accomplished at the mud houses on the Shell."

Stroud was wishing the dance was over. This one always had tired his leg muscles and he was out of practice be-sides. "Don't wager your horses on it," he said. He won-dered why it was these slow, crouching dances half killed a white man. Yet any trapper worth his salt could cover forty or more miles a day on foot, if he had to, and outrun any Indian except for short distances.

Belle, aware that Stroud's attention had wandered again, said accusingly, "You are thinking of the trader's daughter." At Stroud's look of surprise she added, "The one who has gone to the white man's village."

"No," Stroud denied. His surprise that Belle knew of his attentions to Evie Pryce was only momentary. Evie Pryce, the half-Welsh, half-Sioux daughter of Emlyn Pryce, *bourgeois* at Fort Laramie, had been in a convent school in St. Louis for the past two years. Stroud realized that probably every Sioux of an age to gossip knew that for five years now he had been going more and more frequently to Fort Laramie and often was seen there with Evie. Except for the last two years, of course. No sense in hanging around the fort with Evie in St. Louis.

"Perhaps she will not come back," Belle said.

"She is back now at the big mud house." At least she should be. She would have come in with the trade goods caravan. Stroud had wanted to ask the men from Fort Platte just to reassure himself, but he was damned if he would. She was there all right, waiting, while he wasted a week trying to lose Reeshar and two days chasing the Snakes. But it was as much for Evie as for himself now. She'd look good in those St. Louis frills. And Shonka's beaver would buy galore.

"In the white man's village perhaps she found another sweetheart," Belle persisted.

"No," said Stroud. Evie had as true a heart as ever beat against a man's shirt. Not that she ever mentioned her virtue, no more than if she didn't have any. Amused, Stroud smiled down at Belle. She was ready for a man, for a fact, and it appeared she had set her sights on a white one. He couldn't blame her. The trappers' wives had a much easier time of it than they would have in their own villages. "And what of Eahsapa? Are you not promised to him?"

"*Yu!*" The girl made a derogatory sound and subsided into a sulky silence. Stroud thought impatiently of Evie waiting at the fort; then conscious again that his legs were protesting, he settled down grimly to the endurance contest which the dance was becoming.

It was after the third of the scalp dances that young Wyatt had the irresistible desire to massage the calves of his legs. He retreated beyond the circle of light from the large fire and sank to the ground. When his eyes had become accustomed to the comparative dark, Wyatt glanced around and discovered that Reeshar was standing a little behind him and to one side. Reeshar was watching the dancers intently, and Wyatt decided that Reeshar's eyes were following Stroud. Without having acknowledged Wyatt's presence, Reeshar said abruptly, "I still think you'd better come with us."

Wyatt shrugged. "I see no reason."

"As you like," said Reeshar, "but before this party's over, you'll wish it was to hell and you were to home." He turned and went off into the dark.

After a while Wyatt returned to the dancing. Following the fourth phase of the scalp dance, he and Stroud stood together and watched the galloping buffalo-bull dance. The women, having tied their deerskin dresses up above their knees, revealed glossy bare legs above the knee-length leggings. By the time they finished, the first glow of dawn was lighting the sky.

Just as the dance ended, the camp crier began to chant, "*Hípelo, hípelo!*" He was an old man, but his voice was clear and steady. He pointed to Stroud. "Five Scalps has come to us for trade. He has proved himself brave in battle. Those who wish may trade with him in the lodge of Man-Who-Wishes-To-Die. The packs of Five Scalps are bursting with blue blankets, black blankets, white blankets, knives, beads, whiskey. Five Scalps will trade first with the women. *Hípelo, hípelo!* The trader known as the Yellow-Haired-One is also here. He will be in the lodge of Bull Hump."

Stroud had a feeling of satisfaction. The wording of the crier, whether the crier's own or suggested by Shonka, all but guaranteed that Reeshar, the Yellow-Haired-One, would get very little trade. At the completion of the announcement, Stroud saw Eahsapa stride up to Shonka and speak angrily. Then Eahsapa glanced across at Stroud. It was clear even from a distance that Eahsapa's grudging tolerance of a fellow warrior was at an end.

Five

Stroud was seated facing the entrance of the lodge, waiting patiently while the Old Woman, Winuncala, deliberated in her selection from the trade goods. "Any more?" he called.

Wyatt, who was stationed outside to keep order, looked in. "No one in sight."

From the lengthening shadows Stroud judged it to be past mid-afternoon. The whole camp would come to life soon. The squaws would have plenty of time to go off and hide before the whiskey trade with the men got rough. Stroud spoke again to Wyatt, who had now come into the lodge. "Is your sign language up to asking Shonka about those guards?"

"I'll try." Wyatt hurried away.

Winuncala had made her choice, and she watched Stroud as he evaluated the assortment she had selected. Without comment Stroud removed a palette of vermilion and a handful of hawk's bells. To be overgenerous would have every squaw in camp dissatisfied and distrustful. Stroud held the hawk's bells in his hand for a moment. Then he remembered Belle's request, and he said to Winuncala, "Tasina did not come to trade."

"She fears Eahsapa's wrath," Winuncala replied.

Stroud knew Winuncala to be a relative of Shonka's. "You are here," he observed.

"I do not have a sister whose husband would lodgepole me because I come." Winuncala gathered up her trinkets in the folds of her skirt and got slowly to her feet.

Stroud scooped up some more hawk's bells and tied them

in a generous piece of crimson cloth. "For Tasina," he told Winuncala.

Her wrinkled face broke into a toothless grin. She jingled the bundle. "They will make a proud sound for Tasina."

As the stoop-shouldered old squaw walked away, her last remark echoing in his mind, Stroud was reminded of another young girl who had been partial to hawk's bells. When he first saw Batchika at the rendezvous there on the Green River, she had had hawk's bells fastened to the fringe at the edge of her skirt—one tiny bell no bigger than the cup of an acorn to each thong—and when she moved they had made a gay, tinkling sound. It was only lately that Stroud had realized how very young Batchika had been. At the time he hadn't thought much about it one way or another. He hadn't been so old himself—nearly twenty he guessed, though Reeshar had been ten years older. More difference in age than between him and Wyatt. Ey God! but Reeshar had had a big advantage—not in living off the land maybe, but in everything else. A twenty-year-old boy didn't know much; he only thought he did. It made Stroud wonder why Reeshar had picked him to go off with in the first place. Maybe it had been the girls that decided him. Batchika and Wicarpi, in their short buckskin dresses and best fofarraw, and with their flirty ways, were enough to catch the eye of any man—even Reeshar. If Reeshar had regretted their decision to leave rendezvous with the two girls, he hadn't shown it. Not clear enough for a twenty-year-old boy to notice anyway. More likely, Stroud decided, having once gone with him, Reeshar had been careful not to show what now appeared to have been a growing contempt for him and his "sturdy virtues." Reeshar had used him the whole time to provide such comforts as he could. Stroud remembered it was only now and then that he had felt used and he hadn't minded much. He guessed he had been too happy to see what was before him, though it angered him to realize it now. He picked up Winuncala's peltries and tossed them to Mozay at the back of the lodge.

"Eahsapa couldn't've kept many squaws away," Mozay remarked.

Mention of the trading was a welcome distraction. "No," Stroud agreed. "Some of his soldiers will stay away, but not enough to fret about." He eyed the mounting piles of furs and robes. Maybe this trade with Shonka's band would be the turning point. Stroud had long since come to the conclusion that the ability to make money was a natural gift like good aim or a strong bladder. Being blessed with the others, he hadn't yet decided whether he had the money gift or not. If he did, he had been almighty slowed, somehow. He turned away, and in the parflêches behind him he hunted until he found two uniforms, which he removed from the box and shook out. They were of red, yellow and blue with heavy gold braid, and with them were two plumed military hats in scarlet and black. The distinction of wearing a gaudy Mexican uniform was the best way Stroud knew to guarantee the loyalty of an Indian guard. He wished Wyatt would hurry up and bring the guards so they could get the trading over with.

Mozay paused in his work of tying the furs in packs to examine the uniforms. "If anything could strike a man blind, these would," he remarked.

"They serve," said Stroud. He hung them on a lodge-pole.

Greenberry pounded a spigot into a whiskey barrel. Then he hunted up a huge camp kettle and started drawing off whiskey into it. He leaned close and inhaled the fumes. "In a week you can drink your belly full," Stroud reminded him. He went outside. The lodge was at a place in the camp farthest from the stream and facing it. Behind, the ground sloped sharply to a shallow ravine. Stroud looked impatiently for Wyatt; then after a moment he went back inside to wait. Partout came in, carrying fresh water in two large containers made from the paunch of the buffalo. Partout stood for a moment while his eyes adjusted to the change of light.

"Over hyar," said Greenberry. As he looked up, his glance fell upon the gaudy uniforms. He studied them as if he had never seen them before. "Them Mexicans are peculiar a heap."

"Their fandangos are purely a pleasure." Mozay strained on a leather thong he was using to tie the pelts. After he finished the tying, he tossed the bundle on top of a sizable pile of robes and furs. "Last one I invited myself to, I caught a right smart chance of broken ribs and the purtiest señorita you'd ever see." He looked over at Greenberry. "You ever steal one of them Taos beauties, Greenberry?"

Greenberry turned off the spigot of the barrel and looked critically at the whiskey in the kettle. "A fourth full or I'm a gone coon," he remarked. To Mozay he said, "They're worse'n squaws, do 'ee hyar?"

Partout handed one of the water bags to Greenberry, who started pouring from it into the kettle. "*Enfant de garce!*" the voyageur said to Mozay. "Señorita slip off *le* hook?"

"Threw her back, you might say," Mozay replied.

The little Frenchman seemed both puzzled and distressed. "*Diable!* How it is you do this?"

"Easy," explained Mozay. "Her brothers were gainin' on me."

"*Sacré!*" Partout said wistfully. "Me, I never go raid to Taos."

"You must be the only trapper that ain't," said Mozay.

"Water," said Greenberry. Partout handed him the other container, and Greenberry finished filling the kettle.

Stroud stepped back from the lodge opening. "Guess Wyatt's signs worked. Here they come." Shortly Wyatt entered, followed by three Indians, each naked to the waist.

"The biggest ones are the guards," Wyatt announced. "Cetan Hupahu, whatever that means . . ."

"Hawk Wing," translated Stroud.

"And Itazico." Wyatt indicated the second.

"Has-No-Bows," said Stroud. He motioned the two guards forward. At the first sight of the uniforms the Indians clapped their hands over their mouths in astonishment. Stroud waited while Wyatt helped them into the uniforms and the Indians had preened and strutted for a while before he gave his instructions. All knives and firearms were to be collected and piled in the middle of the camp area before the trading with the men began. Shonka would see that the weapons were kept under guard. Hawk Wing and Has-No-Bows were to return to help Stroud.

As the two departed, Stroud motioned to the third Indian. He was without distinction except for having an extraordinarily large mouth. Stroud looked over at Greenberry. "Is the whiskey ready?"

"*Ti-ya.*" Greenberry took a metal cup, dipped it full from the kettle of watered whiskey, and carried it to the Indian, who poured the diluted whiskey into his mouth, allowing the liquid to distend his cheeks. He rolled his eyes and then half danced, half ran from the lodge. He went through the camp, squirting small amounts of whiskey from his mouth into the mouths of those he met. He returned several times for more whiskey, and in a short time there were many braves waiting to trade.

The trading went slowly as always. Mostly they brought in a robe or two at a time or a few furs. For a good robe the

73

price was three cups of whiskey. Few of the men were interested in the trade goods. When the effects of the drink began to wear off they would return with just enough more furs to get what whiskey they wanted. At first the camp was disorderly only in a festive sort of way, with much singing and dancing and harmless quarreling. Even so, for Stroud and his men the strain was great. There was no night or day, only an almost unceasing procession of Indians. Stroud seized an occasional nap during a slack period and got up red-eyed and weary to continue the barter. He was surprised at nothing except the number of furs that gradually made their appearance. Knowing he would need extra pack animals, he traded for them, too, getting twelve. It was reported by the guards that only Eahsapa and a handful of his followers were trading with Reeshar.

It was near the end of the third day that Stroud had his first premonition of disaster. The women of the band, tired of hiding out, began to return to camp and to drink with the men. The squaws showed up to trade again, this time for whiskey, bringing even finer skins than they had before. Stroud decided that Shonka's band had even more furs than he had estimated. "How much whiskey do we have left?" he asked Greenberry.

"No more'n a day's trade," said Greenberry.

"Then put tallow in the cups," ordered Stroud.

It was several hours after the reappearance of the women that trade suddenly ceased altogether, though the noise and confusion in the camp increased. Knowing that a white man was no longer safe wandering about the camp, Stroud sent a guard to investigate. The guard returned with the information that Reeshar was giving away whiskey—all his whiskey.

"We better hit for timber," said Hobart.

"When we've finished," Stroud said. He stepped to the

lodge door. From what he could see of the camp they were all so blind drunk they couldn't tell themselves from a side of bacon. "Reeshar didn't have much more whiskey than I did to start with," Stroud estimated, turning back. "A couple of days' worth, giving it away and with the women helping. They'll want more before it's worn off."

"Ye've got little left, do 'ee hyar?" said Greenberry.

"Dilute it some more." But there was a limit as to how much he could water down the whiskey without the whole shebang blowing up in their faces. It was a ticklish business, trying to gauge how much rum foolery everyone could stand.

Stroud lay back on a pile of furs and listened to the drunken clamor. He had a feeling that this was only the beginning of the trouble Reeshar would cause before they got out of Shonka's camp. Damn him. He'd call a halt one day to his meanness. If only Batchika or Wicarpi could be located. Such a possibility wasn't entirely hopeless. There were only a limited number of Sioux tribes that could likely have picked up Reeshar and the girl, Stroud reasoned. It would almost have to be a band that was camped near the Bear Lodge Mountains that winter, maybe on the Belle Fourche or the Powder River itself. Those would be the camping places nearest the route he and Reeshar and the girls had been taking to winter rendezvous on Powder River. The thing to do was find out what bands had been camped in that part of the country. He couldn't for the moment question Partout; he'd told him to take the horses and women away from camp for safekeeping. But he could question Hobart and Mozay. They were able to remember only one band that had camped near the Bear Lodge Mountains the winter of '37-'38—No Heart's.

Mozay remembered No Heart's band well. "That's Madame Jack's band," he explained. "She figured on seeing her relatives a heap, but the snow was so deep and then some, she only went visiting twice."

"Weren't there others?" asked Stroud.

"Oh, others were roundabouts. But with everybody snowed in, can't recollect who they was. Only time a body hardly bothered to go outside was to chase the buffler out of camp. Godalmighty! So numerous they was a plaguetaked nuisance." And that was the extent of Mozay's information. But it was something to go on.

Stroud waited impatiently for the trade to resume, and one cause for impatience began to nudge another, like a string of pack mules bumping head to tail as they slogged downhill. All that he'd planned about marrying Evie Pryce and taking her back to St. Louis would have to wait now until he could get the past straightened out between himself and Reeshar. He'd thought that the tangles by which this particular part of his past once bound him had been loosened for good. And it was Evie, of course, who had done the loosening, though she didn't know it.

Just being with Evie made him feel right. Like their last day together before she left for the convent school in St. Louis. They went for a ride up into the hills along the Laramie with the excuse of rounding up some of the fort's horses that had strayed into the brush. They rode farther than they expected, not finding any sign of the horses, and came upon two young Oglalas crouching below the river bank, and two young squaws holding their four ponies. Evie knew them. The Oglalas had sighted a herd of antelope grazing toward the river and were waiting till they came out of the brush to get a shot at them. The men each picked out a good one, and Evie watched to tell them when to fire. They found a level, grassy place in the shade, roasted the ribs and had a big feed. Then they talked for a long time. Afterward the Indian couples left but Evie had seen trout in the stream and wanted to fish. Stroud had hooks and lines, and they had a contest, Evie catching nine to his five. They were all big. Then they had stopped fishing, and before they knew it the sun went behind the hills and they heard the clop of horse's hoofs. It had been a man from the fort. Their horses had strayed back, and Pryce had sent every man out over the hills looking for them. It seemed an ordinary enough day judged by what they had done. But Evie somehow made everything seem special. She had a steady kind of happiness that warmed a man and seeped through him almost without his knowing it.

Stroud thought of a big old sponge his mother used to scrub him with when he was little. She'd get it out of the cupboard, all shriveled and hard-feeling, and then when he squeezed water through it the rough edges would go away and the pits and ugly craters would swell together until it seemed whole and alive. That was sort of what Evie did to him—filled up the emptiness in him so that he was complete. Whatever it was, that last whole day with her was good to remember. The next day Evie went back with the year's fur catch to St. Louis, and he forgot to give her the beaded moccasins he'd had made for a going-away present. That was the last time he'd seen her. Now she was back, waiting at the fort, and here he was, waiting for a passel of savages to get sober enough to want to get drunk again.

For two days he waited, and his guess proved accurate. Reeshar ran out of whiskey at the end of the second day all right, and the trade started up again. Partout made a brief appearance at dusk. Hearing the noise and nagged by the fear that Stroud and the others had been killed, he sneaked back into camp. He brought the news that Reeshar's party hadn't yet left.

"That doesn't shine," said Stroud. Pressed by demands for trade, he pushed the thought of Reeshar from his mind.

He looked up as Partout was leaving. "Better picket the saddle horses back of the tipi. Bring the pack string in after dark tomorrow."

It was the next afternoon that two Indians turned up in succession demanding whiskey but with nothing to trade. They were still drunk enough that they could have been given the watered stock, but then every Indian in the whole band would want free whiskey. With considerable difficulty they were persuaded to leave. Stroud turned to Wyatt. "Go help Partout with the pack animals. Then circle the camp with the women and Hobart's boy and wait for us downstream."

The trading continued fitfully but uneventfully until an Indian by the name of Sitanka, Big Foot, entered. He had done his early trading with Reeshar, Stroud was sure. The Indian had a deep burn across one side of his face. Pushing aside a squaw who was trading, he threw down some wolfskins and demanded whiskey. Stroud picked up the pelts. They shone in the firelight, the heavy white hairs parting at the folds to show the fine creamy undercoat. But Stroud wasn't wasting any of his whiskey on wolfskins, no matter how prime. He tossed them back at Sitanka. "Get him out of here," he said to the guards. Before the guards could act, Sitanka drew a knife from his blanket and leaped at Stroud, knocking him to the ground. The others were on him, kneeing the knife from his hand and dragging him off.

Stroud stood up and watched for a moment while the guards propelled Sitanka away from the lodge; then he picked up the knife. It was a shiny new Green River. Knives were a staple item in a trader's merchandise, but no trader would ever let one get into the hands of a drunken Indian. "Knives," Stroud said, half to himself. "That's why Reeshar's waited." As he stood there, he thought he could sense a change in the noises of the camp. Above the mounting commotion the screams and wails of women could be heard, and Stroud realized he'd been done to a crackling. Reeshar had timed it just about right. He had withheld the knives until he was sure that Stroud's whiskey was as good as gone and that the Indians were liquored up enough to put them to use.

Stroud looked at his men, but their only reaction was to work faster in packing the furs. Partout had returned earlier with the horses, and now the packs of furs were being pushed from the back of the tipi and rolled down the slope.

There was a sudden and alarming lack of trade, and Stroud had started to help tie up the furs when Eahsapa showed up. In front of him was Belle, urged along by the firm grip he had on her arm. In his right hand he held a new knife. Eahsapa's eyes were red-rimmed and slightly out of focus, but his coördination appeared to be only slightly affected. Stroud wished the soldier-chief were drunker. He was feeling mean as a gut-shot coyote.

"Whiskey!" demanded Eahsapa. The guards had entered the tipi also. Eahsapa was aware that they had followed him in. "You dogs," he said without turning his head to look at them.

Stroud watched Eahsapa, who rocked slightly on his heels. This was one Indian he'd rather see trade with Reeshar. "Go trade with the Yellow-Haired-One."

Eahsapa looked at Stroud scornfully. "The Yellow-Haired-One made many gifts of whiskey and knives. But he has gone."

Stroud wasn't surprised. Reeshar had used up his whiskey and cleared out while the clearing was good. "My whiskey is not for giving away," Stroud said.

"I am no beggar." Eahsapa gave Belle a rough shove toward Stroud. "You favor her with hawk's bells. Is she not worth much whiskey?"

Stroud studied Eahsapa, trying to decide if the Indian really expected to get anywhere with such a damn-fool offer. Maybe the gift to Belle had in some crazy, drunken way given him the idea. Indians did trade their women sometimes. But this didn't shine. "*Wan k'eya!* It is ridiculous," said Stroud. "She is not yours to trade."

"I could take her for my woman," Eahsapa said. "It is the same."

Stroud glanced at the girl. She should have kept out of Eahsapa's way. She should have been asleep hours ago. Stroud didn't know what time it was, but it must be nearer morning than midnight. "You will take her to her father," he said.

At the reference to Shonka, a slight look of concern clouded Eahsapa's eyes. It only seemed to make him more impatient. "Whiskey!" he repeated. He made a motion with his knife toward the keg. "All the whiskey."

"Eahsapa's heart is black," Belle warned.

Stroud looked down at Belle, for the first time really searchingly. She must be fourteen or fifteen, he decided. Old enough that Eahsapa could have claimed her before now if he'd wanted to—unless she objected. "Now I know what ails him," Stroud said in English. "She won't have him."

"*Ti-ya,*" agreed Greenberry. "And Shonka won't force her."

As Stroud continued to look at Belle, he had a growing uneasiness, a feeling that this was more complicated even than talking a drunken Indian out of a fool notion. "I do not trade for women," Stroud said angrily to both Belle and Eahsapa.

"You gave a gift of hawk's bells. You were not displeased then," the girl replied.

Stroud doubted that he had heard right. Surely the girl

knew he wasn't bound by a trifling gift. Yet crazy as it seemed, she must in some way be a party to this plan. There was no knowing how much Belle was to blame for planting the notion in Eahsapa's whiskey-swelled skull. "Damn those hawk's bells!" Stroud exploded in English.

"Don't get your paw in that trap," Greenberry warned. "She cheated against Reeshar in the 'hands' game."

"So that's the way her stick floats!" Stroud muttered. "She'll find it takes more than tricks to get a husband!" As if dealing with an unruly child, he began to propel the girl toward the opening of the tipi. "I'll take her to Shonka myself."

Eahsapa had maintained a surly silence, hopeful that the girl would get whiskey for him. Now he grabbed Stroud by the arm, at the same time raising his knife to strike. Stroud seized him by the wrist and twisted the knife from his grasp as the Indian guards moved in to help.

Belle, to one side of Stroud, said quickly, "Beware the medicine iron!"

With his left hand Eahsapa struck Belle on the side of the head and knocked her backwards, causing her to trip over a pile of furs. Then he reached into the blanket around his waist and withdrew a pistol. But before Eahsapa could point it, the Indian guards clubbed him from behind. The pistol exploded as Eahsapa sank to the ground, and Belle, who was struggling to her feet, fell back with a cry.

Stroud turned to Belle; she was making no effort now to rise. He kneeled beside her and saw that her left foot was twisted beneath her. She protested as Stroud started to straighten it. He noticed blood soaking into her deerskin dress. He pushed her dress back above her leggings and saw that the blood was pumping out of a bullet wound in her thigh.

"*Yun!*" Belle whispered. "The medicine iron strikes with a tongue of fire."

Stroud pulled the crimson cloth from her waist and made a tourniquet of it. He glanced up at Greenberry. "Any whiskey left in the barrel?"

"*Wagh!* A little." Greenberry went to the barrel and gave it a shake. "A quart or two, do 'ee hyar?"

When the tourniquet had stopped the bleeding from Belle's thigh, Stroud drew a half-cup of whiskey and filled the cup the rest of the way with water. He helped Belle to sit up and handed her the whiskey. "Drink it," he ordered. Belle choked and coughed but did as she was told. Stroud refilled the cup from the barrel and put it aside, then turned to the Indian guards. "Carry the soldier-chief to his lodge." He took up the whiskey barrel and handed it to Cetan Hupahu. "For when Eahsapa regains his senses. Keep him quiet. The bright clothes are yours."

The guards looked down at their uniforms and smiled. "*Haho haho!*" Itazico lifted Eahsapa by the feet and dragged him out.

Mozay picked up the pistol which had fallen from Eahsapa's hand. It was an ancient smoothbore. "I can piss farther'n this thing can shoot," he said.

Stroud glanced at the pistol. A good-sized ball would be lodged in Belle's leg. He knelt again beside her and examined her more closely, probing with his fingers around the wound and along the back of her leg; then with his knife he ripped off the girl's legging, exposing a swelling ankle.

"More bent than broke," diagnosed Mozay.

"Go keep watch," Stroud said to him. "And somebody find some wire." Mozay, taking up his rifle, went to the door and stood just outside. Greenberry and Hobart began hunting in the scattered remains of the trade goods for wire.

Stroud probed again with his fingers, feeling for the bullet. It had entered the inside of Belle's thigh a few inches above the knee, and Stroud located it near the back, where it had ranged down and lodged not too deeply beneath the skin. He loosened the tourniquet, and while he waited for wire he tore some cloth into strips.

Some copper wire was finally located under a bundle of furs and Stroud tightened the tourniquet and turned Belle on her side. He made a probe of the wire and held it, together with his knife blade, over the fire. "Get the rest of these furs out of here," he said to Hobart. "And Greenberry, you cut me some splints from a parflèche." Stroud made an incision, and then with the wire probe he managed to extract the bullet. He poured the whiskey from the cup into and over the wound and bandaged it. Then he turned the girl onto her back. She had stood all this quite tolerably and was still conscious, though Stroud noted that her color was not good. He felt her pulse. It was regular but slow. After loosening the tourniquet for a moment, he studied her ankle. He didn't know whether it was seriously hurt or not. If it was broken, it didn't appear to be out of line. Certainly a splint couldn't hurt, Stroud decided, and it might do good.

There was a sudden intensification of the screeching from the camp. "That's wailin'. Somebody's gone under," said Greenberry, who was on his knees sawing with his knife at some tough parflèche. He finished and handed the strips to Stroud. Greenberry looked down at Belle, whose eyes were now closed. "*Ti-ya!* She got more'n she gambled for. What'll ye do with her?" Hobart pushed the last bundle of furs out the back of the lodge and disappeared after it.

"Take her back to Shonka," muttered Stroud. "What did you think?" He began encasing the girl's ankle in splints and bandage.

Greenberry gave a snort of disapproval. "I think ye could leave her here." Hurriedly he started gathering up odds and ends—sacks of beads, looking glasses, cheap jewelry—and stuffing them into a parflêche container.

Mozay stepped inside. "Here comes Partout," he said.

The Frenchman burst in excitedly. "*C'est temps de s'en aller!*" he cried. "*Les* dam' Sioux! They kill their chief!" He noticed the recumbent figure and recognized Belle. "*Sacré!*"

Stroud stared up at Partout. "Shonka murdered?"

"*Oui!*" Partout was still looking down at Belle.

Greenberry dropped the container and grabbed up his rifle. "Do 'ee hyar? Now what'll ye do with her?"

Stroud didn't answer. He was thinking of how his whiskey would be blamed for Shonka's death. With Reeshar gone they would forget it was his knives that caused the killing. There would no longer be immunity in the name Five Scalps. Reeshar had sown better than he thought. "Get the pack animals moving," he said. Greenberry, Partout and Mozay went out, and Stroud turned back to Belle. He worked rapidly and when he had finished with the splint he stood up. With a glance at Belle, whose eyes were still closed, he started for the door. Then he looked back. "Damn those hawk's bells!" he said aloud. Turning back, he stooped down, lifted the girl in his arms, and carried her from the lodge.

Six

Stroud glanced back at the others riding behind him. Even in the twilight he could see that each face was haggard, as his own must be. They had pushed hard for two days and a night with only brief rests, nagged by the worry of pursuit, and this on top of the sleepless and harried nights of trading. Since leaving Shonka's camp in the early morning dark, they had followed the North Fork of the Laramie downstream as it cut through narrow defiles lined with shingly rock and bristling with pine and spruce. This was the most direct passage through the mountains to the Platte on the other side, though a slow one, particularly with a pack train. Stroud turned his attention to the pack animals, stumbling along at an irregular pace and clearly used up. They were still two days from the forts. The animals needed rest—and if Eahsapa were on their trail, he'd have jumped them by now. Stroud glanced around the bowl-like meadow they were entering. "We'll camp here," he called back. He dismounted and began removing saddle and bridle. The others followed his example, too tired to talk.

Wyatt spread a robe for Belle and lifted her from the litter they had fixed up of lodgepoles and buffalo robes slung between two mules. Young Hobart was interested in the proceedings. "Come on," Wyatt said to the boy. "Let's fix her a crutch."

"How?" asked young Hobart.

"A forked stick with a beaver plew to pad it," said Wyatt. The boy smiled at the idea, showing the space where his tooth had come out.

The others, including Stroud, were busy unburdening the pack animals. There were twenty-five now, including those Stroud had traded for in Shonka's village. When the animals had rolled in the grass in the luxury of being free from the chafing, corsetlike *aparejos*, they were hobbled and allowed to spread out to graze. The riding horses were picketed close by. No one complained about camping cold and eating pemmican. They were all too tired to care. Hobart volunteered to keep first watch, and soon everyone was stretched out asleep, except Stroud. He looked up at the dark, moonless sky, his mind on Reeshar. The man had tried to get him and his whole party killed back in Shonka's camp. Stroud wondered what he would do next.

It may have been an hour later—or it may have been only a few minutes later—that Stroud suddenly sat bolt upright, reaching for his rifle. He saw Hobart dive behind a bundle of furs. Then a volley of shots shattered the quiet of the meadow, wild yells following close upon the shots and lead splattering all around them. The horses neighed and strained at the picket pins and everything was confusion as they all woke with a shock and scrambled for shelter behind packs and saddles. Stroud rolled a couple of packs on either side of Belle. Then he noticed that Mozay had not sought cover but seemed to be struggling to move. The attackers, after sneaking through the meadow and firing the first surprise volley, had mounted and were now charging down on horseback no more than fifty yards away. Stroud crawled quickly to Mozay, whose mouth worked as if he were trying to speak, but no sound came. Mozay's eyes rolled and he seemed to be choking. Stroud pulled two of the large packs of skins close to Mozay and just had time to flatten out behind one himself as the attackers swooped in, discharging their bows from beneath their horses' necks and leaving the whine and whump of arrows behind them as they veered away. Then the trappers were on their feet.

Three guns roared almost simultaneously, while Stroud and Greenberry held their fire. It was too dark to do anything but pull the trigger and pray. The attackers wheeled quickly and came in again. Both Stroud and Greenberry fired their rifles. One dark shadow disappeared off a pony. Stroud emptied his revolver at them and saw another shadow drop. The Indians charged a third time, though they swerved away at a safer distance and sent only a scattered flight of arrows.

Stroud waited for another charge, realizing now he had fired his last cartridges in the Colt. There was no sound from the trappers save the rattle and thug-thug of their ramrods as they reloaded. When the charge didn't come, Stroud gave his attention to Mozay. A glance was enough. His throat had swelled and turned blue as the choking blood ascended. Apparently the bullet had ruptured a lung, for there was little external bleeding. Mozay's Madame Jack was moaning softly and holding her face in her hands as she knelt beside Mozay. Suddenly the blood began gushing from his mouth, and Mozay turned his face against the pack of skins. He still grasped the rifle he had reached for at the alarm. There was a long, bubbling exhalation; then he lay still and the rifle slipped from his hand.

There was nothing anyone could do except listen to the Indians whooping as they cut the hobbles of the pack animals and drove them off. The bodies of the slain Indians were too close to the trappers' camp to be retrieved by the war party. As soon as the enemy had disappeared, Stroud and Greenberry went to the bodies. With his foot Stroud turned over the first dead warrior he came to. There was a livid burn across his face. It was Sitanka, the brave who had tried to knife him in Shonka's camp because he wouldn't take his wolf pelts. Greenberry drew his knife and bent down. He grasped the Indian's scalp lock, cut quickly, gave a yank, and held up the dripping scalp. Then he went to the other body.

There was digging to be done as soon as it was light. Not that there was any hurry. Eahsapa, with the loss of two of his Bowstring Soldiers, would have no further stomach for a fight, but would content himself with having run off Stroud's pack animals. He would be more content had he known he had killed Mozay. A grave was dug and Mozay was buried and the two scalps with him. Silently the men piled the grave with slabs of rock. Stroud was sorry about Mozay's death—sorrier still that his own entanglements had caused it. He continued to pile rocks until Greenberry inquired, "How big you calculate these wolves'll be, now?" Stroud looked up to see the others standing and watching him. Then he looked at the stones piled unnecessarily high. All the while Madame Jack had made the men edgy with her wailing, which kept up until she whacked off a finger at the first joint with an axe, to testify to her grief.

Stroud turned his attention to the packs of beaver, mink and otter, and the bulkier packs of buffalo robes, which were scattered all around. It was disheartening. The catch of a lifetime—his lifetime anyway—and no pack animals to carry them in. There was no way out of it but to dig a cache. His glance moved over the packs again and the surrounding meadow. This was the first place Eahsapa would look for a cache. Or Reeshar when he heard about it. While the others waited in camp, Stroud and Greenberry rode back up the river until they found a high, dry bluff overlooking the mouth of a tributary creek. It took them the rest of the day to dig a hole and to transport the furs in relays on the few horses that Eahsapa hadn't got—those that had been picketed—and Maud. She was too ornery even to get stolen. When all the furs were put away in the bottle-shaped excavation and spread over with leaves and branches, the hole was covered with dirt, the sod was replaced, and the extra dirt thrown into the river. That night they built a fire over the cache. Anyway, with no pack train, they'd make the forts tomorrow.

During the night they were awakened by a miserable, cold rain blowing in from the north, and by afternoon of the next day the temperature had dropped thirty degrees. They were bundled in coats and robes as they rode down off the last of the foothills that rolled away from Laramie Peak.

Before them unfolded a familiar panorama. In the foreground, facing west, was Fort Laramie, situated on the north bank of the Laramie River at the tip of an eliptical-shaped plateau. Two miles to the east was the juncture of the Laramie with the Platte, and less than a mile up from the juncture was Fort Platte, facing southeast down the Oregon Road. Except that Fort Laramie was bigger, the rival trading posts were similar, with adobe bastions at two corners, smaller wooden blockhouses protruding over the entrances, American flags fluttering from tall masts. Their whitewashed walls rose imposingly against the background of hills covered with coarse grass and scattered with pines and cedars. Crowding the plain between the forts were several hundred Indian lodges. The course of each stream was dotted with growths of cottonwood, ash, willow and box elder. Behind Fort Laramie, and offering an incongruous touch of domesticity, was about a four-acre patch of cultivated ground.

Stroud pulled in on the reins and came to a halt. He glanced back. There was no pack train of mules strung out behind now, no bundles of furs which meant the end of his years in the mountains. Stroud noticed that the squaws, Mozay's Madame Jack and Hobart's Emma, along with

Belle and young Hobart, were considerably behind. In his eagerness to get to Fort Laramie Stroud guessed he must have ridden faster than he intended. Madame Jack and Emma had been slowed down some anyway by Belle's litter, which was now slung between the horses of the two squaws; since the mules had been stolen, the loads which the squaws' horses formerly carried on the pole drags had been combined and packed on Maud. Maybe it was just as well they didn't all go into the fort together, Stroud decided. It would give him a chance to explain to Evie about Belle.

The other three men had come up beside him now and they sat in silence for a moment, gazing at the prospect before them. It had been two years since they'd been to the forts, and the adobe walls looked mighty hospitable. At least Fort Laramie did. They couldn't expect much hospitality from Fort Platte, now that Reeshar was in charge. In the four years since Platte had been built, there'd been no real trouble between the forts. Fort Platte hadn't been a keen enough competitor for that. But with old Charles Wyatt's decision to start a trade war, and with Reeshar showing up as the instrument for waging it, things could get awkward, especially for young Wyatt.

Stroud glanced at him. There was bound to be considerable interest in Stroud's cache when they got to the forts. Any one of his outfit could multiply his share in the cache by helping Reeshar find it. With around twenty thousand dollars' worth of furs in that bottle-shaped hole in the ground, here was one piloting job that would bring a good price, considering the shortness of the trip.

But Stroud wasn't much worried about the loyalty of any of them. He hadn't spent every day with them for the last two years without knowing pretty well how their sticks floated. Take Wyatt, now. Although Wyatt was too practical to antagonize his uncle to the point of being cut off without a penny, he'd never shown any inclination to toady to him. At most, Wyatt tolerated the old man, whom he rather good-naturedly considered a blackguard. Wyatt wouldn't resort to pirating to please his uncle. Stroud had never regretted permitting Wyatt to join his party two years ago, and there had been no reason to refuse the boy's request to be taken on. Though the hired personnel of the two forts maintained a half-hearted rivalry at that time, everybody else—free trappers, Indians and travelers—plied back and forth between the forts at will. Actually, Stewart, the Scot sportsman, and his party from St. Louis, including Wyatt, had shown a preference for Fort Laramie and had spent most of their time there. Moreover, Wyatt wouldn't want any part of trouble. He'd split himself up the middle being a fence sitter before he'd take a hand in anything but poker. And Hobart, Greenberry and Partout—ornery enough, for a fact, but they'd been in the mountains too long to have the low-down meanness in them.

Besides, there was a far better reason than these why none of them would talk. The reason was Reeshar himself. Reeshar had tried to get them killed back in Shonka's camp, and they'd all see Reeshar in hell before they'd sell out to him. No—they'd not desert now. Not after two years together, freezing and frying and risking their hair.

Anyhow, there was one good way to eliminate all risk. "We'll dig the cache up after we've wet our drys for a couple of days," Stroud said.

"The first thing we ought to do is go to Fort Platte after that son-of-a-bitch Reeshar," said Hobart.

Stroud had been expecting somebody to get that idea. It was a likelier cause for worry than being sold out. "No we don't," Stroud said.

"Then I'll go it alone," said Hobart. "Nobody can try to kill me and stay healthy."

"I don't want you or anybody else going over to Fort Platte and starting trouble," Stroud stated emphatically.

"What I do now ain't your say-so," said Hobart.

"It is if you go after Reeshar and start a fight between the forts. I don't want the blame for that. Catch him out if you want and beat the bejesus out of him, but stay away from Fort Platte," Stroud said.

"I'll go to Fort Platte when I feel like it," Hobart announced.

Stroud gave Hobart a steady look. "You try it and I'll stop you." Hobart grinned insolently but said nothing. After a moment Stroud glanced at young Wyatt. "Maybe you'd better stay away, too. Pryce would be glad to put you up." Stroud and Wyatt had talked before about the position the boy was in now with Reeshar. They'd wondered what old Charles Wyatt would have thought if his nephew had been killed as a result of Reeshar's doings. Recent happenings showed how much more ruthlessness the trader could muster than old Wyatt had bargained for.

"Reeshar ought to be relieved enough to see me alive that he'll let me alone," said Wyatt. "Anyway, the trade caravan must have brought mail. I'll go on over and see what kind of reception I get."

Stroud didn't say anything, though he doubted that Reeshar cared a tinker's damn whether Wyatt were dead or alive. Stroud was struck by the thought that what had been a simple life a few weeks ago had now built up a full head of complication—Reeshar, Belle, a trade war, a small fortune in furs buried in a hole in the ground.

They all sat gazing at the scene before them—the forts, the white-skin tipis, the streamers of smoke like thin pennants against the sky, the teeming life. Finally Greenberry said, "This coon's half froze for hot bread and brandy."

Stroud's thoughts turned to Evie. He forgot his troubles and kicked his horse into a run. Greenberry, Hobart, Partout and Wyatt were instantly on his heels, and the five men, firing their rifles and piercing the air with high-pitched cries of "*Owgh-owgh*," rode at a dead run toward the forts.

They dipped into a hollow, losing sight of the forts for a mile or so, then ascended a steep, twenty-foot embankment and came up before the main gate of Fort Laramie with its impending blockhouse. With a wave of his hat, Wyatt kept on toward the other fort. Hobart, with surprising agility for a man who was not small, raised himself to a standing position on his horse's hips. His flaming beard and long hair blew wildly in the wind as he leaned forward, knees bent. Several gaily bedecked squaws and their half-breed children peered down from between the pickets. Others were gathering to witness the approach of the trappers, and especially the red-bearded one who rode standing up. Encouraged by his audience, Hobart took off in a ride around the fort, continuing his high-pitched yells.

Stroud went on at a canter through the arched passageway beneath the superstructure of the blockhouse. Even though there was considerable noise from the squaws and children on the wall as they tried to watch Hobart, Stroud was aware that the small coutryard—some twenty-five yards square—lacked its usual bustle. There were no trappers in sight. In the center of the court the baling press stood idle. To Stroud's right, just south of the entrance and in front of a large storeroom, was the only sign of activity. There the last several mules of a Mexican pack train were being relieved of sacks of flour, corn, pinole and dried pumpkin. After each mule was unburdened, he was driven into the corral by cries of "*Hu-a! Vaya!*" from a pair of Mexican traders with broadbrimmed hats and bright serapes. Farther down the west side, beyond the storehouse, were the shops of the carpenter and the blacksmith, the ring of hammer on anvil sounding loud in the quiet of the courtyard. A gate at the southwest corner led into the corral, which was simply an area formed by leaving a space of about fifteen yards between the buildings and the wall on the south end of the fort. Small cell-like lodging rooms formed the north and south side of the fort, each with its door and tiny windows opening out onto the courtyard. Directly opposite Stroud, who had reined in his horse just inside the entrance, a flight of stairs led to a gallery and second floor above the building on the east side. It was on the gallery and second-floor rooms that Stroud settled his attention.

Descending the blockhouse stairs behind Stroud and holding a spyglass in his hand was a man in his late thirties —a good ten years older than Stroud. He was distinguished by a trim brown beard and brown eyes, and his gray cassinette pants and red flannel shirt set him apart from the buckskin-clad trappers. It was Amer Bostwick, who as chief clerk was second in authority to Emlyn Pryce. Bostwick had been in the mountains some fifteen years, sent out from Philadelphia by his family, who couldn't bear to see him die at home of lung fever. The climate had cured his lungs but it hadn't done anything to improve his disposition. "Where is everybody?" Stroud asked, dismounting.

Bostwick tucked the spyglass under his arm, and with a nod of greeting to Greenberry and Partout, he advanced to meet Stroud. He did not smile as he shook hands. "Evie's not here," he said.

Stroud let the remark pass. "How are you, Amer?"

"No complaints. Emlyn went down the road to meet the dragoons," replied Bostwick. "Evie went along."

"They're here so soon?"

"Sooner than expected."

Stroud glanced toward the gallery again. Evie's not being here was a big disappointment, but he didn't blame her for going down the trail. It was the first time any part of the U. S. Army had come to Fort Laramie. "When will they be back?"

"Before dark." Bostwick glanced around the group. "Have the first drink on the prairie."

Stroud tied his horse to the stair railing and moved toward the trading house, picturing in his mind the meeting of Evie and the Army. It'd be some if she wore St. Louis clothes. Stroud stopped at the entrance to the trading house, which occupied all of the west wall north of the main gate, and looked back. The others were following. Hobart was just riding into the fort.

The interior of the trading house consisted of two connecting rooms, each about twenty-six by thirteen feet. The half into which Stroud entered contained items which were especially popular in the Indian trade. It was also used for liquor dispensing. A window in the south wall of the room opened into the passageway of the main entrance, permitting trade with the Indians without allowing them into the fort. There was a counter across the south wall, and another across the west side, with shelves behind. Near the angle of the counters was a ten-gallon keg of whiskey. The other room, Stroud knew, was stocked with hardware supplies and staples.

It was all striking evidence of what had happened to the fur trade even in the nine years Stroud had been in it. No brigade captains any more leading trapping parties through the mountains all winter. No caravan captains to manage the trade at rendezvous. No distinction between company trapper and hunter, the skilled craftsmen of the fur trade, and the raw-handed *engagés* recruited at such miserable wages they couldn't afford to quit. Now the *bourgeois* ran everything from the fort, assisted by his chief clerk, and an *engagé* was any trapper or hunter who worked for the Company.

Bostwick walked across to the counter. A junior clerk had just finished waiting on an Indian through the window that opened into the passageway. The Indian had paid for his whiskey with a buffalo robe, and the clerk rolled it up before dropping it underneath the counter. The clerk was hardly more than a boy with rosy cheeks and light hair slicked straight back. Bostwick raised the hinged board which jointed the counters and stepped behind. He was pre-occupied as he began pouring whiskey into pint-sized tin cups from a jug which he took from beneath the counter.

Stroud regarded the young clerk. "Hello, Hiram. Thought you'd be gone back to the States."

The young man grinned. "No, sir. I signed on for three years more." Stroud guessed there wasn't much reason for Hiram to go back to the States. His folks were Mormons and he'd run away from home in Nauvoo, tired, Stroud supposed, of belonging to a persecuted sect, though some would say it was a lack of dedication. Anyway the boy had sneaked out one night, jumped onto a barge, and floated down to St. Louis, where he'd got a job in the fur warehouse. Serving drunken Indians in a howling wilderness was better than dodging "gentiles," so when he got the chance he signed on as a post clerk.

A voice at the window said, *"Minnewakan!* Whiskey!" It was another Indian, who pushed a buffalo robe and a container onto the shelf built on the inside of the window.

"You'll be eating parflèche and lariat before you're

done," Stroud said to Hiram. He watched the young man measure out the whiskey—three full pints—and pour it with the aid of a funnel into the Indian's container.

"You haven't done so bad," replied Hiram.

"I don't work for the Company."

Bostwick didn't raise his eyes from the cup he was filling. "Not everybody has your luck."

Stroud didn't say anything. If Bostwick had ever paused for a charitable thought, he'd paused in vain. Stroud was more interested in what Hiram was doing. "Three pints for a robe?" For some time it had been standard barter that a buffalo robe brought three cups of three gills each.

"Thank Reeshar," said Bostwick.

"I'm goin' to Fort Platte and thank him with this," said Hobart, doubling up his fist.

Stroud turned to him. "I told you if you tried it I'd stop you." After a moment he looked back at Bostwick. "What's beaver bringing a plew?"

"I don't know what Emlyn'll give you with this price war on. Last catch he paid seven," Bostwick said cautiously. He pushed a filled cup in front of Stroud and each of the others. Stroud decided Bostwick was putting it low. Reeshar had offered him that much, knowing Stroud hadn't heard about the trade war.

"Can't drink beaver," Greenberry said. He picked up his cup and sniffed the contents. "State brandy. Luck to ye, boys." He drank deep and then set the cup down and wiped his mouth. "It shines," he said. "I was weaker than a goat in spring, now."

Bostwick studied Stroud from the other side of the counter. "I heard how you got Shonka's trade. You must feel good enough to dance Injun."

Stroud knew what was on Bostwick's mind. It was the absence of pack mules. That was the first thing Bostwick would have noticed when he sighted them through his spyglass. "Some of our customers weren't quite satisfied," Stroud said.

Bostwick glanced around the group, the thought growing on him that someone was missing. "Where's Mozay?"

"Rubbed out," said Stroud. Rubbed out. Gone under. Buried under a pile of rocks to keep the wolves from cheating the worms. "Life's chancey enough wherever you live it." He downed his brandy.

Bostwick had been trying to appraise Stroud's situation, "You cached your furs?"

"That's right."

"Well, then, there's no worry," Bostwick said. He corked the jug of brandy and put it away under the counter. The door opened and Stroud looked around to see Jake and Belco, two old mountain men who had hired out to the Company a couple of years back. At the sight of them Greenberry gave a piercing war cry and started dancing around in a circle, patting his belly with the palms of his hands and chanting, "*Hi-Hi-Hi-Hi, Hi-i-Hi-i-Hi-i-Hi-i, Hi-ya-hi-ya-hi-ya-hi-ya . . .*" With answering whoops Jake and Belco took up the chant. After a moment Bostwick lifted the counter board. "Your credit's good," he said.

"Obliged," said Stroud. Bostwick left the room and Hiram refilled the cups—not from the State brandy, which was private stock, nor from the adulterated alcohol traded to the Indians, but from a keg of respectable churn-brain reserved for those who could pay a respectable price. Stroud picked up his cup. Whiskey was whiskey at any price. It had been a long time. A man who valued his hair never drank on a hunt, except to outpoison a snake bite. He needed all his wits, and sometimes even that wasn't enough.

Stroud took a long drink, then watched Jake and Belco for a moment. With their unkempt beards and flowing hair and greasy buckskins, they were as alike as two beaver. There was something a little pathetic about them. He guessed it was from trapping for the Company. Let a man be told where to trap, and how long, and when and where to turn his catch over to a Company messenger; it did something to him. Being allowed a few weeks at the fort didn't make up for the loss of the old free life. The three old *compañeros* ceased their dancing and began pummeling each other in an effusion of greetings. Another Indian came to the window for whiskey, and as Hiram folded more robes and stuck them under the counter, Stroud remarked, "You're asking for trouble, trading whiskey when the Army's due in."

Hiram shrugged. "Platte keeps right on trading it so we might as well."

"You're apt to get your liquor confiscated."

"The Army's a durn fool anyhow," Hobart said. "Some of this mountain dew may come from Taos, but a heap is hauled straight past Fort Leavenworth."

As Jake and Belco came up to the counter, Stroud motioned to Hiram to put out two more cups. "Heered how you got Shonka's trade, old hoss," said Belco with his eyes on the whiskey cups. "We never even broke open a sack of beads. Met Reeshar and his men on their way back."

"I don't suppose they told you they handed out knives before they left," said Stroud.

"Did they, now!" said Jake. He looked questioningly at Stroud. "I heered Reeshar was a friend of yours."

"Hell's full of friends," said Stroud. He watched Hiram filling the cups, aware that Jake and Belco were still looking at him. If it was information about Reeshar they were hoping for, they were barking up the wrong tree. Stroud remembered that he was out of cartridges. "You have any cartridges for a Colt?" he asked Hiram.

"Sorry, Mr. Stroud. We ordered some, but they didn't come with the shipment," said Hiram.

Belco downed his drink. "This knocks the hindsights off Taos awardenty," he said, wiping his mouth on his sleeve.

"Yessir!" Jake agreed. "That Taos brandy's got so much taste of corn it makes ye think ye're a hoss feedin' for plowin' time." He pushed his cup out to be refilled.

Stroud looked back at Hiram. "Just what is it the Army plans to do out here?"

"They're to protect the emigrants and scare the Indians. Going to South Pass and then back by way of the Arkansas to do a little scaring for the freighters on the Santa Fe trail."

"The Army's acting as an escort as far as South Pass?" asked Stroud.

"Well, no," said Hiram. "They're to ride ahead and look intimidating to everything they come across. Starting with the Pawnees, I guess."

"Ain't no army needed for that," Hobart said in disgust. "The Sioux already done it." He pushed his cup out to be refilled.

"That's right," said Jake. "Last time the Pawnees riz up to amount to a damn was spring of '38 when they rubbed out Paints-His-Face-Half-Red at the forks of the Platte. Killed the lot. Even the squaws."

"*Wagh!* That was the Skidi Pawnees," said Greenberry. "Traded hyar a time or two back afore the Sioux had 'em on the run. It's the Sioux needs scarin'."

"The Army intends to throw a big scare into them," Hiram confirmed. "An Indian runner came in yesterday with a dispatch to Mr. Pryce, asking him to get all he can in for a conference. Not much time, but two bands straggled in today."

"Thought there were more camped between the forts than usual," remarked Stroud.

"Bullets whinin' is the only talk an Injun can hear now." Greenberry finished his drink and shoved his cup across to Hiram.

"What does Mr. Pryce have to say about a conference?" asked Stroud.

"Not much," said Hiram. "He's too worried that the Army'll want the fort." There was a surprised silence.

"For a military post?" asked Stroud.

"Yep. They're supposed to consider sites on the Oregon Road."

"Ey God!" said Stroud. "How many movers do they expect?"

Hiram shrugged. "Polk got elected on the slogan 'Fifty-four forty or fight.' They'll expect enough to start a stampede."

"*Sacré voleurs!*" said Partout. "*Les* dam' *emigrés!* They go Oregon bang! *Toute la journée.* They scare *le* bison, he run to *les montagnes!*"

"Movers! *Wagh!*" said Greenberry. "They'll be swarmin' through like a plague of locusts, the green not even rubbed off a little, rollin' their eyes at an Injun yell as if a whole tribe was on 'em, and pickin' up a beaver trap and askin' what is it, and pokin' their noses in every nook and cranny."

"Place's goin' plumb to hell," said Belco. "Movers! Soldiers!"

Stroud agreed with Belco. Through the wide opening into the other room, Stroud could see that the shelves were filled and overflowing onto the floor with stock mostly for the emigrants. And the warehouse bulging, too, likely. He guessed the items were useful enough, but it didn't seem worth it by a dollar and a half to get the Army out to clear the road for wagons bogged down with tons of hardware and foodstuffs by emigrants that ought to know better. At least Pryce knew what he was doing. Independence was six hundred miles and seven weeks behind the movers by the time they got to Laramie, and it was their first opportunity to buy supplies and pay for repairs. The other three forts—Bridger, Hall and Boise in the twelve hundred miles between here and the Dalles—would no doubt do a brisk trade, but Laramie and Platte had the first and best chance at the movers. Jim Bridger and his partner Louis Vasquez had only last summer built their rickety excuse for a post four hundred miles to the west on Black's Fork. Stroud motioned with his nearly empty cup toward the other room. "You'll ruin Bridger's business."

"There'll be enough for everybody." Hiram grinned. "You'll all be throwing away your traps and waitin' on the movers before it's over. Gant and Clyman have already gone back to guide movers through."

"*Wagh!* That ain't the holler tree for this coon," said Greenberry.

"No siree!" objected Jake. "Give this child a little 'bacca, some powder, lead, a Green River knife and a sack of traps, and it's hurraw for the mountains!"

"That's all any man needs," agreed Belco. "Sometimes not even that. I recollect once in the Peaks, with a party of *ciboleros*, we run buffler with nothin' but lance and bow, in belly-deep snow, and killed five apiece." He shook his head. "Runnin' meat for emigrators as don't know fat cow from poor bull's too tame and then some."

Stroud knew now where it was Jake had got the notion he and Reeshar were friends. It was from Belco. They had run across Belco that winter in the country of the Spanish

Peaks. In his memory Stroud could see Raton rearing its head so close on the left that it seemed more towering than the peaks opposite, and the valley of the Purgatory between. It seemed fitting somehow that he had first known Reeshar in the valley of the Purgatory. *El Rio de las Animas Perdidas en Purgatorio*, the Mexicans called it—the River of Lost Souls in Purgatory. Funny what tricks a few drinks played on a man, sometimes making him see things he'd overlooked before, and other times getting him so addled he was ornery as a bull pecked with lances. Stroud was reminded of Hobart, and he leaned forward a little to see the red-bearded man better. Hobart didn't look exactly happy, but at least he hadn't carried out his threat about going after Reeshar. It was a good thing he was thirsty. Another drink or two and he'd forget it entirely. Stroud looked closely at Jake and Belco again. The two men were not as old as they appeared, yet now they were almost outdated, clinging to the past. In a way old Merk, crazy as he was, was better off. He and the past would expire pretty much together.

"Did Merk come in?" Stroud asked.

"Ain't seen that old hoss since afore you went out," said Belco. "Figure he's gone under."

"We saw him in the Medicine Bow country with a good catch. He should've been in by now."

Jake shook his head. "Ain't seed his old scaly hide."

The conversation drifted then to news from the States—mostly of the joint resolution of Congress admitting Texas to the Union, and of the inevitability of war with Mexico. Stroud wasn't interested in a war to extend slavery, if that's what it amounted to. His father had never owned slaves—claimed that like most other immoral indulgences it cost too much.

Stroud finished his drink and had his cup refilled. He had a feeling of growing impatience. This coming into the fort wasn't just an end of two years in the mountains. It was the beginning of something else. He wished Evie would come. The waiting was hard. His mind wandered then to Reeshar. There hadn't been much he could do about Reeshar while he was getting Shonka's trade, but there would be time now —time in which to look for Batchika or Wicarpi, time after seven years to find out what Reeshar wouldn't own up to.

Stroud asked Hiram what Indian bands were camped at the forts. Among those Hiram named was No Heart's village. Stroud had a feeling of satisfaction. No Heart's was Madame Jack's village, Mozay had said, and Mozay had been certain that they were camped near the Bear Lodge Mountains the winter of the blizzards. It was a place to start, and maybe luck would be with him—or he could make his own as he'd had to often enough.

The door opened behind Stroud, and Hiram looked toward it. Stroud turned and saw that it was Billy Pitcher coming in. Billy was a handsome young half-breed who acted as clerk, sometimes trader and general handyman around the fort. He was a trifle below average height and inclined to be stocky. A neatly trimmed mustache gave him almost a dapper appearance.

"Where you been?" Hiram asked.

"Out seeing the herder. Bostwick's afraid our milk cows'll get mixed in with the Army cattle when they show up."

"*Le diable!*" said Partout. "He is joke? *Ha! Ha!* With cows and bulls there is *la différence.*"

"Tell Bostwick," said Billy. He looked at Stroud. "Passed your women. Isn't that Shonka's daughter with the bad ankle?" Stroud nodded, and Billy said, "Whatever you traded for her, she's worth it." Before Stroud could ask what gave him the idea Belle was traded for, Billy said, "Bostwick tells me you had to cache your furs."

Stroud motioned to Hiram to put out another whiskey cup. "That's right. We traded those Indians out of everything but their spite."

"Too bad." Billy watched while Hiram finished filling his cup, then he took a drink. "*Gracias*," he said to Stroud. After a moment he asked, "What'll you do about pack animals?"

The question didn't make much sense to Stroud. "You mean to bring in the cache?"

"Why yes," said Billy.

"I supposed Mr. Pryce would let me use some of the fort mules for a few days," said Stroud, sounding puzzled.

"Sure he will, soon as they get back," said Billy. "If you want to wait."

Stroud put his cup on the counter with an air of exasperation. "Just what the devil are we talking about?"

Billy looked at him. "Didn't Bostwick tell you? All the pack animals we have are down-river."

"What for?"

"Mr. Pryce sent wagons down the trail to haul back the spring shipment," Billy said. "It got stuck again."

Stroud wondered why Pryce didn't give up trying to navigate the shallow Platte. Every year Pryce tried to float his furs down to St. Louis, and every year they got stuck, though usually far enough down so that wagons could be sent out from St. Louis. But with the furs grounded so far upstream this time, it would be easier to haul them back to Fort Laramie and then freight them to Fort Pierre on the Missouri. From there they could be sent by boat to St. Louis. "When did they leave?" Stroud asked.

"Yesterday. It'll take a couple of weeks to make the trip."

"Two weeks!" said Stroud.

"The boats are stuck more'n a hundred miles down," explained Billy. "Reeshar didn't even try it. He's going to freight his."

"And you don't have any more mules?" Stroud asked. Billy shrugged. "Three or four."

"What the hell kind of a makeshift business are you running?" said Stroud. "And what ails Bostwick he didn't tell me when I first came in?"

"You know Bostwick. Answers what he's asked," said Billy.

"What's happened to Mr. Pryce he's so short?"

"It ain't his fault," Billy explained. "The Crows raided down here twice lately—got more'n half our animals." He gave Stroud a steady look. "They didn't bother the Fort Platte herd. Reeshar must've put 'em up to it."

Stroud picked up his cup again and emptied it, then banged it down on the counter. "I don't want to wait," he said irritably. "I better get some ponies from the Indians." He was suddenly tired of Billy Pitcher, of Hiram, of all the rest of them. He was tired of problems.

He went outside and headed for the stairs. He was a little unsteady as he climbed to the rooftop. The ridgeline to the northwest seemed to tilt. In that direction the gray sky had darkened and a cold wind had blown up, carrying the smell of rain and snapping the flag on the mast atop the blockhouse. Reeshar again. Because of Reeshar he had no pack animals and neither had Pryce. Reeshar must be irritating Pryce plenty, too. With Reeshar using every trick he knew, it was no wonder he was getting more than his share of the trade. At least by the way Laramie looked, the free trappers must be doing business mainly with Fort Platte.

From the Indian villages between the forts more than the usual din of an Indian camp filled the air. Stroud could see that the plain was churning with fun, foolery and mean whiskey. There was one thing to be said for this price war.

From the looks of the camps, the trappers were trading their hairy banknotes for more doings than he had seen since his first year or two in the mountains.

Stroud turned to look down the broad road to the southeast, already rutted permanently by just four summers of travel. The tracks dipped and disappeared and reappeared among the barren hills to the right of the slate-colored Platte. There was no sign of anyone moving up the road. Stroud had an unreasonable feeling of disappointment. He'd been so sure somehow that when he looked in that direction he'd see Evie riding in with the Army. Rode like a man, she did.

He looked again at the Indian camps, worrying about horses and wondering what he would find out about Batchika, refusing to let himself think that he might not find anything, speculating, remembering, conjecturing, giving way to a solid, searing hate of Reeshar.

Stroud had been on the wall a good half-hour when the clatter of hoofs in the courtyard attracted his attention. Hobart was reining his horse around toward the main gate, followed by Jake and Belco mounted bareback on mules. "Where are you going?" Stroud called down suspiciously.

"To Fort Platte!" Hobart turned in his saddle, half slipping as he did so. "I'm goin' to drag Reeshar out of there and split his head plumb to the swaller!"

Stroud realized that the cold air must have sobered him some, for he could see how drunk Hobart and the others were. "You damn fool! Come back here!" he yelled. "You'll start a fight everybody in both forts will get in on." Hobart rode on toward the gate. Stroud shifted his attention to the two older men. "You better keep out of this."

"Hyar we are and we don't turn," announced Belco.

Stroud had no time to say more as the three disappeared into the passageway and then came loping out on the other side and veered toward Fort Platte. He watched them angrily for a moment, thinking it would be a wonder if they all didn't fall off and break their necks, for they had kicked their mounts into a gallop. Stroud turned and ran down the stairs, steadying himself by keeping one hand on the rail, but feeling uncertain and foolish. At the foot of the stairs he almost ran into Greenberry and Partout, who had just staggered out of the trading store. Partout was singing: " '*Adieu, belle Francoise! Je vous epouserai, ma luron, lurette. Je vous . . .*' "

"Be quiet," said Stroud.

"Did he go off ridin' on his head?" asked Greenberry.

"He's about one drink shy of that," said Stroud. "Why didn't you stop him?"

"Why didn't ye?"

"I'm going to," said Stroud. Muttering that Hobart was the biggest fool dug out, Stroud untied his horse from the stair railing and mounted. He rode out of the fort at a dead run and headed straight through the Indian encampments, scattering dogs and children before him. It added very little to the general chaos. Many drunken Indians, joined by trappers equally drunk, were racing their ponies, singing, gambling, brawling, the broad plain between the forts teeming with a confusion of sounds and motley colors.

It was in front of Fort Platte that Stroud overtook Hobart and the two old trappers. Their approach to the rival fort had attracted some attention. Several men on the wall were looking down at them. Stroud brought his horse across Hobart's path, forcing Hobart to veer away to the left.

"Out of my way," growled Hobart.

"I ought to pour you back in the bottle," said Stroud. He grabbed at the bridle of Hobart's horse.

Hobart pulled hard on the reins and with a curse kicked his horse on. Stroud had to let go of the bridle, but he spurred his own horse and kept in front of Hobart, forcing him away to the left. Before Stroud could protect himself, Hobart cut him across the face with the ends of his reins. Feeling the hot welt rise upon his cheek, Stroud sent his horse leaping ahead. With his left fist he hit Hobart behind the ear, the rush of his horse carrying him on past. Stroud wheeled around and the two charged full upon one another, passing knee to knee and each striking a blow given added force by the momentum of the horses. There was a thwack as they came together. Both men reeled in the saddle, recovered, and turned to charge again.

Greenberry and Partout had now come up, and they joined Jake and Belco as spectators to the fight. No one noticed the men on the wall, whose numbers had increased. One of them pointed down the trail.

The fight settled into a simple, brutal pattern of attrition, of charge and wheel and charge again, the horses spewing up mud and churning the soft ground, each man vulnerable to the other's fist, and the outcome a question of who could absorb the most punishment. A goodly number of Indians and trappers from the camps had come running up, but for the most part it was a struggle carried on in silence, the only sound coming from the fighters and their mounts—grunts and thuds as blows struck face and chest, the breathing of the horses and the squeak of straining leather.

So intent was he, so oblivious to anything but the crash of fists and the taste of blood and the feeling of cold air turning to fire inside his lungs, that Stroud failed to notice the approach of a group of horsemen from down the road. But the others gathered around noticed, and their attention was divided. As the fight continued, the group of riders advanced at a fairly rapid pace from the hills across the Laramie, the closing distance revealing them to be a squadron of dragoons riding in a precise double column and preceded by an officer and three civilians. They splashed into the stream, the water boiling around stirrups and girths.

Stroud was not aware of them until they had approached to within about three hundred feet. Then, as he turned to charge again upon Hobart, he saw them through blood-fogged eyes. The four people in the lead were an austere-looking officer, the heavy-set Pryce, his daughter Evie in a deerskin dress—and Reeshar.

But there was no time for other than a fleeting glance, because Hobart was coming at him again. They sent another exchange of blows smashing at one another. This time Stroud felt Hobart begin to give, the way a cut-bank trembles before a swollen current. When Stroud hit him again, Hobart started slipping from the saddle. Stroud continued to hit him, standing in the stirrups and driving Hobart down and off the saddle, until at last the red-bearded man lay sprawled face up on the ground, one hand still grasping the reins.

Stroud wiped the blood from his eyes and looked around. Blood streamed from nose and mouth and sundry cuts. His shirt was stained with blood and even his horse was splattered. Half encircling him and mounted on matching grays were upward of a dozen dragoons. They wore flat-topped forage caps with a wide yellow band, red and white neckerchiefs, dark blue fatigue jackets with yellow trim, sky-blue trousers with yellow outseam, and fringe-top buckskin leggings extending from ankle to knee. Each was armed with broad Prussian saber, percussion-cap musketoon carried on a sling, and a brace of horse pistols. They had evidently seen enough of the fight to enjoy it, for one of the dragoons, wearing the V-shaped stripes of a sergeant, had a wide grin on his Irish face. Next in Stroud's line of vision was a slender, tight-lipped young lieutenant with a sharp-featured face. Then the massive Pryce. Then Evie. Then

Reeshar. The only sounds were the snorting and blowing of the dragoon horses and the jingling of accoutrements.

"Hello, George." Evie's voice broke the silence. Her pale, coppery skin, deep tinged by the sharp, wet wind into which she had been riding, gave emphasis to her wide-set, bright-blue eyes. Her brown hair was worn Indian fashion, parted in the middle and pulled tight into bundles over each ear, except that around her face it crinkled slightly, giving the impression that if it were turned loose it would curl. In beaded deerskin dress, leggings and moccasins, she seemed exactly right.

Stroud looked then at Reeshar, until now only a shadowy presence. Whether it was for Mozay, or for seeing Reeshar with Evie, or for the past, Stroud wasn't sure. Maybe it was partly because he was still mad at Hobart, or because of the unguarded look in Reeshar's eyes which showed surprise that Stroud had escaped Shonka's camp. Whatever it was, Stroud sent his horse leaping straight at Reeshar, who had time only to raise his quirt before Stroud smashed him in the face with his fist, knocking him backward. Stroud pulled on the reins and wheeled for another charge, but it wasn't necessary. Reeshar was slipping from the saddle.

Evie's voice came through the red haze that seemed to envelop Stroud. "George! Look out!"

Stroud turned in time to see Hobart draw his arm back. Before he was aware of what was happening, Hobart threw a rock. It hit Stroud on the forehead, and he fell sideways off his horse.

Seven

For an instant upon waking, Stroud wondered with a feeling of complete loss where he was. He lay on a pile of buffalo robes, and after a moment he realized that his lodging was the second-story apartment along the east wall of Fort Laramie. Guiltily he had a vague recollection of having earlier heard the call of *"Lève! Lève!"* and he abruptly raised himself to a sitting position. He brought his hand to his forehead and was surprised at the size of the swelling. It was huge. His whole face seemed a mass of cuts and bruises. His memory touched without much satisfaction on the fight the afternoon before; then his attention was caught by several dresses hanging on nails on the wall. Below them, on the floor, were two pairs of shoes. He raised himself gingerly and went for a closer inspection. One dress, of a pale-blue wool, caught his fancy, and another of dark silk he thought had an air of elegance. It had been a long time since he had seen gowns as nice as these. He reached out and touched the pale-blue one, smiling when his rough hand caught a little in its softness. There was a light knock, and at his call to enter, the door swung wide. Evie stood on the threshold. She gave a slow, good-natured smile and stepped inside. In her left hand she held a spyglass.

"Your head's as big as a buffalo's in summer," she said. "Feel better?" Though Stroud had turned as Evie entered, his hand was slow to leave the pleasant feel of the fabric, and as Evie saw this a tightness came about her mouth.

Stroud, seeing Evie mostly in silhouette in the open doorway, was not aware of the change in her expression. He was feeling relief at her pleasant greeting. He grinned. "A heap better and ready for hugging." Obediently Evie crossed to him and with complete naturalness kissed him lightly. As Stroud's arms closed about her, however, she slipped away. Stroud felt both cheated and surprised at her cold reception. He wondered what her reason was. He hadn't thought Evie would question a man's right to get drunk now and then or to fight if he felt like it. He guessed he'd find out in time, whatever it was.

"You're taller than I remembered," Stroud said. The way he spoke made it clear that he had done a lot of remembering.

"Just the same." Evie had turned toward a window that looked out across the inner square of the fort toward the west gate.

Stroud tried again. "You must have been a rare treat to St. Louis."

"Doubt if they ever see anything but mud." Evie shrugged. "Nothing in St. Louis but mud."

Stroud felt a rising irritation. Unreasonable maybe, under the circumstances, but she might have made it easier for him. This not coming out with whatever was wrong was the half-Indian in her. Or maybe the half-Welsh. Or maybe just the all-female. With a show of unconcern Stroud looked over the furnishings of the room—bedstead but no mattress, two chairs, a chest of drawers and a tin pail to hold water. On the chest was a board for cutting tobacco, and above it hung a brass crucifix. Near it, dangling from a nail, was a fairly fresh scalp with coarse, long black hair. Stroud watched Evie, still at the window, adjusting the spyglass. He admired her well-rounded tallness and general air of composure, though at the moment the latter was irritating. Resolutely he examined again the ill-assorted articles in the room—the crucifix left by some one of the missionaries on his way to Oregon—probably Father De Smet; the scalp no doubt a trophy of some favored hunter or trapper who was accommodated for a night or two; and Evie's belongings, which included parflêche boxes of varying sizes. In a corner were Stroud's possible sack, Hawken's rifle, and other personal possessions. Stroud wondered if it was Evie's doings that he had occupied the room for a night, or whether it was a welcome by her father to a trapper with a valuable cache to sell.

Evie seemed finally to have the spyglass adjusted to suit her. "You've seen an Army camp, haven't you?" she asked.

"A long time ago." Near Fort Leavenworth it was, after he left home. He had thought he might join the dragoons until he talked to some of the enlisted men. The posters and the recruiting sergeants had made it sound like a gentleman's tour of the West.

"Then come look," said Evie impatiently. "There's something wrong with this one." Stroud went to stand beside her. She handed him the spyglass. "I wish you had seen them yesterday," she went on. "Riding two abreast they were, and the horses were beautiful—first fifty blacks, then fifty grays, then fifty bays, then chestnuts and then blacks again."

"And any of your ponies could outrun the lot," said Stroud. He put the glass to his eye and looked to the west, upstream, to the so-called Army camp. Only the portions on higher ground were visible, the view of the rest being cut off by intervening swells of ground. Something was wrong. Two or three miles upstream there was visible exactly one wall tent, about thirty feet from the stream, and scattered in every direction were the small figures of men and the larger ones of horses and wagons. Some moved and some didn't, and those who did were hampered by stray piles and pieces of equipment and gear. There seemed to be no order about the movement anyway, the men, horses and wagons all milling about. Cattle and sheep wandering at will added to the effect of complete disorganization. Stroud started to hand the glass back to Evie when something caught his attention. Protruding from the growth along the river and almost in a line from the wall tent to the stream was the flared top of a single tipi. He turned away, thinking that some poor bastard of an Indian must be mighty surprised. "There's something wrong all right," he agreed.

"I'm surprised to see they're camped on the Laramie at all," Evie said. "Last I saw yesterday they rode off up the Platte, planning to camp there."

"The grass is grazed off," said Stroud. The hundreds of Indian ponies had done it. Now even the Indians were having to keep their herds at a distance from the forts, and Fort Laramie's small herd of milch cows had to be grazed on the plain under guard.

"We told 'em that. The dragoons Pa and I rode in with were supposed to pick the campsite, but the others got here before they had a chance to look. I guess Reeshar outtalked Pa because they just went on up the Platte trying to make camp before the rain set in," explained Evie.

"Looks like it was quite a rain," remarked Stroud.

"It started not long after your fight with Hobart. Gentle-like at first. Then after supper it was a regular cloudburst." Evie paused. She turned her head and glanced up at Stroud.

"Whatever you hit Reeshar for, it wasn't jealousy."

"No." Stroud didn't want to tell Evie about it. He never had wanted to. If a man hadn't been able to take care of one girl, it wasn't much of a recommendation. He looked out of the window again.

"The cloudburst must have hit about the time they were trying to get over the ridge between the Platte and the Laramie," said Stroud. "In the rain and half-dark it wouldn't be easy. They should've come back to the forts and gone upstream." He lifted the spyglass again and looked toward the Army camp. Three mounted men in uniform had left the confusion of the camp and were headed toward the fort. A little way back a bunch of Army mules were being herded toward the fort by three or four mounted men. "I think we're going to have callers," Stroud said.

"I expect it's Colonel Kearny," said Evie. "He's coming to see Pa this morning. And to dinner, too." She added, "Pa wants to see you soon as you've eaten."

Stroud refused to show any interest in the colonel. "Was it your father had me put up here?"

"Nobody knew where else to put you. Your horse is in the corral. I rubbed him down and fed him some oats."

"Greenberry could've taken me to camp."

"If you have a camp."

"I must have one somewhere," said Stroud. "Why didn't you ask Greenberry where it is?"

Evie half turned and suddenly smiled her good-natured smile. "It was all right, George. Pa didn't mind your sleeping here. And it was a lot easier than trying to find Greenberry—or Partout, either. They roared around enough when nobody wanted 'em, and then disappeared. In one of the Indian camps, I guess." She paused and then observed, "Greenberry's an old goat."

"What about Hobart?"

"He acted real strange. Pa saw him and his wife and young Hobart all packed up and moving out soon after we got in. Hiram said he picked up a big supply of whiskey. What'd he move out for?"

"Mad, I guess." Stroud was beginning to think Evie was right, that he had no camp. She had accounted for everybody but Mozay's Madame Jack and Belle.

As if sensing his unasked questions, Evie said, "Madame

Jack found some cousins, I heard. I don't know where the girl is—with Madame Jack, I expect."

Stroud felt a certain relief that Evie had finally brought Belle into the conversation. "Belle's a problem," he said cautiously. "I'll have to find a place for her for a while."

"She can stay with me," Evie offered. "I heard all about her."

"You're kind." Stroud was glad that apparently it wasn't Belle that Evie was put out about. Anything else could be straightened out easy enough.

"No, curious. Besides, I'd like company," said Evie.

Stroud glanced around. "Where are you sleeping?"

"After two years behind walls? I've been down at the camps with some of Mama's people—Grandfather Big Road, mostly." Big Road was chief of one of the Oglala tribes camped between the forts.

"Then Belle can stay with you there."

"No. I'll move in here. It would please Pa and be a change for the girl."

"Her band'll show up soon."

"They always do when they've nothing left to trade."

"Trading was good."

"Come tell me about it while you eat." Evie started for the door.

"What time is it?"

"The second table already finished. If you expect to see Pa you'd better move." Evie led the way along the gallery, down the stairs and to a lower room that was used as dining room and kitchen. The furniture consisted of a large rough table with stools, and along one wall there was a narrower table for preparing food. Near by was a door leading into a pantry and larder. Opposite the entrance a window looked out into the corral. The cooking was done in a fireplace.

Standing in front of the fireplace with a half-filled coffee cup in his hand was Evie's father, Emlyn Pryce. He was a large, heavy-set man, almost shapeless in his bulk, with an air of rugged independence, a voice that rumbled, and eyes that were unexpectedly gentle. Orphaned at sixteen, he had left Wales for Canada, entering as a lowly *engagé* with the Northwest Company at Grand Portage, and after ten years had worked up to *bourgeois* of a small post on the Saskatchewan. The future had seemed good and his rise with the company automatic, but the Northwesters had combined with the Hudson's Bay Company and Pryce was one of nearly a thousand men who had been cut loose. He'd been glad to start over again with the American Fur Company as a clerk. Stroud had always admired him. He was an ornament to the mountains in his fair dealings with the Indians, though he could drive a good bargain when he had to. Seeing Pryce, Stroud was reminded of what his father used to say—that there was no man with ambition who was content. And Pryce was content. It did limit him some, Stroud guessed.

Pryce was plainly glad to see Stroud, and Evie was plainly surprised to see her father in the kitchen. "Never knew Pa to be so impatient to see you," Evie said slyly.

"And a pretty fool I'd be not to." Pryce shifted his cup and extended his hand, his glance traveling over Stroud's bruised and battered face. "We're both glad you're in," he said as he shook hands. "You were slow in coming."

"I had trouble finding Shonka and more trouble getting his trade," explained Stroud.

"I heard," said Pryce. "How much did you get?"

"Thirty packs—mostly beaver and mink—and I already had nearly half that much," said Stroud.

Pryce gave a low whistle.

Evie, who had gone to push an iron kettle into the coals, turned toward the men. "Don't you two get started on anything long-winded, Pa. We saw the colonel from the window."

"We'll all see more of him than we'll like before he's out of here," Pryce said impatiently. He took a swallow of coffee, then set the cup on the table, pulled out a stool and motioned to Stroud. The two sat down opposite each other. "Besides," added Pryce, "what George and I have to say doesn't depend on long-windedness."

Stroud smiled. "What are you paying?"

"Eight dollars a plew for prime beaver," Pryce said. "It's the same price you'd get for them in St. Louis."

"It'll shine." Stroud admitted to himself that it was more than he'd hoped for. Evie came and put down a plate of dried buffalo meat and a small pewter pitcher of tree molasses, boiled down from the sap of the box elder.

"Reeshar'll pay more though, and I couldn't blame you if you want to deal with him," said Pryce.

"I know," Stroud said. "But I don't."

"That is good." Pryce paused. "I should have gone out myself after a big trade like Shonka's, instead of sending Billy Pitcher." Pryce was plainly feeling guilty. He finished his coffee and pushed the cup aside; then he smiled at Stroud. "I'll admit your catch will help me with the Company. With that and the emigrant trade—I've stocked heavily on that—they may not be so quick to sell the fort."

Evie set a cup of coffee in front of Stroud. "Of course they won't, Pa. I can't believe they really intend to anyhow."

Stroud could believe it. Fort Laramie had always played second fiddle to Fort Union up on the Missouri. And with the fur trade not what it used to be, the Company might sell it to the Army rather than face abandoning it in another few years. Fort Union could handle what was left. And as for Fort Platte—it was nothing but a bothersome fly that was easier to move away from than to swat. Stroud understood why Pryce might be extra sensitive on the subject, having lost a job as *bourgeois* with the Northwesters when they merged with Hudson's Bay Company twenty years ago. But it wouldn't trouble the Company, back in their offices in St. Louis, that Fort Laramie was home to a Welshman and his half-breed daughter; that Pryce had seen to the rebuilding of the fort and had put some of himself into each sun-baked adobe.

Stroud poured molasses into his coffee, took a spoon from the mugful in the center of the table, and began absently stirring. He wondered about the trade goods for the emigrants. Chances were Pryce had ordered them under the same arrangement he had for the Indian goods—ordered what he thought he could get rid of, and if there were any miscalculation he would take the loss. Working for the Company a man had all the drawbacks of being in business for himself without so much chance of gain.

Stroud realized that Pryce was talking about the mules that had gone down-river to bring back the spring shipment of furs. "I don't think I'll wait," he said. "I'll trade for some Indian ponies. Meant to yesterday."

"You might have yesterday," Pryce said. At Stroud's quizzical look he added, "Kearny's raising hell about the whiskey trade. That's all he talked about yesterday."

"Won't the Indians trade for anything else?"

"They've traded for necessaries."

"I can try. I'll get some somehow." Though Stroud admitted that Pryce could be right. To an Indian horses were money in the bank. It was discouraging. Seemed like everybody and everything were conspiring against his getting his furs in. First Reeshar and Eahsapa, then the Platte River, and now the United States Army. He took a mouthful of coffee and savored it a moment before he swallowed. He hadn't had a cup of coffee since God knows when except at the feasting in Shonka's camp. It was too valuable a trade item to be squandered. He looked across at Evie who had pulled up a stool and sat near her father. "This is good coffee. What did you do to it?"

"It's some I brought from St. Louis," explained Evie.

"I can't be any help in getting horses," Pryce said apologetically. "Right now I'm about as popular as a polecat. The Indians have thought I was all-mighty and they can't see today why I just don't ignore Kearny." He paused and then said in disgust, "I should have gotten horses a week ago. But I thought I had enough to get by until I found out what was going to be done about the fort. . . ."

"What about Evie's grandfather?" Stroud asked.

"Big Road? I've tried him," said Pryce. "Went out early this morning. He looked at me as if I were the first white man he'd ever seen."

Evie laughed, then said reprovingly, "Pa! You know good and well why Grandfather's upset."

"I know. He's lost face with his people because I can't control the Army."

Stroud knew that Big Road liked to get his people back to their usual ways as soon as possible every summer. Now they'd likely hang around, hoping somehow to get their fill of whiskey. "He'll get over it," said Stroud. But it wouldn't be in time to do him any good. Stroud was convinced that if he wanted horses he'd have to try to get them himself. After a moment he said, "I'm not surprised Kearny's raising hell about the whiskey trade. But will he do anything but talk? Anything permanent, that is."

"I don't know," said Pryce. "I gave him my conclusions on the matter." Though the Indian agents and the military had been trying to bring the liquor trade under control for twenty years, they hadn't even been able to slow it down, and Pryce had long since come to the conclusion that the methods used were downright ridiculous. One agent for the Upper Missouri had the impossible task of keeping watch on several widely scattered trading posts and nine tribes of Indians—all the bands of Teton Sioux, the Arickarees, the Gros Ventres, the Mandans, the Poncas, the Cheyennes, the Crows, the Blackfeet and the Assiniboines—numbering upward of fifty thousand and roving the wilderness from the Missouri River to the Rocky Mountains and from Canada to the Platte.

The trading posts were only carrying out orders from the Company and owners in St. Louis. Any *bourgeois* who refused to trade for liquor would soon be replaced by one who would. The place to stop the liquor trade, Pryce had told Kearny, was in St. Louis—by taking action against the Prattes and Chouteaus and other leading citizens of St. Louis, whose fortunes were being built, or at least helped along, by the liquor trade. Pryce had pointed out, too, how it might have been stopped years ago by bringing to task Ashley in St. Louis and Astor in New York, who had started it all by claiming that the liquor trade was necessary in order to compete with the British-owned Hudson's Bay Company and Northwest Company.

Certainly, attacking the trade at its source, when known, would be more effective than chasing around the wilderness seizing a keg or two of whiskey here and there. Pryce had stated bluntly that much of the whiskey was hauled right past Fort Leavenworth—that it was loaded into wagons at Westport or Independence in broad daylight even though there were two government agents at Westport. It was then openly hauled into the territory, where it often remained a week or more awaiting the arrival of somebody to deliver it to the trading posts. "I told Kearny quite frankly," concluded Pryce, "that only last summer the

Company had smuggled enough whiskey, hidden in flour barrels, past the agent at Bellevue to keep the Indians on the upper Missouri drunk all summer."

"What did Kearny say to all this?" asked Stroud.

"Nothing," said Pryce. "But he quit lecturing me."

"What's he going to do about the whiskey you have on hand?"

"I don't know," said Pryce.

The door flew open and Hiram, the clerk, stuck his head in. His fresh young face was pinker than usual, either from excitement or the exertion of running across the courtyard. "Kearny's just riding in, Mr. Pryce."

Pryce stood up. "At least I'll find out what he's going to do." He went on out.

Stroud finished his cup of coffee. He was interested but he'd been disappointed too many times before to think anything much would come of Kearny's concern. Stroud watched Evie cross the room, aware of the easy way she moved. The whiskey trade and his concern over getting pack animals were forgotten. He wanted to go and hold her in his arms and find out what it was that had come between them upstairs, but he wasn't sure whether it was the right time for it or not. The whole truth was he didn't know much about women. There had been Batchika, and that was about all. He only knew that he wanted Evie and that this coming into the fort had been complicated by so many things that nothing seemed to be going the way he had imagined. It had seemed natural enough upstairs to hold out his arms to Evie after two years away. But he felt awkward now.

He went to stand near her and watched as she pulled the iron kettle from the coals. He was pretty sure that he smelled biscuits and it was reassuring. It was a certainty the second table hadn't had biscuits and he doubted even that the first had. Evie had made them just to please him. "You doing all the cooking?" he asked.

"Only helping out." Evie knocked coals from the top of the kettle and lifted the lid off with a poker. "Pa just bought a Navajo couple from some Mexican traders. They're so glad to get free they're willing enough, but the woman hasn't got the knack of biscuits yet." She reached to the cook table for a plate and a long fork. "Don't just stand there. Get some milk."

Stroud smiled and took a pitcher into the pantry. The crock of milk was cold in his hands, and the cream slid over the edge and broke in thick clots. He remembered getting milk for his mother from the springhouse. Cool and moist the springhouse had been and heavy with the ancient smell of leaf mold.

While he ate the dried buffalo meat, biscuits and milk, Stroud told Evie of his trading. "There's enough, Evie, we can go on to St. Louis soon as I finish my business here," he concluded. "It'll be a good start."

Evie, who had waited to eat with him, stopped a biscuit halfway to her mouth. "You want to live in St. Louis?" From her tone of voice it sounded as if she had not considered this possibility.

"It doesn't have to be St. Louis. Wherever we want," said Stroud.

"It was those dresses hanging on the wall that set you to thinking about St. Louis," said Evie. "I saw your look."

Stroud was puzzled. "I was thinking of you. How pretty you'd look in the blue one, the color of your eyes, how . . ."

"No," Evie interrupted. "You were seeing a woman—in St. Louis or some such place—toasting her feet on a brass fender in front of a fire, or standing at a window watching the carriages in the street through lacy curtains. Maybe her eyes were the color of mine. Maybe she even looked like me. But it wasn't me, George. Not me, picking sarvis berries, or pounding pemmican, or mending your moccasins."

Stroud had a guilty feeling that maybe Evie was right—at least partly right. He didn't remember that his thinking had gone that far—but it might have if Evie hadn't come in when she did. "You don't have to do those things. And it doesn't have to be St. Louis," he repeated.

"Money can be put to good use out here," suggested Evie. "Jim Bridger's new fort now . . ."

"Doesn't interest me." Stroud paused and then reminded her, "We've talked of this before."

"You have," said Evie slowly. "But that's all I thought it was—just talk."

"Didn't you really expect we'd go back to the settlements?" Stroud had stopped eating and was studying Evie quietly. Maybe it was a mistake to have mentioned St. Louis so soon. Especially when she was distracted by the Army.

Evie appeared not to have heard. "Is that why you've been so bent on getting money—just so you could leave?"

Stroud abandoned any pretense of eating and shoved his plate back. He and Evie sat looking at each other across the table. "*Hell* bent's what you mean, isn't it?" Stroud said defensively.

"You needn't be touchy. Anybody could tell you didn't intend to pack traps the rest of your life."

"Then why act surprised if I intend to leave?"

"I thought you liked it here. I thought that'd make a difference when the time came."

Stroud hadn't really thought much about whether he liked it or not. He had felt at home in this country, which was maybe the same as liking it. "I came to make myself a stake and I've finally made it," said Stroud. "Not as much as I'd once hoped, maybe, but I've made it."

"And that's the only reason you came—just to make money?"

"I'm not the first." Stroud saw no reason to admit that he almost gave it up once. That it took all his determination just to make himself stay.

"Most boys come for adventure, or their health, or because they're running away. Pa says you don't feel a need for money until you're older."

"Not this child," said Stroud. "I felt it by the time I got to St. Louis." It had taken him that long to figure out why it was, really, that the neighbors had come for his father that time. It boiled down to a simple matter of money. A man was allowed eccentricities if he had money enough.

"Don't look so glum about it. You'll figure out something." Evie paused and then added, "But don't take a notion to go to Oregon."

Stroud gave a short, harsh laugh. "I won't. You didn't even see the movers that came through two years ago. Or last year, either." They were all alike. He'd run across them on the trail last year, looking wan, sallow, underfed, poorly clothed, their eyes filled with distrust and indecision, making up in plain damn foolishness what they lacked in gumption.

Evie's expression was puzzled. "What's wrong with 'em?"

"They're mostly low-ignorant. They're the kind that arrested my father once for witchcraft. Or maybe it's 'wizardcraft.' "

"That isn't done any more," scoffed Evie.

"Yes it is," said Stroud. "Fentress County, Tennessee, 1835." He could still feel the confusion and terror of that night when he had been awakened by neighbors he had known all his life pounding on the door and threatening his father for "bewitching" a girl.

Later they admitted, half proud and half ashamed, that

their guns had been loaded with silver bullets—the only kind that would kill a wizard. Stroud could still hear the tap, tap of his father's peg leg on the bare floor as he went to let them in. That was something those ignorant-crazy people had temporarily forgotten—that for a while they had been proud of Squire Billy Stroud and his part in the battle of New Orleans with Andy Jackson. That night they only remembered that Squire Billy read most of the time and who could tell what mischief he learned? To Stroud's way of thinking, Squire Billy's questionable pursuits would have been overlooked had his land been paying for itself instead of lying fallow. His father had never intended to work the land. He had bought it as an investment, expecting to sell at a profit. But for thirty years the only explanation he gave out, when pressed, was that the land was too valuable to plow. It probably hadn't helped any that what little his father had was spent in giving his sons a "right smart chance of learnin'."

"Who was it that your pa was supposed to have bewitched?" asked Evie.

Stroud gave a flicker of a smile as an apology for his silence. "Some young girl who was suddenly taken ill. Something the doctor couldn't diagnose."

"Was he judged guilty?"

"He wasn't brought to trial. They found out in time the girl had a fairly common ailment." Stroud decided against telling Evie it was a very bad case of anonymous pregnancy. Damn fool thing they hadn't figured it out in the first place. Stroud wondered what difference it would have made. It wasn't long after that fearful night that his older brothers struck out for themselves. Most likely they would have anyhow about then, for when he asked his father why, Squire Billy had said it was a good idea. People could say what they liked about Fentress County being in its infancy

—the whole truth was that it was stillborn. With his father's blessing he himself had left the following spring.

"How was he afterwards—your father?"

"The same." Stroud had wondered about that, too. Squire Billy had gone back to his reading just as if it had never happened. "He didn't even seem to care."

"Then there was no harm done. There's worse things than ignorance."

"There are different kinds," Stroud conceded. "Anyway I'm not going to Oregon."

Evie stood up and picked up the biscuit plate. After a moment she said, "Do you want any more biscuits?"

"I guess not," Stroud said.

Evie studied him, standing with the plate in her hand. "What would you do in St. Louis?" she asked.

"Why," said Stroud slowly, "I haven't decided exactly. It's been a long time since I was in the settlements."

"You wouldn't like being a shopkeeper," said Evie.

"Lord no!" said Stroud.

". . . or an innkeeper, or a banker, or an undertaker . . ."

"Don't be ridiculous. There's always something interesting for a man with capital to invest. I'll have to go to St. Louis and look around a little."

Suddenly Evie's good-natured smile appeared. "I don't believe you'll go anywhere much—not back to the settlements anyway. Pa says once you're this side of the Purgatory you never go back."

"Have you ever seen the Purgatory? It's a thin, snaky little stream that gets lost in a couple of wide bends of the Missouri."

"I know," said Evie. "The name just caught Pa's fancy, I guess."

"I think your father's got it confused with the River Styx."

Evie began stacking the breakfast things with a clatter. Her pretty mouth and chin set in stubbornness. "You better go finish with Pa, if you haven't already. I've got the colonel's dinner to worry about."

For a moment Stroud had the feel of a tie rope around his body and Maud pulling on the other end, then his exasperation found vent in another direction. "Doesn't the Navajo woman do anything?"

"She's gone to dig some wild turnips. Besides, she can't make biscuits yet."

"You already said that."

Evie crossed to the worktable and banged the dishes down. "At least it's something I wouldn't have to worry about in St. Louis," she said with a note of triumph. "Dinner for a colonel."

Stroud clapped his hat on his head and left, and was no sooner outside than he was tempted to go back. *You'll figure out something*, Evie had said. He shouldn't have let that remark stand. He'd been thinking for nine years, and it was back to the settlements for him. But maybe he'd better wait until the Army cleared out and Evie could get her mind on other things. Eyes on the ground, Stroud sidestepped a puddle of water without really seeing it. Although it was not raining at the moment, the sky was overcast and there had been intermittent drizzles. He was walking diagonally across the courtyard when a dragoon sergeant came out of the corral. The sergeant looked at Stroud, appreciating the bruises on Stroud's face and forehead. "It's a hard head you have."

Stroud vaguely remembered seeing the sergeant with the group that had watched the last of his fight with Hobart. "Hard enough," he replied.

"Where's the red-bearded fellow?" asked the sergeant.

"Off sulking." Stroud was about to go on, then he paused and looked at the sergeant again. "What happened to your camp?"

The sergeant pushed back his forage cap, showing a fringe of curly hair. He had long, curly lashes, though his square, rugged face and busy mustache gave him a very masculine appearance. "Why," he explained, "just after the bungs was pulled from them hogsheads up above, the whole camp was struck by lightning—Taos lightning." He grinned and then added, "I was the soberest man there, and I could hardly navigate."

Stroud was mindful that the sergeant was eyeing a group of squaws sitting outside one of the doorways, blanketed against the cold wind. They were laughing and chattering. Outside the door of Pryce's office a mounted private held the reins of two horses. He, too, was eyeing the Indian women. "Not them," said Stroud of the squaws. "Just take a bottle of whiskey over to the Indian camps."

"The prettiest one ever is camped upstream," said the sergeant.

"Whiskey'll be just as good there," said Stroud.

"I tried that last night," the sergeant said. "I offered her some but she wouldn't have anything to do with me."

"Oh, hell," said Stroud. "You give it to her husband."

"Haven't seen any husband. I found her there by herself and she still is."

"That tipi spang in the middle of the Army?" asked Stroud. "A squaw by herself?"

"She looks pretty young," the sergeant grinned. "Regular little hellcat and no mistake. The minute I stuck my head in the door she tried to take it off with a forked stick."

Stroud had a strange feeling somewhere around the pit of

his stomach. "Could the forked stick have been a crutch?"

"It could that."

"And her leg's in a splint?"

"Her ankle, it is."

"Ey God!" said Stroud. So it was Belle settled in the middle of the U. S. Army. His lost camp was found, all right. But where were the others? Stroud wondered how many more fixes Belle could get herself into. Damn her anyhow.

Eight

Through his irritation and concern at Belle's predicament, Stroud heard the sound of a voice—not Pryce's but coming from Pryce's office—and snatches of words, something about "Army's deplorable condition," "uncoöperative action on the part of the vendor," and "place the blame somewhere." Almost immediately the door was opened by a moon-faced young lieutenant. Then an older officer strode out. Stroud recognized the older officer as Colonel Kearny, though Stroud had had only a few fairly distant glimpses of him that summer at Fort Leavenworth when he was on his way west. Kearny was tall, with a rather long nose and deep-set, large eyes, and so far as Stroud could tell he had aged very little in the nine years. Stroud tried to remember what he knew of the man but it wasn't much.

Kearny had just been promoted that summer nine years ago to Commanding Officer of the First Dragoons at Fort Leavenworth. There had been considerable doings at the fort, Stroud recalled, and it had freshened old gossip about Kearny. Mainly about his marrying the beautiful stepdaughter of General William Clark several years earlier. The wedding had been postponed, with the guests already assembled, by the unexpected return from school at West Point of the bride-to-be's stepbrother, Meriwether Lewis Clark, who apparently had been hoping to marry her himself.

Stroud decided that that was probably what had interested him in Kearny in the first place—the relationship to William Clark, even as distant a relationship as stepson-in-law. Clark, a legend during his lifetime, had been dead only seven years. And it was only forty years ago that he and

Meriwether Lewis had been the first Americans to cross the continent—the first to see the vast, empty prairies and river valleys and mountain ranges. Stroud wondered whether, even through such a weak relationship, something of Clark's temperament could have rubbed off on Kearny. Certainly as Indian agent, Clark's interest in the Indian's welfare might explain Kearny's impulsive and unorthodox action—it had also been part of the gossip that summer—in burning out a liquor trader and destroying his stock near Fort Des Moines the year before. What Kearny had done since that time, Stroud didn't know, but he looked like a man bound for something fairly big. Just outside the door Kearny paused to glare at the lieutenant.

"I'm sure no one will hold you responsible, sir," said the lieutenant. "The senior officers will make it clear that it was their fault." His remark was meant to be soothing, but it only seemed to irritate Kearny.

"I don't know whom they'll make it clear to," said Kearny. "I'm declaring these forts out of bounds." The horse holder had brought the horses into position, and Kearny swung into the saddle. The lieutenant took the reins of his horse and quickly mounted. Colonel Kearny's glance rested for a moment on Stroud, the large, brooding eyes seeming to look clear through him. Then Kearny spoke to the sergeant. "Garrow . . ."

"Yes, sir."

"I am going to arrange to use Fort Platte for shoeing also. Select another fifty mules and herd them there."

"Yes, sir." As the officers and the orderly started off, Garrow said in disgust, "Saint-forsaken, ugly picture! If there's anything worse than a rat-tailed, hammer-headed, cat-hammed mule, it's the unchristened bog-spawn of humanity that tends to 'em." Having grumbled, Garrow went off fairly cheerfully toward the corral.

Stroud, noticing that Pryce was standing in the open doorway of his office, went to stand beside him. Together they looked after the departing officers. "Is he going to confiscate your liquor?" asked Stroud.

"No need. He's leaving three officers and a hundred men to keep peace until he gets back from South Pass—thirty days, he says." As Pryce watched Kearny and his lieutenant and the orderly ride through the gate and turn in the direction of Fort Platte, he said, "Wouldn't you like to come to dinner, George?"

"No," said Stroud. He wasn't interested in socializing with the Army.

Pryce knew how Stroud felt. He wouldn't be entertaining Kearny unless it was expected of him.

"Has Kearny made any mention of buying the fort?" asked Stroud.

"Not yet," Pryce said.

"Then what's he so all-fired busy about?"

"Mostly nonsense about the conference." Pryce shrugged. "It was an inspiration he had two-three days back when he ran into Bull Tail's Brûlés. He thinks the sight of the dragoons put the fear of God into them, so he invited them up for a conference and trusted we could get enough Oglalas to make it impressive."

Pryce paused and then said irritably, "I don't know what a conference'll do to the Indians, but I can tell you what it'll do to me. It'll finish off what little trade there is left. Kearny plans on handing out gifts."

As if the conference were too depressing to dwell upon, Pryce abruptly changed the subject. "Pierre and his wife left this morning. You're welcome to their room. You and one of your men." He indicated the middle compartment on the north side, the door of which stood open.

"Much obliged," said Stroud. "I'll get Greenberry." He'd move his things in later. Right now he'd better get Belle out of the Army camp. "I need an extra horse for a while. Can I use one of yours?"

Pryce nodded. Then he said, "Evie took pleasure in your coming. I hope she'll have no cause to regret it."

"I'll give her none." Stroud wondered what the devil Pryce had heard about Belle and hoped it was the truth. Stroud walked across the courtyard to the corral. If Pryce had heard the truth, it'd be the first thing that had gone right since he arrived at the fort.

The corral was a rectangular area behind the south-side buildings of the courtyard, an area narrower but longer than the courtyard because there were no buildings against the walls, although the smithy did extend a few feet into the corral at the west side. The walls and buildings at this corner of the courtyard were not connected, leaving about a fourteen-foot passage into the corral. Stroud unhooked the gate of split cottonwood logs, noting as he did so a muscular man, bare to the waist, with silver bands around his arms at the biceps and a beaded headband to hold back his long black hair. His dark skin gleamed in the light of the forge. Stroud decided it must be the Navajo man whose woman hadn't learned to make biscuits yet. Another man, bare to the waist also but wearing a leather bib apron, was shoeing a mule. Forty or fifty other mules milled about in the corral, squealing, biting and pawing each other and generally being cantankerous enough to harass two dragoon privates who tended them. Stroud guessed Garrow must have brought the mules in while he and Evie had been talking in the kitchen. Stroud's big stallion was standing aloof with three other saddle horses in a corner. Stroud led his own horse and one other to the saddle shed at the end of the smithy and saddled up. He led them out the corral gate, closed it after him, and mounted his horse. With the extra horse in tow, he headed up the Laramie.

The gray sky had lightened some, though the overcast was still solid. The Laramie surged swift and dark past the front of the fort, its banks full from the rain. There'd be rough fording today. The thought struck Stroud that a toll bridge across the Platte, always too swift and deep to ford, would make money for somebody if the emigrants kept coming. That was how his father had made the money to buy all those worthless acres—a toll bridge. Squire Billy had built one just west of the Cumberland Gap. The thought interested Stroud only in theory and he dismissed it. The trail took its course back from the Laramie a hundred yards or so, and the bed of the river, marked by the cottonwoods and tall grasses of the bottomlands, would disappear and then reappear as Stroud loped over the hilly plain. Ahead of him the land rolled in waves up to the foot of Laramie Peak, its crest now hidden by clouds.

Here was where the plains met the mountains—where white men and red had met in barter and carousal even before the forts were built. Yet not long ago, either. It had been less than twenty-five years ago that an obscure French-Indian trapper, with the help of the Sioux, had named it with his life. And already the streams had been trapped out by one-hundred-and-fifty-man brigades, year after year, until beaver and mink and otter and muskrat were as scarce as fat bull in spring. And now the movers were coming through, more each year, and the Army was thinking of setting up forts. It didn't take long for a place to change. Stroud supposed most people would call it progress.

Gradually the disagreement he had had with Evie and the worry about getting his cache out had ceased to be uppermost in Stroud's mind. Near the river he could see cattle and sheep grazing under guard. The Army had made some progress anyway.

Stroud proceeded upstream as fast as the led horse would permit. He heard a bell jangling, and up over the ridge in front of him came Sergeant Garrow, riding a saddle mule and leading a white bell mare. Lined out behind was a string of Army mules, and bringing up the rear were two private soldiers mounted bareback on mules. Garrow raised his arm in passing. The mules trotted past briskly, each with the brand "US" on its left flank.

A little later as he topped a knoll Stroud could see the Army camp ahead. Wagons straggled down from the direction of the ridge between the rivers. The absence of tents was explained by the fact that the supply wagons had failed to reach camp the night before—or at least not many of them. From the campsite came a strange, confused murmur, and as Stroud entered upon it he saw men and wagons all jammed together on a gentle rise from the river. They looked as though they had made the fastest trip on record to the center of mud, chaos and discomfort, and right now the whole outfit wasn't worth the sorting. The ground was worked up into deep mud and the men were covered with it; the horses and wagons were bedaubed and spattered. Directly in front of Stroud were the carbines, pistols, swords, saddles and bridles of perhaps twenty men stomped into the mud. Everywhere was mud. Just beyond Stroud about thirty men were crowded around a fire, trying to cook. Those doing the cooking were hampered by others who were trying to dry themselves. Some were still quite drunk and all were miserable-looking from being periodically wetted by the morning drizzles.

Stroud paused behind the ragged circle of men and through a break in the lines saw that one dragoon was roasting coffee; his iron frying pan was full, and while he stirred, the beans smoked, sweating with the heat. Stroud discovered that it was the effort of the coffee roaster that was causing much of the noisy talk.

"You're going to burn it again," one of the men complained.

"Ain't done yet."

"Done or not, get it off," ordered an angular man, holding a coffee grinder in the crook of one arm. When it was clear that his order was being ignored, others in the circle took up the cry, but the coffee roaster continued stirring.

Also on the fire tended by other men were several large skillets containing sizzling beefsteaks. One of the men cooking steaks looked helplessly around the circle. "Why don't some of you go and find your own messes?" His request was greeted by hoots and jeers.

Stroud looked up the slope and saw other fires surrounded by similar groups of quarreling men, while many strayed about between the groups. Then his glance moved down to the stream again and he lost interest in the Army. On the bank of the stream, between it and the one wall tent and nearly concealed in a willow thicket, was the single tipi. Stroud started on, but before he had made much progress, his way was partially blocked by a mounted officer—a young second lieutenant—who was surveying the chaos in a listless manner. He was carrying a fawn cradled in his right arm. On impulse Stroud remarked, "This ought to impress the Indians."

The lieutenant, a young man barely out of his teens, had straight dun-colored hair and an incongruous black mustache that looked as if it were painted on. It seemed to take him a while to grasp Stroud's remark. Then he said, "Thank God the weather has kept those beggars away." The fawn struggled feebly and whimpered. The lieutenant glanced down at it. "Poor little thing. It's badly bruised. It was in one of the wagons coming over the ridge." He looked Stroud over carefully. "If you're hunting for Mr. Fitzpatrick, he's down at Fort Platte."

It was the first Stroud had heard that Old Fitz was scouting for Kearny. Tom Fitzpatrick was one of the first of the mountain men. He'd been in the fur trade for more than twenty years, mostly with the Company, though for the last three or four years he had turned to piloting—some Catholic missionaries and the first emigrant party in '41, then the government map maker Frémont, and now this. It surprised Stroud that an old grizzly bear like Fitzpatrick would take orders from the Army.

"No," said Stroud. "I came to get the girl." He gestured toward the tipi. He noticed that the lieutenant's eyes were bloodshot, and his brow was creased in a frown as if he had a headache.

The lieutenant looked Stroud over again. "Through our interpreter we have offered to move her anywhere, but she refuses. Just keeps saying that her husband will come."

"Obliged. I'll get her moved," said Stroud. There wasn't any use trying to make it clear he wasn't her husband.

"If there's anything we can do . . ." the lieutenant offered politely.

"No," Stroud said, feeling angry at Belle. Then he changed his mind. "Maybe your surgeon would have a look at her ankle."

The lieutenant glanced about him and called to a private who was headed toward the stream with a kettle and two dirty frying pans. "Here, you!" The private stopped where he was and made a half-hearted effort to juggle the cooking equipment so that he could salute. The lieutenant ignored his difficulties. "Find Dr. Whetsell on the double and send him to the tipi."

"Yes, sir." The private dropped the pans with a clatter

that made the lieutenant wince. "Just saw him." The private started off at a slow jog in the direction from which Stroud had come. The lieutenant looked at the pans thrown into the mud and then looked away again. A teamster, driving his wagon and team through the confusion mainly by the strength of his curses, caught sight of the lieutenant.

"Where do you want this?" the teamster bawled.

"What is it?"

"Tents for Company B!"

"Upstream about a quarter of a mile," the lieutenant called back with an effort. "We're moving camp." The teamster got his animals under way, and the lieutenant looked distastefully at the mud churned up by the wheels.

A chesty captain came riding through the chaos of men and horses and wagons, intent upon some duty. His appearance was surprisingly tidy. He glanced at the lieutenant as he passed. "Haven't you anything to do, Mr. Love, except nurse that fawn?" He directed an appraising glance at Stroud and rode on.

Stroud watched him as he made his way through the mud. The captain was a tight-knit man of medium height and middle age. In Tennessee he'd be judged a fellow with damned little weevil in his wheat and mighty small chance of water in his whiskey.

Stroud took his gaze from the captain and said to the lieutenant, "He appears to be the only man around here, besides the colonel, who didn't build up a head of steam last night."

Lieutenant Love slanted a hangdog glance at Stroud. "That's my company commander—Eustis. Sometimes I think he and the colonel have no comfortable human failings."

"I heard the colonel say he was declaring the forts out of bounds," Stroud said.

"He'd have done that anyway. It's about all he can do. He can't fire the teamsters or court-martial the whole outfit. We were all in it. It was quite dark when the men got over the ridge, soaked to the skin, half frozen and no food since morning. They tried to make the best of it until the wagons came in. Two or three came in a bunch and the colonel's tent had just been put up when that cloudburst hit. The men just sat in the mud and water with tarpaulins over their heads—to keep from drowning, I guess. God knows they couldn't have got wetter. One of those first wagons must have had whiskey aboard. Some of the men probably bribed the driver to pick it up as he came past the forts." The lieutenant started walking his horse toward the tipi, and after a moment he continued. "I expect it worked the same way on everybody. The first few drinks didn't do a thing—didn't even warm us up—and we thought the stuff was diluted, so we kept drinking more. That was a mistake." He laughed suddenly.

"The colonel was snug in his tent and didn't stick his head out until this morning. You should have seen him. Shocked speechless—for a while anyway—for the first time in his life, I'll wager. If I get drummed out tomorrow it'll have been worth it." The lieutenant laughed again. They were nearing the wall tent, and as Stroud looked toward the river he noticed that a sentry was posted outside the tipi. It was a relief. Lieutenant Love stopped his horse and looked around.

"Here comes the doctor," he said. As Stroud turned, the lieutenant indicated a muddy, rumpled man sloshing and sliding through the mud on foot some distance behind them. He carried a small black satchel. "Whetsell's his name," said the lieutenant. He rode off upstream in the direction of the new campsite, holding himself and the fawn carefully.

When the doctor came up to him, Stroud dismounted and introduced himself. "My first patient was an Indian," the doctor said genially. "Glad you sent for me." He stood very straight—too straight, Stroud decided. He was neither as drunk as he had been nor as sober as he thought he was.

Stroud led the way inside the tipi. There was a fire going. Belle was sitting near it on a buffalo robe. Beside her was the crutch Wyatt had made. At the sight of Stroud, she said irritably, "*Nakos!* At last!" She began to complain about being neglected.

Stroud cut her short. "*He wastéko lo sni.* It is not good. Why are you camped here?"

Belle went into a detailed though rapid explanation. Stroud gathered that it was Hobart's Emma who chose the camping place. Hobart had told her that he did not want to camp with the Indian villages near the forts. The camp had not long been set up, according to Belle, when she was left with Emma and young Hobart. Mozay's Madame Jack had gone to the Indian villages to find cousins. Then Hobart had come, bloody and drunk and angry, and struck his lodge. He had taken his wife and the boy to Cedar Point and asked that Stroud let him know when they were to return for the furs.

"And Madame Jack did not come back?" Stroud asked.

"It rains very much," Belle replied.

"You shouldn't have been left alone," said Stroud. It was the custom that no young Indian girl was ever left alone. But the part of Belle's account that interested him most was Hobart's request that his lodge should not be set up near the forts. Stroud asked when it was that Hobart told his wife where to camp.

"Yesterday, while we still traveled," said Belle.

Stroud was silent. That would be before he had the fight with Hobart. Stroud wondered what Hobart had in mind, putting himself so far from the whiskey supply. It didn't seem sensible.

He'd better go down to Cedar Point and see Hobart as soon as he got Belle into the fort. It was a new irritation. Cedar Point was about ten miles down the Platte, where the broad bottomlands made good camping. He had planned to spend the afternoon in the Indian camps trying to buy horses and at the same time starting inquiries about a white man and a Crow woman who might have lived with some Sioux band the winter of '37. But he couldn't feel easy in his mind until he found out why Hobart was acting so unsociable. Why the devil couldn't anybody be where he was supposed to? Stroud explained then to Belle about the presence of the doctor. Belle looked at the untidy big man and didn't seem favorably disposed. "He will make sure you will not be lame when your ankle is well," urged Stroud.

"*Ha,*" Belle finally agreed. "I understand. Five Scalps does not want a wife who is lame." She fell silent, watching the doctor suspiciously.

Dr. Whetsell kneeled with difficulty beside Belle and examined the splint, running his fingers over it. "Broken?"

"Don't know," said Stroud. "I splinted it just to be safe." He watched as the doctor began unwinding the strips of cloth that held the splints in place. "She's got a bullet wound in her thigh, too," said Stroud.

"That first Indian patient of mine," said the doctor as he continued to unwind the bandages, "was a big old Yazoo called Tubba. Not as pretty as this one. Didn't get very professional treatment, old Tubba." He finished removing the bandages and held up one of the splints quizzically.

"Parflêche," said Stroud. "Buffalo hide."

The doctor tossed it aside and began examining Belle's ankle. "Tubba hung around the back door of old Doc Hill's office in Tupelo. Showed up one day, sicker than a dog, when the old doc was out. I'd been a student about three weeks. Only read as far as castor oil, cathartics and cupping. Didn't know whether to purge, bleed, stimulate, or open his windpipe. Took me so long to diagnose he recovered on his own." Whetsell moved Belle's foot back and forth and watched to see if she showed pain. "The stoics of the wilderness," he said, "the race without a tear."

An exchange with the sentry outside caught Stroud's attention and he looked up to see Captain Eustis enter. Eustis introduced himself and then said, "I'm glad you've come for her. She's quite a responsibility."

"I didn't know she was camped up here till a while ago," Stroud explained. He watched the doctor manipulate Belle's foot some more.

"Was her ankle swollen?" asked Dr. Whetsell.

"Some."

The doctor grunted and started to push up Belle's deerskin dress. His attention fastened on the fringed edge of her skirt. After a moment he looked up at Stroud. "Do they wear anything under these?"

"Young ones like this generally wear chastity belts," said Stroud. He wished the doctor would quit wasting time.

"Shades of my grandmother!" muttered Dr. Whetsell. He pushed the dress up with elaborate care, showing the bandage on Belle's thigh.

"She isn't your wife?" asked Captain Eustis. His voice

had a cautious sound as if he weren't sure that he had interpreted Stroud's remark accurately.

"No," said Stroud.

"Then why isn't she camped with her people?"

"Her band hasn't come in yet." Stroud was aware that this left the question open as to why she was here ahead of her band, but he didn't say anything.

After a moment Eustis remarked, "At least there are enough Indians here for a conference."

"Maybe," agreed Stroud. "Trouble is they aren't the right ones." There were four bands of Sioux camped between the forts, some two hundred and fifty to three hundred lodges in all, totaling perhaps a thousand or twelve hundred people, with each band forming a separate camp. They were Oglalas, and in addition were all Smoke People—Oyukhpes, Bad Faces, Hunkpatilas, True Oglalas. None of the Bear People division of the Oglalas, to which Shonka's band belonged, was camped at the forts now, nor the Brûlés, the Hunkpapas, the Miniconjous, the Sans Arcs, the Blackfeet Sioux, the Two-Kettles. "The ones camped here are likely about a twentieth of the Teton Sioux—the most friendly twentieth."

"It's too bad even a twentieth of them are friendly," said Eustis. "It'd be better for them in the long run if they had nothing to do with the whites."

Stroud was mildly surprised. "You talk like some Indians I know." He was thinking of Indians like Shonka and Big Road, who never liked their people to be around the whites.

"I know what's going to happen to pretty beggars like her"—he nodded toward Belle—"and to her brothers, if she's unlucky enough to have any."

Dr. Whetsell glanced up. "The wound's healing fine," he commented. "Whoever took the bullet out did a good job." He leaned over again to put the new dressing on.

"Where did you come by this forewarning of doom?" Stroud asked Eustis.

"From the Indians along the frontier. All you have to do is look at them. They're a poor, drunken, dishonest, miserable race. The farther you get from the influence of the whites, the more respectable the Indians are. Education hasn't done anything but make the few educated ones worse scoundrels than those who stayed at home. It's next to impossible to win an Indian from his natural filth and idleness. All he learns from the white man is the white man's vices. And it's the educated Indians, and the half-breeds, who are the most rascally part of the population. Agents and missionaries can devote their whole lives to the welfare of the Indians, but if white men are continually waking their worst attributes, and ruining all their energies by keeping them filled with liquor, what good does it do?"

Stroud was forced to admit to himself that the captain had a point, and that he was included in it. "What would you do about it?"

"I'd keep white men from living among Indians. And I'd enforce the law against selling liquor to the Indians. Any man caught doing either would be sent to the penitentiary."

If Eustis were running the show, Stroud figured, he'd be eligible to spend just about the rest of his days behind bars. "You're right about the liquor," he said. "But as for living among the Indians, we trappers don't try to influence them. We do things their way. It's the movers coming through that'll cause trouble here. They don't even know what the Indian way is and wouldn't care if they did."

Stroud turned his attention to Dr. Whetsell. What had started as an idle exchange with Eustis was turning out to be unsettling, and Stroud didn't much like it. It was easy enough to sit back in the States and solve all the problems west of the Missouri. Stroud noticed that the doctor must have finished with the dressing on Belle's thigh, because he had pulled her dress down again and was running his hand the length of her bare leg. Belle was looking resentful and Stroud wondered himself if the doctor couldn't locate her ankle in a more professional manner.

"Can she ride yet?" Stroud asked.

"She hasn't since the injury?"

"No. We carried her in on a litter."

But the doctor's mind wasn't on the question. "How do they get their legs so shiny?"

"Bear grease," said Stroud shortly.

Dr. Whetsell leaned over and sniffed. "Perfumed?"

"Herbs of some kind," verified Stroud. The doctor gave a noncommittal grunt and fastened his attention finally on Belle's ankle.

Eustis began speaking, continuing the conversation as if there had been no interruption. Stroud looked around at him. Ey God, he was tenacious. "We have to see that the movers get through without trouble," Eustis was saying. "You must know it's vitally important that we claim Oregon and freeze the British out."

"And the Indians along with them," said Stroud.

"It's inevitable," replied Eustis. "A time will come when the Indians'll all have to be limited to certain areas."

"Do you really think the government would try it?" asked Stroud. "You couldn't keep a Sioux confined anywhere. Besides, there are a hell of a lot of Indians scattered around west of the Mississippi."

Eustis shrugged. "Anything can happen. Five years ago all the experts—including the government engineers—said it was impossible to get wagons to Oregon. Settlers couldn't be got there overland. And the very next year Mr. Fitzpatrick took a wagon train through with sixty-nine emigrants and some missionaries. Now they're going through every year by the hundreds—four-fifths of them women and children. Oregon being claimed for us by women and children! Nobody can estimate how many'll go before it's over. But you can be sure that laying a claim to Oregon will affect all the territory between it and the States."

"Ey God!" said Stroud. "I'm no Indian, but if I was told to stay put, I'd start thinking of some stream I hadn't trapped for a while or some mountain park I hadn't hunted. There'd be so many places I had to go I wouldn't know which to pick first. Places I hadn't seen for years, or I hadn't thought of one way or another when I did see them, would come up so clear in my mind I'd have to pack up and go and nobody could stop me."

Just to mention it brought to mind that lake in the Wind River Mountains he'd always intended to look for again. He could see its rocky cliffs with growths of fir and pine jutting sharply into the water, and above the lake the mountains looking wind-driven and changing color through the day—frosted silver in early morning, blue at noon, and shades of madder at sunset, and the lake repeating it all upside down. "If the Indians ever got together," Stroud added, "you nor the emigrants nor anybody else'd ever get a foot on this side of the Missouri."

"But they won't," said Eustis.

"No. They fight amongst themselves all the time."

"Exactly," said Eustis. "And when the time comes, they will defeat themselves. They won't be able to discipline themselves to form a sufficiently large force to be invincible."

"Not invincible maybe," said Stroud. "But enough of them can agree to cause a lot of trouble."

Eustis shrugged. "Without discipline any group is helpless. That's the trouble with the emigrants—they're nothing but mobs. They elect captains and make rules and then ignore them. Every wagon train we passed was ready to split apart. If they can't discipline themselves they ought to stay home."

"How far along are they?"

"We passed the lead train four days ago at Chimney Rock. Though I'll never understand how they've gotten this far. They hardly know where they're going or why."

"They should be in soon then," said Stroud.

"We'll have to have the conference tomorrow to keep ahead of them."

The doctor had snapped his bag shut and was struggling to his feet. "Far as I'm concerned she can do anything. Nothing wrong with that ankle."

"Sometimes even Army discipline isn't enough," Eustis remarked as he observed the doctor. "Last night was a sad example of that. Those teamsters deserve to be set loose on foot."

Stroud noticed that Belle was looking at him. "*Ya nipi k'ta*. You will live," he said dryly. "You will live to make pemmican."

Stroud wondered if she had been scared into thinking her ankle was really hurt, or if the mistake had been his. The way things were going in Shonka's camp at the time was enough to confuse anybody. "Yes. Now you can go back to your own people."

Belle shook her head. "You have made a bargain."

"We will speak of that later." Stroud's jaw was set and it stayed pretty much that way while he expressed his thanks to Dr. Whetsell.

As the officers left, Eustis smiled at Stroud. "Have a look at the conference tomorrow. We have quite a program planned."

Stroud returned the smile. "Fine," he said, "but I'll be surprised if the Indians follow it."

When he and Belle were alone, Stroud looked around the tipi, wondering if he should take it down or just leave it for Mozay's Madame Jack to get. It was her tipi and taking it down was squaws' work, but it might be ransacked or she might be timid about coming to the Army camp to get it. Maybe Belle was well enough to help, and he'd seen them taken down often enough so that he guessed he could do it. At least Madame Jack hadn't unpacked everything. The backrests weren't up nor the mattresses unrolled. Most of the utensils were still packed away in parflêches, and the extra robes rolled up. Obviously Madame Jack had been in a hurry to get to the Indian camps between the forts. "Come on," Stroud said to Belle. He held out his hand to help her up. "You'll have to take out the lodge pins." She reached for his hand rather reluctantly and let him pull her to her feet. The lodge pins were wooden skewers which held the edges of the lodge skins together, like the seam of a skirt, and were usually fastened on by a child—young Hobart in their case—who used each pin he inserted as a rung on a ladder to step up on and insert the next one clear on to the top. Sore leg or not, Belle had to help, and Stroud boosted her up above the unpinned part which served as a door. She protested, but she climbed to the top easily enough and removed the pins from the top down. Soon Stroud had the semicircular lodge covering off its frame of poles. Stroud had the poles down before he remembered to explain to Belle that she was to stay at the fort until he could get her to her people. All in all, it was a good half-hour before the lodge skins, cooking equipment and other sundries were loaded onto the pole drag and they started for the fort.

Stroud resumed the earlier conversation as though there had been no interval. He had scarcely talked to the girl since leaving Shonka's village, making only those exchanges which concerned her welfare, and telling her as much as he knew and had deduced about her father, Shonka. It hadn't seemed kind then to make her position clear, but it was certainly high time now to set things straight. "You are mistaken if you think I made a bargain," he said sternly.

"*Han!* You have forgotten the firewater you gave to Eahsapa."

Stroud glanced at Belle, wondering what the devil she was thinking. Did she really believe she was traded for? They were often terrible teases, these Indian girls. Batchika had been. That had been part of the fun at first. "It was a gift," Stroud said.

"You gave it for me in trade. Even my father the chief would have said it was done."

If Belle were teasing, Stroud decided, she was carrying it too far. Somewhat warily he studied her, a shapeless, blanketed figure hunched on the horse. His scrutiny netted him nothing except that she had her crutch across the saddle the way a mountain man carried his rifle. He reached over and took it, removed the beaver-plew padding, and threw the forked stick to the ground. It made him feel better, but not much. Whatever she had in mind, he wouldn't tolerate much teasing—it had a way of getting out of hand. He had learned that from Batchika.

Batchika's teasing had caught up with her once. They had left the rendezvous there on the Green River—Stroud and Reeshar and Batchika and Wicarpi—and had moved leisurely up Green River, through Jackson's Hole, then along the eastern shore of Yellowstone Lake and on to the headwaters of Clark's Fork where it turkey-tailed out into numerous little creeks. It would have been a pleasant and happy time anyway, but Batchika kept things lively with her teasing—sometimes mimicking one of them, sometimes planning funny little surprises, always managing to make the rest of them laugh when they showed signs of being out of sorts. They had stayed several days in a bowl-like valley almost encircled by snow-capped mountains where bighorn sheep grazed along the slopes and from which rivulets flowed clear and cold, Stroud remembered. They had pitched their lodge and stayed over, partly because there had been no mosquitoes or flies. There had been no trouble up to this point and even for some time afterward as they trapped the Big Horn and the Rosebud. They had intended to stop at Fort Van Buren at the mouth of the Tongue for supplies before proceeding to the trapper's winter rendez-vous on the Powder River. But news of the smallpox had turned them back. Tribes as far south as the Yellowstone had fled that summer before the epidemic.

Instead they had gone east to the Belle Fourche and it was here that Batchika's teasing finally caused trouble, though it shouldn't have, now he thought of it. It was Reeshar's lack of humor that had caused the trouble and spoiled Batchika's joke. He had laughter and a way with words, but not much humor, really, though it took a while to understand this. The trouble developed the night Batchika and Wicarpi changed beds. Batchika admitted later it was her idea and it was innocent enough fun—or should have been.

Stroud and Reeshar had left the lodge to see what was exciting the dogs. When they came back Stroud knew im-mediately that it was Wicarpi in his bed, even though the robes were drawn up until only the top of her head showed, for she was lying with her back toward the fire, facing the lodge skin, and she didn't turn to look at him. Batchika al-ways did. Even if she were asleep she seemed to know when he entered the lodge and she would open her eyes to watch him with that shiny soft look until he slid in beside her. But he hadn't said anything when he saw Wicarpi in Batchika's place. He had crawled in between the buffalo robes beside Wicarpi, talking nonsense about how cold his hands were, and had waited for Reeshar to discover the joke so they could all laugh together. But Reeshar had pretended he didn't know that it was Batchika in his bed and before long she had hit him and clambered out to stand angrily by the lodge fire until everything was smoothed over.

Batchika was more careful about her fun after that, but it was clear that Reeshar missed the innocent humor of the joke and thought—or pretended to think—that Batchika was putting at him. Not long after that Reeshar suggested that they swap women. At the time Stroud had thought it a coarse jest and not a particularly funny one. Now he realized that his refusal to consider it seriously was probably one of his "sturdy virtues" that had annoyed Reeshar. Stroud wondered how many other incidents he had misunderstood at the time. His thoughts were interrupted by Belle.

"My father the chief would also have said that you bought me cheaply."

"There was no intention of a trade," Stroud said. "I plan to take a wife soon. . . ." He gestured toward the fort. "You know that."

Belle dropped her eyes. "It is not yet done," she said. After a moment she added, "But a brave warrior needs many wives. This one will be the second."

"There is more to being a wife than traveling together," Stroud pointed out.

Belle ran a finger delicately over her bandaged leg. "That will come. Occasionally even the marriage bed is shared for many days before."

Stroud had the fleeting notion that some of these barbaric customs were mighty strange. He studied Belle again and admitted for the first time that she reminded him a great deal of Batchika. Belle had the same quick ways, the same knowing innocence. Having once admitted a likeness, Stroud had a feeling of resentment, as if the resemblance somehow made him responsible for Belle. But that was ridiculous. Teasing or not, she'd have to find herself some other man to cope with her tricks. The only thing regarding Belle that seemed entirely clear to Stroud was his conscience.

"You shall live with your people," Stroud repeated doggedly. "And if you say at the fort that I am your husband, I will lodgepole you good." This mess was something else to thank Reeshar for. If Reeshar hadn't horned in on the "hands" game, it was unlikely that all the trouble with the hawk's bells would have got started. Stroud glanced toward the fort, pulling ahead of Belle. Wyatt was just riding in through the gate.

When Stroud and Belle entered the courtyard, Wyatt was still mounted and talking with Billy Pitcher in front of the office. Stroud rode up to the two men. Billy watched Belle with frank admiration. "I never seem to come back with anything but furs," he complained.

"Or the beads you went out with," said Stroud. He was watching Wyatt.

At the sight of Stroud, Wyatt had turned and begun to untie a small roll of antelope skins he had secured back of his saddle. Now he straightened around and allowed the skins to unroll, hide side out. "I'll have that buckskin suit yet."

Stroud noticed immediately the mark burned on each— a mark resembling a three-tined pitchfork. "When did Merk get in?" he asked.

"Why, I haven't seen him," said Wyatt. "I took these from the men at the baling press over at Platte."

Stroud looked at the skins again and then turned to Billy. "Has anybody around here seen Merk?"

"No," said the half-breed. "He hasn't come in. I'd have heard. Old Merk is always news."

Stroud recalled coming upon old Merk sitting by the boiling springs and his talk of devils and his insistence that he was coming into the forts to trade. And Reeshar had been following close behind them. He was bound to have come across Merk, too. "Did Reeshar know you took these?" Stroud asked.

"I don't suppose so," said Wyatt with a puzzled expression. "Though I'm sure he wouldn't care."

"Probably not," said Stroud slowly. "Reeshar'd claim he bought them." And there wouldn't be any way to prove he didn't, Stroud was certain.

"You think he didn't?"

"You heard Merk. He was set on coming in to trade."

As Wyatt began to follow Stroud's line of thought, he asked, "Would anybody else use the same mark?"

"No," said Stroud.

Bostwick's voice came from the office door. "Nobody would steal from Merk—or kill the old man for a few hides."

Stroud looked around. Bostwick stood in the doorway as if he had been there some little time.

"You don't know what Reeshar'd do. And neither do I. But so far as I know he was the last one to see Merk alive. And now Merk's hides show up at Fort Platte. It doesn't shine."

Stroud turned his back on the chief clerk and looked again at Wyatt. "The hides'll make a fine suit." Wyatt hesitated and then glanced at Belle, who was sitting patiently on the borrowed horse. "Do you suppose she'd make it?"

"Belle's going back with her people when they show up,"

Stroud said. This was the fourth set of hides Wyatt had bought with the idea of having a suit made. The third set—the ones he had traded for with Merk—had been a total loss, soaked with Mozay's blood, when they'd used the packs as barricades in the fight with Eahsapa. Wyatt himself had thrown them into the fire Stroud had built over the cache.

Wyatt was using sign language to make his request of Belle. The girl seemed pleased at the prospect of a familiar occupation. She measured Wyatt expertly with her eyes. "*Econpíca*. It can be done. He is tall and straight like the young pine on a hilltop. Like Five Scalps," she added, looking at Stroud.

"What did she say?" Wyatt asked.

"That your suit'll fit Stroud," said Billy Pitcher.

"She can't see anybody else," Wyatt admitted.

Stroud leaned over toward Belle and helped her down from the horse. Wyatt smiled at her and handed her the buckskins, and again in sign language started negotiating as to what the charge would be. Behind him Stroud heard the office door shut.

Stroud wondered if he had convinced Bostwick that Reeshar had killed old Merk. Not that Bostwick's opinion mattered. Thinking of Merk, Stroud had a feeling of urgency, of the need to act without having anything exactly to act upon, a vague feeling of impending disaster, as if this was not yet the worst of Reeshar's crimes. Stroud felt again that he hadn't really known Reeshar. Certainly he wouldn't have thought the man capable of murder. Finding out what happened to Batchika was no longer a matter of satisfying his curiosity—of putting his house in order. It was something that had to be done.

Stroud waited, and when Wyatt was finished with Belle, Stroud asked him if he would take the tipi and the other belongings to Mozay's Madame Jack. "I have to go down to see Hobart," Stroud explained. "He's down at Cedar Point."

Wyatt reached for the lead rope which Stroud handed him. "What about the horse?"

"It's Pryce's," said Stroud. "Bring it back here and put it in the corral."

Stroud turned his horse and was headed toward the gate when Wyatt asked, "What about Belle?"

Stroud half turned in his saddle to address Billy Pitcher. "Tell Evie she's here." He rode on out.

Nine

Once through the gate Stroud turned to the right. Before long Wyatt caught up with him. "That was a rough way to treat Belle," he said, pulling his horse down to a walk.

"She can look out for herself," Stroud said shortly. "Can you?"

"I'm going out with the fort hunters in a day or two," said Wyatt. He looked over at Stroud. "Fence sitting makes for a sore crotch."

Stroud thought the boy showed good sense; the farther he got away from Reeshar the better. "Reeshar's been after you?"

"Lord, yes! That cache is bothering him. He's waved everything in front of me but the flag. Money, my uncle . . ." Wyatt laughed. After a moment he added, "You know, Reeshar's not at all like my first impression. Quite personable once you get to know him."

"He wants something from you," Stroud said. Reeshar hadn't changed; he always did believe in being agreeable to someone who could do him a favor and not to the damn fool who had already done one.

"Well, he won't get it," said Wyatt. He veered off to the left and headed for the Indian camps, trailing the led horse carrying Madame Jack's possessions. Stroud went on to the Oregon Road and down to the Laramie ford. The current was strong, forcing mount and rider downstream as the icy water foamed around his legs. He emerged about forty yards downstream, the raw northeast wind cutting through his wet clothing.

He had ridden the crests of only a half-dozen of the grassy ridges rolling away to the south when at the top of the one just ahead appeared two or three Indian horsemen, then several more, followed by people on foot, and suddenly there was a swarm of people and animals spilling over the crest and down the slope in a surging, disorganized mass. Horses were burdened with pole drags, bundled lodge skins, painted parflêche cases and children perched three in a row. Dogs scampered between the legs of the horses or darted away yelping in pursuit of jackrabbits. Paint-streaked warriors with lance and shield rode on their shaggy ponies. Women trudged along singly, leading a pack horse, or carrying an infant on a cradle board, or worrying with the dog travois, or doing all three at once. Old men wrapped in buffalo robes walked ahead in solemn dignity.

It was a whole village on the move, and Stroud didn't make any effort to get out of its way, but just pulled up and let it flow around him. He recognized them as Bull Tail's Brûlés, the band Kearny had personally asked to the conference. Stroud estimated the camp to be one of about thirty lodges, comparatively small. Bull Tail was full of talk about tomorrow's conference. He was going to tell the soldier-chief that he, Bull Tail, was angry with the whites who had driven the buffalo away from the Shell, forcing the Indians to go west of the Laramie Mountains to hunt. The old man strode on, very dignified in his resentment.

Stroud kicked his horse into motion and began to move against the current of the camp until soon the nomads had passed, and there was only the wide, fresh trail, plowed up like a scar on the sodden earth.

Stroud went on to Cedar Point, where the driftwood always caught and piled up on a finger of land jutting out into the river. Here was one of the best camping spots on the North Platte. A dozen tipis, remnants of earlier camps, were scattered back from the river. Identifying Hobart's lodge by its familiar markings, Stroud headed toward it.

Young Hobart saw him approaching and with a gap-toothed smile of recognition ran to meet him. Stroud kicked his horse into a lope and leaned out from the saddle. Sensing his intent, the boy stopped and reversed his direction, looking back eagerly and holding up his arm. Stroud reached down as he passed and swung young Hobart up behind him onto the horse's back.

Hobart's Emma stood before the lodge, smiling at this playfulness. "*Ya!*" she called out in pretended alarm. "You will make the boy too soon a man with such tricks." Stroud reined in, and young Hobart slid to the ground laughing.

Stroud glanced around. "Where is Hobart?" His question was answered by the appearance of Hobart in the lodge door. His eyes were red-rimmed, his face still bruised. For a moment it appeared to Stroud as if Hobart was going to start their fight all over again. "What are you doing camped way down here? And why did you leave Belle alone up on the Laramie?"

Hobart ignored both questions. "What about the cache?"

"We may have to wait for Pryce's mules." Stroud started to dismount.

"I'll take my share now," Hobart said abruptly.

Stroud sat back in the saddle and stared at the shaggy, red-bearded man. "How in hell can you till we dig the cache up?"

"You got money."

"Our agreement is to get the furs to a buyer. Any buyer I choose."

"And I choose to go down to Bent's Fort," Hobart countered.

A feeling of bewilderment replaced Stroud's mounting anger. "What ails you? A fight's a fight. Nothing to hold a grudge about. Besides, you were planning to camp up the Laramie before we ever had a fight."

Hobart refused to comment. "Pay me now," he insisted.

"I'll pay when you help bring in the furs," Stroud said shortly. "And if I didn't know you better, I'd think you were down here to make it easy to sell information to Reeshar about my cache."

Hobart glared at Stroud as if he wanted to hit him, and Stroud was pretty sure that if he hadn't been mounted Hobart would have. "I'm damned if I care what you think." Hobart said, then retreated from the lodge door and disappeared inside.

Stroud looked at Emma, who shrugged. "*Itancanyankel.* Like a chief," she said dryly. She smiled at Stroud. "I make coffee." She turned to young Hobart. "Bring wood for the fire." The boy picked up several sticks of wood from the pile near the lodge while Stroud tied his horse. Then both followed Emma inside.

Hobart was drinking from a bottle, but he didn't offer to share it. Young Hobart inspected his father critically. "Ain't you drunk enough to ride on your head yet, Pa?" Hobart made no reply and after a moment, with a disappointed sigh, the boy turned away. Hobart continued his solitary drinking while the others ate. Nearly everybody was having to eat dried buffalo meat. Even the hunters at the forts were having to go fifty miles or more for fresh meat.

Stroud stayed for nearly an hour, finding the fire comfortable and hoping to learn why Hobart hadn't camped near the forts in the first place. But Hobart said nothing. Stroud took his leave then, telling Hobart that he would let him know when he was ready to dig up the cache.

Stroud started back up the trail, realizing he knew no more about Hobart's activities than he did when he had ridden down, yet feeling somehow that the trip was worth the time because for some reason he was convinced that

Hobart's choosing to isolate himself had nothing to do with the cache.

Stroud glanced around. Ahead, the trail followed the unending undulations of the barren prairie. Now that he was to leave soon, Stroud perversely found the gloomy expanse of prairie beautiful. It looked as though the Creator, having taxed himself making thousands of square miles of rugged mountains, grassy valleys, rocky cliffs, timbered slopes and jeweled lakes, had finally run out of ideas and flung down what was left into a vast, unadorned sea of sandy soil and buffalo grass, made impressive by the enormous waste of it all. Stroud looked up at the gray sky, trying to decide what time it was. He guessed it was about mid-afternoon. He should be back at the fort in time for supper.

He was anxious to get back and straighten things out with Evie. It was no wonder talk of St. Louis upset her when she had just spent two years there and had made a long and tiresome journey to get back home. Besides, after two years apart, it was a ticklish affair to pick up without mishap the invisible threads which bound one person to another. He was a clumsy fool.

Upon reaching the Laramie, Stroud found it was already less deep and swift than it had been earlier in the day. He forded it and went on up the Oregon Road a short distance. He was just about to angle off to the left in the direction of Fort Laramie when ahead of him he saw the Fort Platte herd of mules and horses being driven up from the bottomlands in a tangle of manes and tails by two Mexican herders whose long hair flowed in the wind.

Stroud stopped and watched as the herders brought the animals in to corral them for the night. There were more than a hundred animals, Stroud estimated bitterly. There was certainly no shortage of pack animals at Platte. As he sat watching he heard the clanging of the bell at Fort Platte announcing supper, and then faintly, as if it were an echo, the supper bell at Fort Laramie. With a last look at the Platte herd, Stroud kicked his horse and started off again, angling left. He looked ahead to see Reeshar riding toward him. A little distance to Reeshar's left, but heading directly toward Fort Platte from the Indian camps, were Cebull and Old Man Rem. Reeshar had cut off from the other two, Stroud decided, just in order to intercept him. He reined in and waited. "I'd be glad to sell you some horses," said Reeshar as he stopped a few feet away.

"You came out of your way just to say that?" Stroud asked. Reeshar's jaw was noticeably swollen from Stroud's blow of the day before, and Reeshar raised a hand to it as if by way of comment. "If you want to try to finish what I started, this child's free right now," said Stroud.

"I don't fight with my fists and you know it," Reeshar said. "I wanted to point out you have no reason to feel abused."

"You don't think I should feel abused when you try to get me and my men killed?" asked Stroud.

"You were too greedy in Shonka's camp," Reeshar said.

"Maybe," Stroud admitted. "But you didn't find Shonka by yourself. By all rights you shouldn't even have been in his village."

Reeshar ignored this. "He would have come into the forts to trade—and I would have gotten his furs—if you hadn't gone off acting the hero, chasing those Snake horse thieves."

"What did you expect?" said Stroud. "That I'd step aside and let you have the trade?"

"Those furs should be mine," Reeshar said.

Stroud was silent a moment. There was no use reminding Reeshar that Shonka himself hadn't wanted to come to the forts to trade in the first place. Reeshar really believed what he had said—or wanted to. It was typical of his warped way of reasoning. "I suppose you'd like me to share my cache with you."

"No," said Reeshar. "I'll get it all."

"Like you got Merk's furs?" Stroud watched Reeshar for a change of expression, but there wasn't any.

"Shonka's furs are mine," Reeshar repeated. "That cache belongs to me."

"Then find it." Stroud gave Reeshar a steady look. After a moment he touched heels to his horse and headed for Fort Laramie. He wasn't interested in listening to any more of Reeshar's twisted logic. Though Reeshar had settled one thing. There was no use in trying to buy horses. Horses alone wouldn't be enough to bring in his cache; he'd need men to protect it. And most of Pryce's were downstream. He'd have to wait for both horses and men.

There was something to be said for the delay. It gave him the time he had been needing to try to find out what happened to Batchika. As Stroud neared Fort Laramie it occurred to him that he was going to have to swallow his pride and tell Evie and her father about Batchika—explain why he had to ask questions around the Indian camps. Certainly it shouldn't come as any surprise to them that a man who'd been in the mountains for nine years had had an Indian woman somewhere along the line. He should've told Evie sooner, he guessed. But it was the kind of thing that no man would choose to tell on himself.

On reaching the fort, Stroud saw that the inside gates were still open, and he remembered that the supper bell had already sounded. As he rode through the passageway he noticed through the trading window that Billy Pitcher was tending store. In the otherwise deserted courtyard several squaws and a half-dozen children idled, already waiting for the second table to be called. Because he was late, Stroud tied his horse to the stair rail instead of going to the corral.

Supper was already begun, and Stroud joined Pryce, Evie, Bostwick, Hiram—and Belle. Stroud had forgotten about Belle. At the sight of her he had an anxious moment and his eyes sought Evie's. But Evie responded with a smile as she brought the coffeepot to the table.

"It was mean of you just to leave her with Billy," she said accusingly as Stroud seated himself in the vacant place to her left. She looked at Belle in a friendly, companionable way and remarked, "She's very pretty."

Stroud smiled at Evie. "I hadn't noticed." As their eyes met, Evie gave him a look of understanding, as if she, too, contrite because the day had got off to a bad start, was determined to make amends. After a moment, Evie's glance dropped and she started pouring the coffee.

Though it was Sunday, known to the Indians as the day the white man did not work, supper was undistinguished except that Pryce, Bostwick and Hiram wore ties and coats. It also accounted for the dumplings Evie had dropped into the pot of warmed-over beans and venison. Stroud regarded her as she filled the coffee cups, her neck bare to the curve of her shoulders, the light from the lamps playing a coppery shine on her dark hair, and the steam of the coffee forming a moving veil before her face. Pretty as a hen canary, he thought, and the remarkable thing was that she didn't appear to know it.

The savory dumplings reminded him of his mother's, and her attitude toward meals in general. She was a rich believer in real circuit-rider's suppers—chickens cut up and fried in yellow butter, hot biscuits made with cream, fried ham in slices big as your hand, pickled beets and cucumbers and roasting ears and sweet potatoes, scalding coffee strong

165

enough to float an iron wedge, and milk as cold as a miser's heart, and on the sideboard a potbellied bottle of peach brandy. "There's more in the cellar," she'd say.

Stroud cleaned up the dumplings on his plate while he watched Evie. Aware of his attention, and noticing, too, that he had eaten his dumplings first, Evie said, "I'll fix you some pancakes for breakfast." She pushed a cup of coffee across the corner of the table.

Bostwick looked up. "Let him buy his flour."

"Oh, Amer!" Evie smiled at Stroud with open affection. "Pancakes as full of holes as a sifter, with strained honey to fill them."

Hiram gave a noisy sigh. "If Evie'd look at me that way I wouldn't know what I was eating."

Stroud glanced across the table at Hiram. "That's a foolish statement. My mother used to lecture us on how we should never be tempted to marry any girl unless we'd seen her cook and eaten her cooking."

"The way you told it to me once," said Evie, "was 'never be tempted by money or sweet hugging to marry any girl unless you've seen her cook and eaten her cooking.'"

Belle looked up quizzically for a moment as if she were trying to understand, and then resumed eating. Stroud, noticing this, realized that she must be eating with a fork for the first time. But she was doing such a good job of it, you certainly wouldn't know it.

"At least Evie's money'll never tempt anybody," Pryce said. He paused and looked at Stroud. "Though if it's any encouragement, things have bettered around here since morning. Kearny isn't going to recommend buying the fort. Not now at least. Had his mind made up before he came."

"I'm glad," said Stroud, "but I'm surprised."

"He's making a mistake. He can't protect the emigrants for long by having the dragoons ride out every summer

166

with gifts," said Pryce. He smiled wryly. "I feel a little of the fool myself for all my worry about the fort being taken over by the Army, but at least I'm a relieved one." Pryce took another bite of stew, and after a moment asked, "How was your day?"

"Nothing much," Stroud said. Now was the time to tell them about his run-in with Reeshar; that horses wouldn't be enough to get the cache in and that he would have to have extra men. And after dinner, as soon as Hiram and Bostwick were out of the way, he'd tell Evie and her father about Batchika and how he needed to use his time until the horses and men got back from downstream.

In the moment that he hesitated, Stroud heard one of the squaws in the courtyard scream and then cries of "Meester Pryce! Meester Pryce!" Stroud reached the door first, with Pryce and Hiram close behind him. As he threw open the door and stepped outside, Stroud almost bumped into a squaw who was running toward him, still yelling for "Meester Pryce."

Across the courtyard at the door to the trading store Stroud could see several more squaws and a knot of half-breed children. He ran toward them, aware of Pryce lumbering after him; then pushed through the group at the doorway and went inside the store.

Behind the counter Billy Pitcher was backed up against the shelves, and in front of him with his back toward the door was an Indian with a knife. "Whiskey! Whiskey!" said the Indian, making a slashing motion with the knife. Several feet to one side of Billy was another Indian who was pulling stock from the shelves and dumping it on the floor. "Whiskey!" the Indian with the knife repeated. Stroud crossed the small room in a couple of long strides, and just as the Indian brought the knife up again as if he intended to carry through his threat, Stroud put one hand on the counter and vaulted it, aiming a kick at the Indian. Stroud's kick violently propelled the Indian the length of the counter, where he crashed into the angle of shelves at the end. Billy grabbed the knife from the floor where it had been jolted from the Indian's hand. The Indian who had been slashing the sacks and dumping merchandise on the floor, seeing the door blocked by Pryce and Hiram, ran for the trading window and climbed out. Stroud pulled the other Indian to his feet just as Pryce stepped behind the counter.

"Give whiskey, him," said the Indian.

"No whiskey," said Pryce. He started pushing the Indian toward the door. For an instant it seemed as if the Indian were going to resist, but Stroud's kick had gentled him and he allowed Pryce to escort him out and through the passageway. An altercation with a troublesome Indian was always a ticklish affair. To strike one with a fist was an insult that would only lead to more serious trouble.

Pryce met Jake and Belco and another of the fort trappers coming in, and by the time he returned to the store, the three trappers were all inside, along with the squaws and children and those who had been eating supper. "Everybody who hasn't eaten, go do it," ordered Pryce irritably, "while the rest of us clean up this mess." He waited by the door until the room was cleared of everyone but Billy Pitcher and those who had been eating when the alarm was sounded. Actually the damage was not extensive. There hadn't been time enough apparently for the Indians to rip open a great many bags, though considerable merchandise had been overturned or pulled from the shelves. Awls, wire, beads, cloth, blankets, coffee, sugar, flour, tobacco and other items were strewn on the floor behind the counter for almost the whole length of the store. Pryce surveyed it with distaste.

"These weren't ordinary Indians wanting whiskey."

"No," said Hiram. "They're hired by Reeshar to keep the trading peaceful over at Fort Platte."

"You're sure of this?" asked Pryce.

Billy verified Hiram's statement. "Been working for him for about a month."

Pryce swore at length and with vigor. "I haven't paid enough attention to Reeshar. His predecessors over there have been so inept I've gotten in the habit of mostly ignoring them, I guess. But if Reeshar wants to be childish, I can play that way, too." He glanced around. "How'd they get in? Through the window?"

"Well," explained Billy, "one came to the window wanting whiskey, and while I was arguing with him the other just walked in the door. I didn't even see him at first. And when I went to put him out, the other one climbed through the window."

"In the future we'll keep at least two men in here all the time," said Pryce. "And we'll close the inside gates at sundown. They can always be opened for anyone who wants in." He paused. "You go on and eat, Billy." Billy Pitcher went out and Pryce, eyeing the empty spaces in the shelves, stepped behind the counter and into a pile of flour. He swore again.

Evie had already started to shake out the blankets and refold them. "Don't worry, Pa," she said soothingly. Then she laughed. "I'll get it up and use it for George's pancakes." Bostwick, who was standing apart looking at the floor, seemed not to hear.

His huge bulk a handicap to himself and the others in the confined space behind the counter, Pryce went around to the other side and sat in a chair. Hiram and Bostwick began replacing the undamaged merchandise on the shelves, while Stroud lined up a half-dozen empty kettles and knelt to sort out the smaller items. Belle, with the ecstatic preoccupation of a child in a sweet shop, picked her way around the others, examining everything. Having finished with the two blankets that had been thrown down, Evie picked up a bolt of calico that was partially unwound, put it on the counter and began rewinding it, the bolt making rhythmic thump thump thumps as she turned it.

"It's hard for me to understand a man who'd instigate purely malicious mischief like this mess tonight," Pryce said as he watched the others work. "What did Reeshar do before he came to the mountains?"

Stroud tossed a spool of floury copper wire into one kettle and an awl into another. "I don't know. He used to talk considerable about New Orleans." He paused and then added moodily, "Reeshar was a rare good talker. He could make you see places you'd never been and taste foods you'd never eaten. One minute he'd have you dancing on a steamboat and the next you'd be sipping whiskey on the wide veranda of a plantation house. It made a man forget Reeshar's arrogance, or the way he used people, or his mean streak that showed up every now and then. His faults went pretty much unnoticed until he wasn't around to bedazzle a man with words."

"I believe you. Yesterday he talked the colonel right up the Platte, grass or no grass," said Pryce. "I'll repay him for this. But I don't understand him. To see him, you'd not take him for a man who'd steal or kill to get furs."

Stroud, his hands wrist-deep in flour as he felt for foreign objects, looked up. "You heard about Merk?"

"Yes. From Billy Pitcher," said Pryce.

"There's no proof the furs were stolen from Merk," said Bostwick. Nobody paid him any heed.

"Old Merk taught me to set my first beaver trap," said Pryce.

"Old Merk was a Nor'wester?" asked Stroud.

"Yes and no. More than thirty years ago it was. He showed up and worked for a year or two for the North-westers a couple of times. But he had been down around here first. Living with the Sioux, I think, though nobody really knows. He was strange even then. I figured he had gone under half a dozen times, but after the merger I found him down here again. He led a charmed life—walked in and out of disaster and it never touched him. He had wintered with the band of Paints-His-Face-Half-Red before they were wiped out by the Pawnees, but he happened to wander off just before the massacre, I heard." Pryce paused for a moment. "Appears that his medicine finally wore out."

Stroud glanced down at the littered floor. Without Reeshar, old Merk's medicine would still be working. Stroud started scooping up the flour and sugar into separate kettles, being careful not to mix them and not to get any dirt. He filled several before he looked up. "Here in the middle the flour and sugar are all mixed," he said to Evie. "And something else is in with it. Looks like dried pump-kin."

"Leave it all together," said Evie. "I can sift out the pumpkin and make something out of the other—cake maybe." She put aside the bolt of cloth she had rewound and picked up another from the floor.

"I'll take this out of Reeshar's hide," Pryce remarked. "I'm not a man to dodge a fight with a competitor. But why can't we have it out without teaching the Indians any more of our meanness?" Pryce paused. "I wish Drips would get on out here and do something."

Drips, the new Indian agent for the Upper Missouri, was a former Company man, and Stroud suspected he would show far more interest in curbing the use of whiskey by the

Company's competitors than he would in stopping it altogether.

"You know Drips won't do much," said Stroud, "and he couldn't if he wanted to." He scooped up some of the flour-and-sugar mixture and put it into a clean kettle. "Give the agents time and they might control it, though I don't think the Indians would be much better off."

"How do you mean?" asked Pryce.

"I was talking to a Captain Eustis up in the Army camp today. He thinks that the Indians will all be confined to reservations."

Evie was brushing flour off the bolt of cloth. "Not the Lakota," she said.

"Eustis thinks so," said Stroud. "Already it's happening as close to home as the Pawnees."

Evie stopped brushing off the flour and turned to Stroud. "The Pawnees aren't the same," she said scornfully, "with their shaved heads and their earth lodges and their scrubby garden patches! Even so, nobody's been able to stop them from hunting."

"I doubt if anybody has tried too hard," said Pryce. "The buffalo'll settle it. They're keeping farther west all the time. They'll soon be out of reach of the Pawnees."

Although he didn't say anything, Stroud secretly had a certain sympathy for the Pawnees. Ten years earlier when Laramie was newly built and was called Fort William, the traders brought the Sioux down from beyond the Black Hills and into conflict with the Pawnees. At about the same time, the Pawnees, hoping for the protection of the government, made treaties agreeing to stay within specified limits. Every summer when the Pawnees went out from their permanent earth lodges along the Loup to hunt buffalo below the Platte and west to the forks, Sioux marauders plundered the defenseless villages, ravaging the young crops of corn and beans and pumpkins. The government had pledged to help the Pawnees but had still done nothing, and the efforts of the missionaries and the agents only confused things.

Evie began rewinding the second bolt of calico with another series of thump thump thumps. "The Pawnees are not good warriors," she said. "They can't protect themselves from anybody. The Lakotas will not give up their hunting grounds without a fight."

"Probably not," Pryce agreed. "But violence is no way to settle anything. And certainly violence directed against the United States would be futile in the long run. Though it may come to that." He glanced at Evie. "Nothing ever stays the same. If the change is gradual it's peaceable, but if it's sudden it's apt to be violent. Didn't you learn enough history in St. Louis to see that? And none of us can stop change—or run away from it, either."

Evie finished with the second bolt and stacked it on the first. She stood for a moment running one hand up and down the fold. "You're right, I suppose. It is much changed here already," she said slowly. "Mama often told me what it was like before the white man brought trade goods and whiskey and smallpox—and other things." They all knew it was syphilis she referred to.

Evie's remark about change set Stroud to searching his mind for a thread of thought he had had earlier in the day, and he found it. It was the notion about a toll bridge over the Platte. It was upward of two hundred years after Jamestown was settled that his father built the toll bridge just west of the Cumberland Gap. It had taken nearly two centuries for the frontier to move a few hundred miles west. And now less than fifty years later the frontier was the Mississippi, and a toll bridge would be useful six hundred miles out in the wilderness.

With Oregon settled, which appeared likely come hell or high water, there would soon be a nation with a frontier on both sides. And frontiers couldn't be depended upon. They had a way of moving. He guessed Eustis and Pryce were right. Ey God! It wasn't just that the beaver was giving out—everything was headed slam-bang for eternal smash.

An exclamation from Belle attracted everyone's attention. She stood silhouetted in the wide doorway leading into the other half of the store—the half with merchandise for the movers. Hiram was with her and had been explaining to her the uses of various trade items that had caught her fancy. Belle held up in one hand a pair of scissors and in the other a piece of deerskin she had cut off her sleeve. She was smiling proudly.

"There's your answer," Pryce said to Evie. "Whether the big change here comes in five years, or ten years, or five times ten, it will be sudden. To Belle, that thing in her hand seems a marvel. But for her and the thousands like her to bridge the gap between a pair of scissors and a locomotive would take a hundred years."

"Then they should have a hundred years," said Evie. "Can you imagine Grandfather Big Road agreeing to stay put?" She leaned against the counter, her eyes fixed on the open doorway as if she were seeing far beyond it.

Stroud had a pretty good idea what she was thinking. He'd been with villages when they moved. For the Indians moving was always a gay time, beginning when the crier rode through the camp at sundown announcing that tomorrow the people would move. The women would gather at lodge doors to hear where the next village would be set up, and the children would laugh with excitement, and there would be happy talk around all the lodge fires far into the night. Long before sunup the horses would be driven in, hundreds of them, shaking the earth and making a great noise, their manes and tails flying. The people would be busy then, taking down the tipis, packing up, loading pole drags. Then there was the traveling, with the women gossiping as they rode, the children scampering with the dogs, the young men testing bows and racing their ponies. At the end of the journey the work of unpacking and setting up lodges at the new camping place was still a glad time, and the work was of no matter, for when it was done there would be dancing and merrymaking.

After a moment Evie gave her attention to the bolt of cloth on the counter, flopping it over slowly. "I can't think the government will put a stop to the moving—not for a long, long time."

"The government won't have much choice," Pryce pointed out. "Too many people are pushing through here too fast."

"You're too trusting, Evie," said Bostwick as he lifted a kettle of awls to the shelf. "You can't believe that anybody will do anything except what he ought."

"I am not that trusting," protested Evie.

"No," said Pryce. "But I know what Amer means. You're a pet around here. Even in the Indian villages people show you their best sides. They have given you a more lofty opinion of the human race than it deserves."

"But most people *are* good. Those who aren't I do give the benefit of any doubt, if that's what you mean," said Evie. "But that's only natural."

"Not for me," said Bostwick. "Or for most people I know." He glanced at Stroud. "Take George, for example. He thinks Reeshar killed old Merk for a bundle of furs—and your father is ready to believe him."

Belle came on into the room and her glance fell on the bolt of blue cloth. "*Lecómi*. I like this. It would make me a pretty dress." She picked it up and held it in front of her admiringly.

"Put it down," Stroud said. Belle did as she was told and Evie picked it up along with the others she had straightened and placed it on a shelf. Hiram had resumed his work at the far end of the counter.

Bostwick, reaching for two of the kettles Stroud had filled, jerked his head toward Belle. "Belle's another good example of what I mean. I'll wager, Evie, you've never questioned George's story as to how he happened to bring Belle along." As Bostwick hefted the kettles, his eyes, with a look of sly amusement, met Stroud's.

"George hasn't told me anything about Belle," Evie said over her shoulder. "Greenberry explained before George ever had a chance." She turned away from the shelves and smiled at Stroud.

"And you believed what you were told with no questions asked," said Bostwick as he set the two kettles on the shelf.

"Why shouldn't I?"

Stroud had taken up a broom and was sweeping the unreclaimable flour into a pile. He stopped and looked at Bostwick. "What are you getting at?" he asked with a note of threat in his voice.

"I'm not getting at anything," answered Bostwick placatingly. "I was only trying to prove how trusting Evie is." He turned around and bent to pick up two more kettles.

"However Evie is, I wouldn't have her changed," Stroud said with a tone of finality.

"Of course you wouldn't," said Bostwick, straightening up. "Any man likes to be trusted. And most of them need to be."

Stroud's eyes narrowed. "What do you mean by that?"

176

"It was just an observation," said Bostwick. "It strikes me, though, that you're taking this too seriously."

"It strikes me, Amer," said Evie firmly, "that you're trying to be as irritating as you possibly can. I'm not so simple and trusting I can't see that. Though I don't know why."

Bostwick shrugged. "You must admit that George's showing up with a young squaw is open to question."

Evie's tolerant good nature snapped. "Not by you it isn't," she said angrily.

"You've carried this far enough, Amer," Stroud said. He leaned the broom against the counter.

"Perhaps I'm just disappointed," said Bostwick. He glanced in Evie's direction. "I'd expected an invitation to dance at your wedding before now. You can't much blame me if I've begun to wonder."

Stroud took a step forward but at the same moment Pryce's voice rumbled from the other side of the counter, "You heard George—the discussion is closed."

"Not quite, Pa," said Evie, her eyes bright. "If Amer wants to know bad enough to go to all this trouble, I'll set his mind at rest!" She turned toward Bostwick. "George and I have scarcely had time to talk it out. It's only been about twenty-four hours since he got here. And a girl usually likes to choose her own time to state her plans. But I guess now's as good a time as any if it will put an end to this. We did mention at breakfast this morning getting married soon as the cache is in."

Stroud stood looking at Evie. He had an almost ungovernable impulse to kick the chief clerk and to keep on kicking until he was clean out the front gate. Bostwick's suspicious nature had pushed Evie into declaring in anger something that should be said in joy, and no amount of talk now could set it right. Bostwick said something, but Stroud didn't notice what it was. Of a sudden, Stroud felt as if he had stepped into a trap he had set himself. He maybe didn't know much about women, but he knew once a wedding date was more or less fixed, a man didn't suggest it might have to be postponed while he prowled around trying to find out what had happened to another woman—one he had never owned up to.

It was too late now to tell Evie, or Pryce either, about Batchika. It was too late to do anything but ask questions around the Indian camps like a tater-nosed sneak, hoping Evie wouldn't find out. And if Billy Pitcher's estimate was right, he only had about two weeks in which to do it. Two weeks before the horses and men would be back from downstream. Two weeks before he went after his cache.

Outside, the yells of the children and the sound of voices indicated that the second table had finished with supper. Stroud heard Jake and Belco talking as they went out through the passageway, headed for the Indian camps, probably for a night of gambling. Whatever they played for, the stakes would be piddling compared to his. He would be gambling Evie's happiness and his own against the hope of finding out what had happened to Batchika. But Reeshar had made it a gamble he had to take. Reeshar and his own stiff-necked pride in not telling about Batchika before it was too late.

Ten

Stroud had his pancakes the next morning. He claimed he could have tasted them clear down to his trouser pockets, if he'd had pockets. In other respects, though, the mealtime was unsatisfactory. Pryce had eaten earlier and had left the fort for reasons which he didn't mention. Stroud was still angry at Bostwick, and Bostwick's presence was particularly irksome because the chief clerk was in rare good humor, as if elated by his success in upsetting everybody the night before. Bostwick gave considerable attention to Belle, conversing with her in Lakota. Observing Belle, Evie remarked after Bostwick had left, "She does have a way with her. Knowing Amer's suspicious nature, I can almost believe he honestly thought I should be worried."

"Nonsense," said Stroud. "He was only trying to get at me."

"I expect so," Evie agreed. After a moment she said, "Greenberry told me, I guess, but I've forgotten. Why was it you couldn't leave Belle with relatives?"

Stroud looked at her in surprise. "Because there wasn't time to find any. She was unconscious, and it was either bring her along or leave her by herself."

"You couldn't do that," said Evie. "You did the right thing." She began clearing the table.

Stroud had lingered after breakfast hoping for an opportunity to kiss Evie, but his hopes came to nothing because of the presence of Belle. For the same reason his goodnight kiss of the night before had been furtive and sketchy, and he wondered if this arrangement, which had seemed so ideal when Evie suggested it, was going to prevent him from ever seeing Evie alone. This alarming thought was pushed from his mind when he remembered that it was the day of Kearny's talk with the Indians, and if he wanted to make inquiries of any of them he'd better hump it.

As he was leaving, Evie asked him what his plans were for the day. He'd been afraid she'd ask that. "I'm going to see if I can get some horses from the Indians," he said. It was a lie, of course. But Stroud had decided that the pretense of trying to buy horses was the only excuse he could give for going on his search among the Indians. "I'll be back in time to take you to the conference," he promised.

Stroud hurried out, saddled up and headed for the Indian villages camped between the forts. He felt in luck that the clans most likely to have camped the winter of '37-'38 in or near the Bear Lodge Mountains—the route he and Reeshar and Batchika and Wicarpi had been taking to winter rendez-vous—were the ones that traded at Fort Laramie and Fort Platte. Most of them he had traded with at one time or another. But it was possible to trade with a band and still not be aware of a captive woman. And he was in luck, too, that one of those bands at least was camped now between the forts. Mozay had been sure that Madame Jack's band—No Heart's—was camped there the winter of the blizzards. It seemed a long time ago to Stroud that he had got this information from Mozay back in Shonka's village, but he figured it was just about a week. Ey God! Now that he wanted time to stand still, it'd go as fast as liquor on election day. Stroud kicked his horse into a trot, deciding the place to start was with Mozay's Madame Jack.

He found that her lodge had been set up beside that of her cousin and the cousin's husband. The latter—a fine young warrior named Tahiska—was sitting beside his lodge fire plucking the hair from his face with the aid of bone tweezers and a small looking glass. Aside from informing Stroud that Madame Jack was out to fetch water, the young warrior had continued his plucking. Tahiska was sullen because the blue-coat soldiers had said there was to be no whiskey to trade.

Shortly Madame Jack came up from the river carrying two large skin containers tied to the ends of a stick which rested across her shoulders. After suspending the water bags from lodgepoles inside her tipi and putting wood on the fire, Madame Jack sat down and motioned to Stroud to sit beside her. Thinking of the time when the village would move, he asked her if there was anyone she wanted to marry; maybe he could help her.

"No one," she replied, looking at her left hand. He noticed the bandaged middle finger—the one she had cut off at the first joint when Mozay was killed. Stroud made no further mention of finding her a husband. He should have remembered that only widows who had been happy with their husbands cut off their fingers.

He asked her then who among the old men of her band might have the best eyes for seeing into the past. She mentioned Hetopa and the winter count he kept by painting pictures on an elkskin. For seventy years Hetopa had kept this winter count, the record dating back to the times when the Teton Lakota still wintered east of the Missouri. He asked Madame Jack where he would find Hetopa, and as soon as he could, Stroud took his leave and went to look for Hetopa's lodge. At least it would be a year easy to recall, Stroud was thinking as he walked his horse through the camp—the summer when the smallpox swept through the tribes of the Upper Missouri, followed by a winter of blizzards and freezing moons.

Stroud made his way around the circle of lodges, three or four deep, until he had arrived at the horns of the circle where Madame Jack had told him Hetopa pitched his lodge. In response to Stroud's call, a wrinkled, white-haired man shrouded in a huge buffalo robe came to the lodge door. Stroud looked down from the saddle at the dried-up little old man and said, "*Hóu-kola.* Hello, friend." He leaned over and offered Hetopa a fresh carrot of tobacco. It was all the introduction needed.

"*Hokahê.* Welcome," the old man responded as he accepted the tobacco.

Stroud dismounted, secured his horse to a peg, and followed Hetopa inside. The old man sat down on his bed at the back of the lodge and indicated that Stroud should join him. Careful to observe etiquette by turning to the right, Stroud moved around the fire and sat at Hetopa's left. "I want to talk of snows past. The time of snow following the white man's sickness."

The old man nodded, and in a thin voice said, "Bring the elkskin!"

A tiny woman emerged from the recesses of the lodge. From a parflêche box she handed Hetopa a rolled-up skin. Hetopa spread the soft elkskin on the ground. Spiraling counterclockwise from the center was a succession of pictographs drawn in colors. The last picture in the spiral represented strips of meat drying on a scaffold. Stroud knew that last fall there had been an abundance of buffalo on the plains. His eyes followed the spiral toward its center. The first entry resembled three rows of sticks. The second entry was a drawing of a head and torso covered with black spots. About fifteen or twenty pictures farther up was a similar drawing, this one spotted red. Smallpox or the measles, probably. But there was no such drawing for a more recent time to suggest the smallpox epidemic of 1837. Many of the symbols were simply cryptic reminders which only Hetopa understood, and probably in some instances there was more than one symbol for each year.

The old man studied the symbols, pointing to the first

entry. "When I was a very young warrior," he said, speaking slowly, "we killed thirty Arikara, charging among their earth lodges." He pointed to the third symbol, an inverted U. "From the traders of the north we stole many horses that had iron shoes—the first we had seen."

"You do not count the time of the smallpox," Stroud said.

"Here was sickness," replied Hetopa. "And here." He pointed to the spotted figures.

"I mean the sickness that nearly swept the Mandans from the earth."

"*Hou*," Hetopa grunted in agreement. "That one. But it did not touch my village. I count only what I see." He thought a moment, consulting his records. He pointed to the drawing of a figure shrouded in a red blanket and wearing a headdress. "It was for us the time when the brave Itela was killed by the Shoshones."

"And after that, when the snows came?"

"The horses starved."

Stroud's pulse quickened. That would have been the time of the blizzards. "Was a lone woman found—a Crow woman? Or a white man?"

"Crow woman? There have been no Crow women in our camp. Nor a white man." Hetopa looked down again at his calendar. "But see next. Three hundred horses we stole, on our spring hunt, from the Pawnees."

Stroud had a feeling of hopelessness as the old man rambled on about the time when people were drowned by the swollen river, or the time Mato raped a virgin, or the time the lake burned, or the time they had the cramps, pointing in each instance to a symbol on the elkskin. This could likely take forever. "Not even a white man?" Stroud repeated.

Hetopa considered for a moment, then nodded slowly.

"I have heard of a white man who lived for a time in the camp of the Oyukhpes." The old man referred to another of the Oglala villages now camped at the forts.

"And they were camped near the Powder?" But the old man couldn't remember. Stroud couldn't even be sure that Hetopa wasn't just trying to say what he felt Stroud wanted him to say. Yet it wouldn't hurt anything to see the Oyukhpes.

Stroud searched out the camp of the Oyukhpes. An hour with a self-important old medicine man yielded only conjectures about the forthcoming conference but a great deal of talk about a young warrior, a Hunkpapa Sioux, who was visiting cousins in the Oyukhpe village. The medicine man pointed him out to Stroud—a boy, only fourteen, who was already ranked as a warrior, having counted his first *coup* in battle and having earned the brave name of *Tatánka Iyotáke*, Sitting Bull. It took another half-hour to learn that the white man Hetopa had mentioned as living for a time with the Oyukhpes was a French Canadian. He had been torn to death by a grizzly the autumn Fort Laramie was rebuilt of adobes. That was nearly four years ago. But to take the place of this faded hope was the medicine man's recollection of a captive Crow woman having lived among the Brûlés of Bull Tail's village.

Stroud spent some time in Bull Tail's camp. Bull Tail was still as voluble on what he intended to tell the soldier-chief at the conference as he had been the day before when Stroud met him on the trail, but he knew nothing about a captive Crow woman. He did recall that Istamaza's band of Oglalas had camped on the Powder River the winter of the blizzards. He remembered it well because the following spring Istamaza had carried the war pipe to all the Teton Lakota in an effort to organize an expedition against the Skidi Pawnees, who had caught the small Oglala band of

Itehepi Sakiya Tiapa, Paints-His-Face-Half-Red, hunting buffalo near the forks of the Platte and had killed them all. But there had been smallpox among the Skidis and the plan was abandoned. No, Bull Tail did not know where Istamaza was camped.

Stroud talked to several other Indians in Bull Tail's village, hoping that they might have further information, or at least know where Istamaza was camped, but he had no success. It was well past noon by this time and having nothing more definite to pursue, Stroud made his way leisurely through another of the Oglala villages, questioning at random Indians whom he knew about the winter following the smallpox epidemic and asking where Istamaza might be camped. He learned nothing helpful and decided that he was wasting his time. It was impossible to question individually all the Indians camped between the forts. He felt no discouragement, however, for more strongly than ever did he have the stubborn conviction that he was on the right course. So preoccupied was he that he would have ridden right past Greenberry and Partout, had not Partout hailed him after a fashion. "*Enfant de garce!* He stomp his friends in the ground, this one."

Stroud reined in and discovered Greenberry and Partout sitting Indian fashion in front of a tipi. Greenberry held a half-empty bottle. Partout's squaw apparently had welcomed Partout home by braiding ribbons in with his hair. "There's a room for you at the fort," he said to Greenberry.

"I ain't no sickly squaw. And I ain't so infernally old I'm ready to be put in a hole." Greenberry lifted the bottle and drank. "*Owgh! Owgh!*" he yelled with his head still tilted. "Hurraw fer scrimmage-seed and raise-devil!"

Stroud looked Greenberry over, wondering if the old man had done anything but drink for the past two days. "You ever eat, Greenberry?"

"*Sacré!* He bring flour"—Partout gestured loosely toward his tipi. "She cook. Dam' good."

"Time you settled down, Greenberry, and quit working other men's squaws," said Stroud.

"Ain't a one of 'em ye can trust, do 'ee hyar?" In a burst of drunken generosity Greenberry added, "Anyways hardly a one." He raised his head and looked blearily at Stroud.

"Ever think that Mozay's Madame Jack's pretty lonely now?" Stroud asked. He dismounted and hunkered down beside the two trappers.

Greenberry's reaction was very positive. "I'd as lief be shut up in a sweat lodge with two hundred pounds of lard."

"*Une veuve*—how you say?—widow—what she not know is not worth to know," Partout pointed out.

"Partout's right," said Stroud. "Widows can save you a power of time and trouble."

But Greenberry was taking another pull at the bottle. "Hurraw fer summer doin's!"

"Can you stand up?" asked Stroud.

Greenberry limply flexed one knee. "Touch of the ague." Partout reached for the bottle Greenberry held.

"What you need," Stroud suggested to Partout, "is a second wife. Mozay's Madame Jack now . . ."

"*Non!*" interrupted Partout. "One is pretty near too much, by gar!"

"Ye better forget Madame Jack and worry about your own women," Greenberry said to Stroud.

"Woman," corrected Stroud. "Evie."

Greenberry waggled his head. "Likewise Belle, and if ye keep ferritin' around, ye may have another, do 'ee hyar?"

Stroud shifted uncomfortably. It was a thought he tried to avoid. "It isn't likely," he said shortly. Damn Greenberry anyway. Couldn't he let a man have any peace? Stroud had

"Yes," said Stroud. As long as he was telling a lie, he might as well make it a good one. "Thought I'd ride out a day or two from the forts. Maybe find a village that isn't sulking because the whiskey trade is cut off." The moment he said it, Stroud knew he should have worded it differently but he went on. "Do you know where Istamaza is camped?"

"You mean you want to take some whiskey out to trade?" asked Pryce.

"I hadn't thought of that," said Stroud. He'd thought of it all right, but he'd hoped Pryce wouldn't. That would guarantee he'd get horses which he had no use for at the moment.

"I could sell you a cask," said Pryce thoughtfully. "Nobody'd know the difference if you use it away from the forts."

Stroud was casting about for a way to ease out of this difficulty when unexpectedly Wyatt came to his aid. "I don't suppose my opinion is worth much," said the young man, "but if you'd heard Kearny over at Fort Platte yesterday laying down the law about trading whiskey you wouldn't risk it."

Pryce reluctantly agreed that it probably would be a risk, and to Stroud's relief Pryce didn't pursue the matter. They heard singing start up among the Indians at the conference site. The women were making up songs of thanks, and Stroud knew that the men would join in soon. Yet a little while ago they were drawing back in fear of the dragoons. Like children, the Indians were quick to anger, quick to hate, quick to be happy, quick to forget. Only maybe the forgetting part wasn't quite accurate, Stroud decided. They only appeared to forget. They were quickly diverted, but the memory of having been afraid and the humiliation of having shown it would be held in until there was more remembering to go with it. Then it would all bust out in a God-knows-how crazy way.

Pryce didn't give his attention to the singing for long. "Without whiskey Istamaza's as good a bet as any," he said. "Did his trading early."

"Where is he camped?" asked Stroud.

Pryce shook his head. "I think he started for Goshen Hole, but I'm not sure."

"*Le tuku he?* What is this?" asked Belle. "Why do you speak of the Iron-Eyed-One?"

"I wish to know where he is camped," said Stroud.

"And you learn where his camp is?"

"No."

"*Han!* It is because you do not ask one who knows."

Stroud looked at Belle. Her eyes were sparkling. "And you are one who knows?"

"I know of the camping place from a sister of Istamaza, who visited an uncle who is also a relative of mine."

"Where is it?"

Belle glanced away. "I could take you there."

"I will find it myself." Stroud paused and regarded Belle closely. "Sometimes he camps up the Shell."

"The Iron-Eyed-One is not camped on the Shell."

"Three summers past his village was on Cherry Creek."

"I have much time and little to do. . . ."

"I shall ask someone who has little time and much to do," said Stroud. He was irritated, and Evie's interest in the conversation did nothing to improve his disposition.

"That one may be too busy to listen," said Belle.

Stroud gritted his teeth, and Evie laughed. To Belle she said, "How far is his camp?"

"A long day's ride."

In his mind Stroud began checking possible camping

places. His calculations were interrupted by Evie. "Belle shall show you, and I will go along," she decided.

Stroud realized he had been saved from Pryce's offer of whiskey only to land in a worse mess. "Aren't you needed here?" he asked.

"The Navajo woman can manage," Evie said. "Besides, if you get horses you'll need somebody to help drive them back."

"All right," Stroud agreed. There wasn't much else he could say.

They were nearer the conference site and could see that the Indians were taking places for dancing. Wyatt motioned Belle on. "I'll have her back early," he promised. "I'm leaving tomorrow myself with the fort hunters." The two of them rode off at a trot, and the others went on toward Fort Laramie.

Evie looked at her father. "Pa, did you have the Fort Platte horses run off?" Pryce smiled. "You went out awfully early this morning," Evie prompted.

"Those horses are scattered all over the hills. Reeshar won't find some of them for a week. He'll have to unload his furs unless he wants to put a guard on his wagons." Pryce laughed.

At another time Stroud would have laughed with him. But it had occurred to Stroud that in order to keep up appearances, he would have to pack some trade goods on Maud and take her along when they went to Istamaza's village. There was no knowing how it would all end. He glanced at Evie riding beside him. She seemed to have forgotten her displeasure with the conference and her dislike of the children's game. Either her father's having the Fort Platte horse herd run off or the prospect of a couple of days away from the fort seemed to have cheered her up. She looked as pleased as Belle.

Eleven

There was a general exodus from the forts the next morning. All but a hundred dragoons rode off at daybreak with provisions for twenty-eight days to cover the march of seven hundred miles to South Pass and back. As Stroud, Evie and Belle, with Maud in tow, rode out of the fort, they noticed, too, that all the Indian villages were moving out except the camps of Bull Tail, Big Road and one other. Big Road had announced that he was staying at the forts to see his granddaughter married.

Stroud and the girls headed up the Laramie, past what remained of the Army camp, where they forded the stream. Stroud was feeling put out that Belle still wouldn't tell him where Istamaza was camped except that the way led partly up the Laramie. Belle's spirits were undampened by Stroud's brief displeasure. She chattered on about the dancing after the conference. The people had many gifts from the blue-coat soldiers. She thought it good of the blue-coat soldiers to give so many gifts. It was good, too, that Wyatt was going to be generous with her for making his buckskin clothes. She concluded that many good things came from living at the big mud house.

Belle talked herself out finally and rode in silence for a while, thinking how it would be pleasant to live at the big mud house all the time. Everyone there treated her kindly and she did not go in fear as she often did in her own camp. Though her father had not forced her to marry Eahsapa, as was the custom, often she felt afraid of Eahsapa because he was proud and cruel and angered that she would not have him. He teased her cruelly, too. A brother-in-law was permitted many privileges with his wife's sisters. That was because it was expected that the sisters would also marry him when the time came. Belle would not have minded these familiarities had she wanted to marry Eahsapa, but she did not want to. She hated most the times when he flipped her skirt up in passing, laughing loudly to call attention to her nakedness before she could pull her skirt down again. Now that her father was dead, her uncle would be glad to take horses from Eahsapa and insist that she marry him. Her uncle had said many times that her father, Shonka, was foolish to listen to a young girl who did not know what was best for her. No matter what her uncle said, she would not marry Eahsapa. She would throw herself down from the Shell River bluffs first.

All morning and into the afternoon, Stroud, Evie and Belle traveled upstream, sometimes losing sight of the Laramie, then seeing it snaking along below them through bottoms overgrown with cottonwood and ash. The weather gradually cleared, and it was a pleasant ride through country bright in many hues of green. Toward sundown they came upon a pretty place to camp, a place known by both Evie and Belle. White chalk bluffs half hidden by bushes overhung the far bank of the Laramie. On the near side rank grass and scattered trees extended for a mile in each direction and along the course of a little tributary stream called the Chugwater, flowing in from the south. Overhead a big old cottonwood spread its limbs. At their backs the barren prairie, greener than it would be again during the year, stretched away to the south with unimpeded view. It was late afternoon, and Belle had admitted that they wouldn't find Istamaza until tomorrow. By this time the day had turned out unusually fine, warm and windless, as if the weather were trying to make up all at once for the lateness of summer. Stratus clouds reflected the setting sun in shades of madder and pink.

At first, on approaching the camping place, they hadn't noticed a lone tipi half hidden in a grove of hawthornes. It turned out to be the lodge of an old couple, and Stroud had been pleased to see them, thinking he could find out where Istamaza's band was camped and thus spoil Belle's fun. But it turned out not pleasant at all, for at a glance they could see that the woman was fatally ill. Unable to keep up with their moving village, they had been left behind. The man sat by her side, emaciated but otherwise all right. They didn't know anything about Istamaza. Evie had noticed suckers and whitefish swimming around at the mouth of the creek and suggested they catch some fish for the old people. So while Stroud tended the animals and hung a shelter of robes from the lower limb of the big cottonwood tree, the girls gathered willow shoots with which to weave a net.

Later, Stroud reclined beneath the shelter, smoking a pipe and watching Evie and Belle. "With a hook and line I'd have had enough fish by now to feed a camp meeting," he said. The girls had woven a net about fifteen feet in length and three in width. At the moment they were using strips of bark to fasten a long stick to each end of the net. This had been Evie's idea, and it was a pleasure to watch how confidently she worked.

"I could have worked faster with sinew," Evie said without looking up. "Anyway, you don't have a hook and line."

"How did I know you'd take a notion to fish?" asked Stroud.

Belle finished fastening the stick she was working with and glanced up at Evie and Stroud. "*Wokíya ye Lakóta.* Speak Lakota," she admonished, "or the Iron-Eyed-One will not be seen even tomorrow."

Having tied the other stick to her end of the net also, Evie got to her feet and began rolling up the net loosely, so as not to pull it apart. "*Hokúwa mni kte.* I go to fish.

You gather some wood and borrow a kettle," she instructed Stroud and Belle. She moved off, dragging her bulky net toward the creek a few yards away where it flowed into the Laramie.

Stroud gathered wood while Belle went over to the lodge of the old ones to borrow their camp kettle. When he returned she had the kettle full of water and hanging from a tripod. Stroud built a fire, and then there was nothing to do but wait for Evie. Belle sat down, one leg out straight and the other folded beneath her, causing her soft deerskin dress to be drawn tight across her legs. Her body was small and quite perfect. Stroud regarded her for a moment. This one was pretty as a hen canary, too; only she knew it *"Ehunun,"* said Stroud. "Truly. If you ever do find a husband, the first thing you will get is a lodgepoling."

Belle looked up at Stroud for a moment. "I would not claim for a husband one whose hair is like the feathers of an owl with the wind at its back." Stroud laughed. It had been a long time since his hair had been braided. "If I had a comb and water I would fix it," Belle added.

Stroud shook his head. He knew better than to stick his foot into that trap. A man didn't let anyone else braid his hair if he had a sweetheart around to do it for him, and Belle knew it. Full of tricks she was, although he had to admit she'd been behaving herself since moving in with Evie. "It is good that you have not tried to pretend at the big mud house that I am your husband," he remarked after a moment.

"Not because of your threat," Belle said scornfully. "It is as you said. The small amount of whiskey could only have been a gift to Eahsapa. I am worth many horses."

"A great many," agreed Stroud. "But not of mine."

"Five Scalps is poor in horses. Besides, there are many at the traders' house who look on me with favor."

"And many of them look through eyes old enough to be your grandfather's," he reminded her. Stroud glanced down at the stream where Evie was now catching the fish and tossing them onto the bank. "You finish with the fish," he suggested to Belle, "and let Evie braid my hair."

Belle looked at him rebelliously for a moment, then went to the stream where Evie, barefooted and barelegged with her dress tucked up, was trying to grab a slippery white-fish. A water turtle and several flopping fish were on the grassy bank. "I will finish," said Belle.

"I don't mind," said Evie without looking up.

Belle sat down on the bank and began taking off her moccasins and leggings. "No," she said. "Five Scalps wanted his hair braided, but I told him I would finish with the fish."

Evie straightened up. "He asked you to braid his hair?"

"Yes."

Stepping out upon the bank, Evie scooped up her moccasins and leggings and started toward the campfire. She was surprised and hurt, though it was silly, she told herself, to be bothered by such a trifle. Perhaps George didn't know better. He ought to, though. She had braided his hair for him before she left for St. Louis, and for two years it had been a happy memory. At the campfire she found Stroud stretched out in the grass, his eyes closed. She wanted to ask what had been in his mind that he suggest Belle fix his hair, but when he opened his eyes and saw her standing over him with her deerskin dress still tucked up above her knees, he smiled at her with such open admiration that she couldn't bring herself to say anything. Certainly she didn't wish to appear small and mean, and George couldn't have intended any hurt. "I should have fixed your hair sooner," Evie said.

Stroud sat up. "Belle told me I looked like an owl."

206

"You do," said Evie. "Fetch a bowl from the old ones while I put on my moccasins."

Stroud went to the tipi of the old ones, and when he returned with an earthen bowl Evie had her comb and mirror, which she carried with other personal effects in a deerskin container tied to her saddle. She took the bowl, scooped some water out of the kettle, and sat down cross-legged. She patted her lap and Stroud obediently stretched out and settled himself. Evie began loosening his braids, making sounds of disapproval.

Stroud closed his eyes, conscious of this intimacy. Indian girls always made quite a flirtation out of combing a man's hair. Batchika had done his first braids, teasing him because his hair was almost too short to braid, but he had insisted. Later, when his scalp felt as if it were pulling off, he had had to waken her and have her loosen them. Evie was Indian enough—or maybe it was just female enough—to make the most of the job. At least she had before. He opened his eyes and smiled up at her. "Aren't you forgetting something? Seems to me last time you braided my hair there was more to it than combing and clucking."

Looking down at him, Evie was glad she hadn't said anything. He did remember, though in a way that made it even harder to understand why he would suggest that Belle braid his hair. Or perhaps he hadn't. Perhaps Belle had been mistaken. Evie smiled, and as she bent her head forward, Stroud reached up and pulled her head down to his, and their lips met. This was the way Belle found them as she walked through the long grass carrying her moccasins and leggings in one hand and with the other holding up her dress, in the folds of which she fetched the fish. She let loose her skirt, dumping the fish, some still flopping, together with the water turtle, over Stroud's feet. "You will never comb out the snarls that way," remarked Belle.

Stroud let go of Evie and sat up. "There'll be plenty of time for combing out snarls while you clean the fish," he said, pushing and kicking them free of his feet. He put his head down again and Evie finished loosening the braids. She laughed and handed the mirror to Stroud. His hair stood out straight on each side of his head. After a critical look in the mirror he handed it back to Evie. "I look like a buffalo ready to shed his winter hair."

Evie began working with the comb, patiently untangling the snarls. "After you bring your cache in, I'll do it for you again. I'll wash it and braid ribbons in it."

The ribbons would be for his wedding, Stroud realized. "You're not getting much of a bargain," he said.

"Not much choice," said Evie. "It was either you or Belco." At the thought of Evie with the whiskered old mountain man, Stroud laughed.

"*Wokíya ye Lakóta*. Speak Lakota," Belle reminded them. She was looking quite out of sorts, but Stroud and Evie hadn't noticed. She had cleaned the turtle first, killing it by sticking its head into the fire, after which she slit open its side near the hind legs and drew out the entrails. Now she stood it upon the edge of its shell before the fire to roast, and then began cleaning the fish.

Evie finished combing one side of Stroud's hair and ran her fingers through it, testing for tangles. Stroud saw a hawk sailing motionless above them with pinions spread, looking down in scorn. It was a large, red-tailed hawk, its wings spreading more than four feet. Suddenly it bent its body earthward, clapped its wings close to its sides, and came down to not more than a hundred yards above them, wheeling and circling. The temptation was too much for Stroud. He sat up and reached for his rifle and with a shot brought the hawk plummeting to the ground close by with a force that split it open. While the shot echoed from the bluffs across the river, magpies screamed, squirrels scampered from limb to limb in the cottonwood, and a large bull elk went crashing through the underbrush along the foot of the bluff.

"You shouldn't have killed him," said Belle, her eyes wide.

"Belle is right," said Evie. "The hawk looks both backward and forward. He sees all that has happened and all that is to happen." She pointed to a gnarled tree on top of the bluff. "He made his nest up there."

"He may have been coming to talk to us," said Belle. "My mother was a wise one. She knew the language of the hawks. There was a song she used to sing." In a true, clear voice Belle sang the song of the hawk she remembered from her mother. The song was sad, full of foreboding, because the hawk, having looked ahead to what was to come, saw only whirlwinds and thunders and enemies crouched in the wood. After a moment, Belle picked up another fish and slit it open. "I wonder what the hawk knew about me," she said. Stroud glanced at her, touched by her tone of concern. Since coming upon Belle gambling in Shonka's village, she had aroused in him at various times feelings of amusement, casual admiration, vexation, anger and irritation. Now he felt sorry for her. He supposed her future did worry her some, and possibly it was largely due to him.

Evie had resumed her combing. "My mother sang a song much like Belle's," she remarked. "Though my mother always wondered why it was, since hawks see both good and bad, that in the songs about them they always saw only unhappiness." She looked around. "We camped here once. That's how I knew of the nest.

"I remember one time," continued Evie, "Mama sent me and my cousins to get water to keep the hides damp until they could be fleshed. I talked the others into taking a swim.

We removed our clothes and were about to dive off a fallen tree when I saw a hole in the bank deep under the water. I wanted to see where it led. The others were afraid, but I swam under the water into the hole. It was dark, and I felt something large and soft pass by, going out of the hole. Then I saw a light, and a few feet farther on I raised my head. I was in a beaver house. I was afraid to go back, so I broke a hole in the roof and climbed out. I was in the middle of a growth of wild roses, and I was much scratched up, all naked as I was, in getting out of the bushes."

Evie and Belle chatted on about their girlhood. Their conversation was an insight into the training of Indian girls —the self-effacement and self-control they were taught by the example of their mothers, the skills they learned in cutting moccasins and applying quills and making bead-work and dressing hides and drying meat and pounding pemmican. Evie talked with more zest, maybe because she knew the life only as a summer interlude and not the year round, Stroud supposed.

"Did your years in St. Louis mean nothing at all?" Stroud asked her.

"I think what my father said about Belle is true of me," said Evie. "I am not ready for locomotives yet myself. I would not have stayed a day in St. Louis had it not been for getting an education." She paused. "All the way back with the caravan, I kept thinking about the places I knew, and the good times I had with Mama. I understand better now how important it was to Mama to get back with her people part of the time. Often in St. Louis I wanted to do the same thing. A city—or a fort, either—is not a good place when one is troubled."

"The 'St. Louis'—what is it?" Belle asked.

"A very large village—larger than you have ever seen— far down the Big Muddy," said Stroud.

"It is a very large tribe?"

"No," Evie said. "It is many of the white man's tribes all in one village with big, thick lodges much like the big mud house on the Shell. There is much quarreling, and when the lodges get dirty they cannot be moved about."

"That is not good," said Belle. "And the buffalo—are they not frightened away by the quarreling people?"

"Yes," said Evie. "But the people do not hunt. They trade for their meat in small pieces, not knowing how long it has been killed and whether it is poor bull or fat cow, and it is butchered across the grain so all the juice runs out."

Stroud laughed. "The meat is not as good as buffalo."

"It is no wonder that so many of the white men leave their village," decided Belle.

"St. Louis is just one white man's village," explained Stroud. "There are many, many more across the Father of Waters. There is much to see, and many good things to eat. And many of the women wear fine dresses and have little work to do."

Belle considered for a moment. "I had heard there were many white men, but it is hard to believe. I would like to see these strange villages."

"No, you would not," said Evie. "The air is heavy and the water tastes bad. And the dresses are not so fine as ours. I remember the first grown-up dress Mama made me. It had a loose body and long sleeves. Sleeves and collar and bosom were all ornamented with beads, with beaded belt and beaded moccasins to match."

"I remember my first one, too," said Belle. "My father had traded for some flour in a loose, seamless sack, and he made me carry it across my saddle. All day I rode, getting flour on my new dress and spoiling it more and more."

Stroud was reminded of Evie's dresses hanging on the

wall of her room. "You never wear your St. Louis dresses," he observed.

"I hate those dresses, George. I will not wear them—not ever."

"The dresses are very pretty," said Belle.

Stroud, taken aback by the intensity of Evie's feeling, felt a stab of annoyance. Was this Evie's way of saying she wouldn't go back to the settlements? What with the ever-present Belle and his own doings, they had never had a chance to talk it out. Evie was finished with his hair and he sat up, continuing to turn it over in his mind as they waited for the fish to boil.

Stroud and the girls ate in the open, beside the fire. It was well past dark when they finished. Stroud built up the fire before they rolled up in their robes, the girls beneath the shelter and Stroud in the open, feet to the fire. He lay for a while with muddled thoughts of Evie and Belle running through his mind. Presently he drifted into sleep. Sometime later he seemed to be walking in a rose garden with Evie—a rose garden such as he'd never seen before—and she laughed when the briars tore at her trailing dress. They were walking hand in hand toward a large, white, comfortable-looking house with fluted pillars, but as they walked the house got farther away instead of closer. Then quite suddenly they were inside, only the house wasn't comfortable at all. It was drafty and the wind whistled through the cracks, most particularly a wide one in the floor of what appeared to be a large dining hall. In silent agreement they started stuffing the large crack with torn clothing—strips of fur garments—which were handed them by a third person whom Stroud could not see clearly. But the stuffing did no good, and slowly the crack began to widen and the wind blew colder. And there was not just one wide crack. As he looked about, Stroud could see many cracks all growing slowly wider, and it became of great importance to decide where to stand, so that when the cracks became huge chasms he would be in a safe place. Evie whined when she saw the many cracks—a strange, animal-like whine that tingled along Stroud's spine—yet he was powerless to comfort her. Through her whines Stroud heard a loud knocking on the door, and with leaden feet he went toward it, panicky that he wouldn't get there in time—in time to bar it, for the door must be barred. When he finally reached the door, he found there was no door, for what he had thought was a house was a vast tipi with many chambers. At the door-that-was-not-a-door, with his fist raised to knock again, was a large wolf. Yet it was not a wolf but a man with a wolf's head. Behind and around it were other wolfmen, and with a feeling of intense chill, as if the cold wind blew through him, Stroud recognized the large wolfman with the raised fist as Reeshar. The others were harder to identify and yet he did it swiftly. There was Greenberry, and Jim Bridger, and old Fitz, and Partout, Jake, Belco, Wyatt, Billy Pitcher, and many others—some of them trappers who he thought had gone under. They all held Green River knives menacingly in their hands, only the blades were of silver that gleamed in the moonlight. The cold wind was very strong and it flapped the ears of the wolf heads ludicrously because the heads did not fit very well—except Reeshar's. The ears on Reeshar's head were erect and pointed slightly forward as they should be, and somehow this seemed infinitely horrible. The wolf-who-was-Reeshar grinned and said, "I've come for the other one, the other one, the other one." Stroud tried to bar the door-that-was-not-a-door with his body. The wolf-who-was-Reeshar put a hand on Stroud's chest and started pushing with a firm, insistent pressure, and Stroud had the hopeless feeling that he would eventually give way. Protectively he put an arm around Evie's shoulders, who stood now at his side. Her strange whining had stopped—he didn't know when—but she had hurt her foot in one of the cracks, for it was bandaged and she used a crutch. As the pressure against his chest increased, Stroud realized he was dreaming, and forced himself awake, though it was difficult, for he couldn't rid himself of some parts of the dream.

He opened his eyes, and for a few moments he knew real terror, for the wolf-face of Reeshar was still before him, and so was the insistent pressure on his chest. Stroud lay unmoving. Gradually he realized that he was in reality looking up at a large white wolf who sat with one paw on his chest, watching him intently. The fire had gone cold. With a sudden, violent motion Stroud sat up, flailing his arms at the same time. The wolf drew back a few feet, and Stroud's hand searched the ground for a rock and found it. As he pulled back his arm to throw, the wolf turned and the rock hit him a glancing blow on the flank. The wolf slunk away and Stroud found he was breathing hard. He lay back thankful that the wolf hadn't attacked him. Though maybe it wasn't surprising. He couldn't recall anybody really being attacked by a wolf.

Stroud built up the fire and then remained awake, remembering his dream clearly, and he pondered over it, finding the idea of Reeshar with the head of a wolf quite fascinating. Now that he thought of it, Reeshar was like a wolf in a lot of ways. To be fair to both Reeshar and the wolves, Reeshar had their intelligence, grace and strength. There was a rhythm to Reeshar's motions unexpected in a large man. He had sociability, too. These were the things a man liked first about Reeshar—the easygoing strength and the good mind. The friendliness with his own kind, though, was not necessarily good—in either a wolf or Reeshar. It was most usually a matter of convenience—for mating or food-getting—a banding together of a large pack for a special reason. Right now Reeshar had gathered a pack at Platte sure enough. And the intelligence hid other traits, such as cunning and treachery.

The cache now—that would appeal to Reeshar as a worthy prize. He had even admitted as much.

Stroud decided that even Reeshar's eating habits were wolflike. Reeshar gorged when he had the chance—ate and ate until he was almost stupefied. And in a pinch anything would do. Greenberry said once a wolf would eat anything from a mouse to a buffalo, if hard put to it, and Stroud had found this to be true of Reeshar.

Something else came to Stroud's mind, too; an odd incident that happened after the fight with the Bannocks at that first rendezvous he and Reeshar had gone into together. Reeshar had pulled up the body of a Bannock who had been killed, to sit on while he ate. Since then, Stroud felt this should have indicated to him something in Reeshar's character. Now it, too, appeared somehow wolfish, like the scornful way wolves urinated on some enemy they had killed and didn't want to eat. Or maybe more like the way he had seen them wallow in carrion. They rarely ate carrion, but whenever they came across some, like as not they'd roll in it. A sort of reveling in flesh—in carnage. This comparison was so disturbing that Stroud tried to steer his mind to other things, in an effort to court sleep. And he did sleep finally, toward morning.

He awoke out-of-sorts and impatient. Evie and Belle were quick to notice his change of mood, and they were silent and hurried as they broke camp. The holiday spirit of the day before was gone, the outing being now reduced to finding Istamaza's band as quickly as possible. The old man had eaten the night before. Even the women sipped some of the broth. Now Stroud gathered some more wood

215

for the old people, and also killed two rabbits he came upon, which he skinned and hung in a tree outside the lodge. With the boiled fish, they could get along a few days until somebody else came by.

Belle led Stroud and Evie several miles up the Chugwater. Here low bluffs a quarter of a mile apart bordered the stream. Some twenty-five lodges were scattered along it. It was Istamaza's band, all right. They were engaged in the usual early-summer tasks of drying meat and thinning hides.

Belle had relatives among the band with whom she visited, accompanied by Evie. Stroud sought out Istamaza, named for his glowering countenance and piercing gaze, which neither age nor obesity had softened. There had never been a Crow woman living in his band, he said. He was certain he had no recollection of one at any time, nor a white man, either, under the circumstances Stroud mentioned. He remembered the time well enough. It had been a winter to remain close by the lodge fire. Many of the people had gone snow-blind, and the medicine men had cured them by putting snow on their eyes and blowing on the backs of their heads. But most of the bands had wintered within the protective folds of Pa Sapa, the sacred Black Hills. There were no villages other than those already known to Stroud that had camped along Powder River or near the Bear Lodge Mountains that winter. Of this Istamaza was sure. And none of his men remembered differently. They were so sure of this that Stroud went back again to questioning them about a Crow woman and a white man who wintered with some Sioux band, patiently rephrasing his questions, explaining that the white man he wished to know about wouldn't have come into a Sioux camp until about the time of the third of those early blizzards that winter.

"*Hou,*" grunted Istamaza, remembering. "That was a very bad storm. Some of our horses strayed and we spent several days looking for them, riding to the east and north." After a moment he said, "While we were hunting our horses we did see two white men with an Indian woman, but I do not know where they went."

"But the woman was not a Crow woman?" asked Stroud. Two white men with an Indian woman was too commonplace to arouse much interest. It could have been any two trappers with a squaw.

"I was not close enough to tell," explained Istamaza. "We came to the top of a hill, looking for our horses, and in the valley below us we saw the two white men and the woman. The snow was so deep we did not go closer, for we could see our horses were not in the valley."

"Perhaps the men were Indian also," suggested Stroud.

"No," said Istamaza. "The woman was riding ahead on a mule with packs of furs. Behind her walked one of the men and the other followed him riding a horse. The horse had a white man's saddle. Also, the hair of the man walking was not in braids but hung down over his shoulders so that we could see it clearly against the white snow. It was yellow."

Istamaza's evidence was so unexpected and so conclusive that for a few moments Stroud said nothing. It couldn't have been anybody but Reeshar with the yellow hair— not wandering around at the exact time and approximate place where Stroud would expect him to be. And the chances were that it was either Batchika or Wicarpi with him. If the Indian woman whom Istamaza saw had belonged to the other white man, she would likely have had a horse of her own. She wouldn't have been riding on top of the packs.

217

"You did not see them again? You do not know where they went?" asked Stroud.

"No. They were traveling west."

"And the other white man—the one riding the horse. Could you tell how he looked?"

"No. With his hat like yours and the distance, it might have been any white man. It was only the bright yellow hair of the other that we could see clearly. I have told you all I know."

And it was quite a lot, Stroud told himself. He was on the right track. It would appear that Reeshar and the woman had somehow come across some trapper who had sheltered them during the blizzard, and then they had struck out together. But who was the trapper? And where were they headed? What band of Sioux did they subsequently stay with? For Stroud was more sure than ever that they— the two men and the woman now—had probably wintered with some Indians. But where could they have been camped that none of the Indians he had talked to had run across them?

There was clearly nothing more to be learned from Istamaza, so Stroud asked about horses. He had decided he would have to trade for some if the Indians were agreeable, in order to avoid making Evie suspicious. He would worry later about the complications it would cause. But for the second time that day Stroud was in luck. No one was interested in trading horses. There was little they needed, for they had done much trading at the big mud house. Perhaps some coffee and flour in exchange for buffalo robes? Anxious now to get back to Fort Laramie, Stroud inwardly chafed at the time it took to let the Indians look over his trade goods and see if there was anything they wanted. However, there was very little, and at the end of an hour or so he was free to hunt up Evie and Belle.

Stroud hurried the girls into the saddle. He took the shortest way back. On their outward ride they had made almost a right angle, having gone straight southwest along the Laramie nearly twenty miles to the mouth of the Chugwater, then about ten miles south. Now he completed the other side of the triangle, setting a fairly brisk pace. An hour before sundown he struck the Platte a few miles below the forts and took the Oregon Road northwest. He was surprised to be overtaken by a patrol of dragoons. The officer in charge was Captain Eustis. He nodded at Stroud and touched his cap to the girls. He looked as if he would have liked to ask them to ride along with the patrol, Stroud thought, but he led his men on past without another glance, their accoutrements jingling a smart tune. Stroud watched them pull rapidly away and disappear beyond a hill. He couldn't get used to this symbol of United States authority. He wondered whether the presence of troops was quieting the Indians or galling them.

When Stroud and the girls splashed through the Laramie and came up to the flats above, they saw that the first emigrant train had come in. About thirty wagons were corralled over near Fort Platte. Smoke from their fires spiraled up into the quiet air of late afternoon. Children romped about, a few people were going in and out of the fort, some of the wagons were blocked up with their wheels off, a few oxen and horses were being shod. The wagons in their tight little corral seemed to be huddled up against Fort Platte. Stroud noticed also, as his glance swept the dusty plain between the forts, that another band of Indians had come in to make camp. It was easy enough to tell from the lodge markings whose band it was. He turned to Belle and was surprised to find that she was no longer riding between him and Evie. She had slowed her horse and was some fifteen or twenty feet behind, her eyes fixed on the camp of the newly arrived Indians.

"There's one thing certain," Stroud said, mostly to himself. "He hasn't much to trade but my mules."

"Who?" asked Evie.

"Eahsapa. Shonka's band." He motioned ahead. "They've come in."

"That should please Belle," said Evie. "She can go to her sister now."

"There's no hurry," said Stroud. "They'll be here a while."

Twelve

Stroud, Evie and Belle rode on to Fort Laramie, its location on a bend of the Laramie River facing west by north requiring travelers from the Oregon Road to approach it from the rear and come up to it along the north wall. They had just turned the corner and were riding along the west wall toward the main gate when Pryce rode out. He was so preoccupied that he wasn't aware of them at first, even though he was headed right at them.

"Where are you going, Pa?" Evie called.

"No horses?" Pryce asked, pulling up.

"No," said Evie. She noticed that her father was plainly out of sorts. "What's wrong?"

"Considerable. You saw where the first emigrant train is camped?" asked Pryce.

"Yes," said Stroud. "Huddled up against Fort Platte."

"And not one blasted emigrant has set foot in Fort Laramie," Pryce said angrily. The others stared at him. "What's more," he went on, "not one of them intends to."

"Why not?" asked Evie.

"Because I'm an ass," said Pryce bitterly, getting more and more worked up. "All day yesterday I sat around laughing every time I thought of Reeshar's horses scattered all over the countryside. And when somebody reported that the herders and some of the *engagés* straggled in with only twenty-five or thirty yesterday afternoon, I laughed fit to kill."

He paused and then went on even more violently than before. "You want to know where Reeshar was while I was pleasuring myself? He was riding down the trail to meet the emigrant train. He met it, too. Yesterday afternoon, with me standing on the wall watching, the train came in piloted by Reeshar. What's worse, he'd convinced the lot of them that Fort Laramie was nothing but a den of thieves."

"Couldn't you convince them Reeshar lied?" asked Evie.

"No," said Pryce. "They 'don't aim to find out' whether he did or not."

Stroud could imagine how apoplectic Pryce must have been the day before, with his warehouse bulging with supplies for emigrants that were doing all their trading at Fort Platte. Stroud could imagine, too, the blank, withdrawn expressions on the faces of the emigrants. It was a fact that once they set their minds, no appeal to reason could change them.

"What are you going to do?" he asked Pryce.

"Meet the next train myself," said Pryce grimly, "and tell them there's smallpox at Fort Platte."

"*He wastéke lo sni!* That is bad!" said Belle, recognizing the word "smallpox," her eyes getting round with fear. "The white man's sickness will kill us all."

"*Ma k'eya!* Nonsense!" Evie said impatiently. "It is only a trick."

"How far down the trail do you expect to find the next train?" asked Stroud.

"They're reported to be two days behind. Should get in tomorrow. I figure they ought to be camped tonight a few miles below Cedar Point," explained Pryce.

"Hobart's camped down at Cedar Point," said Stroud. "Let him talk to the movers. They'd be quicker to believe the word of a simple man."

"Aye," said Pryce. He thought about it for a moment and then asked, "You think Hobart'd do it?"

"He doesn't like Reeshar any better than we do. Just

offer him some credit for whiskey," said Stroud. Pryce nodded and rode off.

Stroud and the girls tended to their horses, and then while Evie helped the Navajo woman with dinner Stroud unloaded Maud. After dinner Evie and Stroud played cribbage with Hiram and Bostwick till nearly midnight while Belle worked on Wyatt's buckskins.

As a result of having stayed up late or being talked out, they had little to say at breakfast, though there was mention of the first wagon train of emigrants having moved out that morning. For half the morning Stroud sat on a bench in the entrance passage, smoking a pipe and fighting off a feeling of hopelessness. Reeshar could tell him what he wanted to know in two minutes. Instead he had to go poking around like a hen scratching for seed in last summer's garden patch. Four days spent trying to find out which Indians had camped on the Powder River the winter of '37-'38, and now he had to start all over again trying to find what band might have been camped to the west—the direction in which Reeshar had been headed with the white man and Indian woman. Stroud decided he might as well start his questioning with Jake and Belco, who were in the trading store already beginning the day's drinking.

As he stood up, Stroud noticed an Indian on horseback approaching the gate. Stroud recognized the Indian as one of the old men who had sat in council with Shonka. The Indian pulled his pony to a stop just inside the passageway and looked down at Stroud with a cultivated absence of expression. "*Hóu-kola*," he said in greeting. Stroud waited for the Indian to make his purpose known. After a moment the old man said, "I speak for the warrior-chief Eahsapa."

Whatever was on his mind, Eahsapa was going about it formally, Stroud was aware. It was also a matter that might lead to a ruckus, as the sending of an old man indicated.

"I hear thee, Old One," Stroud replied.

The old Indian's face was about the color of cured tobacco leaf, and as full of wrinkles. "Eahsapa says he cannot walk with pride until he has been offered the filled pipe."

Stroud was puzzled. "The filled pipe is for a wife stolen."

The old man nodded. "For Tasina. She lives with you now."

"She is wife to neither of us," Stroud replied. "Nor is she stolen." He knew the custom. To send a filled pipe would be a public admission of woman-stealing; if the wronged man smoked he was agreeing to a settlement, but if he refused the pipe he was angry and would seek satisfaction. Stroud couldn't believe that Eahsapa was really sincere in claiming that Belle was his to be stolen. More likely it was a trick to make Stroud vulnerable to some refined extortion. "Eahsapa has forgotten. He offered Tasina in trade for whiskey."

The old man nodded. "The warrior-chief was drunk, and his heart was black. You cheated him, he says. He demands the pipe, or there will be blood on the ground."

"*Hoh!*" said Stroud. "Tell Eahsapa I send him no pipe. Let him think of the mules he stole from me. Thirty mules for one maiden. It is I who was cheated. *Iyáya yo*. Be gone, and tell him that." Stroud didn't much want to be responsible for sending Belle back to her village against her will. Not just yet, anyway.

The old man nodded solemnly. "Then go about with care."

Stroud watched the Indian ride away. It had galled him that he had let Eahsapa make off with his mules. He should have had them back at any cost, if for no other reason than to have discouraged an Indian from thinking he could get

224

away with anything. Was he growing cautious, now that he had made enough to leave the mountains?

As Stroud walked into the courtyard and toward the trading store, the memory of an instance when he had recovered stolen horses—he and Reeshar—forced its way into his mind. It was the time a hunting party of a half-dozen Crows had come upon him and Reeshar and the women camped. Several of them knew the women, and there had been a great show of friendliness as they camped together for the night. But he and Reeshar had been awakened in the morning to discover the Crows trying to make off with their horses. Although the Crows had fled when fired upon, Reeshar had not been content. He had fired again, knocking one Indian off his horse and breaking his thigh. Anyone else would have killed the man, but Reeshar always had been a poor shot. He had sat down beside the Indian, promising him he must die, making him smoke a pipe, telling him to take a last look at the bright new day, and then he put a bullet through the Indian's head. Batchika and Wicarpi had hidden their faces and did not see Reeshar take the scalp and then lick his knife clean before returning it to his belt.

Outside the trading store, Greenberry was stretched on a bench, snoring loudly, an empty bottle on the ground near him. Stroud went on past him, opened the door of the store and slammed it closed behind him. Jake, Belco and a Company trapline rider were at the far end of the counter. They all looked around as Stroud entered, and Hiram, who was across the counter from them, set out a bottle of whiskey. "I hope you didn't wake up Greenberry," he said. "He's used up his credit and is getting cantankerous. Offered him a gill to keep him quiet, but he said that was like offering a freezing man an inch of cordwood."

225

"Looks like he's got enough whiskey in him to swim a skunk," said Stroud.

Hiram talked on as he rearranged some stock on the shelves, commenting on how the Indians had been pretty ugly at being refused whiskey. Luckily their interest in trading with the emigrants had kept them too busy to cause any real trouble—that and the presence of the dragoons.

Stroud only half heard Hiram's talk. He poured himself a cup of whiskey and as soon as he could he asked Jake and Belco about the winter of '37-'38—if there were any Indians known to have camped that winter west of the Powder River. It was the trapline rider who answered. "Wasn't no Injuns camped anywheres around there," he said positively. "I rode all through there in the spring."

"Not around the Big Horns? Maybe Crazy Woman's Fork?" asked Stroud.

The trapline rider shook his head. "I was through there just after the first thaw. Warn't nobody."

Stroud finished his drink and poured himself another, feeling as if he had had a horse shot out from under him. He supposed it was possible a band could have broken camp and left before the thaw, but it was unlikely. And he didn't know any place west of the Powder, except in the foothills of the Big Horns, where the Sioux were in the habit of camping. Without a specific location in mind, he could ask questions from now till Judgment Day without finding out anything. Unless he could find the trapper who was seen with Reeshar and the Indian woman, it began to look as if he might as well give up. He had already considered trying to find out who the trapper was, but it seemed hopeless. Trappers who were around seven years ago were scattered all the way to California and Oregon. Besides, trappers came and went—and went under. Who could the trapper have been? Who wouldn't have talked? Somebody who had gone under, more than likely.

The conversation turned to other things and Stroud drank quietly and steadily to blunt his discouragement while his reason picked and nagged at a mental list of trappers he compiled. Both pursuits were interrupted by the sound of voices from atop the walls of the fort crying, "The families!" They all went out, except Hiram, curious to see if Pryce had been successful in getting this wagon train away from Reeshar. Even the emigrants would be an improvement over his own worries, Stroud decided as he climbed the stairs.

Evie, Pryce and Belle were on the wall, he found, as well as Bostwick and some squaws and children. Stroud took a place between Evie and Pryce. They were all intent on the approaching caravan. "I hope Hobart was a good liar," said Pryce apprehensively. The two lead wagons had reached the Laramie and were hesitating at its brink, the swift current causing some trepidation. Behind them was a double line of canvas-topped wagons strung out along the trail—Stroud counted thirty—flanked by people on foot and a few horsemen, and followed by a herd of thin-looking cattle. The lead wagons finally plunged in and began fighting the current. This was the fourth year wagons had come into the forts, wagons other than those of the trade caravans and the few missionaries, the first year bringing fewer than a hundred emigrants, then the number jumping to a thousand for each of the past two years. Kearny had said there would be nearly twenty-five hundred souls in all this year, though estimates of some of the dragoon officers ran as high as four or five thousand.

Several of the mountain men were picking up easy money guiding emigrant trains through, Stroud knew. And there was Jim Fitzpatrick, who was acting as scout for Kearny. It wasn't the first time Fitzpatrick had acted as a guide, so he must like it, but just because it appealed to old Broken Hand didn't make it desirable in Stroud's opinion. Stroud knew that the future wasn't in beaver any more. And he wasn't going to get caught in the backwash like Jake and Belco, or even Greenberry, for that matter. But acting as a guide didn't line a man's pockets, either. With the whole place headed God-knew-where, the thing to do was get out. Even if a man were going to stay, there'd be ways to make money after the beaver was gone besides taking orders from stiff-necked Army officers or gumptionless movers. With a couple of hundred head of well-grazed oxen now, a man could make a good trade for the scrawny animals pulling these movers' wagons. Or a man could haul supplies to the new settlements. Or there were any number of other things that a man could do. But why think about staying when he had got what he came for?

A cheer from the others on the wall drew Stroud's attention to the wagons again. The lead wagons had crossed the river safely and had turned off the trail and headed for Fort Laramie. "That is better," said Pryce, his tension relieved.

Evie leaned across Stroud and spoke to her father. "Pa, can I go see them, soon as they're corralled?"

"You'd better wait," said Pryce. "Bull Tail will be out with a delegation before they even get unhitched." He explained that Bull Tail had managed to get a feast from the first emigrant train. "With that encouragement he'll bedevil them all," Pryce concluded.

"I'll take you and Belle to the emigrant camp tomorrow," Stroud offered. "I need cartridges for my Colt."

"I didn't say anything about Belle," Evie remarked.

"You know she'll tag along whether we like it or not," said Stroud. "Can't get away from good old Belle." Evie gave Stroud a searching look, then glanced back at the wagons.

"Fine," agreed Pryce absently. "Hobart certainly seems to have been worth the hire."

Stroud watched until about half the wagons had crossed the Laramie and started crawling across the mile-and-a-half distance between the ford and the fort. Then, deciding he needed something more to drink, he went back to the store. Greenberry still slept on the bench, and Stroud's bottle was still on the counter. Belco had returned to the store before him.

Stroud settled down again, trying to reason who the trapper could have been who brought Reeshar and the Indian woman into a Sioux camp. What trapper would have been trapping alone seven years ago? What trapper, probably long since dead, wouldn't have talked?

It was only a matter of time until Merk's name came to Stroud's mind. Merk was one of the few trappers he had ever known who was in the habit of camping alone. And Merk wasn't apt to have talked. He might have remembered, and he might have told if he had been asked. But nobody would have. Nobody knew enough to ask. But he wasn't long since dead. He had been killed recently by Reeshar, and that, more than anything else, made Merk the most likely candidate. He was killed not for his furs, but because he knew too much.

It was enough to drive a man crazy to think that old Merk, when he had come on him there by the soda springs, could probably have told him all he wanted to know. Stroud emptied his glass again, and then, aware of a clamor of voices outside, he went to the door, followed by Belco.

Emigrant families were straggling into the fort, a tired, disorderly swarm. Men and boys wore cotton shirts and pants of homespun, held up by copperas-dyed suspenders, fastened front and back by big pewter buttons. The women were dressed in somber linsey-woolsey. Some of them wore straw sundowns or caps of coarse, knotted twine like cabbage nets, while others were bareheaded, with hair tied in tight knots at the nape of the neck or plaited and piled up on top of the head. Both the young boys and girls had close-cropped tow hair.

The emigrants scattered through the courtyard, opening doors and examining the various compartments without hesitation, saying little. They eyed Greenberry snoring noisily on the bench, the half-breed children, and the squaws in their paint and fofarraw.

Like the hub of a wheel, a lean man dressed in dusty black stood in the center of the courtyard, peering about suspiciously. He looked like the cussedest circuit-riding preacher out of jail. "I can see that sinners are as thick hyar as black bugs in spiled ham, and gamblers and whores and thieves skitin' about like weasels in a barnyard!" he said. "It's the devil's own garden patch!"

Stroud and Belco, not wanting to chance being the text for a sermon, went back into the store. Stroud commenced drinking in earnest. It was too late to talk to old Merk. Pretty soon it'd be too late to marry Evie. Stroud was hardly aware of the movers, who soon invaded the store in goodly numbers.

Not long after Stroud and Belco went back into the store, Evie came out of her room and cast an angry look over the emigrants in the courtyard. Then she descended the stairs and crossed to her father's office.

Pryce was seated at his desk talking to Bostwick about trading fresh cattle for the footsore animals of the emigrants, with cash and a substantial amount of sugar to boot. "If it's only split hoofs they have, we can treat them with soap and boiling pitch," Pryce was saying. "They will be good as ever in a few weeks." He looked up as Evie entered. She seemed put out about something. "What is it, daughter?"

"They stole my shoes," she said bluntly.

"Who?"

"These prying movers."

Bostwick stepped toward the door leading into the store. "I'll have a look at the cattle then?" he asked.

Pryce nodded. "And see if Hiram and Billy need help in the store."

After Bostwick left, Pryce turned to Evie. "Your moccasins?" His expression was mainly one of bewilderment.

"Shoes," Evie said impatiently. "My St. Louis shoes."

"These people are overcurious," admitted Pryce. "But there's little lost. You never wore them."

Evie advanced toward the desk. "It was stealing, Pa. Stealing ought to be punished."

"That would be silly. I have to trade with these people."

"In a Lakota village a thief would be flogged half to death and his horses killed!" Evie said angrily. "I want the gates locked and the people searched."

Pryce was plainly perplexed. "You are being spiteful, daughter," he said slowly. "That isn't like you."

It hadn't been easy since Evie's mother died. There had been nothing in his own past calculated to help him raise a daughter. When he'd been a young man, children had been farthest from his mind, though he guessed he'd planted a few of his own up around the Saskatchewan. He'd been too busy in those years to pay much heed to anything but work. As the *bourgeois* of a small Canadian post, he had known what it meant to be busy; particularly during those first fine days of spring with a wind fresh but mild from the west, the snow inside the fort all melted, the men boiling back fat for the pemmican and preparing hoops and staves to make

231

kegs for the grease, the women sewing bags to put the pemmican into. And when each day's work was done, there was always a Blackfoot girl to cook his meals and warm his bed with her firm brown body. Nothing much there calculated to help him raise a daughter. Particularly a daughter neither white nor Indian. Like sassafras tea brings out the measles, he'd hoped St. Louis would bring out the white in Evie. But at the moment he wasn't sure what had been brought out. He looked at her with a worried expression and said, "What is it, daughter?"

The anger seemed to die within Evie as she regarded her father. Tears welled in her eyes and rolled down her cheeks. "I don't know, Pa. I don't know." She was silent, made contrite by her father's concern, then turned and left the office.

Toward noon the next day, when Stroud left the fort with Evie and Belle, headed for the emigrant camp, he knew that Evie was upset about something. He was pretty sure it had nothing to do with his drinking of the day before. True, he had only a hazy recollection of events after the arrival of the emigrants, but he did half remember Evie putting him to bed with a satisfying degree of patience and solicitude. Today she was pleasant enough whenever he spoke, but the shine was gone. She hadn't even made much effort to fancy herself up for going visiting. Nothing like Belle had, anyway. Stroud glanced at Belle, who walked on his other side. She had on a tight-fitting bodice of red cloth worked with beads and porcupine quills, a full blue skirt, and red leggings, also embroidered. She had put a fresh vermilion part in her hair and fresh spots of red and white on her cheeks. Stroud had to admit to himself that the effect was good. Looked like the most got-up trapper's wife in all creation.

He glanced ahead again, his mind abruptly veering to his conviction of the day before that it had been Merk whom Istamaza had seen with Reeshar and the Indian woman. Even sober, Stroud felt it made sense, though he kept having the notion that there was some other connection concerning Merk and the winter of '37-'38 that was eluding him—something that he had just about put together the day before when Merk, and all his other problems, had ceased to worry him. All morning the half-remembered train of thought had persistently plagued him, though he tried not to think of it, for it only made his headache worse.

They were approaching the opening of the wagon circle. Stroud saw that inside the circle numerous cook fires were burning, each tended by what appeared to be a single family. The wagon at the right of the opening was blocked up and the rear wheels were off. A man holding a bucket glanced up. He was a hawk-billed, weasel-eyed man with a ragged beard, who looked like he wouldn't know his britches from a pair of bellows. He shook a blob of yellow grease from his hand, wiped his hand on his trousers, and reached for his rifle.

Before Stroud could speak, a woman holding an infant said from beside the fire, "One of them French Injuns. One woman ain't enough for 'em." Her eyes held on Stroud. Since coming in from the mountains, Stroud had shaved, and his smooth face and dark braids were misleading. The woman looked again at Evie and Belle. "Bedizened. Shoo 'em off, Mr. Sikes," she ordered her husband.

"Who's your captain?" asked Stroud.

Disconcerted, the man studied Stroud from head to foot, then lowered his rifle. "Reckon you ain't Injun. French neither. A body can't much tell."

Belle's eye had been caught by a poke bonnet—a red one

—on the tailgate of the wagon. She stepped toward it. "*Wapáha sa bite*. Red warbonnet," she said, smiling and reaching out to touch it.

"She'll get lice on it, Mr. Sikes!" said the woman. Her husband obediently snatched the bonnet from Belle's reach. The woman shifted the infant on her hip and turned to stir something on the cook fire. Silent and tight-lipped, Evie started to go on, and Stroud motioned Belle to follow. But Belle's attention had been captured by Mrs. Sikes' hair. It was silky and corn-yellow, and though stringy, it was Mrs. Sikes' best feature. Belle put a hand to her own coarse hair and then touched Mrs. Sikes hair lightly. The woman screeched and turned on Belle, a heavy, long-handled spoon held threateningly.

"Put it down, Mrs. Sikes," said a voice behind Stroud. "She ain't aimin' to scalp ye." Stroud looked around to see Moses Hawley, a mountain man he had seen off and on for years and who wasn't considered very bright, though he was agreeable enough. The little man gave Stroud a snaggle-toothed grin. "Howdy, old hoss," he said. He touched his battered hat to Evie. "Miss Evie." He indicated Mrs. Sikes, who had lowered the spoon but still watched Belle suspiciously. "Mrs. Sikes here allows every female Injun wants to lift her hair just because a Pawnee squaw tried to cut off some for a keepsake."

"You the pilot for these movers?" Stroud asked.

"Takin' 'em clean to Oregon," said Moses.

Knowing Hawley, Stroud thought the movers would be lucky if Hawley didn't get them lost. "Where did you run into Pawnees?" Stroud asked.

"Near the forks, two, three weeks back," Hawley answered. "Startin' out on their summer hunt."

"That's where it used to end," said Stroud.

"Things have changed, boy, even in your time," Hawley

said. "The Pawnees were headed for the Republican. Talked like they might have to go as far up as the mouth of the Arickaree to find buffler."

"I've been trying to find out who your captain is," said Stroud. "I need some ball cartridges for my Colt."

"Palmer's his name," said Hawley. "But I can tell ye right now the only man in this train with a Colt's revolver is Parson Wirt." Hawley rolled his eyes heavenward and added in a pious voice, "Just a plain unlearnt preacher called to prepare a perverse generation for the comin' day of wrath."

Stroud laughed. "Where do I find him?"

"The Westerfields look after him. Their wagon is acrost there." Hawley indicated a wagon at the opposite side of the circle. "I'd find him for ye but I'm huntin' the captain. Got to interpret for him."

"Obliged," said Stroud. "I won't have any trouble." Stroud and the girls walked on through the camp. Most of the women were busy with preparations for feasting the Indians, though there was considerable indignation about it. Pots of coffee boiled over fires, and fresh-baked bread and cake cooled on tailgates. Out on the flats, a short distance beyond the circle of wagons, Stroud could see that the Indians were assembling. Some of the emigrant women were already carrying food out to the meeting place, where buffalo robes had been spread on the ground.

Stroud found Parson Wirt without trouble, but Wirt refused to sell or trade any of his cartridges, for the Lord had said to "come with your slaughter weapons in your hands." Recognizing the futility of opposing the Lord, Stroud gave up trying to get cartridges, and he and the girls walked on out to the feasting place.

The Indian chiefs—some from each village to a total of about forty—were being seated in a semicircle around the buffalo robes, and the emigrant men were forming another half-circle facing the Indians. Behind the chiefs was a row of young warriors, and behind them squaws and children. Unintentionally the emigrants were arranging themselves similarly, the women hovering behind their husbands and their many children crowded as close as possible.

Trappers from both forts mingled with Indians and emigrants. There was constant shifting and milling of the crowd around the fringes. On one side were Captain Eustis and a half-dozen dragoons. Stroud and the girls stopped at a point where the two half-circles joined. Stroud saw Moses Hawley and a genial, well-bred-appearing man, whom he judged to be Palmer, sitting in a place of prominence among the whites.

Bull Tail, looking impressive, stood up and began making a speech, with Moses Hawley interpreting. It was no doubt the same speech Bull Tail made to the first group of emigrants, Stroud decided, and it was probably the same one he'd make to the other three wagon trains yet to come through. Bull Tail talked about how his white brothers traveled through the Lakota's land, shooting the game and scaring it away. Then he requested food and presents to make up for this, assuring the whites of everlasting friendship and enlarging at length upon the request for presents.

As Stroud watched the circle of seated men, he found himself comparing the appearance of the Indians and emigrants. The Indians were attired in their ceremonial clothes of white deerskin embroidered with beads and dyed porcupine quills. Many of the chiefs wore trailing headdresses of eagle feathers, and all wore necklaces of elk and deer teeth and fish vertebrae, bracelets of burnished hoop-iron, and hair ornaments of coins and brass wire. In contrast were the drab clothes of the emigrants, made more drab by the stains and wear of travel. As Stroud went on to study

236

the faces of the two groups, he noticed a fierce pride in the faces of the Sioux, but except for Palmer and a few others, the movers had a down look. Stroud wondered if in some sort of groping way it was pride the movers hoped to find in Oregon.

Stroud felt a first glimmering of respect for them. By the time they'd inched their way across a continent and made a go of it in Oregon, they could look themselves in the eye all right, and any man, for that matter. Stroud was reminded of certain small animals that migrated in vast bodies —squirrels, or marmots maybe—overcoming with patient energy but great loss every obstacle which they blindly encountered, urged onward by some instinct. This blind migration of the movers—was it maybe a providential instinct? Was it the same that two hundred and fifty years before had caused thousands to brave the dangers of an ocean-crossing to gain a foothold on a hostile continent? Perhaps that was what Eustis and Pryce had thought—or even tried to say. That the approaching change out here wasn't the end of everything, but only the beginning of something else. If this was so, the Indians would get caught in it, of course. Sudden change always caught somebody, and that would be a pity. But when a country started changing, the best didn't always come out at first. He'd seen enough in Tennessee to know that a changing country was fertile soil for bringing out the shiftiness in people. The question was, how long would it take for the change to be a change for the best?

Some movement to Stroud's right claimed his attention. He noticed that where the ends of the two semicircles joined, Eahsapa sat across from the white man called Sikes. Two more likely disturbers of the peace couldn't possibly have been paired off. Stroud realized then that Evie and Belle, who had been standing at his right, were no longer there. He glanced over the rough circle of spectators and saw that they had moved about ten feet farther along, apparently finding a vantage place more to their liking.

Aware that Bull Tail was no longer speaking, Stroud glanced back at the circle of seated men. Palmer was just stepping to the center of the circle. The genial look Stroud had noted earlier had been replaced with one of patient sternness, giving him the appearance of a schoolmaster facing down troublesome children. Though a man of education, his speech turned out to be about as undiplomatic as Bull Tail's had been hypocritical. Palmer said that the emigrants felt friendly but were ready for enemies, and if molested, would punish the offenders. He refused Bull Tail's request for presents, though he claimed that the emigrants were glad to feast the Indians and talk with them. He concluded by saying brusquely, "We have nothing more than we need for ourselves. Eat the food we give you and be satisfied. We have nothing more to say."

As Palmer sat down, there was a murmur of disappointment and discontent from the Indian chiefs and considerable shifting about and muttered comments from the men who stood behind them. Several Indians, who had been appointed to serve their people, placed cups before the chiefs and handed one to each of the Indians who was standing. Many of the cups were of china. Having an insufficient number of tin cups, those of the emigrant women who had china cups had had to unpack them. Bread, cake and meat were distributed, and coffee poured. The feast proceeded in frigid formality. No one touched the food before him until all were served, when at a signal from Bull Tail the eating began.

Uneasy because of the tension in the air, Stroud looked again for Evie and Belle, but they had moved. His eyes searched the fringe of spectators and found Evie finally, standing slightly behind the line of squaws. Stroud had the strange feeling that she had chosen sides. Belle was nowhere to be seen. Keeping his eyes on Evie, Stroud started to make his way around the outside of the circle, but paused as Eahsapa's voice caught his attention. Eahsapa and the young chief next to him were having a fairly loud conversation, and whatever Eahsapa had said caused his companion to lean forward slightly and stare at the emigrant Sikes. Stroud moved closer to them.

"*Kanghi bloka.* A male crow," remarked Eahsapa, looking with contempt at Sikes.

"As though he were a beaver, he also has two yellow teeth," said the other.

"*Hou!*" agreed Eahsapa. "As though he were a male striped turtle, he also has two red eyes."

Stroud didn't like it. The usually playful comparisons had an ugly sound. Eahsapa and his companion continued to think of more witticisms inspired by Sikes' homeliness, such as his face being flat like a badger's, his nose being sharp like a beaver's claw, his feet being turned out like a mud hen's. The unwavering scrutiny of the pair was having its effect upon Sikes. He stared back at them. When his wife came bringing more coffee, Sikes glanced at her. "They're talkin' about me, sure as shootin'," he said.

Mrs. Sikes stooped and filled the Indians' cups. "Watch 'em, Mr. Sikes," she cautioned. "Those are my best cups."

She moved away, but she hadn't taken more than a half-dozen steps when Eahsapa got to his feet. "*Sehánle!* Enough of it! The white dogs tell us to be satisfied. . . ." He paused and then dashed his cup to the ground. Immediately other young warrior chiefs leaped to their feet. There was the tinkle of broken china.

Sikes jumped up toward Eahsapa. "You ugly nigger!" He hit Eahsapa in the face, knocking the Indian down. Instantly Eahsapa was on his feet, knife drawn. Stroud grabbed Eahsapa's arms from behind. Sikes didn't have to be restrained. He was backing away.

Captain Eustis and two of his dragoons pushed through the circle and faced the Indians. "Go home!" ordered Eustis. The Indians neither understood nor wanted to. A general uproar had developed, with excited talking and gesturing by Indians and whites alike.

Then Big Road stepped out and faced his people, holding up a hand. "*Yaglápi!* Go home!" he commanded. "The feast is over." There was a moment's indecision; then the Indians began to disperse. Palmer had moved up beside Eustis just as Stroud had let loose of Eahsapa. The Indian was quivering with a rage which embraced Stroud as well as Sikes.

"You better not have any stragglers," Stroud warned Palmer. He turned and went in search of Evie and Belle. He found Evie first. She was watching the Indians as they arrogantly left the circle. She appeared angry.

"Eahsapa was right," she said bluntly.

Stroud wasn't sure who was right and who was wrong. He only knew that red and white alike had better make the best of being thrown together. Because Sikes had struck him, now Eahsapa would have to lift hair to salve his pride and save face with his people.

Evie turned to walk away. "I'm going home."

"Wait until I find Belle."

"I don't want to wait," said Evie, turning back to face Stroud. "Can't she find her way to the fort?"

"I suppose she can, but there's no depending on it," said Stroud.

"Isn't that up to her?" asked Evie.

"She'll manage to get herself into some kind of mess," said Stroud.

Evie regarded him and then said slowly, "You made yourself responsible for her, George. It was right of you to bring her into the fort. But I don't understand what's in your mind now."

Stroud didn't quite understand it himself. It was one thing to get Belle out of the camp of drunken Indians, and it wasn't unreasonable to be slow to send her back to her people against her will, considering the way she seemed to feel about Eahsapa. But there was something more—something to do with Batchika in a way. It was a vague sort of feeling, mostly, that if he turned Belle loose to shift for herself without knowing things would be right for her, he would be failing Batchika a second time. If he had failed her, that is. Whatever it was, he couldn't explain it to Evie. "You're trying to make something out of nothing," he said, "because you're mad at the movers." Evie looked at him and then turned and started for Fort Laramie. Stroud watched her for a moment, wondering what had got into her anyhow.

He gave his attention then to locating Belle. With the shifting of the crowd it took longer than he had anticipated. He saw her finally. She was backed up against a wagon by Reeshar, and the sight of them gave him a start that drove his concern about Evie out of his mind. He'd spent considerable time satisfying himself that his men were loyal, but he had completely overlooked the fact that greedy Belle had known all along where the cache was buried. She had watched them build a fire over it and had camped with them beside it that night. Hobart's Emma and Madame Jack knew, too, of course. But Emma wouldn't tell any sooner than Hobart would, and with Mozay dead, Madame Jack would stick Reeshar with a knife if he came within reach of her. As Stroud neared Belle and Reeshar, he was gratified to see that Belle seemed angry. With her back against the

241

wagon, she had a cornered look. Reeshar stood facing her, one arm extended, his hand resting on the wagon. Before he reached them, Stroud saw Belle very deliberately spit in Reeshar's face. Reeshar grabbed Belle by the shoulder, but before he could slam her against the wagon, Stroud came up behind him and clamped his right arm around Reeshar's neck. Stroud felt his bicep knotting against Reeshar's throat. Reeshar flailed his arms and tried to gouge Stroud's face, but Stroud kept his head down. When he felt Reeshar begin to sag, he turned him loose. Reeshar dropped to his knees, but he got up almost at once and leaned against the wagon, looking at Stroud furiously and gulping air.

"He offered many horses and fine gifts, but I did not tell," said Belle, moving over beside Stroud.

Stroud had a feeling of vast relief. Belle was greedy, for a fact, but she seemed to have some sort of principles. "That is good," he said.

"Why the devil don't you go after your cache instead of hanging around here worrying about it?" asked Reeshar angrily. He straightened up, putting a hand to his throat. "You're wasting your time with these Indians anyway. There isn't a one of them can tell you a thing."

"Then why don't you tell me what band of Sioux took you in that winter after the blizzard?" asked Stroud.

The idea seemed to please Reeshar. After a moment he said, "Now is as good a time as any." His eyes lighted with malicious pleasure, and a silky tone came into his voice like the time he told the Crow horse thief to take a last look at the bright new day just before he shot him. "You'd never guess whose band of Sioux it was."

Stroud didn't like the look in Reeshar's eyes nor his tone of voice. Stroud was wondering what the joker was—why Reeshar was telling him anything. "How do I know you'll tell me the truth? Where was this band camped?"

"Crazy Woman's Fork," Reeshar said.

"You're lying. Nobody was camped on Crazy Woman's Fork," Stroud said. "I talked to a trapline rider who was through there just after the first thaw."

Reeshar shook his head. "The Indians broke camp early —before the first thaw—to go on their spring hunt."

Stroud conceded it was possible that Reeshar was telling the truth. That's about where he had expected that Reeshar —and the Indian woman and the trapper seen with him— would have found a band of Indians. "All right then, whose band was it?" Stroud asked warily.

The look of amusement on Reeshar's face deepened. "Paints-His-Face-Half-Red."

Stroud's first thought was that that was the connection he had been trying to make all morning concerning old Merk. Pryce had mentioned how Merk had wintered that time with Paints-His-Face and had wandered away just before the massacre. *The massacre.* "They were all killed," Stroud said blankly. "Even the women and children."

"Fortunate I left them a few days before it happened, wasn't it?"

Stroud looked at Reeshar in rage, feeling the fool for his painstaking search, knowing Reeshar had been quietly laughing at him the whole time.

"Damn your ugly soul!" he exploded. "I see plain enough now why you wouldn't tell me anything there when I was digging out my trade goods. You couldn't tell the truth, and a good lie would have spoiled your fun, wouldn't it? I might have believed you. It amused you to open up old wounds. You wanted to make me suspicious. What could you lose? The truth was washed away in the blood of a band of Indians slaughtered at the forks of the Platte."

Stroud paused, finding it all hard to believe, but knowing it was the truth. "It's an evil joke you've been enjoying,

Jesse," he continued. "But you've overlooked something—your guilt. Somehow I'll find out what it is you've done. There must be holes in your rotten past you didn't stop up tight enough. Like old Merk. He sheltered you during the blizzard and then took you to Paints-His-Face. You thought for seven years he was killed along with the whole band. But he had left them, too. Probably not long after you did. Gave you quite a turn, didn't it, coming on Merk there at the soda springs? Seeing you again, he might begin to remember, mightn't he? He wasn't so crazy people wouldn't listen. So you murdered him."

"You can't prove it," said Reeshar. "You can't prove a crazy accusation like that." He picked up his hat from the ground where it had fallen when Stroud choked him. "You're feeling pleased with yourself. You think you're getting somewhere with your nosing around." He paused and glanced down at the ground, chewing his lower lip reflectively. Then, looking up at Stroud, he said, "It's too bad you'll never be able to find out what you really want to know. Which squaw was with me that winter, George? Was it Batchika or Wicarpi who was killed by the Pawnees? And how did the other one die?"

Stroud leaped for Reeshar, but Reeshar took a long step backward, and at the same time Stroud was hit from behind with a glancing blow on the head that sent him sprawling in the dust. He looked around dazedly and up into the mean little eyes of Cebull, the sagging face of Old Man Rem, and the muzzles of two rifles. Stroud picked himself up, burning with humiliation and rage. "I'll choke the truth out of you yet," he said to Reeshar.

"Be sure you sneak up from behind," said Reeshar flatly, "or I'll kill you."

Stroud turned and started back across the area where the feast had been held. Some of the emigrant women were clearing away the utensils used for the feast. Others, along with their men and trappers from both forts, were milling around talking. Stroud had gone some distance before he stopped suddenly, remembering Belle. He found that she was hurrying along a short way behind him. He waited, reflecting bitterly that he had nothing else to do. Reeshar's trail had come suddenly to a dead end. Just as Belle caught up with him, Moses Hawley detached himself from a nearby group and joined them. Stroud was in no mood to talk, so he started on toward Fort Laramie, thinking it would discourage the old man, but Hawley fell in step beside him.

"Nearly had a ruckus on our hands," said Hawley cheerfully. "Those Sikes'll lose their scalps yet."

"The Pawnees should have saved somebody else the trouble," said Stroud.

"Missionaries have made them Pawnees soft-headed," said Hawley. He shook his head. "The Sikes are an even-yoked pair. Both natural-born troublemakers." Stroud made no effort to continue the conversation, and after a few more comments about the Sikes, Hawley remarked, "Funny thing about those Pawnees. Remember the time they caught Paints-His-Face at the forks?"

Stroud remembered very well, though it was strange that Hawley should mention it. "Why?"

"They didn't kill the squaws and children, like they said. Not near the lot of 'em anyhow."

Stroud stopped and turned on Hawley. "Do you know what you're talking about?" he asked incredulously.

"It's a fact," said Hawley. "Saw some of the Sioux squaws myself."

Stroud still didn't believe it. For seven years it had been general knowledge that nobody was spared in that raid. "If this is so, why hasn't it come out sooner?"

"They kept the captives hidden when anybody come around—until just lately," Hawley explained. "Besides, nobody around here hardly sees the Pawnees any more. They got nothin' much to trade. I tell you I saw 'em with my own eyes. Even talked to one of 'em—the daughter of Paints-His-Face."

"Then why would they boast they'd killed everybody?" persisted Stroud. "It wasn't to their credit."

"Neither was the truth. The Pawnees made a sacrifice out of one of them Sioux gals. Cut her in little pieces and put 'em in baskets and planted a piece of her with every seed when they put their crops in. That's *some* even for Injuns."

Stroud was convinced. It was a known fact that the Skidi Pawnees used to make human sacrifices, but they were supposed to have quit it a long time ago. It was entirely possible they had had a relapse. And they certainly wouldn't want it known. Ey God! Now he'd have to hunt up the Pawnees somewhere on the Republican. It'd take a week or maybe two. What would he tell Evie? Stroud started off at such a fast pace that it left Hawley staring after him, and Belle had to half run to keep up.

On the fringes of the crowd, Stroud came across Greenberry and Partout. For the first time since coming into the forts nearly a week ago, they were entirely sober, though it appeared that they didn't intend to stay that way any longer than they could help. They were bargaining with an emigrant for what Stroud judged to be the best axe of Partout's squaw and several pairs of her newly made moccasins. Stroud motioned Greenberry and Partout aside. "I'm going down around the Republican to locate the Skidi Pawnees," Stroud told them.

"*Sacré bleu!* You forget *le* cache?" asked Partout.

"It'll still be there when I get back," said Stroud shortly.

"It don't shine, George," said Greenberry.

"What in hell do you expect me to do about the cache—go sit on it?" said Stroud. "We can't bring it in yet, so there's no earthly reason why I can't be finding out some things I have to know. It's none of your damned business, but this child intends to get married just as soon as that cache is in. How do you think Evie'd feel if I married her and then it turned out that Batchika was alive and I hadn't even bothered to find out? Evie'd think I didn't consider marriage with an Indian binding. Being Indian enough herself, she'd wonder all her life if I mightn't just pull out and leave her, too. God knows, it's been done.

"And if that isn't reason enough to suit you, a trip to the Pawnees ought to settle Reeshar's hash once and for all. It'll be a better use of my time than wearing out my ass waiting for Pryce's men. That cache has stayed put without my doing anything about it for a week now, and it'll keep on staying put for another week or so providing you keep your eyes open and your mouths shut!" Stroud inclined his head toward Belle. "Keep her here at the fort. She knows about the cache, remember." With Belle in tow he headed again for the fort.

Partout looked after them with a puzzled frown. "This Batchika. What is she to do with the Pawnees?"

"Ye durn fool, why didn't ye ask?" said Greenberry.

On reaching the fort, Stroud left Belle in the courtyard and went on to his room, relieved that Evie was nowhere in sight. Time enough to talk to her when he was ready to leave. It would give her less chance to ask questions that might be hard to answer.

Stroud had gathered his gear, saddled up, and was talking to Pryce in the courtyard before he caught sight of Evie. She came out onto the gallery and Stroud watched as her glance went to his rifle and slowly moved to the other articles indicative of travel, including his horse which he held by the bridle.

"Reeshar'll do what I least expect," Pryce was saying. "He might try to get back at Hobart for telling the movers there was smallpox at Platte. I'd better see Hobart tomorrow."

"Eahsapa's scalp-hunting, remember," cautioned Stroud, his eyes still on Evie. "He'll take whatever he can get." Stroud walked to the foot of the stairs, leading his horse. "I have to go to the Pawnee hunting camp on the Republican," Stroud explained as Evie's eyes met his. "I think they know why it was Reeshar killed Merk."

The statement was only a half-truth, of course, and as Evie looked at him Stroud was afraid that it was the other half that was most noticeable. He had a feeling that, like any string of lies, his had worked fine right up to the last one, which hadn't worked at all.

"What if Belle's band leaves before you get back?"

"Keep Belle here, whether they do or not," said Stroud. "She knows where my furs are cached."

"Why didn't you say so in the first place?" asked Evie.

Stroud made one of the few completely honest statements he had made in several days. "Because I only just thought of it. When I went to get Belle, Reeshar was trying to force her to tell."

There was an awkward silence, which was broken by Pryce. "The wagons from down-river will be back before you are," he pointed out. "I'll have to hold them till you get here."

Stroud didn't need to be reminded that the wagons—and the men, too—would have to wait to help bring in his cache. Besides, Pryce wouldn't want to freight his spring shipment of furs up to the Missouri without including Stroud's. "I'll be back in ten days," he said. "They won't have to wait long."

He looked again at Evie. He didn't know what she was thinking. But whether she believed him or not, she'd just have to take the next ten days on faith, and Stroud only hoped there was enough of it to last. Maybe now was as good a time as any to find out.

Evie and her father watched Stroud as he rode across the courtyard and disappeared through the passageway.

"What's got into George?" said Pryce.

"I don't know. But I don't think he ever tried to buy horses—at least not very hard."

"Why do you say that?" Pryce asked.

"If he wanted horses bad enough he'd get his back from Eahsapa—even if he had to steal them back," Evie said.

Pryce was tight-lipped. "You're right. Then what in hell is he up to?"

"I'll not pry, Pa."

Something in Evie's tone of voice caused Pryce to turn and look at her. His expression softened. "Sometimes, daughter, I don't think you have any Welsh blood at all."

Thirteen

It was the morning after Stroud left that Pryce disappeared. Pryce had started early for the Army camp on business concerning the mules that were shod at the fort, and he had said he was going on from there down to Cedar Point to see Hobart. It was supposed that he would have cut across country from the Army camp and come into the Oregon Road far down. No one had felt alarmed when he failed to return to the fort that first night. Everyone assumed that he had probably stayed with Hobart—possibly even to wait for the next caravan himself. It was only after the caravan came in without him the following day that Evie became disturbed. It was raining hard when the caravan crept in. By the time general concern was felt, there had been so much travel on the Oregon Road that it was impossible to tell whether or not Pryce had reached it. Nor could they be sure he had even headed directly for Cedar Point on leaving the Army camp.

Many of the trappers felt that Pryce's disappearance was Reeshar's doing, or some of his crew at Platte. Others were inclined to the theory that Eahsapa was responsible, or some other Indian who had been provoked by being refused liquor. But there was nothing, really, to support any of these suspicions. True, Reeshar had gone down to see Hobart that same morning. He had been seen at Cedar Point by Captain Eustis as he went by with the patrol. Reeshar had come back up the trail not long after Captain Eustis. But according to Hobart, Pryce had not come down to Cedar Point at all. Evie had gone over the facts many times in her mind those first days as she rode with the men in search of her father.

a sudden desire to leave, and he stood up. "We'll go after the cache about the end of next week."

"You drink, *non?*" Partout asked.

"No," Stroud said. He mounted and rode off, heading for Fort Laramie. As he moved through the Indian villages covering the broad plain between the forts, he noted that many of the Indians were already dressed in their ceremonials for the approaching conference. In the camp nearest the fort, his attention was caught by a familiar voice coming loud and clear from a tipi. Stroud recognized both the voice and the tipi as belonging to Big Road, Evie's grandfather. Stroud stopped to listen. He decided that Big Road was rehearsing his speech for the conference.

It was a good speech, though Stroud wasn't at all sure it was exactly what Kearny wanted to hear—warnings, principally, against accepting the white man's gifts lest in the end they become poor as snakes. Stroud decided to stop and see the old chief. Certainly he owed Evie's grandfather a courtesy call. With the cessation of sound, Stroud dismounted and entered the tipi. Big Road was a stern old patriarch, with iron-gray hair and seamed face and a lean, firm look even in old age. He too was already dressed in his finery for the conference. His clothes of soft elkskin were embroidered in multicolored porcupine quills and fringed from the neck to the ends of the sleeves and down the sides of his leggings with scalp locks. His hair was lifted up and crossed over the top of his head and tied in a large, loose knot with the ends falling free halfway to his shoulders, giving somewhat the effect of a Turkish turban.

After the formalities were dispensed with and there had been a friendly exchange of gossip and good wishes, Big Road said he'd heard about the loss of Stroud's horses and mules, and his expression softened with an understanding benignity. A young man courting should most certainly have many horses if he hoped to succeed. "A good wife is worth many horses to a man," he advised, "for she will multiply his years for him." Stroud smiled at this, and explained that he was courting in the way of the white man, which did not require horses.

Stroud wanted to ask Big Road if he had ever heard of a Crow woman having been taken in by the Sioux during the winter of the blizzards and the smallpox. But the possibility that Big Road might mention it to Evie decided Stroud against it. He did ask if Big Road knew where he might find Istamaza's band. But Big Road didn't know. They talked for a while longer, then Big Road's young squaw came to the lodge door and said that it was time to go to the council called by the white soldier-chief.

Stroud and Big Road walked together through the crowds to the conference site, Stroud leading his horse, and Big Road's two squaws following behind the old chief. Quite an assemblage of Indians was gathering in the angle between the two rivers. Upward of fifteen hundred, Stroud guessed. Some of the young bucks were mounted on their tough little ponies, but almost everyone milled around on foot. Stroud noticed that a screen of buffalo robes, apparently for a windbreak, had been erected. It was stretched between lodgepoles set in the ground, with an American flag raised at each end. The place selected was only about a quarter of a mile below Fort Platte, just downstream and between the Oregon Road and the Platte River. The crowd extended clear back across the road. Stroud thought he recognized some of the white men around the windbreak as Platte *engagés*. Presently they were close enough to the windbreak to see that scores of buffalo robes had been spread on the ground in a great half-circle facing the windbreak. Some of the chiefs in their ceremonials were already seated cross-legged on the robes. Big Road left Stroud and went to sit among the chiefs.

Stroud went up to Fort Laramie then for Evie. She and Belle were ready, waiting on the gallery that ran along the second story outside Evie's room. As Stroud rode in, the Navajo man was bringing their horses from the corral. Stroud walked his horse across the courtyard, looking up at Evie, noting how tall and slim she seemed and yet strong, too, like a tough willow branch. St. Louis hadn't changed her much. She was more grown up of course, more certain of herself, but certainly still as much Indian as white. She was wearing a deerskin dress and her hair hung loose, falling in glossy waves to the small of her back. Except for her lighter skin and blue eyes she looked as Indian as Belle.

Both girls were in a festive mood, which Stroud didn't find surprising since it was the first time any part of the U. S. Army had come to Laramie Fork—the first meeting of the Army and the Teton Sioux. Evie was pleased, too, because her father had been requested by Colonel Kearny to serve as interpreter for the conference. Stroud thought Kearny showed good judgment. No white man spoke Lakota better than Pryce, or better understood the Indian nature. A poor interpreter, or one with a grudge, could cause a sight of mischief.

When they reached the conference site, everybody seemed ready for the council except that Kearny and his staff hadn't yet arrived. The whole arrangement resembled an amphitheater. The screen of buffalo robes was like a backdrop, with benches and seats arranged in front of it and the Indians facing it in a huge semicircular mass; the elder chiefs, including Big Road and Bull Tail, sitting cross-legged on robes, then the lesser chiefs behind them. Among the lesser chiefs of Big Road's band, Stroud noticed the young warrior-chief Red Cloud, sitting quiet and tall in his feathered bonnet. Behind the lesser chiefs were warriors of all ages, and back of them women and children. Behind this massed group many young warriors had remained mounted. Stroud and the girls stayed on their horses, too, choosing a vantage point at the end of the semicircle to the north nearest Fort Platte.

Shortly Kearny and his staff of five officers and an escort arrived, accompanied by several pack mules loaded with presents. Pryce and Reeshar were both along—Kearny was playing no favorites between the forts—as well as Jim Fitzpatrick, the guide, gray and granite-faced and looking older than his years. Riding up near the windbreak, Kearny and his staff dismounted and went to the chairs and benches provided for them, while the mules were unpacked and the presents opened and piled up where the Indians could see them. Then the older chiefs got up and filed by, the colonel shaking hands with each as he was introduced by Pryce. As the chiefs went back to their places, Kearny remained standing and began addressing the chiefs, speaking slowly and pausing for Pryce to translate.

"Sioux, I am glad to meet you. Through your chiefs I have shaken hands with all of you. Your great father has learned much of his red children, and he has sent me with a handful of braves to visit you. I am going to the waters which flow toward the setting sun. I shall return to this place, and then I shall march to the Arkansas, and from there home. I am opening a road for your white brethren. They are now following after me, and are journeying to the other side of the great mountains. They take with them their women, their children and their cattle. They all go to bury their bones there, and never to return. You must not disturb them in their persons, or molest their property; neither must you on any account obstruct the road which I have now opened for them. Should you do so, your great father would be angry with you and cause you to be punished.

"Your great father has warriors as numerous as the sands upon the shore of your river. As we have come to you without difficulty, so could they. But although he is the enemy of all bad Indians, he is the friend of those who are good.

"I am sorry to hear that some of your war parties have killed white men, but we will bury the past. We cannot call to life those who have suffered. In future you must not trouble your white brethren, even though you meet them in an enemy's country. To the Indians with whom you are at war, and whom I may meet, I shall say the same.

"You have many enemies about you, but firewater is the greatest of them all. It is contrary to the wishes of your great father that it should be brought here; and I advise you, whenever you find it in your country—no matter in whose possession—to spill it all upon the ground. The earth may drink it without injury, but you cannot."

Stroud felt a little embarrassed for Kearny at the remark about spilling the whiskey, and there was some laughter among the younger Indians. Kearny either didn't hear the laughter or ignored it. "I wish you to remember particularly," he continued, "what I have said to you—that all of you who have heard me may tell those who are not present.

"Your great father is the friend of his red children, and will continue to be so, as long as they behave themselves properly. He did not direct me to come among you to bring you presents, but he has sent you a few things to help you remember what I have said."

The great crowd had remained quiet during Kearny's speech. Now there was a rumble of talk. Stroud's glance moved over the throng of Indians and back to Kearny, the scene affecting him despite his earlier indifference. There was an elemental wildness in the air. The wind, honed sharp and clean on distant mountains, fluttered the feathers of the Indians like hundreds of small pennants and whipped the manes and tails of their spotted ponies; the sky, turbulent and ominous, darkened the vast, rolling prairie and threatened the handful of people upon it. The uniformed men grouped in front of the backdrop seemed alien and insignificant, yet one of them in a precise and patronizing speech had warned the Indians against trying to protect what they considered their lands. Stroud looked back at the Indians and wondered how it could ever be explained to them that their hunting grounds had been sold to the great white father some forty-odd years before by a little man named Napoleon.

Gradually the Indians quieted and Big Road stood up and faced Kearny. "My father," Big Road said. "Many bands of Lakota are in the country round about us. We here are only a few drops of rain from the nearest cloud. I have come to this place to hear what you have to say. You have made me remember old times. As a young man I went with my own father to visit the great red-headed chief, the man you called Clark. He spoke as you do—that white and Indian must live in peace. But he also said that the Indian must not live off the white man, like magpies cleaning up after the wolves; that the Indian must not learn the white man's vices but remain true to the old-time ways." Big Road pointed to the piles of presents. "I will not insult you by refusing your presents today. But I say this to my people." Here Big Road half turned so he could also address the Indians. "Beware how you accept the gifts of the white man, lest in the end you become poor as snakes crawling upon your bellies in the dust and flicking at flies with your forked tongues." As Big Road sat down there were muttered comments among the Indians, whether of approval, disapproval or both, it was impossible for Stroud to tell.

Bull Tail, the Brûlé chief whom Kearny had first met down the Oregon Road, stood up almost immediately and Kearny nodded to him to proceed. It seemed to Stroud that Kearny's rather set expression relaxed a little. "My father," Bull Tail said, "what you have told my people is right, and it pleases me. I know now if they are good to their white brothers, they will be well treated in return; and we will find that such presents as those they are about to receive will often come." He eyed the presents—big stacks of blankets and cloth and piles of mirrors, tobacco, sacked beads, knives. "You say that you open the road for our white brothers and that they come in peace. We know they bring no gifts as you have done now. It would warm the hearts of my people to be feasted by those who use the road and wish to show their friendship. My people will long remember the words you have this day spoken to them; and as you have said, so always shall they do."

Stroud felt sorry for Bull Tail. All his brave talk and righteous indignation of yesterday was gone up in smoke after a good look at the presents. Stroud felt sorrier for those Sioux who would be counseled by such as Bull Tail. They'd be their own worst enemy. He even felt a little sorry for the emigrants. Bull Tail had sneaked in a joker, and if he made it stick, the emigrants, with their limited supplies, weren't going to take kindly to having to feast the Indians every time a wagon train stopped at the forts.

Bull Tail's last words were barely translated into English by Pryce when Stroud heard a deep, muffled rumbling. Others heard it, too, for heads began to turn; first the mounted braves at the outside of the semicircle and then others, clear up to the older chiefs. Some said it sounded like buffalo running, but there had been no buffalo within fifty miles of the forts all spring. Then riding into view to the west just beyond Fort Laramie came mounted dragoons, four abreast, stretching out into a long column, their sabers rattling against spurs and stirrups. The blue uniforms looked dark in the late, sunless afternoon, and Stroud counted five wind-whipped guidons—five squadrons strung out in column of four's, first a black-horse troop, then a gray-horse troop, followed by a squadron of bays, another of chestnuts, and finally blacks again. At the end were two mules, each packing a mountain howitzer and led by a mounted trooper.

When the first squadron was about halfway between the two forts, it formed in line to the front and came to a halt. Each squadron executed the same maneuver, every file except the first in each platoon obliquing to the left and forming into double ranks, until the entire regiment was formed in column of squadrons. It was a nice maneuver, and as the regiment sat at attention a few hundred yards away, each of the two hundred and fifty troopers and officers motionless in his saddle and controlling his mount, Stroud had to admit it was impressive—a considerable contrast to the muddy chaos of the day before. Stroud heard the commanding officer—it looked like Captain Eustis who was taking Kearny's place at the head of the regiment—give two orders. At the second order, there was a massive clatter as sabers were drawn. The next command, repeated all along the ranks, set the regiment in motion at a trot. For about a hundred yards the regiment moved at a trot. Then Stroud saw Eustis turn his head and heard his high-pitched cry of "sound charge!" The bugles blared their brassy command, sabers were lifted as if to strike, and with fierce cries coming from fifty throats, the double-ranked squadron broke into a gallop, charging an imaginary line about a hundred yards short of where the Indians were assembled, and then veering sharply to its left. Squadron after squadron charged the imaginary line, each unintentionally coming a little closer to the Indians before veering off. At the first charge, the Indians stirred uneasily. At the second and third charges they began to be rolled back as if by a wind, the young men on their ponies retreating clear to the Laramie.

"It's cruel!" Evie said. Stroud agreed it was cruel, though he doubted that Kearny had intended it to be. The council had all but been disrupted.

While the regiment had been executing its charge and re-forming again to the rear, the howitzers had been assembled—little brass cannon weighing about two hundred and fifty pounds and firing twelve-pound shot. Stroud noted that they were the same kind that were installed in the blockhouses at the two forts, a popular type of gun in the mountain country with both the military and the fur companies, because it could be easily transported and assembled. Now the howitzers were rolled out between the regiment and the Indians and aimed across the Laramie to the south. The gun crews began firing alternately, lobbing shells in plain view of the Indians and at a safe distance, though with startling effect. They were firing explosive shells—"hollow shot" the Army called them—filled with powder and rifle balls. Some of the Indians had seen solid shot fired from the cannon at the forts, but this was their first experience with explosive shells. On some the fuses were cut short so they would explode in the air, while some—percussion shells—exploded on hitting the ground, the whole display breeding a tremendous scare among the Indians. The flash of the explosion was visible in the twilight, followed by the *boom—SSSS—BOOM* of gun and shell, clouds of powder smoke, showers of muddy earth thrown up.

It took a long time for the Indians to quiet down, their excitement continuing throughout most of the handing out of gifts. Because there were so many Indians, the presents were distributed through the chief of each clan. There was no doubt in Stroud's mind that the conference was a success from Kearny's point of view. The Indians had been impressed all right. But Stroud still felt that Kearny had made a mistake to take no notice of Bull Tail's demand that the emigrants feast the Indians. Maybe it didn't sound like much, but it was a fool sort of thing that could cause trouble.

At Evie's suggestion, Stroud and the two girls decided to go and look at the shell fragments. As they moved around the edge of the crowd, Stroud noticed for the first time a half-dozen freight wagons lined up outside Fort Platte. Reeshar had let Pryce test the navigability of the river at this season. Having found out it was too low, Reeshar was now ready to freight his furs—as Pryce would have to do with his when he got them back from downstream—over the traders' road along the course of the White and Teton Rivers three hundred miles to the Missouri. The wagons were already loaded with bales of buffalo robes and furs—old Merk's among them, Stroud reflected. Stroud noticed the two Mexican horse herders for Fort Platte walking toward the main gate of the fort. They were muddy and wet and tired-looking, as if they'd just come in from a long walk they wished they hadn't taken. Stroud wondered where they could have been on foot for any distance.

Stroud, Evie and Belle rode on around the crowd and down to the banks of the Laramie. Ahead of them they could see Indians in steady numbers crossing the icy stream to examine the ground where it had been torn up by the exploding shells and to pick up the still-warm fragments.

Close by, a group of a dozen or so small Indian boys played a war game on the banks of the river. Stroud noticed that they had altered their usual game of playing at war with enemy Indians. Now, though divided into two groups, only the one that was charging up the river bank was armed with the customary diminutive bows and arrows, while the other group, farther up the incline and hidden behind some brush, was armed with sticks. These boys, poised as if mounted, suddenly galloped down upon the others, pointing the sticks, shouting "Bang," and scattering the attackers, who retreated down the bank to the edge of the river. The outraged yells of the vanquished were quieted by a pleasant laugh. A young warrior on a wet pony, apparently having just returned from examining the shell fragments, had reined in and was watching the mock battle. Stroud recognized the young warrior as the visitor to the Oyukhpes, the one called Sitting Bull. He was hardly more than a boy himself. He chided the children with the bows. "You deserved to lose. You will never beat the blue-coat soldiers if you let them have the top of the bank. Next time circle behind them and make them fight uphill."

"That is what I told them but they did not hear," said a boy younger than the rest—perhaps no more than five. He had hair that curled and skin light for an Indian. He had not participated in the fight, but stood watching the others. Stroud had noticed the child earlier in the day around the village of one of the Oglala bands.

"Ho! You do not fight, but you tell the others what to do?" said Sitting Bull.

"My bow is in my lodge," said the child. "And I will not carry a stick and be a blue-coat soldier. I will only fight against them."

"And who are you to be so little and talk so big?" asked Sitting Bull. He smiled at the little boy.

"I am called Curly. Though when I become a warrior-leader I hope to be called like my father—the holy man—Crazy Horse."

"Then learn to make yourself heard." The young warrior rode off laughing, and after a moment Stroud heard him start singing a gay song as he headed toward the festivities.

"Little Curly is the nephew of Spotted Tail," remarked Evie in an absent sort of way. They had reined in at the top of the bank to watch the children. After a moment Evie said, "I don't like their game. And I've changed my mind about seeing the shell fragments. Let's go home."

She repeated to Belle in Lakota the part about going home. But Belle didn't want to go back to the fort. She had heard that there was to be dancing after the giving of presents and she wanted to stay. Evie and Stroud agreed that Belle shouldn't stay by herself, and they returned in the general direction from which they had come, trying to locate someone to leave her with.

The decision was made for them by the appearance of Wyatt, in company with Pryce. Wyatt was only too glad to take Belle off their hands. They all moved on together for a short distance. Wyatt said, "I was just telling Mr. Pryce. Some Indians ran off the Fort Platte horses this morning. Set the herders afoot. Cebull just rode out from the fort to tell Reeshar."

"I saw the herders walking in a while ago," said Stroud.

Wyatt looked from Stroud to Pryce with a grin. "I don't suppose either of you knows anything about it."

"I don't," said Stroud, "but I'll probably get the credit."

Pryce shook his head. "Army's making these Indians restless. Makes you wonder what they'll do next." The talk of horses seemed to remind him of Stroud's shortage. "Are you still trying to get horses from the Indians?" he asked Stroud.

She sat now on a chair in her room. The room was much the same as when Stroud had seen it, the only additions being mattress and bedding, and a mirror above the chest. She had a rounded deerskin container open on her lap, sorting through the contents. The receptacle, made gay with blue porcupine-quill embroidery and tassels of dyed horsehair and conical tin ornaments, was about eighteen inches long and fifteen deep—what the trappers would term a possible sack.

Evie was very deliberate in her examination of the contents. She picked out first the many small sacks and cases inside, opening each, and after checking their contents replaced them at one end of the larger container. There was no question about the sack of medicine, or the bag of ornamented plum stones and other objects used for games, or the tough little case containing dyed quills and an awl. A sack of beads and another of sewing articles were returned, as was the one containing hair ornaments—including strips of fur, some of beaded deerskin, and an assortment of ribbons.

The next small case held a plush purse. Evie looked at it a moment and then dropped it on the floor at her side. It was followed by several pairs of cotton stockings, a pair of kid gloves, and a lace handkerchief. Evie bent down and retrieved the handkerchief. It was a pretty thing and perhaps it could be cut up and used for something. Even Belle had a cap edged in gold lace. While Evie hesitated, she glanced out the window toward the west gate, then took a longer look down the Oregon Road through a window across the room. She had placed her chair carefully to make this possible, commanding a view in both directions.

Belle, who sat cross-legged on the floor with her back to the west window, had paused in her work when Evie began discarding the various articles. Belle was working on

Wyatt's shirt, seaming it across the shoulders and down the upper side of the sleeves, sewing with a small sharpened bone and fine sinew. Belle had tanned the skin herself. The trappers' wives had helped with the softening and ornamentation to make the work go faster, though the ornamentation was simple because of lack of time. She watched as Evie picked up a spyglass for a better look down the Oregon Road. "*Toke!* So! It is Five Scalps you watch for now," said Belle.

Evie made no reply, though Belle was right. With her father gone, the fort was no better than a prison and she wanted to be with her mother's people. There would be solace there. Here there was only senseless confusion. She put the spyglass down and glanced again over the courtyard. The last of the emigrant caravans had made camp the day before, and now there was a steady flow of people coming to trade. Then, too, the Company wagons had returned from down-river nearly a week ago, and a number of trappers—nearly twenty now—were at the fort.

They had been sobered at first, and diligent in helping to comb the countryside for any trace of their *bourgeois*, Pryce. But with hope gone and no search to occupy them, they were getting restless and quarrelsome, chafing at being held at the fort to wait for Stroud's furs. They were anxious to start the long haul to the Missouri, for some of them planned to go on to St. Louis. The emigrants would leave tomorrow, Evie knew, and most of the Indians, too. There would be no more caravans this year—no more Yellow-Eyes.

"Will you leave tomorrow whether Five Scalps returns or not?" Belle asked.

"I—I do not know." Evie wished that Grandfather Big Road's people were not striking their lodges. It would be so much simpler if they just stayed in their camp between the forts. But her grandfather had said he could wait no longer for her wedding. His people were restless and needed to go. It made Evie wonder just a little if Big Road thought that George was not coming back.

"What would you do if I left?" Evie asked Belle.

"Five Scalps said I was to wait here."

Evie made no reply. She wished that Belle could stay with her sister, but she supposed Belle had better stay at the fort until the cache was in. Evie looked down and found that she still held the lace handkerchief. Unable to make up her mind, she tucked it under the deerskin container and commenced again with the sorting. She kept her porcupine-quill comb with the beaded strip at the top, but she put several tucking combs in the growing pile on the floor. The tucking combs looked too much like St. Louis. Evie's thoughts were interrupted again by Belle.

"Five Scalps asked that you wait, too?"

Evie looked at Belle in astonishment, but Belle had her eyes on her work. "He would expect to find me here," said Evie. "He could not know how things would be."

"It is sad about your father. My heart is on the ground," said Belle, adding after a moment, "Eahsapa is bad, but I do not think he brought harm to your father."

"It was not Eahsapa." Evie thought that Belle was right; besides, Eahsapa still sulked and watched the emigrants. She had seen him from the window only yesterday, following the caravan at a little distance. Evie almost felt sorry for Eahsapa. Captain Eustis had gone out with all the patrols himself and had done such a thorough job of alarming the movers that it made Eahsapa look quite ridiculous. In his own camp he must be the butt of many jokes.

"I think it was the Yellow-Haired-One," said Belle, referring to Reeshar. "There is blood on the ground between him and Five Scalps."

Evie looked up from her sorting. "Do you know why?"

"No. It started before they came to our village to trade. Though it may have worsened there."

Evie hesitated to accuse Reeshar. There had been no bad trouble with Reeshar—no worse than with others in the fur trade at various times. Whether or not he had killed old Merk, he would have no reason to harm her father. Whatever had happened was caused somehow by the caravans and the soldiers. Since they had come, everything was changed. Hearing the talk in St. Louis, it sounded as though the movers were doing a fine thing. But she hadn't foreseen stolen shoes and broken teacups, Evie reflected bitterly. And that wouldn't be the last of it. Unlike Belle, she knew of the vast numbers of white men who lived beyond the Father of Waters. There would be no end to their coming and no end to the trouble. Her father had tried to make her see it. She wished George would come back. He would know what to do. She glanced out the window again to the east. Ten days he said he would be gone. He should have been back before now. It was ten days ago yesterday that he had left.

Belle was watching Evie again. "I could tell Five Scalps where you had gone," she offered.

"He would know where to find me."

"Then why do you wait? Do you fear he will not search for you?"

Evie felt surprised and bewildered, and then angry. Such a thought had not entered her mind. It had been understood between Evie and Stroud for some time that they would marry when she came back from St. Louis.

Evie thought of the first time she saw George, the time he came to Big Road's village five years ago. She had been racing some of her playmates to the river and had almost collided with George as he rounded a bend in the trail. He had reined in and she had stopped short, and though she was half-girl, half-woman at the time—scarcely thirteen—her heart had skipped a beat when she looked up at this stranger with the piercing eyes of the eagle. Something of her feelings must have showed in her eyes, for George had looked into them long and deep, his glance seeming to run clear through to her moccasins, with a special turn around her heart. Then he had leaned down and tweaked one of her braids playfully. "You are much too young, pretty one," he had said in English. "Go play your own games." He had ridden on into the village then to see her grandfather about trading and did not know until later that she understood what he said. He hadn't known either that because of his daughter, Big Road traded only at Fort Laramie. Evie had seen George next at the fort the following spring when he brought his furs and traded for supplies. He had come to the fort often after that, and it was almost as if he had waited for her to grow up.

"He has been slow to take you for a wife," Belle continued.

"My father's people do not do things the Indian way." Evie was beginning to feel defensive. She looked at Belle uneasily, but the expression on the younger girl's face betrayed nothing. She was sewing again on Wyatt's shirt, making neat, even stitches in the fine white skin.

"Five Scalps knows the Indian way. That is how he got me," said Belle.

"It was not a trade. You said so yourself."

"I do not speak of that."

"What, then?"

"It is since my village came. The day after we returned from finding the Iron-Eyed-One. Five Scalps offered Eahsapa the filled pipe."

"*Ma k'eya!* Nonsense!"

"Ask in my village. Everyone knows."

Evie hesitated, angry and confused. Belle was a flirt, but Evie hadn't thought her dishonest. "You must be mistaken. If Eahsapa asked to be sent the filled pipe, George refused. He has talked many times about returning you to your band."

"At first," Belle pointed out. "But not since that day."

Evie knew without really thinking about it that this was true. Even when they had ridden in with the patrol and had seen that Belle's band was in, George had avoided a direct answer when she suggested that Belle could stay with her sister. And now he said that she must stay at the fort because of the cache, but he admitted he had just thought of that the day he was leaving.

"Ask in the village, if you think I do not speak truly," Belle repeated.

Evie got to her feet, pushing the deerskin container onto the chair. The lace handkerchief fell to the floor and she kicked it into the pile of discarded articles. She wouldn't ask. She couldn't. And she suspected that Belle knew this. She moved swiftly toward the door, wanting to get away from Belle's questions, from her own growing suspicions. Maybe she had been blind. Maybe . . .

"You will take the blue dress when you go?" Belle was looking at Evie's dresses, which still hung on the wall.

Evie had reached the door, but she turned back to look at Belle. Evie had planned to give her the dresses if she wanted them. But not now. "It would be too long for you," Evie replied. "And I have not said yet that I am going." She stepped through the door and ran down the steps and across the courtyard, wondering if Belle were telling the truth.

She went into the trading store. If she was going anywhere, there might be something she would need. It was foolish to believe Belle, she told herself. George wouldn't do anything like that. She had loved him a long time and she ought to know.

Hiram was waiting on two emigrant girls and she browsed around until they left, aware of men's loud voices in the next room, where some trappers were drinking.

"Find what you want, Evie?" asked Hiram.

"I don't know that I want anything," she replied and went out into the courtyard, the echo of Belle's words beating at her. She went on up the stairs leading to her quarters. At the top of the stairs she hesitated, indecisive, not wanting to go back to her room and Belle, yet not knowing what else to do. On impulse, Evie turned to her right along the short catwalk that led to the roof of the rooms against the south wall. She went across the gravelly roof to the wall looking down into the corral and beyond it to the Laramie River. Even at that distance she could still hear the voices of the men in the trading store. In a moment she heard hoofbeats. Riding along beside the river behind the fort were Captain Eustis and several dragoons. Apparently they were on their way from the ford to their camp upstream. Riding in their midst, his hands tied in front of him and his shaggy beard sunk on his chest, was Hobart. She saw him rouse himself and yell something, the sound of which came to her faintly, and then he subsided again. He appeared quite drunk. The river made a sweeping curve around the fort at the corner where Evie watched, and as the dragoons followed along the stream and came nearer, Evie called down to Eustis, "What's Hobart done?"

Eustis looked up and touched his cap before calling back, "He's a deserter, Miss Pryce! He's been hiding out as a trapper all this time, but we finally got him."

The sound of Eustis' voice roused Hobart from his sullen stupor again. He didn't even see Evie on the wall. He was too drunk for that. "You're goddamned right I am!" His voice was hoarse, as if he had done a lot of yelling on the way up the trail. He stood up in the stirrups, wobbling dangerously. "Did you catch the others, Old Useless? How many? Fifty—a hundred? There was plenty, wasn't there, Useless?" Hobart was jolted back into the saddle and silence.

Shocked, Evie watched as they went on upstream. The rhythm of galloping hoofbeats caused her to look down again. To her surprise Reeshar was riding fast after the dragoons, his eyes on Hobart and his captors. Her concern for Hobart outweighing her dislike of Reeshar, Evie called down to him.

"What will they do to Hobart?"

Reeshar reined in. "That's what I want to find out." He looked impatiently after the men. His horse pawed nervously.

Through her own worries and her shock at Hobart's arrest, Evie had the feeling that Reeshar's unexpected interest in Hobart was in some way suspicious. "You scarcely know him," she pointed out.

Reeshar gave his full attention to Evie, smiling up at her. "I can't think he really matters much to you."

"He does to George," Evie said bluntly.

Reeshar gave Evie an appraising look. "George is a fool. He spends his time hunting for a squaw he should have forgotten years ago, when he might be with you." He watched his words take effect before he rode on.

It was a deliberately cruel thing Reeshar had said, Evie knew. But was it possible there was some truth in it? She hadn't quite believed that George had gone to see the Pawnees about old Merk. She didn't know what to think. She turned and walked slowly around the walls to the front steps, knowing she'd better tell the men about Hobart's arrest. At the foot of the steps she could hear that the men in the store were having an argument. More than that, it was an argument about Reeshar and George. The door was open, and she could not avoid overhearing.

"If you heard a pack train come in to Fort Platte last night, why are you so sure it had George's cache?" It was Bostwick's voice.

"Because there ain't no reason for Reeshar to sneak a pack train through less'n he's up to no good. And he was sneaking hard. The hoofs of them pack animals was muffled. If I hadn't been awake and fairly close I wouldn't heard nothin', old hoss." Evie recognized Jake's voice.

"Just where were you?" asked Bostwick.

"Far side of Bull Tail's camp," said Jake. "I tried to see, but it was dark as the inside of a buffalo bull. Dark and still. Comin' from a tipi where there was a fire goin', I couldn't even see Platte. But from the sound, it was a big train."

"That doesn't mean it was George's cache," said Bostwick.

"What is there now to be packed on mules?" It was Belco getting into the discussion. "George's cache, that's all. Reeshar's tradin' is done. His spring shipment of furs was hauled out more'n a week ago. No siree. Reeshar's dug up Stroud's cache, and you can tan my hide for saddle skirts if Stroud's furs ain't stashed away in Fort Platte right this minute."

There was a silence. "Seems to me if any big string of pack animals went out from Platte lately, some of us would have known about it," Bostwick said cautiously.

"Come now, Amer," Evie heard Billy Pitcher say. "Last week we were all looking for Mr. Pryce—mostly down toward Cedar Point. Reeshar could have torn down Platte and we wouldn't have noticed. When did anybody see

Reeshar last, anyhow?" After some discussion it turned out that no one had seen Reeshar since the day after Pryce disappeared.

Evie tried to remember when she saw Reeshar last, and decided, too, that it was the day after her father disappeared. Captain Eustis had questioned him about his visit to Hobart, trying to find out if he had seen her father down toward Cedar Point. Reeshar had answered the questions readily enough. He admitted he had been down trying to bribe Hobart into sending the next emigrant train to Fort Platte, but he hadn't seen anybody but the patrol.

"Maybe you're right." It was Bostwick speaking again. "But anyway it's no concern of mine. George is a free trader, remember. Tell Hobart or Greenberry. They're the ones that ought to know about it."

"Ain't seed Greenberry since day before yesterday," said Belco. "I won his traps on a race, and half a hour later he'd put his saddle up in a poker game."

"That's three times I know of. He'll lose that saddle yet," said Jake.

In her concern over Stroud's cache, Evie had temporarily forgotten her own troubles and Hobart's arrest. She thought Jake and Belco were right. There was no other explanation for Reeshar bringing in a pack train in the night. But how did Reeshar find out where George's furs were cached? After a moment Evie became aware of Bostwick's voice again.

". . . there's a woman mixed up in it, all right," Bostwick was saying.

"Ain't none of our business," said Belco.

"I've made it my business," Bostwick continued. "George's been asking around the camps, ever since he came in, about a Crow squaw. He thinks she was brought into some Sioux village the winter after the smallpox."

"It still don't make sense, him going off after Pawnees," said Belco.

Evie felt both hot and cold all over—seared with hurt and shame and chilled with shock. She couldn't really believe it when Reeshar had told her. But he was right. She couldn't see what connection there was between a Crow woman and the Pawnees, but it made more sense than George's saying he was going because of Merk. It seemed that everybody knew about the Crow woman but her. Why hadn't George told her? Why was he looking for a Crow woman now?

Evie glanced around. She didn't want anybody to see her —not looking like a lost calf. She moved out to the courtyard, remembering her talk with George on the wall the day before he left. How he hadn't said much except that he'd take her and Belle to the emigrant camp. Even at the time it hurt. And the way he'd let her come back to the fort alone, after the feasting, while he looked for Belle. Earlier, when they had gone to see Istamaza, George had asked Belle to braid his hair. Possibly Belle was telling the truth. Perhaps her being so quick to speak out against St. Louis had turned him away.

Greenberry, cold sober, came running through the entrance passage. He was in a highly agitated state. He hesitated, glancing toward the corral and then toward the door of the store. Seeing Evie, he said, "Did you hear about Hobart? He's a deserter! Hobart's a deserter from the Army!"

Though Evie heard what Greenberry said, she was thinking that he must know, too, about the Crow woman. "I know."

Greenberry looked both surprised and puzzled. He indicated the trading store where the men were still talking. "*Wagh!* Do they know?" Evie shook her head. Greenberry cast another look at the corral, torn between the desire to see what was going to happen to Hobart or to be the first to spread the news, a distinction which would doubtless earn him a drink. The prospects of a drink tipped the scales.

Evie watched Greenberry enter the store. The men were probably still talking about George hunting for a woman. No wonder they were all so kind to her—favored her so. They were sorry for her—sorry to see her making such a ninny of herself. She wondered if they all knew about Belle and the filled pipe—that George admitted to woman-stealing. She turned and fled up the stairs to her room, anxious to finish her packing and leave. The door to her room was still open just as she had left it. Her moccasined feet made no sound on the steps, and as she entered her room she stopped.

Belle was wearing the blue dress and had propped on the chair the small mirror from over the chest. While Evie watched, Belle adjusted the mirror so that she could see her feet. It was clear that she was inspecting herself in sections. Her hair was done in a low knot on her neck, like the emigrant women, and held in place by the tucking combs Evie had discarded. Even her skin might have been burnt coppery by the sun. The dress lay on the floor several inches below the hem.

As Belle observed this in the mirror, Evie moved up behind her and said, "I told you it would be too long."

Belle whirled and then smiled, so entranced that she was oblivious to Evie's anger. "I can hold it up in front when I walk." She demonstrated. "I have seen the white women do it when they walk through wet grass."

Evie turned her back on Belle and stared unseeingly out the west window. Little better than a thief, Belle was. Worse than some, for she took from those who befriended her.

Evie had returning doubts that Belle spoke the truth

about George. If she did, that was thievery, too. Either way, she was in the wrong—either a thief or a liar. Evie felt she could have taken the Crow woman on faith—waited for George to tell her. But the Crow woman and Belle, too—that was too much. It left too many questions, too many doubts.

Far up the Laramie a flash of sun striking fire from metal reminded Evie that the patrol was taking Hobart to the Army camp. She picked up the spyglass she had been using earlier and adjusted it. She saw the patrol all right. They were just topping a rise. Evie watched until they dropped from sight and was about to lay the glass down when she caught movement and a touch of color in the thicket along the river.

A mounted Indian came from the thicket onto the well-worn trail running from the fort upstream in the direction of the camp. Both man and horse were painted. It was Eahsapa. He carried a rifle in the crook of his right arm. He pulled up and looked after the patrol for a time, then wheeled his horse and started in the direction of the fort. After a moment he walked his horse into the growth along the river. Evie waited, but he did not reappear.

Evie turned to Belle. With her hair knotted and in the blue dress, she didn't look Indian. In his desire to get a white scalp, Eahsapa wouldn't know who it was he was killing until too late.

"The blue-coat soldiers have bound the hands of Red Beard and are taking him to their camp," Evie said. "Come with me to see what they do."

"Red Beard? Bound?" said Belle in surprise. "Why?"

"Let us go and find out," said Evie. She didn't want to take time to explain about Hobart. Eahsapa might leave.

"Your father told us not to go to the village of the soldiers."

"This is for a purpose. Others will be going." Belle hesitated, stealing a glance in the mirror. "The dress is yours," said Evie. As Belle looked at her, Evie forced herself to smile. "You look very pretty. You will be much admired by the soldiers."

"I may wear it to the camp?" Belle could scarcely believe her good luck.

"Yes, but we must hurry." She helped Belle down the steps and over the short distance which led to the corral. Belle waited at the corral gate, attracting the curious stares of several emigrants who came into the fort. In a few minutes Evie led out two saddled horses and helped Belle up. Evie was anxious to get started—anxious that they not be stopped. They were almost to the gate when Greenberry, Belco and Partout emerged from the store. They hailed Evie, who was much too close to ignore them. They eyed Belle with open admiration but did not immediately recognize her.

The men were moderately drunk, even Greenberry who had cashed in fast on being the bearer of news, and it was Partout finally who exclaimed, "*Le diable!* She is Belle!"

"So she be, old hoss," said Belco wonderingly. To Evie he said, "Where you takin' her in all that fofarraw?"

"To show her off in the camps," Evie said ambiguously, giving her horse a light kick. She didn't want them to take a notion to go along, and there was no time for talk.

Greenberry looked after the girls as they rode through the gate. When they veered to the left he looked vaguely surprised. Partout pulled at Greenberry's sleeve impatiently. "*Allons.*"

"Quit plaguing him, old hoss," protested Belco. "He won't get to talk to Hobart noways."

"*Wagh!* I can try," said Greenberry, "and after that I'm talkin' to Wyatt, do 'ee hyar? It must've been Wyatt that told Reeshar where to get the cache. Hobart wouldn't and Partout's been with me." The three headed for the corral.

Upstream Evie and Belle rode side by side. The trail between the Army camp and the forts was cut by deep ruts, making the horses' footing insecure. Evie looked at Belle. The dress was becoming to her, with its sloping shoulders and wide sleeves, the cross-over bodice tapering to a tiny waist, and the full skirt. She looked very like the young Creole girls Evie had seen riding from the oak-shaded plantation houses of St. Louis. For a moment, however, as she looked at Belle, Evie was not seeing a girl who would be desirable whether she wore deerskin or lace, but herself, Evie Pryce, whose name was the only thing really white about her.

Evie had been watching to the left of the trail, and they were approaching what she was sure was the willow thicket where she had seen Eahsapa. Suddenly she knew that Eahsapa was still there. There was no movement, no sound, but she knew. She struck her pony with the quirt. The quick little horse leaped forward into a run, with Evie hugging its neck. A puzzled half-smile crossed Belle's face. It was a strange time for a race.

As Evie flashed past the willow thicket, she thought she saw the glint of a rifle barrel. She glanced back at Belle, who was having difficulty keeping her seat in the saddle now that her pony had broken into a gallop. She looked a little pathetic. Suddenly the enormity of what she was doing overwhelmed Evie. She reined in her horse and whirled around in a swirl of dust. "Tasina!" she cried, using Belle's Indian name in an effort to warn Eahsapa. "Tasina!"

But Eahsapa did not hear or did not understand. A rifle roared from the thicket and Belle's horse slipped in the rutted trail and went to its knees. Belle catapulted over the horse's head, struck the ground face down, and lay still in the dust, her dark hair coming loose and fanning around her, the dress billowing out into a crumple of blue. The horse struggled to its feet and limped off.

Eahsapa sprang from the thicket, drawing his knife. He ran to Belle, dropped his rifle, and gathered up the loose hair in one sweep of his hand. He hesitated, letting the coarse dark hair slide through his fingers. He turned Belle over and looked down into her face. Then he raised his head in a listening attitude and glanced back down the trail. Evie heard it, too—several horses galloping toward them, and from the singing and whoops of the oncoming riders she suspected it was Greenberry, Partout and Belco. Sheathing his knife and taking up his rifle, Eahsapa started running toward the thicket.

Almost immediately the three trappers came into view, riding hell-bent for the Army camp. Partout and Belco were slipping precariously on their unsaddled horses. They seemed to straighten somewhat on their mounts as the scene before them registered. First Evie, two hundred feet up the trail, looking frightened; then the splash of blue on the ground, and finally Eahsapa, who was now disappearing into the willow thicket. All three trappers sat stupidly for a moment, looking from Belle to the willow thicket. There was the sound of thrashing and then hoofbeats receding from the other side of the heavy growth. Evie started riding back toward the figure on the ground. The trappers walked their horses forward, and Greenberry slid to the ground beside Belle. He knelt, feeling for a heartbeat, then quickly examined her. There was no blood, no wound. He noticed her horse limping at the edge of the trail.

"Her heart's still pumpin', do 'ee hyar?" said Greenberry. "And she ain't hit." After a moment Belle opened her eyes.

Evie had reined in beside Greenberry. "She's all right?" asked Evie incredulously.

"*Ti-ya*. These ruts are good for something, now."

"I tried to get her killed," said Evie. Aware that Belle's eyes were upon her, Evie repeated, "*Hina-hina!* I tried to get you killed." Evie saw the way the three men were looking at her, as if they hadn't heard right, or as if she had lost her mind. "Tell George," she said to Greenberry. She kicked her horse and rode for the fort.

Greenberry stood up and watched Evie ride away. Then he glared belligerently at Belco and Partout. "Git down, ye damned old sots, and give me a hand."

Neither of the men made a move to dismount. "God-almighty!" Belco said in a shocked voice. "What ails Evie?"

"She ain't to be blamed," said Greenberry angrily. "It's George's fault, do 'ee hyar? I told him to leave Belle where he found her. Anybody that could see through a rail fence could see that Belle'll never breed anything much but trouble. And as if bringin' Belle in wasn't enough, George goes off on a fool squaw hunt leavin' Evie and Belle like two wet cats with their tails tied together. He's the natural-est born damn fool I ever did see!" Greenberry turned to Belle.

From down the trail Evie looked back and saw Greenberry helping Belle onto her horse. She didn't know what devil had possessed her, trying to get Belle killed. That she could even think of such a thing made Evie feel sick and scared. Besides, in wanting to keep George, she couldn't have thought of a way better calculated to lose him. He'd have to know, and once he did, he'd never want to see her again. Her troubles seemed overwhelming, the world itself seemed overwhelmingly complex. As she neared the fort, she dug her heels into the pony's ribs and turned off the trail toward Big Road's camp and her mother's people.

Fourteen

It was the next day, around noon, that Lieutenant Love rode out from the Army encampment on his way to Fort Laramie. Behind him was a mounted dragoon leading a horse on which Hobart rode, and another dragoon brought up the rear. Hobart, dirty and disheveled, had his hands tied in front of him so he could hold on to the saddle horn. His shirt was glued to his back with dried blood, and he was still weak from shock, for he had already received part of his punishment for desertion—fifty lashes with a rope's end.

Love glanced back at Hobart, and in doing so he saw a lone rider emerge from the fringe of willows on the far side of the Laramie and splash across. As the rider came out on the near side of the stream just below the Army camp, he recognized him as Stroud. Love recalled hearing that Stroud had gone on a long ride to the Republican River— more than ten days ago—something about seeing Pawnees. He lifted his left foot out of the stirrup and eased around in the saddle so he could watch Stroud. He saw him look ahead in their direction, saw him regard them steadily for a moment, and then as recognition came to Stroud, saw him break his pony into a gallop. Instead of the big stallion Love had seen Stroud ride before, he was riding a Spanish pinto, but it was plainly used up. Stroud was dirty and bearded and alkali-streaked, and in addition he was now wet from the thighs down from fording the stream. It didn't take Stroud long to close the distance. He reined in, ignoring Love, his attention entirely on Hobart. "Ey God!" he said, looking at Hobart's back and at his bound wrists. "What have you done?"

"He's a deserter," said Love.

Stroud glanced again at Hobart's bloody shirt. He remembered Hobart's wanting money so he could go on down to Bent's. And his impulse to sell his share of the furs to Reeshar before they came into the forts. But why hadn't he just told the truth? Nobody would hold it against him. "Why in God's name didn't you tell me?" he asked Hobart.

"Who'da thought these pork eaters'd get here so soon?" Hobart muttered.

"He's to converse with no one," said Love.

Stroud's glance fell upon two lengths of heavy chain across the saddle of one of the dragoons. "You're going to shackle him?"

"Until we get him back to Fort Leavenworth. He has to serve out his enlistment in prison," answered Love. After a moment he added, "Go ahead and talk, but get it over with before we get to the fort." The lieutenant faced front again.

As they all rode on at a walk, Stroud regarded Hobart closely. The sight of the shaggy, rough man, bound and beaten, was almost incomprehensible. Restraint would near kill him. "That bastard Eustis," Hobart muttered hoarsely. "Soldierin' under him was like ridin' a plug that's done nothin' but pull a plow."

"You knew him?"

"Old Useless?" Hobart snorted in disgust. "He was my company commander at Jefferson Barracks. We were both in from the first. I stuck it while we built the stables, though a lot of 'em didn't. Deserters was as plentiful as blackberries in June."

"I'm surprised you stuck it that long," remarked Stroud.

"I was waitin' for the horses," Hobart said simply, "and they was worth it. Army made me a sergeant and put me to teachin' the men to ride. And that's when the trouble started." Hobart paused again, letting out his breath with

269

a grunting sound. "Eustis didn't know a breast strap from a crupper," he continued. "But I kept on and did some teachin' of my own on the sly. Then one day we showed 'em some real ridin', thinkin' Eustis would be pleased. He had me walkin' the river towpath for it, packin' a bag of shot. Said I was turnin' the U. S. Dragoons into a circus!"

Hobart paused again, then his eyes lit and his voice took on new life. "Can you see it, George? I was trainin' him a Injun-fightin' regiment that'd out-Injun the Injuns. They was ridin' hangin' off and firin' under the horses' bellies and every which-a-way, precise as you please, instead of settin' up eight feet tall waitin' to get their guts tore out."

"Sorry," said Stroud. It wasn't much to say, but nothing could help Hobart now. After a moment Stroud asked, "How was it you got caught?"

"Eustis. He come by with the patrol just when I was ridin' on my head. Knowed me in a minute. I did it a time or two in the regiment."

Stroud remembered the times they'd all thought Hobart would fall off, doing that trick, and break his fool neck. But none of them could have guessed it would bring down anything like this. Stroud glanced ahead in the direction of the forts and the plain between. He was surprised to see that the Indian camps were gone, except for one over near Fort Platte. He was too far away to identify the lodge markings, but from the location he guessed it to be Eahsapa's. At least it was where Eahsapa's camp had been when he left. Stroud wondered if Eahsapa had got a scalp yet. The thought occurred to him that if Eahsapa hadn't been after a scalp, Eustis would likely have sent someone else with the patrol instead of going himself. What it amounted to was that Hobart had been caught for desertion because a damned fool mover named Sikes had hit Eahsapa.

"It was rotten luck," said Stroud.

"My luck was about to run out anyhow," muttered Hobart. "Too many people knowed. Garrow recognized me that first day when we was fightin' over by Fort Platte, but he kept his mouth shut. I wasn't worried about him. But with Reeshar findin' it out . . ."

"Reeshar?" Stroud asked.

Hobart grunted in affirmation. "My luck run out, and yours with it."

"What do you mean?"

"Reeshar came down to Cedar Point—the day after you left, it was—pretending he wanted to bribe me to send the next lot of movers to Fort Platte. What he really come for was to beat me into tellin' about the cache. He would have tried it, too—him and Cebull and Rem—but I had to duck inside when Eustis passed with the patrol. It made Reeshar suspicious, and he threatened to call Eustis back." Hobart paused and looked at Stroud, almost pleadingly. "For Christ's sake," he said. "Can't you see? I told Reeshar where the furs were cached to keep him from turnin' me in!"

For a moment Stroud felt stupefied. "You did what?" he said, staring at Hobart. Then, forgetting Hobart's bound wrists and bloody back, forgetting everything except that this man had cost him his chance of going to St. Louis, had cost him nine years of his life, Stroud stood up in the stirrups and smashed Hobart in the face. Hobart toppled off his horse and landed in a clump of low brush beside the trail. He made no effort to get to his feet. With bound hands tangled in the brush, he lay in a twisted, half-reclining position glaring up at Stroud, blood trickling from his mouth. Love and the enlisted men had stopped, too surprised to do anything. Stroud glared back at Hobart. "Nine years of freezing and frying and risking my hair, and you sell me out for what? To save your own hide, and you get caught anyway. Ey God! I ought to kill you!"

"Kill and be damned!" yelled Hobart hoarsely. "And your nine years be damned, too! That cache was partly mine. Why do you think I chanced hangin' around here? Your nine years be damned!"

Love rode back to where Hobart was lying and dismounted. "Let's get him back up," he said to his men. The two dragoons got off and together they hoisted Hobart up to the saddle.

Feeling empty and half ashamed, Stroud kicked his tired pony into a gallop and rode off. As he headed for Fort Laramie, he began trying to piece his world together again. He thought back to what Hobart had said. It was the day after he had left to go to the Pawnee hunting camp that Reeshar had gone down to see Hobart. For a moment Stroud couldn't remember how long it was that he had been gone. He decided that it had been seven sleeps to the Skidi hunting camp. Seven days there and five back, he guessed. Reeshar would have had plenty of time to bring the cache in. But maybe not time enough to get it very far away, if he'd already freighted his spring shipment. Maybe they knew something about it at the fort. He lifted his glance ahead to Fort Laramie. There was no one aloft. The wagons were back from down-river, Stroud noticed, some dozen of them, all parked on the flats east of the fort.

There was activity enough inside the fort, Stroud discovered. As he came out of the entrance passage into the courtyard, he saw a crowd consisting of what appeared to be the entire personnel of the fort, including the squaws, collected in front of the carpenter shop. Greenberry, Partout and Wyatt were there, too, all three appearing angry, as if his arrival had interrupted a quarrel. Stroud glanced up to the gallery opposite the main gate, then to the crowd again, but he didn't see Evie anywhere.

It was then that he saw in front of the carpenter shop, supported on sawhorses, a long, narrow box made of rough-hewn lumber. Obviously it was a coffin. For a moment Stroud had the crazy feeling that in fording the Laramie a few minutes before he had ridden into the middle of a nightmare and soon now he would wake up. He dismounted, not bothering to tie his pinto to anything. The people, silent and awkward, made way to let Stroud through. He went to the side of the box and lifted the lid, letting it slide to the ground. The body inside was wrapped in a blanket. Stroud pulled back the top edge. It was Pryce. His swollen face was a startling white with blue patches. Stroud's glance traveled the length of the blanket. Pryce had been a thick man, but just below what Stroud would judge to be Pryce's chest, the blanket sloped down in an unaccountable way. Stroud pulled the blanket back farther. Pryce had been ripped from breastbone to pelvis and from side to side. Where Pryce's abdomen should have been were four loose flaps of skin, retracted by the severed muscles and exposing a great, gaping cavity. There was nothing much inside him at all. "In God's name," Stroud said, "what happened to him?"

"Young Hobart found him in a deep pool in the river, his belly butchered open and filled with rocks," Bostwick said. He stepped over to the coffin and drew the blanket over Pryce's body and then picked up the lid and put it back on the box.

"Who did it?" Stroud asked.

"All we know is that he disappeared the day after you left," said Bostwick.

The Company carpenter, with a hammer in hand and nails sticking out of his mouth, came out of the shop. He placed a nail on the edge of the lid and drove it in with three deft blows.

It couldn't have been Eahsapa, or any other Indian, who had done this to Pryce, Stroud felt. He'd never heard of an Indian filling a body with rocks and throwing it into a river. This was more like the stories of the Natchez Trace he'd heard as a boy—the brutal and senseless murders and the terrible men like the Harpes and Joseph Hare and Mason and Murrel who committed them. There was only one man around here who was capable of such a thing.

"Reeshar did it," he said.

"Reeshar?" Bostwick looked skeptical. "What reason would Reeshar have?"

Stroud was trying to remember what Reeshar had ever said about himself. He had talked a lot about New Orleans during those long winter evenings around the lodge fire. And about riding along the great rolling Mississippi, and along the swamps and the canebrakes. It had been just about ten years since the steamboats had put the gentlemen of the Natchez Trace out of business. It was about ten years since the breakup of the Murrel gang. Reeshar would have had to start young, but it fit. And it wouldn't necessarily be inconsistent with the fact that Reeshar was an agreeable companion when Stroud first knew him. A man needed friends when he was new to the mountains. He stood a better chance of not going under. Reeshar would have been a damn fool not to make himself agreeable.

"He killed Pryce because he wasn't putting Pryce out of business fast enough," Stroud explained. "Or because he was afraid Pryce might find out that Hobart told about the cache."

Greenberry, Partout and Wyatt had followed Stroud and now stood beside him. "Hobart? Hobart told?" said Greenberry. "Of all the infernal, rot-mouthed, low-down . . ."

Wyatt cut him off angrily. "Now, damn you, are you convinced I didn't tell Reeshar where the cache was? If you'd stayed sober you'd have had no need to try to make a scapegoat out of me." He looked at Stroud. "I came over here as soon as I heard, worried about Evie, and Greenberry accuses me of telling Reeshar where the furs were hid. I only got back with the fort hunters last night."

"What did ye expect?" said Greenberry. "Turning your back on trouble always gets ye into more! Anybody but a snot-nosed dandy'd know that!"

"Oh *vengeance!*" said Partout. "I get my hands on Hobart . . ."

Greenberry turned on him. "It's them furs ye'd better get your hands on, else we'll be trappin' for the Company!"

"Shut up, all of you!" ordered Stroud. "Quarreling isn't getting the furs. Just where are they?"

"*Wagh!* We think they're at Fort Platte," said Greenberry.

"They are," affirmed Wyatt. "I saw them this morning in the warehouse."

Stroud swore. The furs were close enough, but there'd be hell to pay getting them out. He glanced over the crowd, wondering how much help he would get. He remembered then that he hadn't seen Evie. "Where is Evie?" he asked.

Bostwick answered. "She doesn't know about our finding her father. She went out early this morning with Big Road's band."

Stroud felt relief that Evie didn't have to know now. He'd tell her at the right time. But he was distressed about her, too. Evie had been acting strange before he went off to find the Pawnees. "Where's Belle?" He glanced around again. As he did so he had the uneasy feeling that the others had suddenly drawn together. No one moved, yet they seemed to be bunched against him.

"Took her to her sister," said Greenberry.

"She wanted to go?" asked Stroud.

"Didn't ask."

Stroud felt that Greenberry was trying hard to be or-nery. Like Maud when she got dug in. "I've gone to a lot of trouble to keep Belle out of Eahsapa's way," Stroud re-minded him. "Besides, she was supposed to be kept here till the cache was brought in."

"It's in," Greenberry said.

Stroud looked from Greenberry to Bostwick and then at the others again. Whatever it was that they held against him had something to do with Belle—or Evie and Belle. He was just about to demand what else was going on, when Greenberry said, "Ye are done with squaw huntin', now?"

Stroud had been expecting this reproach. He hadn't kept any better track of Reeshar than the others. But it was too late now to do anything but go over to Fort Platte. "Talk isn't getting Reeshar."

Bostwick straightened up. "There's no proof he killed anybody," he said bluntly. His tone of voice somehow im-plied that Stroud's accusation was nothing but fabrication.

"There was Merk," Stroud reminded him.

"Nobody murders for hides," said Bostwick.

Stroud clenched his fists. "He didn't murder him for hides! Besides, he'd done murder before. He'd do it again."

"You know for sure he's murdered someone?" persisted Bostwick.

Stroud regarded the trader steadily, wondering why Bostwick was so determined to discredit him, and why he was wasting time trying to convince Bostwick of Reeshar's guilt. "He's done murder, all right. That's what I went all the way to the Pawnees to find out. Now I'm going after him." He turned to Partout and Greenberry. "Bring that wagon along," he said, pointing to a freight wagon with two mules hitched to it standing just inside the corral.

"Your furs are not the Company's responsibility," Bostwick said. It was as if Bostwick had drawn a line in the dust of the courtyard separating free trappers from Company trappers and had dared his own men to cross it.

Stroud looked at the chief clerk in disgust. "You'd rather ruin me than help yourself. Charge me hire for the wagon if you want." Stroud knew that most of the *engagés* would come along if given a little time to think for themselves. Not on his account maybe, but for Pryce, or for the fun of fighting. But Stroud was in a hurry. He went to his horse and mounted.

Partout and Greenberry had already gone to the wagon and climbed in. Greenberry grabbed the reins and slapped the near mule across the rump. "Git!" he yelled.

Belco gave Jake a shove. "Hyar we are and we don't turn!" The two old trappers clambered into the wagon just as it started up. Without a word, Wyatt gathered in his rifle and sprinted after them. He leaped on the wagon as it went through the corral gate and clattered after Stroud, who had already ridden out through the main passageway.

Stroud rode the mile between the forts at a gallop, not waiting for the men in the wagon. He was surprised that the sturdy little pinto under him had any steam left. He had hated having to leave his stallion back in the Pawnee hunting camp, but the long trip south to the Republican had made him lame. Stroud raised his eyes to the walls of Platte. A couple of *engagés* were sunning themselves on the roofs. A peaceful, drowsy day. He'd fix that. Stroud rode on through the front gate past some Indians trading at the window and pulled up. A few squaws and half-breeds lounged about. It had been at least two years since he had been inside Fort Platte. The *bourgeois'* office and quarters were to the left. He glanced in that direction but saw no one. He looked along the banquettes, and to the roof of the buildings on the north side.

Then he lowered his eyes and saw Reeshar standing in the warehouse door. He held a rifle, and he had a shot bag and powder horn hanging from his shoulder. The two faced each other across the small courtyard. For each, only the other existed. Stroud was aware that the warehouse door was open. If Reeshar got off the first shot, and missed, all he had to do was step beck, slam the door of the warehouse, and reload. Stroud hadn't gone to all this trouble just to have Reeshar fort up where he couldn't get at him. Stroud thought of the blockhouse behind him above the main gate. There were two flights of stairs at an angle and a door at the top. If it was closed, he'd be fair game and no mistake. But if it was open . . . There was a six-pound howitzer up there, like the two Kearny had brought with him. He could smash the warehouse door so Reeshar couldn't barricade himself in there.

"I told you I'd get your cache," Reeshar said.

"To hell with the cache!" said Stroud. "I've found out what happened to Batchika."

"You must be insane," jeered Reeshar.

"You're too arrogant to face the truth, Jesse. But you're cornered. I've talked to Wicarpi."

"You're lying," said Reeshar flatly.

Stroud didn't even seem to hear him. "Wicarpi wasn't killed by the Pawnees. She's living with them. I wanted to bring her back with me, but just the mention of your name makes her want to start running, like she ran from you seven years ago. You didn't leave that camp together. She ran to get away from you, and later—hours later—you tracked her down. She was lucky, though. She had come across old Merk. Why he didn't shoot you on sight and be done with it, only somebody as crazy as Merk could ever explain. But you were lucky, too. He sheltered you through that blizzard—even if it was at gunpoint to protect Wicarpi. In the Sioux camp, as an enemy squaw, she was guarded so closely you couldn't get at her there, either. Everybody had a share of luck except Batchika."

Stroud paused, his eyes on Reeshar, wondering how long he was going to listen.

"You taunted Batchika, Jesse. That day I left to go hunting I was scarcely out of sight before you started telling her that I wasn't coming back—that I was gone for good to look out for myself. It had rankled a long time, hadn't it, that Batchika wouldn't take to you—that she stuck to me and my 'sturdy virtues'? All day you taunted her, and then you seized your axe. What did you ever do with that axe, Jesse? Throw it away? Or did you lick it clean after you killed her with it? And what about your knife? It was when you drew your knife, and Wicarpi realized what you were about to do, that she ran."

From the look in his eyes, Stroud knew that Reeshar was about to shoot. It was a flat, unblinking stare with flecks of light, like the eyes of an animal waiting for the exact moment when it suited him to pounce, yet putting off that moment, fascinated by his prey. Stroud gripped his horse with his knees.

"You killed Batchika, Jesse. You killed her and then, by God, you ate her!"

Reeshar fired, but at the same instant Stroud raked his pony hard, and as the animal jumped he ducked his head and shoulders below the pony's neck on the off side, hearing the bullet whine above him where his head had been, and the slam of the warehouse door and the bar being dropped into place. Stroud figured he had earned himself about fifteen seconds. He wheeled his pony and galloped back across the courtyard, seeing with relief that the blockhouse door at the top of the landing was open. He threw himself from the pony and took the steps three at a time. At the top he dived through the blockhouse door just as Reeshar's rifle roared from the warehouse, the bullet splintering the railing. That was the last shot Reeshar was going to get in this turkey shoot, Stroud told himself grimly.

He got up, leaned his rifle against the wall and swiveled the howitzer so that it pointed through the door. He lowered the muzzle and sighted along the tube. The shot would just clear the narrow landing in front of the blockhouse door; as for his target, anywhere in the warehouse wall was good enough, for the solid ball should cause a whole section to collapse. He struck his tinderbox at the touch hole.

At that instant the warehouse door flew open. Reeshar paused only long enough to throw a shot in the direction of the cannon pointing down from the blockhouse door, then ran for the corral. It was too late for Stroud to withdraw the spark he had struck. The cannon let out a deep-throated whoom! Stroud was not prepared for the second explosion —the explosion with its orange flash of fire that followed when the shot hit the warehouse. Too late, Stroud realized that the howitzer had been loaded with hollow percussion shot, which Reeshar must have got from Kearny, instead of with a solid ball such as both forts had always used. It was no wonder that Reeshar had been in a hurry to quit the warehouse. As the air about him cleared, Stroud saw a cloud of dust and smoke across the courtyard. The warehouse wall was smashed and a portion of the roof had collapsed.

Stroud ran down the stairs, carrying his rifle in his left

hand. Everybody was too surprised to pay him much attention as he pushed his way through the crowd of curious and alarmed *engagés* and women and children to the corral at the north end of the fort. Through the postern gate, mounted on a big roan gelding, galloped Reeshar. Stroud had no time to get off a shot with his rifle before the wall hid Reeshar from sight. Stroud ran to the postern gate, his moccasins throwing out small spurts of dust. Reeshar had headed straight for the Platte river a hundred yards away and was already plunging through the foliage.

Cursing his luck, Stroud went back into the courtyard to his pony. He was mounting when the wagon with Greenberry, Partout, Wyatt, Jake and Belco rattled through the gate. It pulled up and those in it surveyed the destruction. Flames now were leaping from the collapsed roof of the warehouse. The smoke was black and sour-smelling. "*Sacré nom!*" said Partout. "The furs!"

"I need a fresh horse," said Stroud. There was no chance now of getting the furs out. At the moment it didn't much seem to matter.

Greenberry was staring at the smoke and flames and the smashed wall. "Mine's saddled, do 'ee hyar?"

Stroud rode out through the front gate. He could see as he approached Fort Laramie that the crowd from the courtyard had moved to the banquette. Inside, heading for the corral, he noticed that Pryce's coffin was still resting on the sawhorses. He also noticed that the mounts of Hobart and his guards were near it, in front of the blacksmith shop. The only sound in the deserted courtyard was the clean ring of hammer on anvil. Stroud turned his trembling pinto into the corral, pulled off his saddle and threw it into the shed. In a matter of minutes after entering Fort Laramie, Stroud was mounted on Greenberry's barrel-chested roan, which had been tied in the courtyard. It was an irritation to be stopped by Lieutenant Love, and Stroud looked down at him impatiently.

"There's little doubt that it was Reeshar who killed Pryce," said Love. "Hobart admits that Pryce did come to Cedar Point just as Reeshar was leaving. Reeshar followed Pryce and killed him. Hobart heard the shot."

Stroud felt no surprise. "Tell Bostwick that," he said, riding on out. As he passed Fort Platte on the way to the river, the stench of burning furs was strong in his nostrils.

Fifteen

Before climbing the bluffs on the other side of the river, Stroud stopped long enough to load his rifle and study the tracks of Reeshar's horse. The animal had been badly shod; the shoes were too heavy and the heels extended straight back, more like mule shoes. He ascended the bluffs and paused again at the top. The tumulous plain, for the most part barren, though diversified by clusters of pines and furrowed by ravines, extended as far as the eye could see. At first Stroud had no glimpse of Reeshar. Then away in the distance he saw a black dot crawling up a long swell of the prairie. After two weeks of being hurried and driven, he now was quite calm. He could catch up with Reeshar. It was just a matter of time. He set out at a conservative lope. It looked as if Reeshar had decided to follow the wagon route from Fort Laramie to Fort Pierre on the Missouri. Stroud remembered that Wyatt had spoken of his uncle's building a new post on the Missouri below Fort Pierre. Maybe Reeshar had this in mind. But it was a long way to the Missouri—three hundred miles.

By night Stroud reached Rawhide, where the upper waters of the creek flowed through a wide, loamy valley, lightly timbered but lush with grass. He unsaddled Greenberry's horse and let it roll and graze. After making up a small bundle of firewood to take along, he saddled up again, with no thought now for sleep or food, and rode on through a moonlit land, gambling that Reeshar would stay on the wagon route, or pretty close to it.

Shortly after sunup Stroud saw a black cluster on the prairie. It was several wolves gorging on a buffalo carcass. There was not much left but hide and bones. Possibly

Reeshar had shot it for meat, and had taken the meat with him, or consumed it raw, for there was no wood. Stroud needed no reminder of his own hunger. He rode on, scanning the country from every rise until off to the right he saw buffalo grazing. Shortly he shot a fat cow and took the liver and a hump rib. But he didn't stop to eat. He ate the liver raw as he went on. It was a blistering day, and a dry wind parched his lips.

He thought of the buffalo lying back on the prairie for more wolves to gorge on. He and Reeshar had each killed a two-thousand-pound animal for one meal.

About noon the trail came to L'Eau qui Court. Here on its upper waters it was a narrow ribbon flowing between steep banks. There wasn't a stick of timber in sight. Using the wood he had brought along, Stroud made a fire and set the hump rib to cooking. He unsaddled the horse and started to lead it down to the grassy bottom. But the animal tossed his head and pulled back. Stroud saw a dead wolf lying near the stream, some fifty yards away. He let the horse loose and went on down to the river bottom. There had been a considerable scuffle, according to the tracks. The wolf's skull had been smashed. Near by lay a Hawken rifle, the stock broken in two at the breech. The butt was smeared with the blood and brains of the wolf. He could see where Reeshar had dismounted at the stream's edge, probably to drink.

Stroud looked more closely at the dead wolf. It was a large male, better than six feet from nose tip to tail-bone tip and weighing well over a hundred pounds, he estimated. Its muzzle and lower jaw had a mottled look from dried froth that extended clear back to the eyes, which were open and peculiarly yellow. The tracks of Reeshar's horse led away on the opposite side of the stream.

Stroud knelt for a drink and then went back to his fire. All the time he ate he was disturbed by the thought of the dead wolf and the broken rifle. He saved some of the cooked buffalo meat, wrapping it in his kerchief and stowing it in Greenberry's saddlebag. After stomping out the fire, he saddled the horse and picked up the trail on the other side of the stream. From closer inspection of the tracks, Stroud saw that Reeshar's horse had bolted across the river but Reeshar had been able to catch him.

Stroud jogged on, keeping the tracks before him. Far ahead, he could see that the open country was breaking up into rugged terrain. All afternoon he ascended a gradual acclivity toward a high, grassy plateau, beyond which a ridge of pine-covered hills introduced the more distant mountains with their abrupt walls of limestone topped by a black growth of pines. The setting sun promised some relief from the heat of the day, though the wind remained hot. There was not a cloud in the sky. At least there was small chance of rain to wash out Reeshar's tracks. Stroud hunched himself for an all-night ride.

By morning he had come to White River beneath its imposing chalk-white bluffs rising a thousand feet into the thin blue of the sky. For two days he jogged down the valley of the White. Stroud could tell from the freshness of the trail that he was gaining on Reeshar. Reeshar was slackening his pace, but he hadn't always kept to the wagon tracks, so that several times Stroud was slowed down following the trail over rocky ledges or through gravelly ravines.

Before dawn of the third day, at the mouth of White Earth Creek, Stroud suddenly felt light-headed. Berries and roots and plums weren't much to live off of. It had been better than twenty-four hours since he had eaten the last of the meat. With brief satisfaction he thought of how hungry Reeshar must be getting. He wondered what Reeshar thought of when he got good and hungry.

Stroud dismounted by the stream and drank, then lay back, holding the reins in one hand. It wasn't the first time —or the worst time—he'd been hungry, he recalled. That winter with Reeshar and the two women was the worst.

The sudden sharp slap of a beaver tail on water, upstream, brought Stroud to a sitting position. He strained to see in the dark. There was nothing. He dropped the reins and lay down, turning so that he could watch upstream. His eyes searched through the slim white birches. For a long time he waited, hardly breathing, wanting to widen the angle of his vision but not daring to move. Then something—a sound or intuition—caused him to turn his head. Quite close behind him a shadow had detached itself from the birches, a crouching figure running swiftly upon him. Stroud didn't have much time. He rolled on his back and raised his rifle just as the shape, more substance now than shadow, raised its arm to strike. Stroud pulled the trigger, and the flash of his powder illumined for an instant the painted face of an Indian. The force of the bullet knocked him sideways and he fell with his head and shoulders submerged in the stream.

Stroud looked up at the sky. The daybreak star was shining. He lay there for several minutes; then got up, went to the Indian and pulled him out of the water. He rolled him over, not surprised to recognize Eahsapa's features beneath the streaked war paint. Strangely, the warrior's death saddened him. He hadn't wanted to kill Eahsapa, yet there was nothing else he could have done.

As the Indians did for their warriors who fell in battle, Stroud carried Eahsapa out on the prairie, where the wolves and the buzzards could feed upon his flesh and scatter his body to the four directions. Then he looked around for Eahsapa's pony and found it tied downstream. With a change of mounts, he might get this business with Reeshar over with sooner. He removed the crude Indian saddle and led the pony off.

With the painted Indian pony in tow, Stroud pushed on as the sun mounted and gave notice of another blistering day. Sometime around noon he noticed that he had not seen the tracks of Reeshar's horse for some distance. He backtracked and found them leading toward the river bottom. He followed them down to the stream's edge. Here the tracks became confused; then they led back from the river, the horse moving at an irregular pace—running for a while, trotting and finally slowing to a walk. Stroud followed carefully.

The trail doubled back parallel to the way they had come, though closer to the river. Then the tracks returned to the stream. Stroud picked his way slowly and quietly. After a while he heard a noise in the brush. He stopped, and in a moment he made out a saddled, riderless horse whose reins had snared on a branch. It was Reeshar's horse.

Stroud dismounted and untangled the reins; then, with Reeshar's horse in tow also, he retraced his steps to the place at the river's edge where the horse had got away from Reeshar. Following a false trail had cost him some time. But Reeshar, on foot, couldn't be far. He picked up the trail of footprints going off downstream but angling away from the river. The whole thing was getting worse as it went along, Stroud thought. First Reeshar losing his rifle, and now his horse. It was being made too easy.

It was late afternoon, near the mouth of Wounded Knee Creek, when the pursuit came to an abrupt end. Stroud looked ahead and saw Reeshar halfway up a long wooded slope to the right of the river. Reeshar was sitting watching him.

As Stroud paused, Reeshar lifted a hand and made a gesture as if motioning him to come on. The slope was strewn with deadfall and Stroud made his way slowly, wondering what Reeshar was up to, half suspecting that he had another gun. Yet Reeshar must have seen him first and could have got off a shot as Stroud followed down the stream. He watched Reeshar closely as he approached him, and again Reeshar impatiently waved him on.

Stroud went ahead, disconcerted and wary, noting as he got closer that Reeshar's right sleeve was torn and hanging in ribbons. Then he saw Reeshar's face. It was gaunt and lined on one side, livid and swollen on the other. The flesh on the right side had been torn from cheek to jowl. The gashes were now scabbed over, but the wounds were inflamed and swollen. Through the shredded right sleeve, Reeshar's arm was exposed. It was badly lacerated, and it, too, looked swollen and angry. Stroud decided that the wolf had probably been lying in the deep grass beside the stream and had leaped upon him when Reeshar knelt to drink. Stroud reined in about ten feet away and stared down.

"You try a man's patience, George. You really do," Reeshar said with good-humored exasperation, though his voice was thick. "Your only excuse for holding me up this way is that you've never been to New Orleans before. If you had, you'd get a move on." He paused and tried to smile. It broke open the ragged gash on his cheek and it started to ooze. He wiped his mouth on his left sleeve and complained of being thirsty.

"You ever known a wicked and beautiful woman?" he went on. "Plenty in New Orleans, George. Oh, believe me, enough for us both and then some." Reeshar leaned forward in a conspiratorial manner. "Wickedness by itself is sordid. Beauty alone is shallow. But together . . ." Reeshar half closed his eyes in the pleasure of his thoughts.

Stroud sat perfectly still, too surprised and repelled to move or speak. Reeshar talked more then—talked as if they were the best of friends, as they had been that first year. As he sat there on the ground he rambled on about garlanded Creoles, mulatto girls laughing, pigtailed mariners brawling along Chartres Street, black slaves with earrings jangling. He paused frequently to catch his breath and run his sleeve across his mouth.

Stroud realized after a while that Reeshar never swallowed—that he couldn't swallow. The wolf had been mad, all right.

He remembered his suspicions of Reeshar's past. "A fling in New Orleans'll cost us dear," Stroud said, pretending to believe in Reeshar's delusion that they were about to leave for New Orleans. "Maybe if we worked the Trace . . ."

Reeshar looked at Stroud intently, a flicker of awareness showing in his eyes, to be replaced by an expression of withering scorn. "The Trace is no good any more." He paused and then said craftily, "It's old man Wyatt's furs are sending us, George. . . . My furs, really . . ."

Stroud said no more. As Reeshar talked on, Stroud realized that he had lost all desire to shoot him. What satisfaction would it be to shoot a man who wouldn't even know why he was being shot? If he killed Reeshar now, he would only be assuming the role of executioner, and it was a little late for that. The wolf had already done his job for him. He had heard of men bitten by mad animals. For the lucky ones it had been a matter of days—for the unlucky ones, weeks. From the looks of him, Reeshar was going to be one of the lucky ones—though Stroud felt that the wolf had cheated him.

A cooling breeze stirred the dead air, and Reeshar's mood abruptly changed. "It's that wind again," he muttered. "It's nearly skinned me alive." He ran his left hand lightly across his chest and on down his belly and thigh. The touch seemed to cause him pain. As the breeze freshened he groaned. "Do something!" he demanded between clenched teeth. "Can't you see what it's doing to me?" He wiped his mouth on his sleeve and seemed to forget Stroud and New Orleans. He began to explore his body with his finger tips again, muttering something about heavy clothes.

Stroud tossed the reins of Reeshar's horse to the ground. "Suffer, damn you! Suffer and see how it feels." He turned and rode down the hillside, Eahsapa's pony still in tow. Maybe Reeshar could make it to the Missouri, though it didn't much matter. He was dead, all except for the dying. Behind him Reeshar called out, "George!" Then a little later Stroud heard hoofbeats coming after him. Stroud didn't look back.

He dug his heels into his horse's ribs, and he and the led horse broke into a run. After a while he stopped and listened. There was a reassuring stillness. Reeshar could wait alone for Satan to serve his subpoena. Stroud wasn't going to make it any easier for him. Reeshar had lived like an animal. He could die like one. Stroud started back the long way he had come.

At dawn he saw thin pillars of smoke rising into the quiet air. He was on high ground near the river, and out on the plains he saw the camp of a wagon train. It proved to be the wagons from Fort Laramie, hauling the furs to the Missouri. By the time he came to it, the mules were hitched.

Billy Pitcher was in charge, astride a saddle mule, ready

to move out. An *engagé* rode the near-wheel mule in each team. Among the muleskinners were Greenberry and Partout, their expressions anything but happy.

"Your furs were a total loss," said Billy. "But so is Fort Platte." His face broke into a grin. Stroud nodded and rode on past before Billy could ask any questions. Stroud stopped beside Greenberry. The old trapper had a resentful look in his water-blue eyes. Behind him with the next team was Partout.

"Ye lifted hair, now?" Greenberry asked.

"Didn't have to," said Stroud.

"Reeshar, he is go under?" asked Partout.

"In a manner of speaking," said Stroud. Anxious to change the subject, he asked, "Just what happened at Fort Platte after I left?"

"*Wagh*," said Greenberry. "Them *engagés* was as amazed as if they was just born, the way Reeshar lit out. With nobody to tell 'em, didn't hardly know what to do except laugh and holler because our cache was goin' up in smoke. We didn't stay to argify with the varmints—only about as long as a weasel looks at a comin' rock—but I reckon they clean forgot the fire would spread until it was too late. Inside a hour or two they'd all sloped."

"They abandoned Fort Platte?"

"Nothin' left but 'dobie walls and smolderin' beams, do 'ee hyar?" verified Greenberry. "And stink."

"Probably figured they weren't getting enough out of it," said Stroud. "No loyalty. They were a hard bunch."

"Bostwick, he is hard. No more credit. *Voila!* No more free trapper," said Partout.

"Hell's full of Bostwicks," said Greenberry. He was eyeing the horse Stroud was leading. "Where'd ye get the Injun pony?"

"He was running loose." Greenberry glared at him as if to say that was a lie. Stroud ignored him. "You want your horse now?"

"Turn him in with the fort herd," said Greenberry. "We'll be around a heap."

Stroud nodded and started to pull away.

"*Wagh!* Ye got nothin' to tell, now?" prompted Greenberry.

"Nothing," said Stroud. With a gesture of greeting to Jake and Belco farther down the line, he rode off. He supposed they'd heard what had happened at Fort Platte between him and Reeshar. If they hadn't they'd have to find it out from somebody else. He didn't want to talk about any of it.

No wonder that he hadn't figured it out for himself— what Wicarpi had had to tell him. It was hard to believe of any man, under any circumstances. Especially a man of some refinement. But Reeshar was nothing but an animal— like a wolf, predatory, ready to kill and feed on any life weaker than his—even Batchika's—to satisfy his rapacious appetite. Stroud couldn't help wondering if Reeshar had eaten her liver first, perhaps sprinkled with a little gall bitters; if he had torn at the flesh raw, or maybe fashioned a spit of some kind; if he had left anything at all for the wolves. How could he tell anybody what Reeshar had done to Batchika? And how was he ever going to forget it?

For a time as he rode along, Stroud felt empty and without purpose. For the past several weeks, since discovering Reeshar was alive, he had been living in a state of transition, or suspension, as if a new phase of his life could not begin until the old was ended. He had done all he could for Batchika now, and God knew what happened to her was nothing he could have foreseen.

292

Stroud remembered then something of the last day at the fort—something concerning Belle and Evie he had intended to ask about. He looked up and ahead. The trail back to Laramie was long and he was close to exhaustion.

Before setting out after Reeshar, Stroud had ridden five hundred miles in twelve days to the camp of the Pawnees on the Republican and back. He must have traveled another hundred and fifty or two hundred more trailing Reeshar.

Even so, he started out and kept a steady pace until he was again beside the narrow ribbon of L'Eau qui Court. He crossed to the other side, intending to push on. But he made the mistake of resting a moment—of stretching out to relieve saddle-cramped muscles. It was nearly noon, and he hoped to reach the forts by noon the next day. Time enough then to sleep. He closed his eyes briefly to shut out the sunlight.

When Stroud opened his eyes again, unaccountably it was sunset. He sat bolt upright and reached for his rifle, wondering what had awakened him. The sun had left only a red glow. He looked around for the horses. They were safely grazing near by.

The sound that had awakened him came again—the wild, half-human scream of a panther. Stroud stood up. He'd never heard a panther give voice in daylight before. Then across the river he saw movement. Only it was no panther. It was Reeshar, nearly naked, and running up and down the opposite bank, ripping off clothes as he ran. He would stare down at the water, scream, and turn and run the other way. Tortured by thirst and the sight of water he was unable to swallow, his cries rent the air, shrill and full of anguish.

Almost without volition, Stroud lifted his rifle and sighted along the barrel. As he would shoot any animal wounded or crazed with pain, he shot Reeshar. The screams stopped and Reeshar fell forward and lay still.

In the silence that only space can create, Stroud went to his horse and mounted. He glanced once at the white figure sprawled on the bank across the river. Then leaving Reeshar, leaving Eahsapa's horse, leaving everything that was the past, he rode off across the plain.

Sixteen

In the corral at Fort Laramie, Stroud arranged the rigging on the ground beside Maud—*aparejo*, crupper, folded saddle blanket, woolen pad. Wyatt had gone around to Maud's off side and was waiting. Quickly they placed the rigging on Maud and cinched her up. Stroud led her, together with the pinto he had got from the Pawnees, out of the corral toward the store, Wyatt carrying three rolled-up skin *mantas* to wrap the packs in. A couple of trappers idled on the wall.

"What happened to all the stores at Fort Platte?" Stroud asked Wyatt. He had noted after he crossed the river this morning that Fort Platte was indeed gutted and deserted, and furs or no furs, it had given him a feeling of satisfaction. He had spread his robes on the other side of the Platte last night, not wanting to cross over then and sleep in wet buckskins. He had noticed this morning even before crossing the river that the hard-packed barren flats between the forts were empty of Indian camps, and he had wondered where Belle was. But mostly he had experienced a sense of relief. He hadn't really wanted to see Belle just now. Stroud felt that he had shed any responsibility for her sometime these last few days. Partly because now that Eahsapa was no longer a threat, it seemed that he had settled his obligations —if there was anything not already settled.

At Stroud's question about the stores at Fort Platte, Wyatt smiled. "It was the craziest doings you ever saw," Wyatt related. "Those fools over at Platte didn't make any effort to put out the fire in the warehouse. We came back here and went up on the wall to watch. About the time we got here, they seemed to realize the whole fort was catching fire. They opened the corral gates and let the horses out and then started rushing in and out of the fort carrying out stuff—whiskey first—and piling it on the plain. They drank and carried on for an hour, whooping and laughing like it was some sort of carnival. By the time the fort was half burned, they caught a horse or two apiece and loaded them up—with whiskey mostly. Then they lit out. Some scattered like they might be headed for Indian villages, but most of them went off down the Platte in a body. Headed for St. Louis, we guessed. The Indians took what was left. By night there was nothing in the fort or out."

Hiram came out of the store carrying a hundred-pound bag of flour and put it with the pile of other supplies—sugar, coffee, dried fruit, corn, powder and shot—then went back inside. Wyatt was spreading the three tarpaulin-like skin *mantas* on the ground. "You should have seen how fast those Indians broke camp once they got that loot."

"What about the horses?" asked Stroud.

"Indians rounded up what was left and took them, too, I guess. Can't be found."

Stroud made no reply. This would no doubt finish old man Wyatt. Many a fur-trade venture had gone under for less. Stroud was glad it was Shonka's band that got the loot. They deserved some luck. He began apportioning the supplies among the *mantas*.

"Greenberry was right," Wyatt said. "You can't turn your back on trouble without getting into more. Cebull and Rem were ready to shoot me. They thought I'd told you about their stealing your cache."

One of the trappers on the wall leaned over and shouted, "The horse-soldiers!" He pointed toward the northwest.

Wyatt was making one pack out of the bags of sugar and corn. "It's St. Louis for me," he explained.

"So that's the way your stick floats," said Stroud.

"I'm going when the dragoons leave." Wyatt straightened up and watched Stroud put the powder and lead on one of the *mantas*. He glanced over the supplies. "What are you going to do with all this?"

"Feast some Indians, maybe," said Stroud. Hiram came out carrying three Hudson's Bay blankets and several pounds of tobacco. "Where did Big Road go?" Stroud asked him.

"Up the Platte." Hiram looked at Stroud intently. "It's Evie you're going after?"

"If I can get her. Who else?"

Hiram gazed off into space. "She went off in that blue dress."

"Evie?" Stroud asked in disbelief.

"Belle. Evie gave it to her. She looked awful pretty—even if she was still half scared." Hiram seemed unaware that he was holding the blankets and tobacco. "I don't think I understand women," he said.

Stroud took the tobacco from Hiram and placed it with the other smaller items and began wrapping them in the *mantas*. He wondered vaguely what Belle had been scared about. "I forgot fishhooks," he said. Hiram put the blankets down and went back in again.

Wyatt knotted the lash rope on his pack and glanced at Stroud. "How about a good buckskin suit? Hiram's got one for sale."

Stroud didn't look up. He had noticed that Wyatt wasn't wearing the one Belle had made for him. Too bad. Wyatt had wanted that suit. Stroud glanced down at his buckskin clothes, nearly black now with several years' accumulation of grease and dirt. The fringe on the sides of the trousers was mostly gone, having been used for whangs. He needed some new buckskins, for a fact, he admitted. But Evie wouldn't mind seeing him this way. Maybe she'd make him some new ones. "Mine's grown to me," he said finally.

Hiram was back almost immediately with a packet of fishhooks. He handed them to Stroud. "Man in here a while back bought fishhooks," Hiram said cheerfully. "Preacher with that last bunch of movers. Not at all like that hell-fire-and-damnation one."

Stroud wrapped up the sack of flour in the remaining *manta* and began tying it. "When did the last train go through?"

"Day or two before you got back the first time," said Hiram.

Bostwick came to the door of the trading house. "That'll be a dollar for those fishhooks," he said. He held an open account book in one hand and a pencil in the other.

"I hadn't forgotten," said Stroud. "And don't you forget that Greenberry and Partout are paid up." Stroud wasn't sure they deserved to be bailed out, but he couldn't be letting Bostwick press them into working for the Company. He lifted his shirt and reached into a pocket of his money belt. "Greenberry's to have a set of traps, understand?" Stroud handed Bostwick the money and watched while he made an entry in the account book. Then Bostwick snapped the book shut and went inside. Stroud glanced up at the sky. He judged it was past noon. Time to hit for timber. "Let's pack her up," he said to Wyatt.

They worked silently, slinging the side packs, securing the top pack, passing the lash rope back and forth and speaking only the terse calls. Finally Stroud braced his left knee against the boot and hauled the rope taut. "Take slack," he called, giving off to Wyatt. He couldn't see Wyatt over the top of the pack. "Tie," he called again. He could hear Wyatt tying up, the rope rubbing against itself and making

298

a clean sound. Stroud mounted his horse and took up Maud's lead rope. Maud brayed loudly several times, objecting to the heavy packs. Stroud looked down at Wyatt. Maybe he was ready for St. Louis now. "Luck," he said. "You'll need it." He grinned, thinking of Belle, then turned to Hiram. "Good luck to you, too." He touched heels to his horse and rode out with Maud trotting along behind.

Approaching from the direction of Fort Platte was a detachment of dragoons, some two dozen or more, alkali-streaked and saddle weary. Stroud had no desire to meet the dragoons, but he couldn't very well avoid them. The two in the lead turned out to be a captain and Sergeant Garrow. "See any Indians on your way in?" Stroud asked.

"Seventy-three lodges of Sioux several miles up La Bonte's Creek," said the captain. "We camped near them night before last." He tilted his head in the direction of the deserted and charred fort. "What happened to Fort Platte?"

Stroud hesitated an instant. A story he had heard the Indians tell their children came to his mind—a story about how greedy Old-Man-Coyote broke off all his teeth taking a bite of rock-stuffed duck. "I busted my teeth on some furs." Stroud rode on with a nod at the grimy troopers.

Garrow watched him. "He's beginnin' to sound crazy as the rest of these mountain men," he remarked in a puzzled voice.

The captain put his horse in motion and the others started up behind him. "They are all alike. They have a talent for existing in the wilderness. A simple, uncluttered life is all they ask. Trap a little, hunt a little. But their old way is about gone, I suspect. The country's changing."

"The mountains'll be here till Kingdom Come." Garrow's expression was still puzzled as he turned in his saddle. Stroud had angled away from the Platte and was heading into the barren hills.

At the top of the first ridge Stroud looked around at Fort Platte—or what remained of it—wondering at what he had said to the captain and Garrow. At the time, it was calculated to stop further questions, but it was true all right, he guessed. Though up until now he hadn't thought much about it. It hadn't taken long to lose his furs, but it was taking a while to get used to the idea that they were gone for good. There was an emptiness in him that was slow to fill. The fort was lost from view as he started down the other side of the ridge. He was anxious to get away from it—it seemed to smell faintly of burning fur. Besides, there was thirty miles before he'd hit grass. He'd better hump it.

He had gone about ten miles upstream to the vicinity of Warm Springs when he saw at a distance the main body of troops. It was a moving picture of blue-clad men in long file, each company with matched mounts, and bringing up the rear were the wagons, whose sun-dried wheels gave out agonizing shrieks.

Both his animals were rested, and Stroud kept a steady pace. By nightfall he stopped for water at Cottonwood Creek. He pushed on. It was a warm summer night, starry and moonless. Though he was tired from the many days of strain he had put himself through, his mind was kept wide awake by thoughts of Evie. He couldn't really rest now until he had seen her and knew that things were right between them.

At midnight he stopped in the wooded, grassy bottoms of Horse Shoe Creek to rest his animals. After a while he moved on.

A faint glow of light was breaking over the ridges to the east when he came to the crest of the hills looking down into the narrow valley of La Bonte's Creek. He sat still to watch, as he had countless times, this daily resurrection of the world. While the valley itself was still buried in darkness and shrouded with a thin mist, the light began to spread over the sky. First it touched snow-covered Laramie Peak, the wreath of mist which encircled it gradually rising. Suddenly the dull white of its summit caught fire with a light like burnished silver, and at the same moment the whole eastern sky blazed. Then the sun rose above the edge and flooded the valley with a dazzling light, dissolving the mist. It revealed the white skin lodges of Big Road's village far up the stream.

The village had been awakening since before dawn. Fires were going, and from the lodges gray columns of smoke rose through the still air. Stroud had a growing feeling of impatience. But it wouldn't do to go whooping and hollering into the camp. Indians were hell for etiquette. First he would pay his respects to Big Road and offer him gifts. He rode along the hills parallel to the stream until he was directly above the camp. The rising sun looked down upon a scene of moving people—men and boys going to or from their morning bath in the stream, women cooking, herders going out to drive in bands of horses. As he rode slowly down to the camp and through it to Big Road's lodge, his eyes searched for Evie, but she was nowhere in sight. The camp had a festive air. Because of the cook fires burning, Stroud decided that they must be celebrating an unusually successful hunt—antelope, from the sagey smell of the cooking meat.

Big Road was seated before his lodge. Stroud made the sign for friendship and then said, "I have gifts for the chief. Let us smoke the pipe together."

"*Hokahé, micínski kin,*" replied Big Road. "Welcome, my son." He gave an order to one of his squaws. Stroud dismounted and ground tied the pinto. Maud he tied to a peg. He sat beside the chief and soon one of Big Road's wives brought out a chopping board, tobacco pouch and pipe, which she set before Big Road. Stroud had taken a carrot of tobacco from his saddlebag, and now he laid it on the board. Big Road smiled. "It is good that you tie a mule at my lodge. One laden with gifts."

"I have come to ask for your granddaughter," said Stroud.

Big Road cut off a piece of tobacco and began chopping it on the board. He poured tobacco from his pouch and chopped it in with the other. He filled his pipe. It was a ceremonial pipe with the bowl carved from red stone and the stem made of two slender pieces of grooved wood glued together and wrapped with buckskin. The bowl wasn't much larger than a thimble. One of the squaws lighted the pipe for him with a brand from the fire. He blew smoke to the earth, the sky, and the four directions.

As he puffed at the pipe he talked, recalling that it was twenty years ago that a young white man had come for his daughter. He went into a detailed account of Pryce's wooing of Evie's mother. Stroud found it hard to keep his mind on the old man's rambling story. He was impatient to find Evie. Then, too, at the far side of the camp Stroud caught a glimpse of some young men clowning. They had ridden into the camp yelling and shouting, belaboring a spavined old horse, ludicrously painted. The young men were daubed with mud to make them unrecognizable, and one was dressed and padded to look like a pregnant woman. Stroud wished Big Road would come to the end of his recital so that he could go and watch the fun. The crowd around the young men was so thick it was impossible to see what they were up to. Stroud was passed the pipe, and became conscious suddenly that Big Road was talking now about Evie. "She has suitors in the little time she has been in my lodge. Painted Crow has offered ten horses."

"She is promised to me," said Stroud.

"You have been slow to see the promise fulfilled." Stroud took the rebuke in silence, remembering that when he went off to see the Pawnees, Big Road was camped at the forts, waiting to see his granddaughter married. Stroud puffed on the pipe.

Presently Big Road said, "You do not bring horses?"

"The mule and its pack are yours," Stroud offered. "The blankets, the flour, the sugar, the corn. And five pounds of tobacco." There was over four hundred dollars' worth of supplies packed on Maud. He hadn't intended it all for Big Road. He returned the pipe.

"It is good to have many gifts," Big Road said, taking the pipe and puffing on it. "But it is the number of horses that will be remembered and talked of."

It wasn't cupidity that prompted Big Road, Stroud knew. Whatever he gave the old man would be more than compensated for by presents from Evie's relatives. It was a matter of prestige that was at stake—the public knowledge that Evie was desired by a man willing and able to give. "I am poor in horses," Stroud reminded the old chief.

"In my youth," said Big Road, "my friend Kicking Bear was poor in horses and spurned by his sweetheart's father. Kicking Bear stole a hundred horses from the Crows and drove them all, in a great cloud of dust and a tangle of manes and tails, right up to the lodge of his sweetheart's father. They crushed the tipi and the father was angry. But Kicking Bear got his sweetheart. It was a brave thing. I helped him in this."

Stroud reached under his shirt into his money belt and brought out a handful of gold and silver coins, which he poured on the ground. "This will get many horses—perhaps more than a hundred."

Big Road studied the coins silently for a moment. "It is not the same. Besides, it would be hard to find anyone that would trade even one good horse for trinkets."

Stroud wondered if Big Road was pulling his leg. But even so, the old boy was just about right. "I can get horses," said Stroud, "but it will take time."

"Patience is necessary to all good things," said Big Road. "Ten horses?"

"Ten horses." As an afterthought he said, "The mule and nine."

"It is not the usual way," said Big Road. After a while he smiled. "But it is good. You have always kept your promises to my people. That is well known." Big Road picked up the pile of coins. "It will be good to have a shiny necklace," he decided. He poured them from one hand to the other, admiring the glitter. "My granddaughter has gone with the boy to bring the herd to water."

Stroud mounted and rode away, thinking of the glittering coins and all he had done to get them. He wondered then what Big Road would regard as gifts of equal value to give in return for near five hundred dollars in gold and silver coins. Ey God, a man did strange things!

Stroud rode along the open slopes above the river, looking for Evie. The many herds, having grazed all night in scattered places, were being watered and driven to fresh pasturage for the day by young boys—poor boys or orphans—who did the work for food and lodging. He saw Evie and a lad in his early teens driving a band of some thirty horses out of a grove of cedars near the top of the ridge. Stroud pulled up and watched them come down, Evie on one side of the herd, the boy on the other. She rode a man's pad saddle, and like a man she had the long end of the reins of the war bridle coiled up and stuck in her belt. With her right hand she held the reins at the honda, and her left arm hung loose at her side. As the horses came down onto the open slope, a few of them broke off and started to run and kick up their heels. Evie put her horse into a run and cut in front of them. Stroud thought he never saw a girl ride so well or look so good on a horse. "*Huh!*" *Huh!*" she shouted as she headed the horses back in with the rest of the band.

Stroud rode on to intercept Evie and came up beside her. She looked at him in her open, honest way. "I wasn't sure you would come," she said. The lead mare was out in front now and had slowed the band to a trot. It was a motley band of grays, blacks, buckckins, sorrels, pintos— tough little horses, some of them unbroken either to saddle or pole drag.

Stroud felt surprise. "Why not?"

"Didn't Greenberry tell you?"

Stroud jogged along in silence a moment, remembering there was something about Evie—and Belle—he had intended to ask Greenberry about. "No."

"It was something about Belle and me," said Evie.

Stroud remembered the feeling he had had at the fort when everybody seemed lined up against him—something concerning Evie and Belle. Whatever Evie had on her conscience, when the time came for unburdening, he had a sight more to unburden than she did. "Let's don't talk about it now," he said. "It wouldn't matter anyway."

"I suppose it wouldn't to you," said Evie. "And whatever they thought at the fort doesn't seem to matter. My opinion of myself was the worst damage. It isn't what other people think of you, George, that's important—it's what you think of yourself."

Some of the horses started to run again. The boy headed them back. "*Huh!*" he cried, waving his arm. "*Huh! Gray Horse Crazy! Huh! Little Flop Ears!*"

When the band was drinking and snorting in the stream, and as they waited while their own mounts drank, Stroud said, "Everybody must be some damaged."

"Grandfather thinks so," said Evie. "He says the truth has two faces. One is sad, and the other laughs." She was watching the water swirl past her horse's legs. "How did you get on with grandfather?"

Stroud smiled. "He drove a hard bargain. You'll hold it over me."

Evie looked up at him straight and steady. "I would have run away with you."

"I know."

"So did grandfather."

Stroud laughed. After a moment he asked, "What is this about Painted Crow offering ten horses? How many times did you talk to Painted Crow?" He knew that a girl could refuse to talk with a young man and thereby make it clear she didn't wish him for a suitor.

"I don't want to talk about that, either," said Evie. "I may not be ready for locomotives yet, but I found out one thing. I'm way past scissors." She still watched the water. "There's no place for me at all."

"There's plenty of time and plenty of room," said Stroud. "We'll make a place." He paused and then added, "Though we won't be starting out like I planned. My furs burned— and Fort Platte along with them." Stroud realized he hadn't thought about his furs all day. It was a good feeling.

"I thought you'd get them back."

"Why?"

"I don't know," said Evie. "I expect because you can do anything you set your mind to."

"Not this time," Stroud said. Though it didn't seem important now. Funny the notions a man saddled himself with. He'd got along out here for nine years without much

306

of a jingle in his pockets. And nothing could have helped that winter of the blizzards. There was no security against bad luck—or bad judgment, either. A man's only security was inside him, he guessed—his own capabilities or maybe just faith. And it was enough. He pulled his horse's head up from the water. "Let's get started."

What a fool he'd been! For nine years he thought it was money he wanted, when the only things worth a damn were Evie's belief in him and his own respect for himself. With these, he could get up from off his all-fours no matter how many times he was tripped. His father always had said that a fellow could get along somehow, provided he had gumption and didn't live too far from a stillhouse or too near to a jail.

"You going somewhere?"

"Not anywhere much," said Stroud. "How far along is that last wagon train now?"

"Not far. About to the Sweetwater," Evie estimated. She gave him a sudden oblique glance. "Who told you about the preacher?"

"What preacher? I still need cartridges."

"Evie's slow, good-natured smile appeared. "It would have pleased Pa."

"Then come on. Let the boy finish with the horses."

"No hurry," said Evie. Stroud studied her face, puzzled. "They'll be fixing a marriage lodge in the camp," she explained. Her guileless blue eyes met Stroud's again. Without his being particularly aware of it yet, the emptiness in him was gone. It looked as if Evie was going to live by all the rules, both white and Indian—or at least those that suited her. Stroud had a warm, half-crazy impulse to laugh, thinking how he'd never know what to expect. Like now. Evie couldn't have picked a better time to turn Indian. If she chose first to follow the Lakota custom of considering herself married when she was carried into a new lodge, it was all right with him.

The boy made a loud clucking sound at the horses and slapped the near ones on the rump. They splashed through the creek, and he started driving them upstream toward the foot of Laramie Peak.

A B O U T   T H E   A U T H O R S

When the Harrises first met in Los Angeles as University of California students, they learned that their fathers were both physicians and both graduates of the same medical school at the University of Louisville. Born in Kentucky, Mrs. Harris (Margaret Plumlee) later moved with her family to the Midwest, where she began her college work at the University of Wisconsin. Her future husband was born in Indiana but reached Los Angeles some years before she did. Except for short terms in journalism, advertising and social work, Mr. Harris has taught English ever since college —first in Maryville, California, until 1946; subsequently at Los Angeles City College.

For some years the Harrises have had a deep interest in historical themes of American life. Their first two novels, *The Medicine Whip*, 1951, and *Arrow in the Moon*, 1953, dealt with the post-Civil War era. The current book covers the transitional crisis of the mid-1840s when the ways of trappers and Plains Indians were being vitally changed by westward emigration.

The Harrises make their home in Los Angeles with their two sons, John, sixteen, and Duff, five.